RETURN TO NINEVEH

RETURN TO NINEVEH

SHARON HOUSE

TATE PUBLISHING
AND ENTERPRISES, LLC

Published by Tate Publishing & Enterprises, LLC
127 E. Trade Center Terrace | Mustang, Oklahoma 73064 USA
1.888.361.9473 | www.tatepublishing.com

Tate Publishing is committed to excellence in the publishing industry. The company reflects the philosophy established by the founders, based on Psalm 68:11,
"The Lord gave the word and great was the company of those who published it."

Published in the United States of America

ISBN: 978-1-68142-333-3
1. Fiction / Historical
2. Fiction / War & Military
15.05.06

Now the word of the Lord came to Jonah son of Amittai, saying, "Go at once to Nineveh, that great city, and cry out against it; for their wickedness has come up before me." But Jonah set out to flee…The word of the Lord came to Jonah a second time, saying, "Get up, go to Nineveh…So Jonah set out and went to Nineveh.

—Jonah 1–3 (NRSV)

PROLOGUE

The fledgling rays of the early morning sun shimmered across the still waters, turning faded pewter into brilliant translucent shades of opal, silver, and bronze. The strengthening shafts of light stretched across the harbor to a battle-scarred ship that was waiting in silence for the sun to warm her decks and playfully dance along shimmering brass fittings. She came to this anchorage to heal the wounds suffered during a desperate encounter with an elusive Japanese destroyer, sent by a merciless conqueror to destroy the last British citizens to flee Singapore.

She waits now, in silence, to feel the pulse of oil pumping life into her array of pipes and tubing as her engines—her heart—come to life and beat in a steady rhythm. Soon her human masters will breathe new life into her, and she will experience the pleasurable taste of salty spray streaming across her sleek camouflage painted hull.

Her name is *Mariah*.

1

Katrin Lee Albright stood alone on the tree-covered hill that overlooked Surabaya Harbor. She and her father, Joseph Albright, an Anglican missionary priest sent from England before the 1929 world financial crisis, went into hiding when the Japanese began their lightning-quick offensive through the small island state. Two nights ago, they witnessed the brutal flashes from dueling ships across the horizon in the distant Java Sea. The few returning ships to the battle-scarred port gave witness to the lopsided conflict of failure and defeat.

Her twenty-two years on earth had not prepared her for the increasing fear she experienced as the Japanese army relentlessly pushed closer to her childhood home. Brushing long golden-brown hair away from her face, she anxiously watched the remaining Allied ships while sailors scurried about, preparing them to sail.

Katrin hoped her father would return before darkness fell and relieve her anxiety. She knew he believed God would protect them, and he prayed with her to place them in His hands. He told her to believe it was already so, and it would be—just as Jesus had promised so many centuries ago. She had to trust the lessons of the Bible that her father taught since early childhood, but fear of being discovered made her tremble.

Katrin felt a shaft of fright penetrate her soul when a sudden rustling in the undergrowth caught her attention. The sound was coming closer, and Katrin held her breath when she saw movement coming toward her hiding place. She waited after hearing the low whistle her dad used to announce his return from searching for lost or wounded Allied soldiers near the Japanese lines. A sigh of relief came when she saw his face emerge from among the trees and recognized the uniform of the tall man following him as American.

"Kitten, are you here?" Katrin heard her dad call before she ran to meet him.

"Dad, thank goodness! All the ships look like they're getting ready to leave. I was afraid the Japanese army was near Surabaya."

"They will be soon, Kat. Captain Logan said the Allies are being overrun. Captain, my daughter, Katrin."

"Ma'am," the captain acknowledged.

"It's going to take years to push them back to Japan," said a lanky lieutenant with dark eyes, from a small group of soldiers emerging from the trees and junglelike undergrowth. "It's like an exploding ant farm, the way they're infesting the East."

"You're right there, Russ," Logan said, turning to Joseph Albright. "Father, we should move on before long, in case a patrol sees signs of our presence in the area."

"We have two choices, Captain. We can go to our base camp a day's hike from here but well-hidden or to the abandoned farm we've used for two nights. I don't think any of the invading forces have gotten close yet, but I can't be sure. I'm afraid a dash to the harbor is too risky with Japanese snipers between us and the town."

Logan ran a hand over his sweat-covered face before answering, "I guess we better go for the closest and move on at daybreak. I'll have Sergeant Ledowski take point. He's the best scout around.

The two British rangers that are with us are pretty bad off, and Private Adams needs a doc soon."

"Katrin, please let Sergeant Ledowski know where our campsite is located," Father Albright said before turning to help the injured soldiers.

Five minutes later, the ragged group of soldiers moved out with their unlikely rescuers along the treelined ridge. Sergeant Ledowski would move out of sight at times and then double back to let Captain Logan know that no one was around to trouble them. Katrin thought it looked like a boy playing hide-and-seek. *But this is real.* She shivered at the unpleasant thought.

The group stopped several times to help the four wounded soldiers and the two British rangers suffering from malaria before reaching the abandoned pig farm. At least the dilapidated buildings still had a usable house and freshwater. Father Albright had found a small unopened can of axel grease, which he used to grease the hand pump in the tumbledown shed so it wouldn't squeak, when he and Katrin first arrived. "God will protect us," he had said. "But sometimes, He asks us to help ourselves as well. He is somewhat busy with more urgent matters than us at the moment."

Katrin listened that evening while Captain Logan and her father discussed their next move. *Will we ever be really safe again?* she thought.

"Captain, I think we need to get these men in better shape before we try to move any farther. We can see the surrounding countryside and would have ample notice if the Japanese were to come this far. They'll most likely be interested in securing the towns and villages before they go exploring these remote areas," Father Albright said.

"I'll have Sergeant Ledowski post some guards, Father, and we'll see how things look tomorrow. I'm anxious to see if your shortwave will reach any of our forces to evacuate you, your daughter, and our wounded from Java."

"I understand. We'll see what God brings us in the morning."

"Lieutenant Crammer, have guards posted and tell them to keep alert," Captain Logan ordered the dark-eyed young man he had come to rely upon as his second-in-command.

"Yes, sir," Russell Crammer acknowledged, giving a perfect salute.

The few able-bodied men rotated the night duty, carefully listening for any unusual sounds beyond the wind rustling the trees. Captain Logan stepped onto the sheltered porch as a hint of light touched the sky the next morning to confer with his trusted sergeant about the approaching day. "Sergeant, all quiet?"

"Yes, sir. The birds ain't even makin' much noise."

"Good. Be ready to move out within the hour," Logan ordered. "I'm not sure the good father realizes how dangerous things are."

"Yes, sir. We'll be ready to move."

"Carry on," Logan stated, returning Ledowski's salute.

Before the small hand of the clock reached the approaching hour, the ragged group of survivors vacated the worn buildings and moved into the jungle after meticulously erasing any sign of their presence. Sergeant Ledowski covered the rear while Father Albright pointed the way to their last chance for sanctuary.

2

"Japan renames Singapore *Shonan*, meaning 'light of the south,'" said the BBC morning-news broadcast. "In just seventy short days, the Japanese military rooted our brave defenders in triumph as the British Empire's most favored city in the East fell to the unlawful attacks against her. Many of her terrorized civilians fled the doomed city on voyages fraught with danger before it fell to this nefarious intruder, only to face peril again when the Japanese bombed northwestern Australia at Darwin on February 19.

"Australia's Prime Minister Curtin has sent a definitive appeal to America's President Roosevelt for support in keeping the Japanese out of Australia, reminding him this is the last major landmass between the Japanese and the American-Pacific coastline. The Malayan Peninsula, along with the Island State of Singapore and the recent attacks upon Darwin, however, does not sate this enemy's appetite. Japan, in her ravenous lust to conquer, continues the brutal, unlawful offensive upon yet more British, American, and Dutch holdings in the East, from the Philippians to Java and into Burma and Rangoon. This is the BBC reporting from Perth, Australia station."

Martin Jamison shook his head when he shut off the radio in his small office. He reflected on the precarious journey he and those remaining at Helen's Landing Hospital on the western coast of the Malayan Peninsula had endured just a few short weeks ago. The quiet life that revolved around the hospital, which was so carefully built by the early residents of the evolving village, had been shattered when the Japanese opened hostilities the previous December. Their swift offensive through the Malay States and into Singapore was said to have even startled their tripartite partners with its tenaciousness.

Dr. Jamison came to Helen's Landing as a young doctor shortly after the end of the Great War, eager to apply innovative methods to treat tropical disorders and complications that sometimes occur with surgeries and disease in the hot, moist climate. He became a reservist in the British Naval Medical Corp to assist in acquiring modern equipment and increase the hospital's capabilities. In time, he convinced the fledgling hospital board to sign a contract that allowed the British Navy to have use of the facilities in exchange for financial support. In later years, the army approached him to arrange for an additional wing in the unlikely event it would be needed.

Over the years, Martin Jamison's reputation grew throughout the region as an expert in his field while his reservist naval rank increased to his current status of rear admiral. The twenty-plus years leading up to this latest conflict had shown that the military contracts were used very little—that is, until the Japanese offensive through the jungles of Malaya.

Dr. Jamison and his colleagues were now attached to an army-navy medical facility along the Timor Sea south of Darwin, Australia, and out of Japanese bomber range. His protégé, Tom Linn, a young medical intern of Malayan birth, had joined other escapees from the Malayan Peninsula in the underground movement that was being formed to undermine the Japanese occupation forces until the East was once again free.

"Dr. Jamison, Dr. Romans and Dr. Patterson are ready for you," Sally Vilmont said, popping her head in the door for a moment.

"I guess I better get moving then," Dr. Jamison said.

"There you are, Martin," Quentin Patterson said. "I was about to send out a search party. I thought after Helen's Landing, you might have become lost in this metropolis."

"Just listening to the latest bit of news about Java. It looks like Japan has no intention of stopping their offensive anytime soon."

"I fear you're right in that assumption, but now that the Americans are involved, we should see a turnaround before long," Dr. Patterson said.

"I hope you're right."

Quentin Patterson left his lucrative London practice to join the navy in September 1939 after England declared war against Germany. He told his shipmates he always wanted to be a sailor and managed to become the medical officer aboard the *HMS Mariah*. Dr. Jamison, a friend since medical school, convinced him to join the hastily outfitted shore hospital and allow younger men to endure the rigors of shipboard life, after the *Mariah* narrowly escaped Japanese bombs in Darwin harbor.

"So have you checked on Lieutenant Nance yet, Quentin?" Dr. Jamison asked his friend while heading for the ward.

"Peter is with him now. He wanted to be sure the fever is really gone this time. I think Arthur will be able to move to a recuperation center soon. I had my doubts a few weeks ago when the *Mariah* found all of you off Bangka."

"Well, let's see what Peter has found, shall we?" Dr. Jamison said as he entered Arthur Nance's room.

"Admiral Jamison, it's good to see you on solid ground," Arthur said with a smile. "When do I get paroled from this place?"

"You're looking much better, Lieutenant. You had us worried there for a bit. Peter, what do his vitals look like?"

"I just checked his temperature, and it's remained normal for the past thirty-six hours. His heart rate appears to be good, but his BP is still a little off," Peter reported.

"It appears things are looking up, Arthur, me boy." Quentin Patterson smiled. "Martin and I will have to confer about your next assignment."

"I'd like to return to my unit, sir," Arthur said with a serious look in his eyes.

"We'll see what the next few days bring. If all goes well, I think you will be released for rest and rehabilitation before being assigned to active duty," Dr. Jamison stated.

Peter left Arthur's ward and thought about the events of the past two years that eventually brought him to Australia. He was also a refugee from Helen's Landing, who escaped Malaya aboard the *Angelica*, a small private yacht belonging to Helen Burns, along with his wife, Jane. He and his friend John Hartman were sent to Martin Jamison in early 1940 by the British Navy to learn about tropical diseases as green lieutenants fresh out of a year's rotation after medical school in London Hospital. They joined the navy the day after England declared war with Germany, feeling very patriotic, and were soon assigned to the growing village in the outer reaches of the empire where doctors were scarce.

Peter first met Jane, a lovely green-eyed American mystery, at the Raffles Hotel in Singapore, where she and her best friend and roommate Sally Vilmont were enjoying a short respite from the rigors of nursing. The idea of seeing Jane again seemed so unlikely, but fate brought him to the small place where she lived. In time, he learned the story about her unexpected widowhood in the United States and her attempt to flee the unbearable pain of her loss. God's grace had restored her wounded soul, with help from Dr. Jamison and her friends at Helen's Landing, and then, by some miracle Peter could not fathom, he grew in her heart.

Jane became Peter's wife in what still seemed a fairy-tale wedding they would never forget. It was held the previous year at Helen Burns's home, which stood at the top of a bluff overlooking the sea. Helen befriended Jane and Sally upon her return to Malaya from England in early 1940 and drew them into the social life of the community. Her friendship and kindness reserved a special place in Jane's and Sally's hearts and, if truth be known, in Peter's and John Hartman's as well. Peter was still in awe of their impending parenthood.

The strength Jane demonstrated on the precarious journey aboard the *Angelica* was only surpassed by her faith that they would be delivered to safety. The miracle was the arrival of the *Mariah* off Bangka Island when it looked like all was lost. Peter shook his head when he recalled the fierce battle *Mariah* fought with the Japanese destroyer and how close they came to oblivion that bright and sunny afternoon.

Wesley Vilmont, an army captain of engineers and Sally's brother, set up what defenses they had, but Andy Burns, *Mariah*'s commander and also Helen's son, was their deliverer that frightening day. Peter looked up from his reverie after a few minutes and thought his mind was playing tricks on him when he saw Wesley walking down the hallway.

"Hi, Peter. How's Arthur coming along? Any signs of improvement?" Wesley asked, shaking Peter's hand.

"As a matter of fact, his fever finally broke. Dr. Jamison and Dr. Patterson are encouraged. They believe if Arthur continues to show more signs of improvement, he'll be sent to a coastal resort that the British Army is using for men to recuperate."

"That is good news. I want to keep Arthur abreast of our unit's current status. As my second, he deserves that much. I really didn't think he would ever fully recover when John operated on him in that shed in Malaya."

Wesley walked toward the ward, remembering that surreal night just a few miles from the battle line when John Hartman operated to stem the internal bleeding that was quickly draining away Arthur Nance's life. He still could not believe his own participation in that life-and-death decision and the fright within him when he saw the blood and John's steady hand repairing what the landmine had destroyed. Turning toward the open doorway, he walked down the ward and saw Arthur engrossed in a book on ancient Byzantine architecture.

"Lieutenant, I see you haven't lost your enthusiasm for building on a grand scale."

"Captain Vilmont! The Byzantines were ahead of their time," Arthur said, laying the book aside. "And I believe we might need to use some of their ideas to fertilize the desert soon."

"You may be more right than you know, my friend. But first, we'll have to see how things go with the Japs around here. Right now, they're claiming seventy-three thousand British troops were taken at Singapore. Churchill told the House of Commons a few days ago that Britain has suffered a serious increase in shipping losses the past two months as well. I've heard rumors that a big battle is brewing in the Java Sea and could spill into the Indian Ocean the way the Japs are moving west beyond Malaya and into Rangoon and Burma."

"That could have repercussions with the Suez Cannel and our oil supplies if things go against us. The Japs could come from the east and the Germans from the west, squeezing us out of North Africa, and we would lose access to the shorter route through the Red Sea and Mediterranean. It could seriously compromise our current oil supply from Iraq and Iran."

"We'll have to wait and see what happens. I also wanted to let you know that the unit is starting to be rebuilt, and, as of now, you are still my second."

"I'll be ready, sir."

"I have every confidence you will be back with us before long. Get yourself well, Lieutenant. I need you to help me rebuild our unit into a strong fighting team to be feared by the enemy."

"I will, sir. We need to reclaim what these interlopers have taken by force and restore order."

"I'm counting on that, Lieutenant. I'll see you back at it soon," Wesley said before he left the ward to search for Dr. Jamison.

* * *

Helen Burns entered the boarding school commandeered as a temporary medical facility and went to the small office where Dr. Jamison was making a few quick notes from morning rounds. He looked up and smiled when he saw his longtime friend in his doorway. "Helen, what brings you out to us today?"

"Well, I've settled into my cottage and helped Jane and Peter set up housekeeping in the one next door. I thought she and I needed to think about working a few hours a week with the patients at the hospital. I know it's different than Helen's Landing, but I think we could be useful in some way. Jane is bored at home, waiting for the baby to come, and the activity would do her good."

"That's an excellent idea, Helen," Dr. Jamison said before a knock on his door diverted his attention. "Well, bless my soul, Wesley!"

"Hello, sir. Mrs. Burns, it's a pleasure to see you again and in much better circumstances."

"Hello, Wesley. I hope we'll see more of you while you're with us. Have you seen Arthur yet? I plan to stop in to see him when I leave Martin."

"I just came from visiting him. As a matter of fact, he's the reason I stopped in. I wondered what his prognosis is for rejoining the unit."

"All I can say at present is that if he continues to show the steady improvement we've seen recently, he'll likely rebound better than we expected. The next few days will tell us more," Dr. Jamison said.

"I see. The new men are starting to arrive, and I'm sure we'll be moved out soon. Corporal Moore is now Sergeant Moore and starting to initiate the new recruits into the realities of army life. Private Jenkins was promoted to corporal and is assisting with the process. Mostly, I've seen a look of awe on faces when they realize we escaped Malaya with you and witnessed a battle at sea. Moore and Jenkins are capitalizing on our little adventure to make sure the new recruits won't be among those numbered as deserters when the Japs try another attack."

"I don't think we'll see that again. The officers of those who panicked and deserted their posts during the first attack on Darwin have since seen the benefit of continual training and more stringent schedules in soldiering," Dr. Jamison said.

"I think I can understand how fear would spread though, Martin," Helen said. "When one or two panic, chaos can escalate quickly, especially with the number of planes that bombed the city and the amount of damage that was done just after we arrived. The Japanese went through Malaya and Singapore so quickly that the soldiers and the town's citizens here must have believed the same thing would happen again."

"You could be right, Mrs. Burns," Wesley said. "But a soldier's first duty is to fight and protect the civilian population. Of course, it's hard to protect a town against what we saw a few weeks ago, but I believe the Japs have stretched themselves too far this time."

"What do you mean, Wesley?" Dr. Jamison said.

"With the Americans coming into the fight, it will change the balance. Last year, America's lend-lease plan brought us a lot of equipment. Now they're in the war, and the American mainland is out of reach for any practical bombing attacks."

"Yes, that's true. When I was there in 1938, I traveled across the country. The farms and small-town factories that I saw were pretty impressive, not to mention the big metropolises, like Detroit, where most of the auto industry is located. I saw barges floating everything from cotton to train cars down a big river called the Mississippi, which runs all the way to the Gulf of Mexico, making it a short voyage to the Panama Canal."

"Jane said her country would be up in arms after Pearl Harbor, and their industrial strength would be at full capacity," Helen stated. "I wonder just how far they're willing to go to put things right again."

"That's what I mean," Wesley said. "The Axis partners are in a war zone, and America's mainland is safe from Axis bombers. If their ships can deliver the goods, the Axis nations might as well quit the fight—they won't stand a chance against that type of supply line."

"We'll have to see how things shape up in the next few months. I tend to agree, though, that America's industry is a tough supply line to beat," Dr. Jamison said.

"I think things will change for the better soon," Wesley said. "Well, I should get back to base and see how Moore and Jenkins are making out." Turning back a moment at the doorway, he said, "I was hoping to see Sally and maybe have lunch together. The matron said she was off-duty today. Will you let her know I was here, Mrs. Burns, and tell her I'll try to see her before we're relocated?"

"Of course, I will," Helen said. "It was good to see you, Wesley. Let me have your address when you've moved so we can keep in touch."

"I will, Mrs. Burns. Good-bye for now," Wesley said, closing the door behind him.

"He's such a nice young man," Helen remarked.

"Yes, I like Wesley," Dr. Jamison said. "As to our earlier talk, I think if you and Jane can coordinate with the matron and maybe have Sally put in a word as well, it would be a great help with the overload the staff is facing right now. At least you can boost morale."

"I'll meet with Jane and Sally and see if I can't round up a few others to see what might be done," Helen agreed.

3

"This is the BBC Perth station reporting," the announcer began. "In recent communiqués between governments, Prime Minister Curtin ended his public address with an appeal and a warning to the United States, stating, 'Australia is the last bastion between the west coast of America and the Japanese.' This comes one day after Japanese prime minister, General Tojo, warned the Australian government it would face the same fate as the Netherlands East Indies if Australia does not submit to Japanese demands.

"In Britain today, Prime Minister Churchill informed the House of Commons, the British Government has agreed to, and I quote, 'a just and final solution,' to India's demands for independence. This is the BBC Perth station reporting."

Peter switched off the radio and came to sit on the small settee with his arm around Jane's shoulder. Drawing her close, he brushed her cheek with a kiss before speaking. "I think, after talking to Wesley and the new colonel at the airfield, the Japanese won't come this far from their home island, so I believe we'll be okay here."

"Don't worry, Peter, we're fine here," Jane said. "I believe America will come here soon, especially after Prime Minister Curtin appealed to President Roosevelt. The Japanese attack on

American possessions has the country up in arms. We're in the right place, and our child will be born in safety."

"Speaking of our little one, how is he doing today?" It still amazed Peter that they would soon be blessed with a child, a small bit of light in this dark time to bring hope for a better future.

"He's fine and starting to kick. I think we might have a ballplayer or a dancer on its way," Jane said with a smile.

"Ballplayer," Peter stated with a grin as he thought of playing catch in a few years. *Of course, a little girl all dressed up in ruffles and lace as beautiful as her mother wouldn't be hard to be proud of either,* he thought.

"I've been thinking about the christening," Jane said. "With New Zealand feeling threatened by Japan and increasing the workweek to fifty-four hours in the defense industry and your father coming out of retirement to work at the shipyard, I wonder if your parents will be able to come."

"I don't know, Jane. It's a long journey and pretty treacherous right now. Civilians aren't even traveling to friendly countries. We can take plenty of pictures and send them. I'm sure my parents will come as soon as it's safe to travel again."

"I thought that might be the case. Your mother's last letter said they didn't think travel was an option right now. Do you have anyone special you want as godparents?"

"We know that John will be the alternate godfather, but we'll need someone to stand in for him since he's now on the *Mariah.* What about Dr. Jamison as godfather? He's been almost a father to us since before we were married."

"I like that idea. He was so good to me when I first went to Helen's Landing. He helped me get through the despair I felt at being alone and helped me learn I couldn't run away from grief. In time, he and Helen Burns helped me to come alive and, in the end, be ready to accept love when it came. I wanted to ask Helen to be godmother. I just hope Sally will understand."

"Why not ask Sally to be the alternate—like John?"

"That's a great idea. I think she'd like that. Oh! Quick, Peter! Put your hand here," Jane said, placing his hand over her swelling abdomen. "Feel him?"

"Yeah." Peter grinned, leaning close. "Hey guy, Dad is waiting to introduce you to this big world. Keep growing and getting stronger. Dad loves you, little one..."

As Peter spoke to the awaited child, Jane reminisced, *I never thought I would see such a happy time after Jim died in that awful accident. I still remember thinking long after the funeral that I'd always be alone. I'd still be a widow in Ann Arbor if I hadn't answered the ad Dr. Jamison placed in 1938 for a nurse with tropical-medicine training. The miracle of Peter's love and the second chance for happiness are such gifts.*

* * *

Wesley, considering the army's next move, entered the temporary barracks near the army airfield. "Sergeant Moore, is the unit ready to travel?"

"Sir, all replacements have reported, and Corporal Jenkins is preparing our transport now."

"Good, we travel overland to Katherine and then by train to Tennant Creek. After we finish training exercises, it could be anywhere."

"Did you find out anything about Lieutenant Nance, sir?"

"I believe Arthur will be among us soon, Sergeant."

"I'm glad, sir."

"So am I, so am I," Wesley repeated, more to himself than the sergeant.

Moore watched Wesley cross the short distance to the field headquarters. He was glad the small unit was moving again in preparation to take the war to the enemy instead of being on the run. He still felt a sense of satisfaction about the small part he and the captain played against the Japanese destroyer off Bangka Island.

Moore packed his duffle bag and glanced around the barracks one more time before heading to the truck that would transport the unit to Katherine. *Odd name,* he thought. *I guess some Aussie had a sweetheart and named the town after her.* Climbing aboard the truck, he noticed Jenkins must have fiddled with the fuel supply. *Just like when he kept the* Angelica *going as we fled Helen's Landing,* he remembered.

"I see we have a couple extra drums attached near the petrol tank. Been moonlighting a little on the side, Corporal?"

"Figured it couldn't hurt none. I don't fancy runnin' short and havin' to walk to where we're a goin'. Lotsa space 'tween here and Katherine by the map."

"You do have a point there, Corporal. Captain Vilmont went to get our travel orders."

"Yeah, seen 'im crossin' the compound a minute ago."

* * *

"Captain Vilmont, come in," Colonel Nolan said, returning Wesley's salute. "I'll give you a brief rundown of what to expect in the next few weeks. As you know, the Americans are in the war now and will be coming to Australia soon. For now, we are going to concentrate on North Africa and run some small campaigns in the East from here. Command was impressed with your ability to improvise in a difficult situation. We might want to expand a bit on that from time to time. In the meantime, here are your orders for Tennant Creek."

"Yes, sir. Thank you, sir."

"You'll be at the training grounds a short time, Captain. Make the best of it."

"We will, sir," Wesley said before saluting once again and joining his men.

The drive to Katherine was long and dusty, punctuated with moments of unnerving swerves over bumpy, washed-out roadways. The unit waited among a mass of uniforms for several hours after arriving in the chaos of backed-up men and equipment to board the overflowing transport trains to Tennant Creek.

Wesley yawned and stretched when he felt the train slowing and looked out the grimy window at the bleak country station, which teamed with military personnel from around the world. Nudging his sergeant, Wesley rose from the uncomfortable seat and moved toward the doorway. He wondered if this was what the Americans meant when they spoke about the *old West* of their country.

Colonel Bastian looked out the window of his office near the train depot and saw the batch of new Australian recruits descending the latest train to arrive. The town was one of several inland settlements being used as temporary training bases away from the threat of Japanese bombing raids. A small British engineering unit was also arriving. He placed his hat on his head before walking the short distance to the station to meet them. He might have a job for them, but time was short if the information was accurate.

"Captain Vilmont?" Wesley heard from behind him.

"Yes."

"Colonel Bastian, Australian Army, Captain. Welcome to Tennant Creek."

"Thank you, sir," Wesley said, while shaking the extended hand, and wondering why he was being singled out among all those arriving at the overworked depot. Wesley figured the town had never seen so much activity and would welcome a time when things returned to the normalcy of everyday life. *Will we ever see a return to the way things were?* Wesley wondered before turning his attention to the Australian major greeting him.

"Bring your unit across the way, Captain. We need to converse before sending you into the outback," Major Bastian said.

"Sergeant Moore, gather the unit and follow me," Wesley ordered.

"Sir," Moore replied, snapping a perfect salute before this mottled mass of disheveled soldiery.

Wesley followed Colonel Bastian into his office and noticed another officer in an American uniform seated on a corner chair.

"Captain, I'll be brief," the man said. "Command heard about your exploits in Malaya and your eye to detail in a tight situation. The battles in North Africa are, shall we say, seeing significant challenges. My country, however, does not like to lose. We will be coming to Australia and moving on into the East to reclaim Allied territory. I would say, before the end of the year, we'll be in North Africa as well. The days of hit-and-run are soon to be over. It's time to hit and stay. But in order to do that, we will require a little assistance beyond our own resources. That's where you come in, Captain."

"I understand and agree about staying, sir, but I was under the impression that British General Philip Neame was to replace O'Conner in North Africa," Wesley said. "I believe the change will bring a new battle strategy to the situation in North Africa."

"That's true, Captain Vilmont," Colonel Bastion interjected. "However, we have learned that General Rommel will be taking command of the Axis Army."

"He's only another man in the flow of commanders Germany has sent, sir," Wesley replied.

"That's true, Captain Vilmont," the unknown man said. "However, many of our troops believe him to be superhuman, and that's where your unit comes into play. We want you to design some surprises that the British can use in conjunction with the new equipment we'll soon be seeing in that theater of the war."

"The Germans may have a few surprises as well. The ancient towns in North Africa, with their narrow alleyways, are built over even more ancient and unstable foundations that are perfect for ambushes and stalling an army on the offensive. They are also a perfect setup to ambush an army on the run. There are the marshes off the coast and the Mediterranean to think about as well. It will take a well-coordinated effort to bring everything together, sir."

"Yes, we understand there are issues to overcome. But we need to think about future plans and ways to ensure their success."

"Well, Captain," Colonel Bastian said, "I think that covers everything for now. Your unit will be transported to the training area for the next three to four weeks. We'll be talking again soon."

"Yes, sir." Wesley rose at the dismissal to rejoin his men. "When Arthur, my second, rejoins us, we can work together on some ideas for you. Until then, Sergeant Moore and I will be working with the new recruits."

"Very well, carry on," Colonel Bastian said. After Wesley had closed the door, he turned to the man in the corner. "Well, what did you think, Major?"

"I think our captain is going to be very busy before much more time passes. My understanding is your group will be working out of Darwin?"

"Yes, that's the plan. We'll be working with some of your people and a few British units. I wonder what Churchill will think of the three of us working the same mission."

"I'd be more concerned about MacArthur. I heard he told the Philippine people he would be back, and that he means to keep his word. He won't like the amount of effort that will be poured into North Africa. After all, the Germans didn't directly attack America...the Japanese did."

4

The last note of revelry echoed from shore when Andy Burns stepped onto *Mariah*'s bridge, a tribal-class British destroyer with a complement of 145 men at her current wartime status. Andy's blue-gray eyes, set in a rugged windburned face, swept across the ship with practiced skill at her four 4.7-inch guns, one 3-inch antiaircraft gun, six 20-millimeters–four 21-inch torpedo tubes, and two depth-charge throwers that have served her masters well in this spreading war. He still thought of her as a thing of beauty, with her sleek lines and orderly decks.

The hasty repair welds were barely cooled before fresh camouflage paint was applied to cover her most recent wounds in a desperate need to quickly return the destroyer to sea. Many crew members standing at harbor stations were new to the ship, following the losses in her latest battle, and replacements for those rotated to other duties, including Quentin Patterson, the ship's doctor. Andy would miss the doctor, come sailor, with his quick wit and brusque insights about the politics that led to this unwanted war. A brief smile crossed his face when he remembered how the doctor disapproved of nearly all politicians and the media that reported their actions.

Andy could vividly remember their last battle at Bangka and the Japanese destroyer's shriek at death. The chain reaction from *Mariah*'s torpedoes caused the load of underwater mines intended for the Banka Strait, which the Japanese ship carried, to explode in a spectacular spiral of fire and smoke, ripping the enemy ship apart. The agonized scream at the fate that had destroyed her hung on the empty ocean's rolling surface, well after her bow disappeared to feed the sea's hungry yearning.

"Sir, all hands are at harbor stations," Mason Roden, *Mariah*'s first officer, reported, bringing Andy out of his reverie.

"Very well."

"Engines are on standby, sir. We are ready for sea," Mason continued.

Mason had become *Mariah*'s first officer with the rank of lieutenant when Andy Burns became her commanding officer and requested the temporary officer become his second-in-command. Andy, as *Mariah*'s first officer, respected the fact Mason was concerned for the men under his command as a gunnery sublieutenant, and the former believed the latter would become a first-rate leader. Mason's experience in the merchant marines prior to becoming a junior executive with Lloyds of London before the war made his enlistment for the duration more valuable for his experience as a seaman and a department supervisor. Mason thrived on the demanding duties and knew he had matured into manhood aboard this ship.

Andy returned to his thoughts while waiting for the harbor pilot to board the ship. Yesterday, he accepted a commendation on behalf of the *Mariah* as her commanding officer. It was the dedication of the crew that had earned the plaque, which would be placed in the wardroom. The promotion to captain, the admiral said, was for his impressive record and the navy's growing need for leaders. Andy thought about the lives lost in that desperate battle off Bangka during the ceremony that gave a chance to the ragged civilian convoy escaping Singapore.

The miracle came when his own family yacht, the *Angelica*, emerged from her hiding place off Bangka Island. Dr. Jamison, an old family friend, told him the refugees from Helen's Landing thought it was all over when a Japanese patrol boat appeared before their tenuous camouflage. *Mariah* arrived on the scene, in answer to their prayers just as the patrol boat was ready to lower a launch to investigate the inlet, and quickly sank it. The crew, numbed by the sudden end to the lopsided battle, was taken unawares when the illusive Japanese destroyer *Mariah* sought appeared unnoticed on the western horizon, spitting fire at her British enemy.

Angelica's refugees warily watched the desperate struggle between the two battling destroyers and feared the outcome, with the knowledge their fate hung in the balance. Andy still cringed when he thought about *Angelica*'s dangerous journey as she secretly traveled by night and hid from the day. He discovered his mother and Sally, the spirited nurse he found so intriguing on his visits to Helen's Landing, along with what was left of the hospital staff, their remaining patients, and the last army personnel who narrowly escaped before the town was overrun.

The *Mariah* and *Angelica* sailed from Jakarta, Java, with a hastily assembled civilian convoy to Darwin, Australia, shortly after their arrival in the beleaguered Java Sea port. The ship was ordered to continue on to Fremantle, a sheltered port halfway down Australia's western coast, for repairs that the facilities at Darwin were not able to provide shortly before the Japanese decimated the harbor and town.

"Sir," Mason reported, "the harbor pilot is boarding the ship."

"Thank you, Mr. Roden," Andy said, returning his thoughts to the ship's current needs.

"Single up the ropes, let go forward, let go aft," Andy ordered. "Let go spring." He watched each order become reality in quick succession, releasing *Mariah* from the harbor moorings before yielding to the tug assisting to swing her into the shipping lane.

"Pilot, take us to sea," Andy ordered, turning the bridge over to the harbor pilot.

"Sir, secured from harbor stations, first watch closed up," Mason reported an hour later as *Mariah* stretched her keel across the ocean's surface and tasted the salty ocean spray splattered by the wind's whimsy onto her open decks and hull.

"Very well, Number One," Andy acknowledged. "We're to return to the Mediterranean by way of the Indian Ocean and Red Sea before entering the Suez Canal. We'll be meeting a convoy of oil tankers at these coordinates," he said, pointing to a place on the chart. "From Alexandria, Egypt, we do escort duty for materials being sent to England."

"Looks like we might be going back to the north-south route in the Atlantic like we did in late 1940," Mason said.

"Sir, we just received a coded message from base," a baby-faced radio messenger reported, handing Andy the slip of flimsy flash paper.

"Thank you," Andy said when he took the scribbled sheet of encoded gibberish. "Mr. Roden, you have the bridge."

"Yes, sir," Mason said, stepping to the center of the bridge.

"Helmsman, change course to one-six-four," Andy ordered the man on duty, when he returned to the bridge with the decoded message in hand.

"Aye, sir, changing course to one-six-four. My course is now one-six-four," came the helmsman's calm reply.

"Very well. Increase speed to eighteen knots. Mr. Roden, increase lookouts—both sea and air."

"Yes, sir," Mason answered before leaving the bridge to carry out the new orders.

The speakers aboard the *Mariah* crackled with static before Andy Burns's voice came through them. "This is Captain Burns. We have been ordered to Surabaya to join the combined forces now defending in the Java Sea. I know everyone was looking forward to returning to England. However, we are being called

3 2

on to protect our allies and, with them, ourselves. I know, as you have proven countless times, you will give your all to stop this latest aggression against our allied neighbors."

Andy switched off the speaker and went to his bridge chair. He knew from dispatches that the battle was not going well for the Allies. They were to make a speed run to Java as a replacement for those already lost to the intense sea battles between the Allies and the Japanese. Andy would use all of his skills to keep the *Mariah* from becoming a statistic in a dusty file containing the names of ships and their crews lost at sea.

The *Mariah* arrived at Surabaya on March 3, 1942, before the moon rose to light the night sky. The initial challenge by the two patrol boats guarding the harbor entrance sent a chill into the lookouts' souls, causing the hair on their necks to bristle until the "all clear" was signaled, allowing *Mariah* to enter the harbor. Upon arrival in the battle-scarred port, the crew heard the Dutch report that the Japanese advance on Java had been checked.

"Sir, ship is battle ready. Fuel is topped off," Mason reported.

"Very well, Number One. Now we wait to see what the Japanese will do next. We lost a good deal of our strength when the destroyers *Electra* and *Jupiter* were sunk last week, along with the Dutch and American losses."

"It's been rumored there are few survivors," Mason said.

"I heard Admiral Doorman signaled the *Perth* and *Houston* to leave and not pick up survivors for fear of them being sunk as well," Brian Jones, the ship's navigator, said.

As *Mariah*'s navigator and the only other full lieutenant besides Mason Roden aboard, Brian Jones was third in the line of command should anything happen to Andy and Mason. He was part of the naval reserve known as the Wavy Navy by the regular naval personnel when the war began. His ability to place the *Mariah* at a precise position within minutes of the requested time frame was uncanny. After their first voyage together, Andy wondered if Brian might be related to the mythical Davy Jones, the *Spirit of the Sea*, and whether that much-discussed personage might be a little more human and a little less myth.

"I heard the ships were engulfed, and there wasn't much that could be done," Mason said. "I also heard Doorman went down with his flagship, the *DeRuyter*."

"Whatever the facts are, we'll have to be extra alert in the days ahead," Andy said. "We still have a few straggling survivors coming into Surabaya. We don't want to attack our own, but we also don't want to be on the receiving end of a Japanese attack. The last one was enough for me."

"I'll second that, sir," Mason said. "I plan to have training tomorrow with the lookouts to bring them up to speed on ship identification. I think with our allies also in the vicinity, it would be a good idea for our crew to be familiar with their silhouettes as well."

"I concur, Number One. Carry on," Andy ordered.

"Yes, sir."

Andy went to his cabin after reviewing the latest dispatches to sleep a few hours before daybreak when ship commanders would be given their next battle plan. He lay prone on the bunk, but sleep eluded him when his mind began to wonder how many more may have escaped Japan's tightening fist after Singapore fell. He hoped Admiral Edwards and his staff had gotten out. He liked the blunt-spoken man who commanded the *Mariah* out of Singapore and thought him to be an apposite officer Britain needed right now. He drifted into sleep, thinking that one day the British would reclaim the *Pearl of the Orient*.

5

Eric Edwards and his small staff were among the last to leave Singapore on the eve of the fall. Besides Sublieutenant Gaines, his aide, and a former *Mariah* crew member, he had four ratings who were office staff, a few displaced navy and army personnel, and two male navy nurses whom his friend Martin Jamison had sent from Helen's Landing for evacuation through Singapore. He did not know if his friend and the others at the last allied hospital on the peninsula were still alive. The rumor of a small craft sailing away from the village, just prior to a large explosion shortly after the two male nurses arrived, could not be confirmed due to all communication being cut off when the enemy overran the village.

The small wooden hull boat the evacuees were aboard was a pleasure craft with a diesel engine designed for coming in and out of the harbor, not for steady use over a period of days. The men rotated the eight berths, with the admiral taking his turn on the makeshift sleeping arrangements, lying across the cabin floor.

"It ain't much, sir," a rating said. "But it beats bein' back with them poor sods that didn't make it out."

"Yes, that's true," Admiral Edwards said, looking at the makeshift arrangements.

After five days of hiding in the islands less than fifty miles from Singapore, Admiral Edwards ordered the sails raised and used the wind to send them in short nightly treks toward Singkep, the last island with cover, before facing the open sea to Bangka. It was also the last place it might be possible to purchase some replacement parts for the finicky engine that sputtered and died as often as it ran.

"Sir, the mechanic says it ain't no proper job, but should 'old for a short while. It might get us past Bangka anyway. T'em gaskets we got had da be cut ta fit, and we was lucky to get 'em spark plugs ta fire 'er wit'," a navy rating reported. "T'ems other ones was all corroded."

"Very well, we sail at dusk," Edwards replied, trying to look confident.

Eric Edwards knew the door was closing fast, and they had to get through the Bangka Strait before it became a Japanese thoroughfare, which would end all hope of breaking out to Java. In the Great War, Japan was an ally, and he remembered as a young sublieutenant working in the East with their navy. Time had changed that alliance, and now the British were fighting to survive against this new enemy.

"Aye, sir."

The night of day 12, the small sailing craft left the southern coast of Singkep and sailed the fifty miles to Bangka. Luck was with them, and no enemy ships were sighted. Admiral Edwards thought it was because the enemy was busy securing his newest conquest and searching the small islands just off Singapore for any British escapees. He did not want to chance waiting longer and ordered the engine started at dusk to begin the precarious trip through the Bangka Strait. Twice they had to hide when ships were sighted on the horizon, giving the small misshapen crew a moment of trepidation at being discovered. Four days were spent hugging Bangka Island while cautiously moving south through the strait. Tonight they would make a straight run for Surabaya

Harbor. According to the sketchy intercepted radio reports, the harbor was still in British hands.

"Sir, we are ready to sail," Gaines reported. He wondered briefly if the *Mariah* was still out there. He had served aboard her for nearly a year but found his niche in the stacks of paper files that made the navy function. Now he wanted nothing more than to join another ship and send the enemy running with its tail between its legs, until Japan became the defeated, bombed-out nation that she so richly deserved to be after the misery she caused by starting a war in the East.

"Very well, start the engine. Weigh anchor. Make your heading two-three-five," Edwards ordered.

"Aye, sir. My heading is two-three-five," replied a young helmsman.

Gaines stood the watch, trying to remember everything he had learned while serving as a sublieutenant aboard the *Mariah*. His eyes scanned the ocean constantly, searching for anything that might be something more than rolling sea. Suddenly, the sky turned red in the far distance.

"Flashes to the west," Gaines reported.

"That's not lightning. It looks like a night battle. Our navy must have found some of the Jap fleet with the invasion forces," Admiral Edwards said. "Have we picked up any radio traffic?"

"Very little, sir, but what we just heard doesn't sound good. I believe some of our ships have been damaged," the army corporal manning the radio answered. The radio was hastily grabbed just an hour before their departure from the admiral's Singapore headquarters, when Gaines made a last-minute check for anything significant left for the enemy to use.

"We'll continue on our present course for now," Admiral Edwards stated. "The battle is over the horizon, it looks like. Stand by the radio and listen for any transmissions. Maybe we can find out who is out there."

"Yes, sir," the army corporal said with a salute.

* * *

Morning came with the knowledge that the battle in the Java Sea was going badly for the Allies. The man on the radio had picked up several signals about damaged ships and possible sinkings with heavy loss of life. "Sir, I've just caught a partial army signal. The Japs are landing on West Java," he reported, showing his concern.

"We'll have to turn east toward Bawean Island," Admiral Edwards said after reviewing the chart. "We can shelter there tomorrow and then make a run for Surabaya at nightfall." He tried to sound confident and bury his doubts about their chances for success. He couldn't let the men lose hope and, with it, discipline. It would only take one plane to spot them, and their fate would be sealed.

"Boat!" the army private shouted from his lookout post.

"Where?" Gaines said, running to his side.

Pointing, the army private shakily answered, "There, to the left of us. See it?"

"Yes," Gaines said. "Looks like a life raft from one of the ships in last night's battle. I'll tell the admiral," he continued, before making his way to the cabin where Admiral Edwards was taking his rest period.

"Sir, there appears to be a life raft to our starboard," Gaines reported after gently shaking the admiral's shoulder.

"We better check it to see if there are any survivors," Admiral Edwards ordered as he rose to return to the upper deck.

"Yes, sir," Gaines said, saluting.

He keeps with protocol, even now, Admiral Edwards thought. *Martin Jamison was right. Gaines belongs on the shore.* His mind drifted briefly to his friend Martin. He wondered if he had escaped Helen's Landing with the others who were there when the Japanese bypassed the village and effectively cut it off from the south.

"Sir, there are two survivors. I think they're Americans by their uniforms," Gaines reported a short time later.

"Make sure their life raft is sunk before we move on," Edwards ordered.

"Yes, sir," Gaines said with a quick salute.

Once alongside, Gaines watched two of the ratings aboard their craft jump down into the raft and lift the first injured man toward their craft's rail. He helped pull the unknown sailor onto the deck where one of the male nurses waited to attend his wounds. The second man soon followed before the last rating to leave the raft ripped a hole in the side to sink it.

The sun was peeking over the eastern sea, turning the water's surface from ebony to iridescent opal and bringing hints of a new day, when the small vessel entered a tiny bay at Bowean Island a few hours later. Trees came to the water's edge and hung over like a canopy that would protect the small yacht from being spotted by a casual enemy flyover of the area.

"Engine off," a navy rating responded to Admiral Edward's order.

The men quickly spread the shredded awning and placed palm branches over it to further conceal their presence from the enemy's march through the South China Sea basin. Admiral Edwards looked around the open deck and decided there was nothing more to be done but wait for nightfall. "Lookouts will be posted two hours on and two hours off," Edwards told Sublieutenant Gaines, who would issue the orders and set up the schedule, before going below to see about the two wounded Americans.

"How are they doing?" Admiral Edwards asked Mike, the male nurse.

"Sir, one is still unconscious and has wounds that need treatment from a doctor. The other one woke up briefly and spoke to me."

"Did he say anything about the battle?"

"No, sir. He only asked about his friend. When I asked his name, he just told me Jack before drifting back into unconsciousness."

"We should be in Surabaya by tomorrow. Until then, do what you can for them."

"I'll do the best I can, sir."

Mike sighed and returned to the Americans to administer what medical treatment he could using the meager supplies they had gathered together before their hasty departure from Singapore. He had barely made it to the boat before it sailed when he went back to shore to get what he could from the harbor first-aid station. The last rope was being taken in from the pier when he jumped aboard.

"We are approaching the final leg to Surabaya Harbor in Java," Admiral Edwards said at the radio-room doorway, the last rays of sunlight sinking into the sea. They had taken a short hop the previous night and, after about three hours, had seen silhouettes to the west. He had decided to use caution and found another sheltered place to spend the day before attempting to reach their final destination. "Have you picked up any signals?"

"We've picked up some garbled signals. They sound foreign, sir," the radioman answered.

"Do you mean Japanese?"

No, sir, more like German," the radioman replied.

"It must be the Dutch on Java. There were no reports of any German forces in the area before we left Singapore."

The small ship steadily moved on a straight path toward the Strait of Madura. As each turn of the craft's propeller brought them closer to their own forces, some feared that fate would snatch away the chance of safe refuge while the darkness held them in limbo. When off watch, men's thoughts turned inward and dredged up fear and fancy, which denied them rest.

"Ship off the port bow!" a lookout shouted in the darkest hours of the night.

Running the short distance to the man, Admiral Edwards raised his glasses. For a moment, he held his breath, trying to appear calm, while he viewed the ship crossing their path. "Raise the signal lantern. It's one of ours," he finally said.

"Sir," Roger Barnes said with difficulty as a bolt of fear ran through him. "Signal to starboard, low in the water."

"Small craft to starboard!" another lookout shouted.

Crossing the *Mariah*'s deck, Andy observed the short signal through his glasses and someone waving their arms. "Turn too and close. Gunners at the ready," he ordered.

The *Mariah* closed the distance as the small boat turned toward her. When it came closer, Andy recognized Admiral Edwards standing on the sleek deck. Eric Edwards boarded the *Mariah* and quickly came to the bridge.

"Sir, welcome aboard," Andy said. "It's good to see you here."

"I'm mighty glad to see you, Commander—no...Captain Burns," Edwards said, noticing the new stripes on Andy's uniform. "We have two wounded American sailors we picked up from a life raft two nights ago. One's in pretty bad shape. We need to get him to your Dr. Patterson as quickly as we can."

Turning to Roger Barnes, Andy said, "Have a detail bring the wounded men to the infirmary and get the rest of the survivors on board quickly. Inform Dr. Hartman of the situation. When everyone is off the yacht, sink it so we don't leave any trace for our Japanese friends to find. Dr. Patterson stayed in Australia with Dr. Jamison, sir. John Hartman took his place."

"Martin made it then," Admiral Edwards said with a slight smile. "What about the others?"

"The rest of the hospital staff, along with their last six patients and my mother, escaped with the final army defenders on the *Angelica*, sir, my family's small yacht. They're in Australia now," Andy said.

"I'm glad for you, Captain. A lot of folks didn't get away."

"My family was lucky, but too many others were not so fortunate," Andy said. "We listened to the final BBC broadcast out of Singapore on the voyage to Australia."

"Is Surabaya still in Allied hands?" Admiral Edwards said, after a moment.

"For the moment, at least, but Japanese forces have nearly isolated the base. The damage is pretty heavy," Andy said.

The *Mariah* changed course after sinking the small craft that had served its final master so well. A short time later, she entered Surabaya Harbor with the latest refugees to escape Singapore at the end of another Japanese bombing raid of the city and harbor.

"It's like Singapore all over again," Mason said, walking onto the bridge after seeing Admiral Edwards to his quarters.

"They can't keep outrunning their supplies forever," Andy said. "At some point, we'll stop them, and then we will start pushing them back."

"We kept Germany out of Britain in 1940," Mason said. "I should think, with the number of countries against them now, the Japs would soon reach a stopping point."

Early the next morning, the radioman reported, "Sir, orders have just come in by code." He gave Andy a flimsy sheet of flash paper, with what looked like gibberish typed onto it.

"Very well. Number One, you're with me," Andy briskly stated.

"Sir," Mason replied.

"We've been ordered to the Indian Ocean," Andy said after decoding the transmission.

"What's our mission, sir?" Mason said.

"Two battle groups are being formed under Sir James Somerville. Admiral Edwards is to be part of the command force as well. He has asked that the *Mariah* be his flagship," Andy said.

Eric Edwards emerged from *Mariah's* wardroom after a short meeting with what command personnel remained on Java. The last signal received ordered all ships and naval personnel evacuate Surabaya Harbor and join the battle groups being formed under Somerville. The final order stated Admiral Edwards was to take charge of a separate smaller group.

"Sir, please join us," Andy said when he noticed Edwards step onto the bridge.

"Thank you, Captain. We should be sailing shortly. It's good to be at sea again," Admiral Edwards said.

"Yes, sir, it is. We're honored to have your flag aboard the *Mariah*. She will serve you well," Andy said.

"I'm counting on that, Captain. Yes…I'm counting on that," Admiral Edwards trailed off as he looked out toward the waiting sea.

6

Katrin washed the last dish and put away the few remaining tins of food before joining her father and Captain Logan in the central dining room. The six-hour hike the previous day became a surreal nightmare of fear and sadness when one of the wounded men collapsed. Her father spent the past hour with Sergeant Ledowski in prayer and counsel, after praying the burial rite at the grave of the American soldier the sergeant had carried the last mile to this final resting place. She watched in sorrow as her dad knelt before her mother's grave for a moment after the short service.

Taking a deep breath, Katrin entered the dining room, trying to show a brave face so her father wouldn't worry about her. She remembered when her parents first found this seeming paradise and how the small parish had built the gathering house and cabins as a retreat for church members so that they would have a chance to know God better. Katrin wondered, as she lingered in the doorway, if this quiet place would ever be a paradise again.

The broadcast they picked up the previous evening on the old wireless stated Mr. Churchill had reported to the House of Commons that naval losses during the past two months were significant, indicating that the Indian Ocean was becoming untenable for the Allied forces and may have to be abandoned.

The newscaster continued with reports that the government in India was divided by Muslin and Hindu factions, making the independence articles proposed by England more difficult to enact.

Father Albright looked up to see Katrin and smiled. "Come in, my dear. Captain Logan and I were just discussing how we might leave Java and find some of our own."

"What's left of the navy was spotted in the harbor a couple days ago. If we're quick and lucky, we might find out how we can get the injured, along with you and your daughter, to safety," Captain Logan said.

"Dad, what about the Way of the Cross home?" Katrin said.

"Way of the Cross?" Logan asked, wrinkling his brow.

"It's been several years, Katrin. The entrance might be over-grown and difficult to find—if we can find it at all," Father Albright said with caution.

"But it's still there, Dad. We used to go that way when we'd do an overnight hike with our youth group to get here. I loved it when Mom would come with us, and we would make a campfire in the big chamber. I still think of it as my special place."

"Sir, I don't understand," Captain Logan said. "Are you saying there's a way to get to Surabaya without being seen?"

"There might be, Captain. It would be best to check at daybreak before we get our hopes up," Father Albright said. "We made a door to cover the entrance to keep wild animals out. It's been nearly five years, though, since it was last used. Not since my wife passed away."

"I'll have a couple of the men scout it out first thing."

"I'll have to go with them. I couldn't show you on a map how to get there. I just know the landmarks."

"Very well, Father. But if a Jap comes along, don't try to convert him. And I'm afraid the collar will have to stay here, too easy to spot from a distance. You've been lucky so far."

"Yes, I suppose I have."

* * *

"Well, Russ, did you find anything?" Logan asked when Lieutenant Crammer returned the next morning. "By the way, where is the good father?"

"He's with Sergeant Ledowski getting some knapsacks that were left here to carry supplies, sir. The entrance is a bit small, but about fifty yards in it starts to open up."

"What about dead ends—can we get lost in there?"

"Father Albright says the way is marked."

"Captain Logan," Katrin said, "the trail is unmistakable. You'll understand when we get there."

Father Albright and Sergeant Ledowski led the ragged band of soldiers to the cave entrance before the sun left the day behind. Before leaving the church's retreat, every available canteen had been filled to the top, and the spare knapsacks were packed with useful items—from food to tools—to help them on their journey. Each cabin floor in the peaceful retreat had been cleared of any telltale signs that anyone had been there for some time. Common areas had been brushed with small leafy tree branches, which were taken from high above their heads and carried the mile hike to the cave's entrance. Once the last man was inside, Sergeant Ledowski used the branches to erase any evidence of their presence in the area, well into the mouth of the cave, and carefully draped the undergrowth back over the makeshift doorway as he pulled it closed.

The soldiers were surprised, after crouching to enter the cave, when the rocky floor began to tip downhill and then opened into a large chamber. Father Albright lit a lantern, which was still filled with lamp oil. Captain Logan walked to the far end of the open chamber and noticed a large cross carved on a wall where two more openings appeared, leading into a dark abyss. He turned back to the others and noticed Katrin helping the two British rangers who were still weak from their bout with malaria. Father Albright was able to administer first aid to the remaining wounded Americans and wrapped their arm wounds using an ancient native remedy, which appeared to be working.

"I told you, you would understand *the way*," Katrin said, coming to stand beside the captain.

"So you did," Logan replied, looking into the wide-set hazel eyes and noticing, for the first time, the full mouth and small straight nose that fitted the perfect oval face.

"Sir," Lieutenant Crammer said, breaking the spell, "Father Albright said, if we move on, there's another larger chamber where we can rest a few hours before the trek beneath Surabaya."

The path they followed was marked with the emblems of different-shaped crosses, leading them to a chamber that glowed in soft light and smelled like fresh air and rainwater. Lieutenant Crammer followed the gentle breeze until he found an opening, about eighteen inches across, where the outside air funneled into the open space. Small shafts of light splashed across the chamber, where the lowering sun could be seen filtering through minute holes from the surface. The magical effect lifted the men's spirits for the first time since the Japanese invaded.

Katrin reminisced, while walking the familiar pathway, how her father had used this same pathway to teach her youth group about the Way of the Cross. It seemed such a long time ago, especially after they learned her mother was in the advanced stages of leukemia and was gone before there was time to say good-bye. She smiled, when they reached the large enchanting chamber, at the memories of being here with her parents and friends during an overnight adventure, when she had felt so safe.

"Glory holes, Lieutenant," Father Albright explained when he noticed Crammer scanning the rock ceiling, which was fifty or more feet above their heads. "Early settlers who were looking for precious metals to mine made them. My guess is they were disappointed when their bore holes showed no signs of wealth to be had. But it does make a pleasant resting place with the natural light filtering in.

"How easy are they to spot from the surface?" Captain Logan asked.

"There's only a couple dozen, not enough to be noticeable. I've looked. But plenty to let the sun and moon illuminate our way," Father Albright said. "We're safe here. No one has been here since our last retreat, which was over five years ago."

"It won't hurt to be cautious," Captain Logan said. "We'll rotate the watch at each end should the enemy happen to stumble across an entrance and become curious."

"As you wish, Captain. I hope you and the men will join Katrin and me for evening prayer first though."

Several hours had passed since the short but moving prayers were said. Lieutenant Crammer and Corporal Davis were keeping the second watch. Crammer listened to the silence for a long time and nearly nodded off to sleep when a distant sound made him fully aware of his surroundings. Waiting a moment, he heard it again and signaled Davis to be alert. The sound was starting to echo across the moon-bathed cavern when Crammer quietly woke everyone and signaled for silence.

Joseph Albright cocked an ear to one side and listened for a full minute before he understood the sound was coming from the surface. At first, he didn't know what the advancing odd noise was until a distinctive chatter, followed by a loud booming, echoed through the passages and into the chamber where they all stood. He suddenly realized their small group was taking refuge beneath a battlefield, where soldiers were fighting and dying.

"Father, is it far to where we're going?" Captain Logan asked. "I think the war is catching up with us."

"At least four or five hours. There are torches when we get farther along to light our way."

"We better get moving. I think time is running out."

Five hours passed before the fleeing group of ragged, rescued soldiers and their improbable deliverers emerged from the dark passages to an opening above the sea. The rock-faced hill—covered in dense foliage at the open cave entrance—overlooked the empty harbor, causing their hearts to sink in despair at the new plight they faced. Father Albright went back into the last passage until he reached a marker and then turned to where it looked as if nature had pushed a large dent in the rock.

"Is it there, Dad?" Katrin said.

"Yes, thank heaven. Captain, I'm going to pull the rope, and a ladder should drop down. When you climb up, it reaches the floor of our bell tower. If we can enter the church, there's still a two-way army radio there and some other things my friend Colonel Gherst left with us. I never thought we would need them."

"Lieutenant Crammer, take a peek up top and see if we can slip in and out unnoticed," Logan ordered.

Crammer carefully lifted the trapdoor below the bell tower and looked all around the enclosed square space. He noticed a closed door to the right. Looking up, he could see light filtering through what appeared to be vents about twenty feet above him. Everything was quiet. He quickly slipped into the small space and climbed the wooden rungs to scout the surrounding area before returning to the others.

"Everything is quiet. I didn't see anyone on the streets. I think we can go and get what we need without being noticed," Crammer reported.

"All right. Go with Father Albright and be quick about it. If you hear anything, hightail it back here, and we'll wait for night to come," Logan ordered.

It took nearly twenty minutes to reach the church office crawling on hands and knees through the sanctuary to reach the back hallway that led to the locked office door. Once unlocked with the key Father Albright still carried in his pocket, Crammer cracked the door to look out the office window before quickly shoving Father Albright through and lowering the blind to help conceal their presence. The two men quickly placed the radio equipment into a box left on the office floor from the last Bible-study books to be delivered and returned to the secluded hallway. Father Albright pointed to the back of the church and opened another door before Crammer could catch him. Inside was a large pantry with several tins of food and other items. They shoved the most useful items into what looked like large pillowcases.

"The ladies made these for pew-cushion covers, but the cushions never came," Father Albright said.

It took longer, pushing and pulling their booty, for the return journey to the bell tower's open trapdoor. An air raid was underway when Crammer carefully handed down the precious radio equipment to Sergeant Ledowski. He signaled for a couple of the others to grab the full sacks as he lowered them down. He sent Father Albright down the ladder before grabbing hold of the trapdoor rope and lowering it over his head, as bombs began pounding the northern part of the city.

"Father, you nearly scared me to death when you darted off down that hallway," Crammer said.

"Sorry, Lieutenant, but I knew we needed a few things, and that was the only place to get them. I also grabbed these off the shelf." Father Albright handed Crammer three radio tubes from his pocket. "Captain Logan, we should have enough to last for some time if we're careful. I turned on the water spigot that's concealed in the bell tower as well. We'll have to be careful, but it will give us a freshwater supply. I had the line put in when the children were using the passage to ensure we had water readily available. Over the years, the forming rock has wrapped around some of the pipes, making them hard to see."

"Are there any other surprises that you haven't told me about, Father?" Logan asked.

"No, I think that's it. Do you think the radio will be able to reach our forces?"

"I don't know, but we'll try it tonight. Hopefully it won't be long before someone will come for us."

"I hope so, Captain, for all of our sakes," Father Albright said, looking toward Katrin's small form bent over Adam, a British scout, administering one of the few doses of Quinine that was kept at the church before bathing his sweating body with cool cloths.

7

Intermittent clouds silently crossed the night sky, giving the ocean a patchwork of eerie shadows across the opaque water. Eerie silhouettes slithered across the harbor waters, causing lookouts to scan the sky in search of another enemy bombing raid, which could sink their ship before escaping to the open sea. The closing Japanese ground forces, approaching the war-weary port at Surabaya, were pushing the Allied armies not already overrun into the sea.

"Sir, *Mariah* is ready for sea," Mason reported.

"Very well, prepare to leave harbor. Lookouts to their posts," Andy ordered.

The *Mariah* made her way into the Indian Ocean without the traditional ceremony of leaving harbor between nighttime enemy-bombing raids and quickly took her place among the few remaining Allied ships, turning her bow toward Ceylon. Andy stood at the center of the bridge and scanned the sea, remembering the first time he saw the telltale broomstick-like structure of a periscope as an unblooded first officer. Their task was to join the fleet—based at Ceylon—under Sir James Somerville in order to keep the Japanese out of the Burmese shipping lanes and to protect India from invasion.

"Sir, radio message," the young rating said, handing Andy the clipboard.

"Mr. Barnes," Andy summoned, "tell Admiral Edwards we have orders from Sir James."

"Yes, sir."

Roger Barnes, often called Bunts because of the special bunting he used for signaling between ships, was a regular navy midshipman serving aboard his first ship's assignment on the road to becoming an officer. The ship and her crew were already building a reputation with her battles in the English Channel and North Sea in the early days of the war when he became part of the crew in September 1940, following *Mariah's* covert mission in the Atlantic.

The *Mariah* was transferred to Singapore a short time later, where she spent 1941 serving in the illusion of a peacetime navy until the December invasion of the Malay Peninsula and aerial bombing of Singapore. His young eyes had witnessed merciless attacks, across the shores that bordered the South China and Java Seas, by the conquering Japanese forces. When he returned to England for the next phase of his naval training, he would have a great deal to tell his classmates—if he survived the lopsided naval battles that 1942 brought the Allied fleets.

"Admiral," Andy greeted Eric Edwards when he joined Andy in the map room. "Sir James just sent orders to move west of Ceylon."

"He wants us to sail southwest and form a barrier between Addu Atoll and Maldive Isle," Admiral Edwards said after reading the dispatch. "Have Jones lay out a course and speed to get us there as quickly as possible, and signal the group. If we can keep the enemy from coming through that gap, we might be able to sandwich them and push them into the two fleets Sir James has at Ceylon."

"Yes, sir."

The small group increased to fifteen knots after Brian Jones laid out a direct course to the desired coordinates. Andy sat on his bridge chair and thought about Troy Edmon, *Mariah*'s previous captain. His words, "You don't get a second chance in war," echoed in Andy's mind as he guided the *Mariah* into harm's way.

"Sir, something in the water to starboard," a wide-eyed watchman shouted.

Shots cracked out from the minelayer to *Mariah*'s starboard before the unmistakable wake of a torpedo was seen, which missed the ship by a mere twenty feet. Battle stations sounded, bringing men to their gunnery stations before the reverberating sound faded into the ocean's breeze.

"Sir, torpedo wake to port," Barnes bellowed in warning.

"Hard a-starboard," Andy ordered. "Prepare depth charges."

Tim Parker quickly readied the drumlike cylinders in preparation to launch the depth charges in response to the submarine attack. Tim knew little about civilian life after joining the navy as a naive sixteen-year-old, slowly rising through the ranks. He had served aboard the *Mariah* since before war was declared in 1939 and was promoted to warrant officer under Captain Edmon the spring before hostilities broke out. But it was Andy Burns, a regular navy first officer, and Quentin Patterson, a wavy navy lieutenant and the ship's doctor, who made him welcome in the wardroom when the promotion came through. He stood ready, with the baby-faced newcomers, to pull the cord and launch the first explosive charges the instant Captain Burns gave the order.

"Commence firing," Andy ordered as he brought the *Mariah* across the coordinates that Lieutenant Jones quickly calculated from the torpedo trajectory.

The sea ruptured into spontaneous geysers when the first charges began to explode beneath the ocean's surface. Andy hoped the Japanese didn't hunt in packs like the Germans in the Atlantic's northern shipping lanes. The *Mariah* and her sister ships would be hard-pressed to defend the small group against a "wolf pack." A second destroyer, left from the American fleet that had escaped the Philippines, joined the *Mariah* in pounding the sea to sink the attacking submarine.

Tim watched the charges roll into the catapult to be sure they securely settled into the chamber before being launched into the sea. Showers of water fell across the deck as the two ships worked in tandem crossing the other's path. An oil slick appeared, but Andy thought it might be a ruse and continued the pounding another half hour before changing course toward Addu Atoll.

Mason approached the depth-charge station when *Mariah* returned to her original course. "Do you think we hit it, Mr. Parker?"

"Hard to say. The oil coulda been a trick, but looked ta be more of it when we kept up the depth chargin'. We mighta done some damage and slowed it a bit."

"Keep a sharp eye out for any more of them. I'm guessing those Zeros off Java at our departure, radioed our last coordinates before we lost them."

"Yes, sir. The boys an' me 'ill keep our eyes peeled."

"Carry on, then."

Several days passed without any more enemy sightings while the small group of Allied defenders sailed to their patrol station fifty miles west of Maldive Isle and Addu Atoll. Admiral Edwards ordered the group to begin a north-south patrol of the area before retiring to his cabin to pick up the latest wireless broadcast.

* * *

Martin Jamison turned the dial on Helen Burns's radio, once the tubes were warm until it settled on the BBC station out of Perth, to hear the nine-o'clock report. He and Quentin Patterson had joined Helen along with Sally, Jane, and Peter for a shared evening meal and planning session for the local hospital auxiliary. Helen, in her usual energetic manner, soon discovered the auxiliary of previous years was disbanded, and no one had come forward to resume the activities. With the matron's and administrator's blessing, she spoke with Jane and Sally, and plans were soon underway to start some activities to raise staff morale and cheer the increasing number of patients in the wards.

"I think the Easter egg hunt on Holy Saturday is a good idea, Sally," Helen said. "Using that format, we can hide some fun prizes."

"Even with the shortages, we can get small knickknacks and trinkets for folks to hunt down," Jane said.

"I'm not scheduled until Tuesday, so maybe Jane and I can go into Noonamah and see what's there."

"If you can get a train," Dr. Jamison cautioned.

"Jane, you better check first. I don't want you stranded in your condition," Peter said.

"Don't worry, we'll be all right. Oh, listen—I think the news is starting."

"Good evening from the BBC Perth, Australia, station," the announcer began. "In a candid communiqué, the United States and Britain have informed their citizens that thirteen warships were lost to the Japanese between February 27 and March 1 during a series of ocean battles in the Java Sea. This reporter has learned the Dutch government denied the Axis claim that Java surrendered to Japanese forces on March 8. Sadly, the Japanese Army has since overwhelmed the brave Allied defenders, and Java succumbed on March 9."

Dr. Jamison and Dr. Patterson looked at each other a moment before the newscast continued. Each recognized the same unasked question regarding the *Mariah*'s whereabouts.

"Today, Prime Minister Churchill announced that Sir Stafford Cripps has risked travel to India with a plan proposal—containing Articles of Independence—to settle the Indian problem that is meeting opposition by opposing political factions. In further news of the week, British Foreign Minister Eden and Premier

Tsouderos of Greece signed an agreement in London that Britain will equip Greek forces in exchange for Greek naval aid in the Mediterranean to assist in blockading supplies to the German and Italian armies in North Africa. This is the BBC Perth station. Good night."

"It sounds like the West is starting to consolidate in Europe," Peter commented after Dr. Jamison switched off the radio.

"I wonder if the Allies want to go after Germany by way of Greece again," Sally said.

"I don't know, Sally," Dr. Jamison said. "If they *do* try again, it will take a lot more than what England could provide last year. North Africa, most likely, will need to be resolved before another attempt is made, and the United States might have something to offer as well this time."

"I wonder what will happen with India and the proposal England is presenting to them," Jane said.

"A lot will depend on how strong the political faction currently in power is," Quentin Patterson said. "We'll have to see what might happen with Japan as well. They haven't invaded India yet, but that could change with the present situation."

* * *

Andy Burns continued to patrol with his few companion ships the fifty-mile trek west of Addu Atoll and Maldive Isle. The crew learned that Andaman Island, in the Bay of Bengal, was occupied by the Japanese, putting Ceylon in a precarious position. The off-duty crew was listening at the radio room doorway when a news broadcast reported the heaviest air raid yet on Port Moresby, New Guinea, on March 23 and speculated about its proximity to nearby eastern Australia. Others wondered if rumors of Lutheran missionaries and Nazi-trained natives were advancing along the Markham River Valley to attack Port Moresby from the rear.

"Sir, dispatch from Sir James," the radio-room runner said, handing Andy the sheet of flash paper.

"Very well, carry on," Andy replied. "Force A is regrouping south of India. The battleship *Warspite* and two carriers are with them," Andy read to those on the bridge. "We are to move east twenty-five miles in preparation to lend support."

"Looks like things are starting to happen," Mason said. "We could be back in Surabaya before you know it, with this many ships and air support to defend against the Japs."

"We'll have to see," Andy said. "Mr. Jones, set our course."

"Course to steer is two-one-seven, sir."

"Very well, steer two-one-seven," Andy ordered. "Signal the fleet. Admiral, we should be in place by 1900 hours."

"Good. We'll form a staggered line layered with our destroyers and sloops overlapping gunnery, so the enemy is hit from both sides simultaneously," Eric Edwards said. "Between the dual gunfire and the carriers with Somerville, we should do some damage." He rubbed his hands together in further thought. "We'll see what the next few days bring."

Andy thought about the recent signals between the two forces near Ceylon, searching out the Japanese Navy, while lying on the bunk in his sea cabin. *Mariah's* radio room was manned around the clock, with orders to report the moment the slightest hint the enemy might be nearing the area. The only reports to date were sketchy news intercepts about the formation of an Allied Pacific War Council to take place on April 1 in Washington, DC. The crew learned the proposal from London, for a postwar Indian government was meeting opposition from the Indian Congress and the Muslim League. Sir Stafford warned in a radio appeal to the people of India, if the British offer was refused, there would not be time or opportunity to reconsider until after the war. Andy briefly wondered if Britain would have a say about India's independence articles when the war ended.

Two more days passed before the radio room received a coded message that the Japanese fleet was sighted four hundred miles south of Ceylon. Sir James directed the British warships to sail from the anchorage at Trincomalee, Ceylon, and prepare for battle.

"Sir," Mason reported, "the ship is battle ready."

"Very well. We continue on our current course until Sir James signals to close from the west."

"Signal, sir," the runner said, handing Andy the brief message.

"The Japanese are attacking Colombo, Ceylon, and the air base at Ratmalana. The Zeros are believed to be carrier-based and possibly from the same carriers that attacked the United States' base at Pearl Harbor. Sir James warns to be prepared for aerial attack."

*   *   *

"This is the BBC Sydney, Australia, station, reporting," Admiral Edwards heard the announcer begin when he tuned in the wireless set in his cabin. "In a radio broadcast, Tokyo has warned the Indian government, following Sir Stafford Cripps's appeal to accept the altered Indian Independence plan, to rebel against Britain or, and I quote, 'suffer great calamities.' In support of this threat by Japan, the Indian port cities of Vizagapatam and Cocanada were bombed by Japanese air assaults, shortly after the broadcast, resulting in some slight damage.

"In an effort to resolve the Indian issue and avoid collapse of the negotiations, Sir Stafford offered concessions to India's leaders, including the promise an Indian would hold a key defense post if the rest of the Indian union plan is accepted. This is the BBC Perth, Australia, station. Good afternoon."

Admiral Edwards switched off the receiver. He learned earlier in the day, the British cruisers *Cornwall* and *Dorsetshire* were sunk southwest of Ceylon on Easter Sunday by aerial attack. He also knew British troops were retreating to Prome—forty miles north of Thayetmyo and Allanmyo—under extreme pressure by Japanese forces. He wondered if the government in India was stalling until the battle in the Indian Ocean was decided.

* * *

"Sir," a runner said on the heels of a quick tap at Eric Edward's open cabin door. "We just received a communiqué that the aircraft carrier *Hermes*, along with a destroyer, a corvette, and two tankers have been sunk. It says that some other Allied ships were sunk too."

Admiral Edwards took the quickly scratched-out message from the pasty-faced boy and scanned it for further information. "Thank you, son. Send Captain Burns to my cabin and be ready to bring the fight to the enemy. They can't keep going without supplies, and they're a long way from their supply line."

"Yes, sir," the young rating replied with renewed confidence from his admiral's words.

Andy entered Admiral Edward's cabin. "Sir, you wanted to see me," Andy said.

"Here, read this first."

"It doesn't look like Somerville's fleet is faring well. Are we to join the rest of the fleet to assist?" Andy asked.

"No, Sir James has not ordered us to move in. I wanted you aware of the most current situation. We may be facing a desperate battle if more of the fleet is destroyed. I believe Somerville is a good strategist, but he needs more to work with against the enemy right now."

"If all the carrier and support ships that attacked the American base at Pearl Harbor are here, we'll need considerable air cover to defeat them."

"I believe Sir James is telling the admiralty in London something very similar," Edwards noted.

"I wonder how the message will be received," Andy mused.

"It's hard to say, but history will most likely analyze the decision well after the admiralty has reacted to Sir James's message." There was a tap on the door. "Come," Edwards said.

"Sir, another message from Admiral Somerville," the same young runner said.

"We're to sail to Kilindini, Kenya harbor, to await further orders. Sir James is evacuating the area before our fleet is depleted further," Andy said after reading the brief message.

"Very well, signal the group we sail in twenty minutes. Have Jones set a direct course," Admiral Edwards ordered.

"Yes, sir. Will you join me on the bridge, sir?"

"I'll be along shortly."

Saluting, Andy left for the bridge to inform Mason of the new orders. The *Mariah* turned her bow west a short time later as her stern watched the small island outcroppings sink into the horizon.

8

Quentin Patterson turned off the radio and settled farther into his chair to review patient notes. The only bright spot of the week was having watched Arthur Nance walk out of the ward in renewed health. He had insisted Arthur take a week to relax at a seaside resort before being restored to duty. The army doctor, who was several years younger and in awe of the well-respected London surgeon, gave no argument to his directive.

After reviewing the six charts in his lap, Dr. Patterson let his thoughts drift to the newscast. It appeared the Japs were still advancing, and Bataan was about to succumb to the enemy. *Maybe Martin will know something in the morning*, he thought.

Quentin Patterson entered the hospital early the next morning and went directly to the office next to his friend Martin's. He was still thinking about the previous evening's newscast while he took off his uniform jacket and replaced it with a lab coat and then placed his stethoscope in his pocket. Closing his office door, he knocked on Martin Jamison's door and entered at Dr. Jamison's, "Come."

"Martin," Dr. Patterson greeted his friend. "Have you heard any more about India or how Andy is faring? The news lately isn't very encouraging."

"No more than you, Quentin. Helen might have something to tell us about the *Mariah*. She wants all of us to come to her place Sunday after church. She said to bring a bottle of wine. Apparently, she, Jane, and Sally have combined ration stamps to put a meal together."

"Splendid! It will be like old times," Quentin replied, trying to put some cheer in his voice.

"As close as we can get anyway. Maybe we'll know something by then."

The friends gathered after Sunday mass to enjoy a break from increasingly demanding duties, but John Hartman was noticeably absent along with Andy. Helen welcomed everyone to the cottage, which she had purchased when the coffee plantation at Helen's Landing began to grow and business ties expanded to Australia. She had shipped many of the business records and some personal belongings when Andy indicated concern in his letters about Malaya, after the combined army-navy defenses were built around the growing coastal village.

"Welcome, everyone. Quentin, I'm glad you could join us today," Helen said, smiling at her friends.

"Helen, you've made the cottage look wonderful," Sally enthusiastically stated, entering the sitting room.

"Thank you. I was fortunate to have this place farther down the coast from Darwin. It was spared from the destruction. Jane, Sally, why don't we get things ready and then we can talk over dinner."

"It's wonderful to have some time together, Helen," Jane said. "Peter and I want to talk with everyone. We've started thinking about names and want to run them by you."

The friends soon gathered around the rough-board dining table to the casseroles, breads, and desserts the shortened food supply allowed. It wasn't up to some of the meals that were shared in better times, but everyone's appetite was sated, and a toast was given to the women's cooking ingenuity using the procured

6 3

bottle of wine Martin Jamison had found in a little shop near the hospital. "Our Aussie wines are better than you would expect," the owner had told him when he packaged up the bottle.

"It was like the smorgasbords on family night, back in Malaya," Peter said when he laid down his fork.

"I'd have to agree," Dr. Jamison said.

They got up and gathered around Helen's old radio receiver to listen to the early Sunday broadcast. The dial was soon adjusted to the BBC news hour, which began a few moments later.

"This is the BBC Perth, Australia, station reporting. A brief army news release states the intense Japanese offensive is forcing British and Australian forces out of Prome. And it is confirmed by British and American sources, the Allied navies in the Indian Ocean have vacated the area at this time. On a positive note, the American Army will soon be arriving en masse to bolster the Australian military and join the offensive to push the Japanese out of New Guinea and beyond. This will be my last broadcast as I will be supporting my country, joining the fight to bring order out of chaos. Good afternoon and good-bye, from the BBC radio, Perth, Australia, station."

"It looks like the Japanese are still coveting more territory," Quentin commented after Helen switched off the set.

"Yes, we'll have to see what happens in the next few weeks with the Americans coming. I still believe it will make a difference in the balance here," Martin said.

"The United States is very upset about the Japanese," Jane said. "My first father-in-law, Jim's dad, still writes to us and keeps us up to date about things in America. His last letter said that most of the people he and his sister talk to think the US should fight the Japanese."

"Well, it will depend on what this new council that met in Washington decides," Peter said. "My guess is, Europe will override the East."

"You're probably right, Peter," Dr. Jamison said. "Helen, have you heard from Andy yet?"

"Not in the last few weeks. I'm sure he's fine, or I would have been told. But let's talk about something a bit more cheerful for a change. Jane, you said you and Peter had some names?"

"We have thought of a few. Peter, you want to tell them where we're at right now?"

"Well, I favor Hannah Marie for a girl, but Jane likes Emily Marie or possibly Dawn Marie. As for a boy, all we have is Peter for a middle name."

"I like all of them," Sally said.

"That's the problem—so do we," Jane said with a rueful grin.

"Jane?" Peter asked.

"Yes."

"How about we talk about the christening?"

"Yes, we should," Jane agreed. "Helen, Sally, we want to ask that you be godmothers to our firstborn. Would it be all right with you, Sally, if Helen is first godmother and you are the alternate? You both mean a great deal to Peter and me."

"Sally, what do you think?" Helen asked.

"It's wonderful! I will love being a part of his or her life— Aunt Sally." She smiled. "Jane, thank you so much!"

"It will be a privilege, my dears," Helen answered. "I look forward to being the grandmother influence, but I know Peter's parents want to meet their grandchild as soon as possible."

"When it's safe to travel, I'm sure they'll come," Peter said. "Dr. Jamison, we both would be grateful if you would consent to be the godfather."

"Bless my soul! I would be honored. Thank you both for including me."

"We agreed that John should be the alternate, and he accepted just before the *Mariah* sailed. Dr. Patterson, would you consider standing in?" Peter asked.

"Of course, I'd be glad to. And I'll be available when the time comes as well. I figure, between us, we should be able to bring this baby into the world," Quentin said with a twinkle in his eyes.

"I'm so glad this is settled. Now all we have to do is wait for our little one's arrival," Jane said with a gentle smile.

All too soon, it was time for everyone to return to their temporary homes. Later that night, when the full moon splashed only a dim glow into Jane and Peter's bedroom, they lay beside each other, talking about preparing the nursery.

Across the small town, Sally sat in her small room at the hospital nurses' quarters, wondering where Andy might be and praying for the *Mariah* to be kept safe from harm.

* * *

"I'll see you at morning rounds," Admiral Jamison said in parting to Quentin Patterson as he opened the door to his small rented cottage next door to the hospital grounds.

"Yes, in the morning," Quentin responded before walking the half block to his own three-room cottage across the way. *I wonder when the Americans will get here and when they will begin to show more signs of entering the fight. All that the news talks about are meetings in Washington and this new war council. What we need are soldiers and equipment to get things turning back to normal,* he thought as he prepared for bed.

9

Captain Logan set up the radio equipment that Father Albright's friend, Colonel Gherst, left for him to continue his ministry to the increasing number of troops arriving in Java. Logan said the frequencies were different than the American communication units, but he had hopes it was strong enough to reach friendly ears.

Katrin had learned, since they entered the caves under Surabaya, the names of the other American soldiers and the two British scouts, Adam and Eugene. The two scouts foraged in night excursions around a two-mile radius of her dad's church after recovering from the malaria each had suffered. During one of their outings, they brought back useful household items and medical supplies, which they had found in an abandoned pharmacy. More importantly, they brought news about Japanese strongholds in the city. It appeared, for now, the small church on the cliff top was left untouched.

Captain Logan decided to take advantage of the situation and sent two men up the bell tower at night to check the area. Twice, men entered the church and brought back candles to help light the dark passages. Father Albright warned the men—looking for another way to the sea— to tie a lead line to where they started so as not to get lost in the intertwining passages, where God had twisted his fingers in the oozing lava when the island was formed.

Katrin walked from the makeshift kitchen, setting out of sight to the cave opening above the sea beyond the bend in the rocky passageway beneath Holy Apostle Church. "I brought you some food, Russ," she said, handing Lieutenant Crammer a tinplate.

"Thank you, ma'am, that was very kind of you."

"Please, call me Katrin. We could be here for some time, and ma'am seems so formal."

"As you wish, Katrin."

"Have you heard anything?" Katrin asked.

"I picked up some overlapping chatter earlier, but nothing in the last two hours since the set was turned on. It was in English, but I couldn't raise anyone. I'm sorry, Katrin," Crammer said.

"All we can do is pray for our signal to be heard. Dad said we all need to be strong and trust God's time on this. I'm sure we'll be rescued when the time is right."

"I'm going to try again in about five minutes. You want to wait to see if we get through?" Crammer asked.

"All right," Katrin agreed, sitting down on a nearby rock formation.

Lieutenant Crammer switched the radio unit on, with no volume, until the tubes warmed up, before adjusting the dial. The faint sound of static could be heard before he thumbed the hand mic and began to speak.

*　*　*

The man on duty at the Darwin listening post noticed the blinking light above the radio receiver and increased the volume. He leaned into the speaker to better hear the unidentified caller's transmission.

"This is bravo anchor team. We are trapped near Surabaya with wounded and civilians," the radioman at Darwin heard.

"Sir," the radioman called. "We have that same unidentified caller again."

"Send *identify leader and affiliation in Surabaya*, Corporal, and wait for the answer. If they say Father Albright from the Church of England, tell them to standby," Colonel Bastian ordered.

"Yes, sir," the army corporal replied, turning to his set.

*   *   *

Crammer released the mic button and waited before repeating the message again. He was about to shut the set down for the night when a reply came across the airways.

"Katrin, quick, get Captain Logan," Crammer said.

"Right away," Katrin said, turning to run back to their campsite deeper inside the cave.

"What is it, Lieutenant?" Logan asked when he and Katrin returned.

"Sir, a reply came through claiming to be in Australia and asked for the leader's name and affiliation. They also sent the correct code word for Tuesdays."

"Send the answer, and we'll see what the next instruction is," Logan ordered. "I'll go inform the others that help is on the way."

*   *   *

The receiver in Darwin came to life again as Russ Crammer sent the required answer.

*   *   *

Father Albright came and stood by Katrin by the time the reply went out and squeezed her hand. "God has blessed us tonight," he softly said, looking into her sparkling eyes.

*   *   *

"Sir, the answer is correct," the radio operator told Colonel Bastian and his American counterpart, Fred Palmer.

"Tell them to tune in tomorrow night at nine o'clock for instructions," Colonel Bastian ordered. "Also tell them to keep a low profile and to not alert the Japs."

"Yes, sir."

"I'll have to go back to Tennant Creek tonight," Colonel Bastian said. "I'd prefer to bring these orders in person. I just hope we have a submarine available to get a team in there."

"I'll get with the navy and see what we can shake loose," Fred Palmer, America's intelligence liaison, replied, rummaging through his list of contacts from three separate nations.

* * *

"This is the BBC Perth, Australia, station reporting," Sally and Helen heard when the small set was tuned in. "Today in London, King George IV awarded the Island of Malta the George Cross in a moving ceremony, stating that the courageous citizens of this island fortress in the Mediterranean Sea have thwarted Germany's every attempt to tame the oppositional child. Malta continues to repel German attacks, causing the warring Axis nation to lose men and materials, as the beleaguered defending forces continue to wreak havoc on German shipping from the Boot of Italy.

"In other news, the House of Commons in London has asked Sir Stanford Cripps to prepare a detailed report regarding the failed proposed articles of independence to India. Sir Stanford returned to London after announcing in New Delhi that the All India Congress and the Muslim League have rejected the British plan for postwar India. Good night from the BBC."

Helen turned off the set and gazed out the window a moment in distant thought. She said a silent prayer for the *Mariah* to find safe harbor after learning the battle in the Indian Ocean had seen so many Allied losses. She wondered how long it might be before Andy would be able to send a note. Sally came up behind her and touched her shoulder. She had taken Helen up on using the spare bedroom since the nurses' quarters at the hospital were so small, with two or three women to a room and only common bathing facilities available.

"Helen, are you all right?" Sally asked.

"Yes, I'm fine. I was just thinking about the *Mariah* and wondering how she was faring."

"You would have heard if anything was wrong though," Sally said.

"Oh, I'm sure they're fine. I'm just a little anxious to hear where they might be. But I meant to ask if you had talked with Jane today?"

"Yes, she said she ran across some Americans on leave in town today. They told her that a lot of them were on the way, and Australia would soon have more American soldiers than anyone had ever seen."

"Martin thinks one of the eastern coastal towns will be a jumping off point to send the American Army through the islands. He thinks they'll start at New Guinea and move on from there."

"I guess we'll have to wait to see what the news will tell us in the weeks to come.

"You're probably right, Sally. Well, I'm off to bed."

"I'm going to read a little while before turning in," Sally said.

Sally sat with the open book in her lap for some time after Helen turned off her light. She thought about Andy and how he had kissed her before the *Mariah* beckoned him to tend to her needs that day off Bangka. She knew Andy had meant it when he said he loved her that frightening afternoon when she told him she had killed a man. She still woke in a cold sweat when she dreamed about the oriental attacker seizing her body while panicked fear flooded her senses, that terrible moment before the final few escaped Helen's Landing. "Please, God, not tonight," she whispered into the empty room.

* * *

Several days passed with no word about a submarine being available to begin a rescue effort at Java. Fred Palmer tracked the short transmissions and jotted down what information they had about Japanese strongholds along the shoreline. At least this Logan fellow seemed to have a tight grip on things. He had signaled they were looking for a passage that would bring them out closer to the sea rather than risk overland travel. Palmer was anxious to get a trained team in to see what kind of surveillance might be possible.

"Sir, a call for you," the private told him.

"Palmer here."

"Fred, James Bastian. I've just gotten word it's a go next Wednesday. I tried to get the operation moved up, but no go. Apparently, no boat of any kind will be cut loose for us until then."

"All right, I'll get things in place," Major Palmer said. "We better not tell Logan until we have a definite time. They're pretty vulnerable right now. No point in alerting the enemy if they're discovered."

"You're right, of course. Just don't like leaving them in limbo," Colonel Bastian said. He thought a moment before speaking again "I'll gather the people I want for this and send them north on Monday. I want some engineers to go before we send in the others. I even have one that speaks Japanese," Colonel Bastian said into the telephone receiver.

"I'll wait for your next call and start things in motion on this end," Major Palmer said.

"Very well, I'll send word first thing," Colonel Bastian said before ending the call.

10

Wesley stretched to his full height, just outside the tent flap. Sergeant Moore had driven the men hard the past few weeks and left no illusion that anything except perfection would be acceptable. The best thing was having Arthur back among them. By the end of his first week with the unit, things were taking on a faster pace. Wesley was sure something big was about to happen.

"Sir," Corporal Jenkins said. "I was told ta find ya. The colonel wants ya's up ta 'eadquarters."

"Thank you, Jenkins. Let Lieutenant Nance know where I am."

"Sir, 'e wants 'im too."

Wesley found Arthur with Sergeant Moore going over the day's planned maneuvers. They hitched a ride with a tank commander, returning from night maneuvers a few minutes later.

"Captain Vilmont and Lieutenant Nance, reporting as ordered," Wesley told the aide outside Bastian's office.

A door opened, and Colonel Bastian beckoned them to come into the meeting room. Wesley raised his eyebrows a little at the quick response before entering a large room where three other men were seated at a long table. One was wearing a British major's uniform.

"This won't take long," the major said. "Captain, Lieutenant, we need to send you on a short mission near Surabaya. You will be flown to Darwin and outfitted there. You were chosen because we needed someone that can act quickly, as you demonstrated in February. We also need engineers and someone that understands Japanese. That's where you come in, Lieutenant."

"What about the unit, sir?" Wesley asked.

"The men will be taken care of, Captain," Colonel Bastian said. "Time is short. You will only be gone a week or two."

"Do we get told what we'll be doing?" Wesley asked.

"All in good time," the British major answered.

Wesley and Arthur climbed into a Land Rover outside headquarters and found two small bags with a few of their personal items inside. Whatever was going on, the army was in a hurry. They were driven to a small airfield and soon boarded a transporter, which, along with a dozen other men in a mixture of uniforms, took off as soon as the last man strapped into his seat. They landed several hours later at the airfield south of Darwin, where they were met by the American Wesley had briefly spoken with when he first arrived at Tennant Creek.

"Gentlemen, follow me," Fred Palmer said, leading the way to a building with armed guards on duty.

Once inside, Wesley noticed a manned radio room with the door ajar, which was quietly closed when everyone entered the building. They were led through the antiroom and into a windowless meeting room with several chairs surrounding a large oblong table.

"You only need to know, for the moment, that each of you was chosen because of your individual talents. The mission you will be a part of is top secret and may not be discussed outside this room. If any of you have any doubts, now is the time to speak," Palmer said.

"Sir, I assume you are a sir, what do we call you?" one man asked with a toothy grin.

"Major will do. Anything else?"

"Major, do we get told now what this is all about?" Arthur asked.

"Lieutenant, we needed someone who speaks Japanese. You fit the bill."

"That's interesting, Major. What about the rest of us?" a burley American sergeant asked.

"The rest of you will be divided into three teams. Your mission will be to work with the resistance in the occupied islands and to carry out specific missions when needed. You will work separately most of the time to avoid being detected by the enemy. You will be given specifics at the appropriate time."

"When do we leave?" Wesley asked.

Fred Palmer looked around the table before he answered. He noticed how no one walked away. They only wanted to know when the mission would begin. "When the time is right, Captain," he responded.

The men looked around the table and came to the conclusion that further discussion was pointless. "Major," an Australian special unit's major said, "let's get on with it then."

Wesley and Arthur shuffled out of the room, along with the others, and heard a scared scratchy female voice coming from the radio room. The operator told her to hold on and summoned Major Palmer to join him, then closed the door.

*　*　*

"I said, we heard footsteps overhead last night and then a woman scream. Sergeant Ledowski and Lieutenant Crammer investigated just before sunrise and found evidence that someone was in the church," Katrin repeated.

"Send this corporal," Palmer ordered, handing him a scribbled note with the information required.

"Ma'am, I have to ask, what church?"

"Holy Apostle, Surabaya," Katrin quickly replied. "All the men are searching for a passage down to the sea, away from the harbor. Captain Logan said to let you know and then shut off the radio."

"Tell her help is on the way and to shut down," Palmer ordered.

Katrin listened to the final instructions and shut off the radio before carrying it back to the niche that Sergeant Ledowski and one of the American soldiers made to keep it from getting damaged. She had put off the call as long as possible for fear of being captured by the Japanese that occupied Java.

The scream they heard the previous night was like a knife penetrating her soul. A sense of relief flooded over her when she heard her dad and Lieutenant Crammer return a short time later, relieving her nervousness when being left alone. She ran to the mouth of the tunnel when her dad emerged and felt his arms enfold her shivering body.

"What is it, Kitten?"

"I'm just glad you're back is all," Katrin softly answered, trying to show a brave face.

"It's all right, Katrin. No one is going to find us. Right, Lieutenant?"

"Don't worry, Katrin. We'll find our way out. The British know we're here, and that means the Americans do as well. I'm sure someone will be here in the next couple of days. I'll make sure you're not left here on your own again. Maybe next time you can come on one of the expeditions with your father. What do you say?"

"I think I'd rather do that than be here by myself again, Lieutenant. I never knew how frightening being alone would be, especially after what happened last night."

"Yes, well—I think tonight, I'll have Adam and Eugene do a little scouting just to be sure we're still alone here. I think last night was a fluke and won't be repeated anytime soon."

The meager evening meal passed, and darkness was falling when the two scouts carefully climbed the ladder into the bell tower. Peeking over the open enclosure, Adam looked down to the cobblestone street outside the church. The only sound was from the buzzing mosquitoes and chirping crickets. He signaled Eugene to join him and to look to the other side of the structure. Cautiously edging around the bell, Eugene inched his way to the town side of the church, where he saw a small patrol walking toward the building opposite the church, and opened the door.

Light spilled onto the pavement, and he heard what sounded like American music for a moment before the announcer came on the air. "This is Tokyo Rose...," he heard before the door closed.

"I believe it's a brothel," Eugene whispered and lowered his head below the side of the tower. "We better get back and tell the lieutenant. That's probably what happened last night. Someone got bottled and brought his female companion in here."

Just then, they heard the music again, and Eugene peeked over the side to see a Caucasian woman being dragged by her hair into the street by a Japanese soldier, heading toward the side door of the church. "Let's move," he quickly said, heading toward the ladder.

"No, he might hear us. We wait it out here. Did you shut the trapdoor?"

"Yeah, just in case. I don't much like listening to a rape when I've got a gun in my hand."

"Me neither, but one shot would bring the whole Japanese Army down on us," Adam cautioned.

It seemed an eternity before the side door opened and slammed shut again, but they were spared any sound effects. Eugene looked over the bell-tower sill and saw the man taking the now quiet woman back into the building across the street from the church.

"Let's move, before anything else happens," Adam said.

"I'm with you."

The men quickly lowered themselves out of the bell tower and closed and secured the trapdoor before moving the ladder away from the opening.

"What did you find out?" Logan asked when they returned.

"Sir," Adam said, "there's a brothel across the street. We saw a Jap drag a white woman into the side door of the church. We had to wait for them to leave before we could climb down the bell tower. It looks like they're using the church when they—" He got no further before Katrin and Father Albright appeared to stand beside Lieutenant Logan.

"Go on, Adam. Using the church for what?" Katrin asked.

"Ma'am, it's not pretty. I think they're defiling some of the white women that were captured when Surabaya was overrun."

"I see," Katrin said with downcast eyes. "Lieutenant, I think tomorrow we need to continue searching until we find a way out. I have no intention of being defiled by some filthy Japanese miscreant. I'm sorry, Dad. I know we're supposed to love all people, but this is the work of the devil at his worst," she continued with tears welling in her eyes.

Crammer watched Katrin and Father Albright retreat behind the turn in the tunnel before speaking again. "Whatever it takes, we find the way out. These devils aren't going to get their hands on her," he stated before joining the others.

11

The *Mariah* rested at anchor in Kilindini, Kenya, harbor, with the remaining British fleet. Andy put down Sally's latest letter and smiled for a moment about the woman he was growing to care about and wondered when he might see her again. He contemplated whether the *Mariah* might be sent to the eastern Mediterranean where the island of Malta was proving to be a thorn in Hitler's side. He also knew there were concerns about the large island of Madagascar off Africa's eastern coast.

The Madagascar Strait was the only slim separation between the Nazi-controlled Vichy French island regime and the shores of the east African coast. A landing on the African mainland by Japanese forces, using Madagascar as the jumping-off point, could lead to a drive north into Egypt to aid their tripartite partners in squeezing the British out of North Africa to gain control of the Suez Canal and, with it, the oil resources in Iraq and Iran.

Meanwhile, the battles of North Africa swung across the vast open desert spaces, only to stall and be pushed back to their starting points with neither side seeming able to hold a strategic position for long. Andy wondered if the expected equipment and men from America might turn the battle for North Africa to the Allied forces.

"Sir," Mason said, knocking on the cabin doorway, "we just received a message from headquarters."

"Very well," Andy replied. Reading the message as he decoded it, Andy grinned for the first time since leaving Australia.

"Good news, sir?" Mason said.

"It seems the Americans have brought the war to Tokyo," Andy answered. "Their General Doolittle has led a bombing raid over the Japanese capitol.

"They must have carriers somewhere nearby to pull that off," Mason noted. "I wonder how they got close enough without being spotted."

* * *

"This is the BBC Perth, Australia, station with the week in review," the announcer began the nine-o'clock evening newscast. "In a tenacious move against the Japanese mainland, American General Doolittle has successfully led a bombing raid of B-25 Mitchell bombers over Tokyo on Saturday last. Allied governments throughout the world are hailing the raid as the first move toward what will break the Samurai sword of oppression.

"Meanwhile, the island of Malta continues the fight against the Nazi war machine in the Mediterranean, bringing down thirty-seven German planes. It seems the hard-hitting resistance by this small-island population will continue to be a source of defiance to the evil swastika attempting to sweep across North Africa. This is the BBC Perth, Australia, station. Good evening," the announcer ended.

"It looks like the resistance from Malta will continue to hinder the resupply to the German Army in Tripoli," Arthur commented.

"So it seems," Wesley agreed. "I'm starting to wonder how long we'll be here before something happens."

"Hard to say," an Australian major answered. "A lot depends on intelligence telling command the best time to move out. The Japs are pretty thick in the neighborhood right now."

"Gentlemen," an army captain summoned, "come with me."

"I believe our short respite is about to end," a burly sergeant major stated.

* * *

The men left the small lounge where Major Palmer indicated they were to report daily after their arrival until summoned. An excellent meal of roast mutton and fresh vegetables was served in a small dining hall, followed by coffee and an excellent cigar. Some of the men said it was a bad omen of what was to come, indicating their meals would be sparse from now on. They entered the same meeting room, where Fred Palmer waited to give final instructions.

"You have been separated into three four-man groups by nationality. Major Simons, your Australian group will be first to land at the coordinates you will be given once you are at sea. Captain Vilmont and Lieutenant Nance will follow, with the British group led by Captain Harrold. Major Hill, the American group's job will be to run interference, should the need arise. Any questions? No? Well then, good luck and Godspeed," Palmer concluded.

The small transport plane sped down Darwin's dimly lit runway and lifted into the moonless night just as Colonel Bastian drove up to the small dispatch hut. "I got held up by an unexpected crisis," he told Palmer. "I was hoping to see them off."

"We couldn't wait any longer. The flying conditions could change," Palmer replied.

"I understand. Well, all we can do now is wait for them to report. There's another matter we need to discuss."

Palmer looked at his Australian counterpart and nodded, leading the way toward his car. It was time to start multiple operations to keep the enemy under constant attack from within until the Allied armies could restore order in the East. He looked at the sky one more time before entering the car. He hoped this operation would be one that succeeded.

* * *

Wesley looked out the window once the plane was cruising over the sea on its way to Kupang. It would refuel at the airfield and continue to Penida Island off Bali, as close to Java as thought prudent. Wesley hoped the pilot had a good compass to guide them to their destination; there appeared to be a lot of empty ocean below them.

* * *

"Sir," Anderson said, "Lieutenant Crammer has something on the radio."

"All right, I'll be right there," Captain Logan groggily replied, throwing off his single blanket and feeling the dank chill from the dripping stalactites in this lower cavern hideaway near the sea. "What is it, Russ?" he asked when he neared the rounded opening just a few feet above the sea, where house-sized boulders blocked the shoreline.

"Australia will be calling in ten minutes, sir. The man said we would be receiving instructions."

"Let's hope *this time*, they have something useful to tell us."

"This is Fred calling Mary. Come in, Mary."

Logan nodded, and Crammer thumbed the mic. "This is Mary. Go ahead, Fred."

"It's time to herd the sheep into the pen. Prepare for the shepherd's call."

"Understood. Mary out."

"How soon will the first group get there?" Colonel Bastian asked when the brief broadcast ended.

"The teams board a sea transport tomorrow night and will spend a day and a half getting into position. If all looks good, Simmons will take his team in at 0130. Vilmont and Nance will go at 0230 with the British group if they receive the all clear. They'll have to spend the day in hiding before bringing out the civilians and the wounded. The Americans want Logan and his men back, so it could mean risking a second trip. The equipment the Aussies and the Brits take in should give us a lot of information and make future planning a bit easier."

*   *   *

"Sergeant Ledowski," Adam called. "I've been up top, listening at the tunnel bend for any sign that the enemy has located the caverns. I didn't hear anything, so I inched a few feet farther up. I'm certain I glimpsed a torchlight near the cave opening over the harbor. I think we should post a couple of men near our internal entrance, and we'll have to put out our cooking fire. It would be too easy to see the glow if the Japs stumble into the passage, not to mention the smell of food cooking."

"I'll tell the captain."

Adam nodded and signaled Eugene to join them. After a brief rundown, the two men went up the ancient rock formation into the darkened passage to begin placing the few explosives they had found in their earlier patrols around the city into the natural crevices formed over the centuries. The two rangers were meticulous in their work and carefully connected one explosive charge to the other. If the enemy found the route to this last refuge, the door would be permanently closed.

"Sir, Adam thinks he spotted torchlight up top at the cave opening over the harbor," Ledowski reported.

"Did he see or hear anyone moving about?" Logan asked, narrowing his eyes.

"He didn't say for sure. He did say we should douse the cooking fire though."

"Yes, that's a good idea. I'll tell Father Albright."

Near the place where the chamber opened to the sea, Joseph Albright was gazing at the mass of stars that stretched across the night sky, twinkling like thousands of glistening gemstones. Captain Logan joined him. "You know, I always think God could do no more, and then he gives us this," Father Albright said to Logan.

"Yes, Father, it is very beautiful." Turning to look at him, Captain Logan continued, "Father, we need to talk."

"Are they getting closer?"

"I don't know. I don't want to alarm Katrin, but we do need to douse the fire just in case. Adam and Eugene are putting some explosives in place if we need to block the passage. I'm going to increase the watch. We should hear something by tomorrow. If not, we'll have to move."

"Yes, I thought so," Father Albright said, turning to look at Logan. "I believe God sent me to find you and the others for a reason, Captain. I believe He has placed Katrin and me in your care and will bring us to safety. We'll hear something soon, I'm sure."

12

Wesley and Arthur boarded the small fishing vessel and were quickly herded below decks with the three teams and their equipment. The ensuing day seemed endless in the close quarters with only a porthole opened to relieve the heat of the airless accommodations. Night finally draped the sky in darkness, and the first group of Australian special forces began to prepare for their journey into enemy-held land.

"We'll make radio contact with this Captain Logan just before we cast off," Major Simmons said. "Code word is *shepherd*. Reply will be *lambs are in the pen*. That's the signal to move ahead. The shoreline is rocky, and most of it is obscured by large rock formations sticking out of the sea. It's good for us because even patrol boats can't get in there. The catch is to not run into the rocks ourselves."

"We'll stand by and follow you in," Captain Harrold confirmed.

* * *

Russ Crammer switched the radio on and turned the volume up enough to hear if the call would come tonight. Katrin stood beside her dad, silently praying their ordeal would be over and that rescue was at hand. She shivered at the memory of the horrible screams she witnessed and felt a terrible dread of their meaning.

"This is the shepherd calling Mary," everyone in the cavern heard, turning toward the radio with hopeful eyes.

Captain Logan nodded, and Crammer thumbed the mic. "Lambs are in the pen," he nervously answered.

"Very well, the shepherd will be with you at 0130." And the broadcast ended as suddenly as it began.

"That's all we'll hear. We have two hours to organize," Logan said after Lieutenant Crammer shut down the radio set. "Sergeant Ledowski, set up our defenses here and here," Logan ordered, pointing to strategic places where rock jutted up from the cavern floor.

"Captain Logan, I thought this was to rescue us," Katrin questioned with concerned eyes.

"It's just a precaution. When the time gets close, I want you and your father in the upper tunnel with our recovering soldiers. That way, you'll be safe if something should go wrong."

"I'll tell Dad," Katrin flatly stated before turning her frightened eyes away from the developing scene.

Time seemed to move in slow motion as men unconsciously checked their watches, anticipating what was to come. Katrin and her father gathered the few remaining tins of food and placed them in a knapsack to carry to the newly found upper passage. As the hour drew close, the three recovering soldiers were moved with help from the two men who stood guard overhead. When a signal light briefly flashed low on the sea's surface a few minutes later, Katrin and Father Albright followed the soldiers to the upper passage.

"Flash a quick response, Russ," Logan ordered when he could no longer see Katrin or her father.

* * *

"I see it, Major, just to the right of the formation that's straight ahead," Corporal Drew said, pointing in the direction where the brief flash of light had been seen.

"Okay, here we go then. Have your pistol ready just in case, Drew," Major Simmons responded.

*　　*　　*

"They're gettin close, Sarge," Corporal Anderson noted, holding his fingers around the trigger guard of his rifle.

"The light flashed again, closer in, and Russ Crammer clicked his flashlight one more time. The sound of paddles disturbing the water could be heard and then a low voice, "This is the shepherd," before the darkened faces could be seen when the first small craft entered the narrow entrance from the sea. Two men scrambled out and pulled the vessel onto the sheltered stones before Ledowski and Anderson lowered their rifles when the first one said in a clear Australian accent, "The shepherd is ready to gather his lambs."

Captain Logan stepped from behind the formation, across from Ledowski and Anderson, and responded, "The lambs are in the pen."

"An American," Major Simmons noted. "Signal the others, Corporal, to continue as planned."

"Yes, sir," Drew responded as he eased the safety back in place on his gun.

"Captain Logan, I'm Major Simmons, Australian Special Forces. I thought there were more of you," he said, looking around the dimly lit space.

"Major, a pleasure," Logan responded, shaking Simmons's hand. "My second, Lieutenant Crammer, and over there is Sergeant Ledowski and Corporal Anderson. We have a few more stashed around," Logan indicated when more men emerged from strategic cross-fire positions.

"I see," Simmons said, raising his eyebrows a little.

"Sergeant Ledowski, tell Father Albright and the others they can come down," Logan ordered.

"Yes, sir."

"Major Simmons, Father Albright and his daughter, Katrin," Logan introduced a few minutes later. "It was the good father here that found us to begin with. We got cut off from the rest of our unit and most likely would have been captured if not for him."

"You know the area well then, Father?" Simmons said.

"Around Surabaya and the southern coast fairly well. Our church has been here since Katrin was a small child. When my wife was alive, we used to hike some of the hill country and took the Sunday-school children on outings."

Adam approached the group and reported that everyone was cleared from the upper passage. He indicated Eugene was standing guard for the next few hours before stepping down to the opening, where a second craft was struggling to enter while towing a third that carried equipment and provisions. The two Australian commandos quickly unpacked the radio and signaled the British group to come forward.

Wesley and Arthur strained their eyes, looking into the inky blackness, until a dim formation loomed ahead of them. The two men paddling the low camouflaged vessel skirted the spiraling formation and steered toward the brief signal light that seemed to flash from beneath the sea's rolling surface. A few minutes passed, and the craft floated into shallower waters and seemed to be swallowed by the land before beaching on rough stones where several men waited. Arthur noticed one man appeared somewhat shorter than the others and wondered if he might be a native guide from Java. He caught his breath when the man removed his cap and shook out long golden-brown hair before speaking.

"Welcome to Surabaya, gentlemen. I'm sorry I can't offer you a cigarette or a cup of tea at the moment," Katrin shakily said.

"That's okay, ma'am," Wesley responded. "We're only passing through. Major Simmons, did our supplies arrive safely?"

"Yes, Captain Vilmont, they did. Drew and the others set them over there," Simmons said, pointing to the middle of the open space.

"Arthur, we best get busy then," Wesley said. "We were told on the way in, there's another chamber that has access to the surface. Is that accurate?"

"That's correct, Captain Vilmont," Logan noted. "However, we aren't sure if the Japs have compromised our access. I have a British commando scout watching in an upper passage right now."

"Arthur and I are ready to set up everything, Major. Why don't we find out?" Wesley said. "Captain Harrold, would it be all right to have two of your men help carry the gear?"

"Zagrzebski, Cripps, you're with Captain Vilmont. Keep a close eye out and don't do anything stupid up there," Harrold ordered.

"It should take about four hours once we get there. When do we leave?" Wesley asked.

"I'll be bringing in one of the American's craft as soon as darkness settles in tonight," Simmons said, noting the beginning signs of day approaching. "I plan to have the civilians and wounded evacuated first and follow with everyone else. We have to leave no later than 0200 to be aboard before daylight."

"Then we better get started," Wesley said.

"If possible, might Lieutenant Nance listen a short time up top to see if you hear any of those Jap miscreants talking before you move on to the large chamber?" Major Simmons said. "We might learn something useful about tonight."

"We'll give it a half hour, Major," Wesley agreed.

Wesley and Arthur cautiously approached the cave's vine-covered entrance and peeked out between the tangled bushes before crawling into the undergrowth along the hillside. Carefully climbing through the underbrush, they reached the cliff overhang and listened for any sign of life before climbing the short path that led to the hilltop. About one hundred yards inland, they could see the small church and watched as two Japanese soldiers started for the cliff. Scrambling to clear the path, the two men quickly moved beneath the overhang and quietly waited.

"If they come down, we'll have no choice but to kill them quietly," Wesley said. "I hope I remember what Captain Harrold taught us along those lines."

Feeling every heartbeat, Arthur listened as the men approached, and the sound of their voices became words. He listened for what seemed an eternity until the two men turned away after flicking their cigarettes over the cliff—a few feet from where Arthur and Wesley hid.

"Were you able to understand them?" Wesley asked, a full five minutes later.

"Sir, they plan to explore the cave system tomorrow. It was a captain and his sergeant talking. The captain was giving orders for the sergeant to put together a patrol to start before dawn."

"We have to get back," was all Wesley said.

Four hours had passed since Wesley and Arthur informed the others what they had overheard. They followed the marked path, which Joseph Albright had explained, to the large chamber, where the refugees had spent that first night, with a sense of urgency to complete the mission before time ran out. When they reached the great chamber, each man stopped in sudden awe of what they saw.

It was the first time the tenseness in Wesley's chest relaxed since Arthur translated the Japanese's intentions. Sunlight danced across the chamber floor—in uninterrupted play—from the half-century-old glory holes early prospectors had drilled in hopes of finding riches. He stood in the center of the vaulted opening, appreciating the beautiful display before him. At any moment, he expected fairies to appear in playful flight while angels sang in exultation at the wonders of God's handiwork.

"What do you think, Arthur?" Wesley quietly asked, after a few moments passed in breathless admiration of the magnificent sight.

"I hope we brought a long enough rope. See those depressions near the top? My guess is they're deep enough to set up our equipment. Hopefully, we'll find out in the next few weeks if the area's deserted up top, and the resistance can use it to harass the Japs in Surabaya."

"Father Albright said there was another way into the chamber that's not far from here. Let's hope the Japs don't find the route from the other end," Wesley said.

Two hours passed before everything was in place to Wesley's and Arthur's satisfaction. "We're getting a signal, so the units are working," Wesley said. "The real test will come if we can get one at sea…"

"I'm just finishing up here, sir—," Arthur was saying when a sudden loud noise and the feeling of the earth moving silenced him.

With a finger to his lips, Wesley doused the lantern and pointed for everyone to move to the first tunnel leading out of the chamber. Twice more, they heard and felt the phenomenon, and then—nothing. Wesley waited another thirty minutes before climbing the rope to check the units for damage. He righted one, breathing a sigh of relief when he found it was still intact and the thin wire leading to the surface was still in place.

"We'll have to hustle a bit to get back," Wesley said, picking up the pace when they cleared the first turn.

They worked their way through the twisting passages, following the Way of the Cross that Joseph Albright and his small missionary parish had so lovingly lain out to teach the next generation.

"Sir," Private Cripps whispered, "I see some light ahead."

Wesley slowed the pace and quickly doused their torchlight. He pointed to Cripps to take the opposite side of the widening passage to see if anyone was nearing the final turn. The faint sound of footsteps approaching their hiding place brought a moment of fear mixed with uncertainty, until Adam softly challenged them. Wesley lowered his sidearm and answered the challenge before carefully moving forward—ready to drop and shoot if the voice was the enemy trying to trick them. He rounded the last turn, breathing a sigh of relief when he recognized the British commando he only knew as Adam.

"Sir, we need to move out. We can hear voices overhead in the church. They'll find the cave passages before long," Adam said.

"Very well, let's get moving, men," Wesley ordered.

The first craft the Americans brought was just leaving with the wounded when Wesley and his small party arrived. The British craft was preparing to board Katrin and Father Albright with two enlisted men to help paddle. Arthur walked over to help steady the craft in which Katrin was trying to sit down and caught his breath when he looked into the most beautiful face he had ever seen when she turned to thank him. He held her hand a moment while she lowered herself into the small craft before it slipped away into the night's darkness.

"Captain Vilmont, I want you and Lieutenant Nance to leave on the larger craft. I think we can squeeze in an extra man to lower the number left. Eugene and Adam are still watching up top. I have the other larger one that your equipment was in and the one Corporal Drew and I arrived in. It will be a little crowded, but we'll be gone within the hour."

"Yes, sir. Who else is coming with us?"

Simmons pointed to one of his men and two others who boarded the small dark-colored vessel, which was soon paddling by compass into the dark void until a momentary flash of light responded to their signal. Twenty minutes later, the group was climbing aboard the same fishing vessel Wesley and Arthur had left just twenty-four hours ago. It seemed much longer.

Katrin and Father Albright met them at the upper-deck railing. "Are the others coming?" Katrin anxiously asked.

"Yes, ma'am," Arthur answered. "They should be along shortly."

"Please, call me Katrin. Like I told Lieutenant Crammer, ma'am makes me feel like an old maid."

"My name is Arthur, and you are definitely too lovely to be an old maid," Arthur stammered, somewhat alarmed at his boldness.

Blushing a bit, Katrin said, "You're very kind, Arthur. What do you do for the army?"

"I'm an engineer—at least, for the duration. Before that, I was with an engineering firm in London."

"I think you will have a lot of work when all of this is over," Katrin said.

"Katrin," Father Albright called out, "Captain Vilmont just said we might wind up in Australia for now. I can contact the bishop there and see where we might be useful."

"That's great. Dad, this is Arthur. I'm sorry, I don't know your last name."

"Nance, sir, Lieutenant Arthur Nance, Corp of Engineers, a pleasure to meet you," Arthur said, shaking the extended hand. "You said something about the Australian bishop?"

"I just left my church and parish behind in Surabaya. A lot of memories there," Father Albright said, lowering his head a moment.

"Dad, we'll be back one day," Katrin said. "This madness will stop, and we'll go back."

"Yes, it will stop one day. It will—"

A loud boom echoed into the night, causing everyone on the deck to turn and look toward Java. Even the large formations their rescue boat hid among could not hide the spewing smoke from the direction of the caves before a rumbling shock wave disturbed the surface of the water. Katrin clutched her father's hand before burying her face against his chest, tears splashing down her face in sorrow for the men she had briefly known, left at their last refuge in Surabaya.

"We have another ten minutes. They might have gotten out," Arthur tried to console.

"How could anyone survive that?" Katrin forlornly whispered.

"Wait, look," Father Albright said a few minutes later, pointing at the flash from the sea.

Wesley and Arthur helped bring the last men to escape Java aboard. One man had a gunshot wound to his chest and looked pretty bad. Two others were bleeding from flying rock when the tunnel to the upper chamber was blasted to keep the Japanese patrol from finding the last fleeing Allied soldiers.

"Captain Logan," Father Albright called, "did everyone get out?"

"Adam and Eugene were the last. They blew the tunnel when we were ready to leave the lower cave. Two others were killed in a firefight with the Japs before the tunnel was blown. The blast broke loose some rock from overhead, and Major Simmons and Corporal Drew took a couple of pretty good blows. The other man got too close to the Jap patrol that found the upper cave opening and took a slug in the chest. Adam and Eugene grabbed him and took out a few of the enemy before the rest retreated to regroup and get reinforcements. We loaded up and left before anything else happened."

Two tense days and nights passed with the crowded fishing boat periodically hiding in little known coves to avoid search planes or Jap patrol boats before they made port at Penida Island. Father Albright read the funeral rite the second night out when the man with the chest wound died and was buried at sea. The only knapsack Joseph Albright brought held his worn prayer book, his Bible, and the church tabernacle that contained the Holy Communion vessels and sacraments.

13

"This is the BBC Perth, Australia, station reporting. The United States announced today, American forces in the Philippines have surrendered to the Japanese after the last defenses of Corregidor Island were overwhelmed. It is believed, several thousand American men are now at the enemy's mercy. In the Coral Sea, American carriers have taken on a large Japanese carrier force and left the enemy with one carrier sunk and two severely damaged, stopping the Japanese Army from landing at Port Moresby, New Guinea. This is hailed by the American and Australian alliance at Port Moresby as a decisive triumph. This is the BBC Perth, Australia, station. Good afternoon."

"At last," Quentin Patterson exclaimed after swallowing a bite of his sandwich. "The Japs have hit against something they can't penetrate. I wonder what Germany and Italy are thinking of their tripartite partner now. Maybe this is the beginning of their demise."

"There's a long way to go," Martin Jamison cautioned. "It's one victory at sea against the recent fall of Mandalay in Burma and the loss of the Philippines."

"But it is a victory, Martin. It at least gives Port Moresby some breathing room."

"Sir," a hospital aide said, approaching the table, "a message for you."

Martin Jamison quickly read the scribbled note and looked up at his friend.

"What is it, Martin?" Quentin asked after seeing the change on his friend's face.

"Jane's in premature labor. It's a note from Sally," Dr. Jamison replied as the two men quickly rose from their chairs. "I sent Peter to Freemantle—the day before yesterday—to assist in setting up a receiving facility at the port. With the number of American ships adding to the British and Australian ships coming in, the aid station was overwhelmed. His knowledge about emergency medical logistics was a welcome addition. The Americans were especially anxious to have him there to work with their staff. We thought it would be all right. Jane's not due for at least three more weeks."

Helen was standing at the waiting-room doorway when the two doctors arrived. "Martin, what will happen? Jane was nearly frantic when she came to the cottage. The contractions are so close together. Thank goodness Sally and I were both home."

"I don't know, Helen. Quentin and I are going to check on her now. I'll send someone when we know something. Try not to worry."

"Sally's with her. The matron let her go in because she's a nurse."

Dr. Jamison nodded before he and Quentin entered the ward and turned into the small laboring room where Jane was the only patient. Sally turned care-filled eyes toward them as Jane squeezed her hand during another searing contraction. At the height of the contraction, water gushed from her, signaling the baby's protective water sack had burst. "It's too early!" Jane cried in anguished tears.

Quentin quickly examined her and called for the delivery kit when he saw a small head at the entrance to the birthing canal.

"Martin, I've seen this before. Get an incubator and a pediatric nurse here. This baby is going to be here soon."

"Nurse," Dr. Jamison called after stepping out of the room, "get an infant incubator here *stat* and call down to the nursery for a pediatric nurse right away."

"Jane, look at me. Jane, my friend in London had patients who delivered healthy babies earlier than this. Work with me—don't hold back. This one wants to see the world," Quentin said with a commanding voice.

"I just wish Peter was here," Jane whispered. "I'll do what you tell me. Just please, help our baby," she pleaded before another contraction seized her.

"Keep breathing," Quentin commanded. "Deep breath, now— push! Come on, Jane, you can do this. One more time. That's it. We're nearly there."

He felt Jane's body stiffen a moment later in another contraction before she could feel the birthing pain. That was when a small head presented itself to enter the world. God's guardian angels released their protective arms from the womb, and James Peter Romans emerged, inhaling his first tentative breath of worldly air before crying in protest at the loss of his safe refuge.

"We have a boy!" Quentin exclaimed. "And he appears to have all his fingers and toes."

"He's all right?" Jane anxiously asked.

"I think he'll be fine. I'm going to have him kept in an oxygen-enhanced incubator when he's asleep. But first, here's your son, Jane," Quentin said, placing the small bundle into her arms while he finished the routine work after a birthing.

Jane cradled her baby and looked into his eyes, mesmerized by the sense of wonder at this miracle. *My son*, she thought as a mother's love filled her soul with euphoria. "Your daddy will be so proud of you," she said softly before the specialty nurse gently took him from her arms.

Outside in the waiting room, Helen saw Martin approaching. "Martin?" she asked with concern in her eyes.

"It's okay, Helen. It's a boy, and he seems to be all right. A bit underweight, but that's normal with a premature birth. The next few days will tell us for sure. Quentin delivered him. Jane did what he told her, and the baby is doing better because of it. He said his friend in London talked about this type of thing often, and Quentin picked up some pointers along the way. Quentin said, at one point, he thought about obstetrics as a specialty, but the hours were too unpredictable."

"I'm so relieved. I guess this means we're godparents. How long do you think Jane and the baby will be here?"

"I think two or three weeks. I want Jane with the baby here until they can go home together. And I don't want her to go home to an empty house. She can rest and recuperate, which will give me enough time to get Peter back here. Fortunately, he's under my command. I think, as long as everything is okay here, I can have him finish the mission. I better let him know he's a father."

* * *

"Sir...Lieutenant Romans," a slightly pudgy American private called. "Message came for you."

"Oh, thank you," Peter said, taking the clipboard. He quickly scanned the brief signal while walking toward the new aid station and stopped in the middle of the roadway to read it again. "Yahoo!" he shouted, causing heads to turn. "I'm a father! Hey, everyone, I'm a father!" he shouted before running into the aid station.

"Sir," Peter said, "I need to send a signal to Darwin."

"What's up, Lieutenant?" the American major in charge asked.

"My wife just delivered our son. I need to tell her...well...you know," Peter replied, feeling the heat rising in his face.

"Congratulations, Dr. Romans. Corporal, get a telegram off for Dr. Romans."

"Yes, sir. What you want to say, sir?" the corporal asked while Peter composed himself.

I thought the English were stoic about these things. Guess this one is a little different, the corporal thought. *Better get this thing off before the major gets in a flap.*

* * *

"Jane," Helen softly said when she noticed her stirring in the hospital bed.

Jane's eyes blinked a few times before slowly opening to see Helen and Sally sitting beside her. "Is something wrong? Is the baby okay?" she asked.

"Everything is fine, dear," Helen reassured her. "Sally and I just didn't want you to wake up alone. Besides, as the godmothers, we have our duties to attend to. The floor matron is a real sweetheart and said we could stay if we didn't disturb you. How are you feeling?"

"Well, I think I'm okay. Just a little sore, but with my nurse's training, I know that's normal. I'd like to sit up a little, I think."

Sally cranked the head of the bed up a few inches and watched to make sure her friend didn't go pale on her. A nurse's aide entered a few minutes later and handed Jane a telegram.

"It's from Peter!" Jane exclaimed before savoring the few short words.

"What did he say?" Sally asked.

> Can't wait to see you and James Peter—*stop*—I love you both.—*stop*—Will work harder to get home quickly— *stop*—Love Peter—*end*

"I'm going to put it in Jimmy's baby book. A letter from his daddy on his birthday." Jane smiled. "I'm so lucky Peter will be with us before long. There are so many women here with children who have never seen their fathers because of this awful war. Some of them might never see their fathers."

14

"Sir, signal for you," the rating said, handing John Hartman the flimsy sheet of flash paper.

"Well, I'll be!" John exclaimed after reading the short message.

"What is it?" Mason asked, handing John a gin and tonic in *Mariah*'s wardroom.

The *Mariah* was among the ships anchored in Diego Suarez Harbor—on the northern coast of Madagascar—following a short confrontation with the Vichy French troops, with assistance by bomber planes from the navy's carriers *Illustrious* and *Indomitable*, ending the British offensive action in Madagascar by 4:30 p.m.

"I'm a godfather," John said. "Dr. Jamison sent a signal that my friend Peter Romans had a son that was born earlier today."

"Wasn't he one of the people on the *Angelica*?"

"Yes, he and his wife, Jane, along with Captain Burns's mother, Dr. Jamison, Sally, and Wes Vilmont, and some others."

"I remember," Mason grimly noted.

"Sirs," the rating called from the wardroom doorway. "Captain Burns wants you to report to his cabin."

"Very well," Mason replied.

"John, Mason, have a seat," Andy said when the two men reported. "We have orders to sail to these coordinates inside enemy waters. We are to meet a merchant ship and take on passengers."

"Passengers?" Mason asked with crinkled brows.

"It seems we are to help with some odd mission that has run into a little trouble. John, I asked you to come because there might be some medical issues from what little I've been told. How does the ship stand, Number One?"

"We are fully loaded, sir. There was very little to do after we docked here. When do we leave?"

"Midnight," Andy indicated. "We'll tell the officers a half hour before we sail—and the rest of the crew when we are well out of the harbor. You're dismissed."

"Sir," both men said, saluting.

The *Mariah* sailed without incident and turned her bow eastward.

"Keep a sharp watch," Tim Parker barked to the lookouts under him. "It ain't got no plan to be a findin' Davy Jones's locker."

Two tense days passed while *Mariah* sailed deeper into enemy territory. The uneventful passage gave way to nervous talk among the crew of what might be written in the ship's logbook from this voyage. "His Majesty's warship on a vacation cruise," one rating jested.

On the third night, a lookout yelled, "Small merchant vessel to starboard."

"Mr. Barnes, send the signal we discussed," Andy ordered. "Number One, bring the crew to battle stations quietly. If it's not our boy, we don't want to alert them."

"Yes, sir. Anderson, Davis, get the men moving. Get Mr. Parker on the starboard twenty millimeter," Mason quickly ordered. "Jergens, come with me," he said to the new bridge rating, who was standing openmouthed with the tea ladle still in his hand.

The small vessel continued to close the gap between the two ships, but it did not respond to the initial signal. She looked to be battered and clearly listing to port as she took on a recognizable shape. Andy raised his glasses to look again at the vessel approaching the *Mariah*. He couldn't see any outward sign of guns, but that could be a ploy. When the *Mariah* drew close enough, the side of the other ship could drop, and guns could fire at close range on the destroyer. Other ships had been damaged—or lost—during the same scenario the *Mariah* was sailing into.

"Sir, the men are at battle stations," Mason reported.

"Very well. We'll give it a few more yards and then put a shot across their bow if they don't respond. Mr. Barnes, send the same signal again."

"Yes, sir," Roger answered, lifting his lantern to send the short challenge.

"Sir," Mason said, lowering his glasses, "I see Wesley Vilmont on the deck."

Andy raised his glasses again and saw Wesley, frantically waving his arms and shouting something into the dim predawn light. "Come alongside. Prepare to take on passengers. Mr. Barnes, signal the vessel we are coming alongside. Number One, prepare a boarding party," Andy calmly ordered.

"Yes, sir," Barnes responded, feeling a sense of security by his commanding officer's easy manner of giving orders to bring a situation under control. *Maybe, someday, I'll have as much confidence as Captain Burns*, he thought.

"Mr. Parker, choose three men and prepare to board the vessel," Mason ordered.

"Aye, sir. Bert, Jensen, Perkins, draw sidearms and prepare to board—on the double!"

Two more tense minutes passed before the *Mariah* was alongside the small freighter. Mason quickly led the boarding party onto the stained wooden deck and ordered the men to spread out and be alert. He gave a short sigh of relief when Wesley—and someone he didn't know who was wearing a priest's collar—came to meet him.

"Boy, are we glad to see you," Wesley said, shaking Mason's hand. "This is Father Albright. He and his daughter rescued about a dozen men on Java and managed to hide out until we could arrange to get them out."

"Wes, we need to clear the area. How many are with you?"

"Father Albright and his daughter, Katrin, and Arthur Nance. We also have two wounded with us that needed to be evacuated right away in the hope of getting them to a doctor. We've done what we can for them, but they need medical attention that we aren't qualified to give."

"This ship looks the worse for wear. What about the crew?"

"They intend to return to their homeport. The captain is a native from the islands and says he doesn't worry about the Japs. He says the ship looks too battered to be of any concern to them."

"Very well. Gather your party and let's move before the Japs spot the *Mariah* and figure they've got a nice British sitting duck in their sites," Mason said.

Five minutes had passed before the boarding party and the rest of *Mariah*'s passengers, along with the two wounded soldiers, hastily began transferring to the *Mariah*. Andy arranged for a bundle of extra food to be sent across while the passengers were brought on board. He hoped the small crew would remember to ditch the British tins—as soon as they were empty—to avoid trouble if they were to be stopped by the Japanese.

"Wesley, it's good to see you, my friend," Andy said, extending his hand when Mason brought the four healthy passengers to the bridge.

"And you, Andy. This is Father Albright and his daughter, Katrin. You might remember Lieutenant Nance," Wesley said.

"Of course. Good to see you up and around, Lieutenant. Father Albright, ma'am, a pleasure to meet you both."

"Thank you, Commander," Joseph Albright responded. "Katrin and I are glad to be here."

"We'll do our best to make you comfortable. Number One, arrange a cabin for the lady. Wes, you and Arthur will have to share with Father Albright," Andy said.

"Thank you, Commander. My daughter and I are just grateful to be here," Father Albright said before Sublieutenant Anderson led the newcomers to their accommodations.

* * *

"Father Albright, ma'am," Andy greeted his civilian passengers that evening when they arrived in the officer's mess. "Please be seated."

"Please call me Katrin, Captain Burns. *Ma'am* is so formal under the circumstances."

"Very well, Katrin," Andy agreed with a smile.

"This looks very good, Captain," Joseph Albright said, looking at the fresh bread sitting before him. "By the way, thank you for the clean socks and trousers. Mine were getting a bit worn."

"Can you say where we are going, Captain?" Katrin asked.

"Yes, Katrin. The *Mariah* is currently on a course for Australia," Andy answered.

"Will you and Lieutenant Nance be going all the way to Australia as well, Captain Vilmont?" Katrin asked.

"I believe we will join our unit before long," Wesley commented.

"I believe you're right, sir," Arthur stated. "My guess is, our unit will be spending time in the desert fairly soon." Turning his eyes toward Katrin, he asked, "May I have the pleasure of walking you to your cabin later this evening? That is, if it's all right with you, sir," he said, turning to Father Albright.

"That would be very nice, thank you." Katrin smiled.

"Yes, it would be very kind, Lieutenant," Joseph Albright said with a twinkle in his eyes.

An hour later, Arthur walked with Katrin along the passage leading to her cabin. She asked if they could go up on the deck for a few minutes to watch the night sky. The men on watch were tersely told to keep a sharp eye out toward the sea, but their attention strayed to the young woman looking over the rail alongside the army lieutenant.

RETURN TO NINEVEH

"The stars are so beautiful," Katrin softly said. "It doesn't seem possible there could be a war raging tonight. It seems so peaceful right now."

"Yes, it is a lovely night," Arthur agreed. He didn't know why, but he felt a sense of wonder to be here with this lovely girl beside him, who seemed so easy to talk with. His usual reaction was to be tongue-tied and appear to have two left feet on a dance floor. "I better get you to your cabin before the men on duty get in trouble for watching you and not the horizon."

"All right." Katrin sighed.

Nine ordinary days passed before the *Mariah* approached Sydney, Australia, to disembark their passengers.

"Captain Burns, thank you for a very pleasant and uneventful journey. I believe Katrin and I already experienced all the excitement we can handle for some time to come," Father Albright said, extending his hand to Andy.

"It was our pleasure, Father," Andy replied, shaking hands. "I understand you'll be taking the train to the northeast coast near Darwin. I took the liberty of wiring my mother, Helen Burns, who lives close by. I thought you might need a little help finding some place to stay until it's safe to travel to England."

"That is most considerate, Captain. I'll let Katrin know we have a friend in Dundee Beach. I believe she is saying good-bye to our rescuers at the moment," Father Albright said with a smile at the return of normalcy in an abnormal world.

A short distance from the pier, Katrin was standing with Arthur. "Thank you for being so kind to me," she said.

"Oh, you're welcome," Arthur stammered. Clearing his throat, he began, "I wondered…"

"Yes?" Katrin encouraged.

"Well, just that…uh, would it be all right if I were to send a note now and then?"

Beaming, Katrin replied, "I would like that very much. I don't know yet what our address will be though. Dad said something

SHARON HOUSE

about Captain Burns's mother helping us find a place near her. Do you think she would mind if you sent a letter to her address until we know where we might be located?"

"I'm sure Mrs. Burns wouldn't mind at all. She is a very kind and generous lady. In fact, I might not be here except for her," Arthur said.

"I don't understand," Katrin said, wrinkling her brow.

"It's a bit of a long story, but suffice it to say, our escape from Malaya was only possible because Dr. Jamison thought about Helen's boat, and they brought everyone that was left at the hospital there, but the *Mariah* was our final savior in the end."

"It appears the *Mariah* has repeated that role for Dad and me." Looking pensive for a moment, Katrin continued, "I hope the ship will come through this terrible ordeal. Dad said war is the devil at his worst. I think I have to agree with him."

"It is ugly, and there's a lot of suffering by everyone involved," Arthur agreed. "Maybe one day, we can live in peace."

"I hope so," Katrin said as her father approached.

"We have quarters for tonight," Father Albright said, joining Arthur and Katrin. "Tomorrow we board a train, and Captain Burns was able to get us a sleeping compartment. I understand, Arthur, that you and Captain Vilmont will be traveling with us. We'll have an opportunity to become better acquainted in the next few days. I look forward to a little normalcy after what was experienced the last few weeks."

"We'll have to see about getting some clothing for the journey, Dad," Katrin said.

"Yes, well, we had best see about finding a general store," Father Albright agreed. "Arthur, we'll see you tomorrow morning."

15

"Sir, message just arrived with a priority code," the radio dispatcher said, holding out the flimsy sheet of flash paper.

"Very well," Andy said, taking the message. "You have the bridge," he told Brian Jones as he headed for the map room. "Number One, you're with me."

"Sir," Mason responded, falling in behind Andy.

"We have orders to sail to Alexandria," Andy said after descrambling the message. "Send word all hands are to be aboard by 1900 hours."

"I only gave leave inside the perimeter, sir. The Aussies aren't fond of the British presently. I figured it would avoid a brawl and the need to get our crew out of an Aussie jail."

"Let's hope they don't have a run-in at the canteen," Andy said with a lopsided grin.

The *Mariah* left Sydney's vast harbor with little fuss the following day, entering the Tasman Sea and heading north toward the Coral Sea with her old sailing partner, the *Victoria*. The two ships would join a small group of merchant ships near the Torres Strait at the northern most point near Cape York. The route was a calculated risk with Japanese vessels having recently been near the area. The admiralty was specific though about the ordered route, indicating other ships would join them en route. Andy watched the sea from his bridge chair and contemplated what new dangers the *Mariah* would face as she made her way to the northern coast of Egypt.

Nearly two weeks passed without incident as the *Mariah* and her companions moved into the Indian Ocean with their bows pointed toward the northern coast of Madagascar. Lookouts were on constant watch for any signs of enemy activity. At the week's end, two ships were sighted. Andy ordered battle stations until the challenge was answered before the ships dropped into line with the *Mariah* and *Victoria* and then beginning a speed run for the Suez Canal. Another eight days passed before the group entered the narrow Red Sea approach to the canal.

As the *Mariah* made her way toward Alexandria, there was a greater chance a German plane or submarine could attack. The Indian Ocean might be a Japanese lake, but the Mediterranean was awash with enemy planes and submarines hunting in a small pond by comparison.

"Man your battle stations," reverberated throughout the ship two hours after entering the Mediterranean, causing men to swallow their fear and answer the call. The terse mask of battle covered their faces as breeches were opened and guns made ready, waiting for the order to fire. From the west, four German Stukas appeared as bright shining arrows against the setting sun. Gunners squinted against the glare—with a curse on their lips— at the enemy's ploy to inflict as much damage as possible while the defenders struggled to hit their targets.

Andy watched the planes approach and noticed no bombs attached to the undersides. He wondered if they had attacked Alexandria and were returning to their base when they spotted the *Mariah* and her charges approaching. Andy remembered the loud squawk of the diving German planes at Dunkirk, intended to instill fear in its victims. He steadied his breathing and waited until *Mariah's* guns could reach out and destroy the ugly mechanical birds with their shrill shriek.

Mariah's gunners responded with lethal force when the order came to fire against the swiftly descending swastika. "Watch your aim, up one hundred, fire," Mason ordered from the aft four-inch guns when the planes came into range. "Reload, fire!" he bellowed above the din of noise from the firefight.

The enemy planes diving toward the rear guns stitched the water with cannon shells and strafed the deck, causing deadly splinters to fly through the air and clang against metal armament before turning to climb for another pass. The 20-mms added their staccato voice to the deafening sound, clipping a wing and causing an engine to cough and begin to smoke before it disappeared over the horizon.

The *all clear* sounded a short time later, and Mason returned to the bridge. "No casualties, sir. I have the men clearing the decks and making ready—if they return—or send a friend."

"Very well. They were getting low on fuel, or else they would have stuck around for longer. We'll stay at battle stations for a bit to be sure."

"Yes, sir."

The sun was settling beneath the sea when *Mariah's* crew stood down and breathed a sigh of relief that today wasn't their time to die. "We'll be in Alexandria in a few hours," Andy noted. "Have the watch keep a close eye out for any enemy activity this close to the port."

"Yes, sir," Mason replied before issuing the necessary orders.

The moon was rising over the distant desert when the *Mariah* dropped her anchor in the British-held harbor to await her masters' next orders.

* * *

"Mexico declares war on tripartite partners," the evening broadcast began. "In a statement to the world press, Mexico's president announced on Monday last, the country's intention to support the Allied nations by declaring a state of war against Germany, Italy, and Japan. In other news, England reports German planes bombed Canterbury Sunday night in retaliation to over one thousand RAF planes bombing Cologne, Germany. And this just in: after a grueling battle at sea, American carrier forces have soundly defeated an attempt by Japan to land troops at Midway Island. The details are sketchy at this broadcast, but it appears the Japanese suffered heavy losses. This is the BBC Perth, Australia, station reporting. Good evening."

Peter turned off the radio and peered into the nursery where James Peter was contentedly sleeping. He turned into the bedroom and sat down beside Jane with a wide grin. With Helen's help, he had brought his family home today.

"Is he sleeping?" Jane asked.

"Like a lamb. I have everything ready for when he wants his two-o'clock feeding. Dr. Jamison said he wouldn't need me at the hospital for a few more days."

"Peter, it's wonderful to have our family together. We are so blessed, compared to so many families this awful war has separated. Sally and Helen thought Wesley would be coming back to Australia, but Sally received a letter today that he's not sure now where he'll be next. Sally and Andy Burns correspond regularly as well, but she doesn't know when she will see him again."

"I know," Peter acknowledged. "I had a note from John when he heard about Jimmy's birth. John said he expects several pictures since he doesn't know when he'll see Jimmy. He also said to send a detailed letter about the christening."

"Helen also asked about it when you went to the pharmacy. She wondered when we wanted to have the christening," Jane said.

"I think we should wait a little while. It will give you time to get fully rested and Jimmy time to get used to his mom and dad," Peter noted.

"Mom and dad." Jane sighed. "Oh Peter, that sounds wonderful." She smiled before Peter leaned over to give her a kiss.

* * *

"...the BBC, reporting from Sydney."

Joseph Albright turned off the radio and sat back in the boarding-room chair. He and Katrin had spent the day shopping to replace necessary items left behind in Java. Their train was scheduled to leave early the next morning. Whispering a prayer, he reached for his prayer book before turning in for the night.

"Katrin," Father Albright said, knocking on the adjacent door the next morning. "Are you ready to go down yet?"

"I'll be right there, Dad. I'm just finishing my packing so we can leave right after breakfast."

* * *

Arthur entered the screened-in porch used as a breakfast room arranged with small tables and chairs. He was surprised to find hot coffee available and poured a cup of the aromatic beverage that had become scarce over the past three years. He looked up from his cup in time to see Katrin framed in the doorway a moment before he rose to greet her.

"I guess we're ahead of everyone," she said, taking the seat he held for her. "Dad thought I would be the slow one."

Wesley and Father Albright soon joined the two young people who seemed unable to stop looking at each other. "Well," Father Albright said, "I look forward to a journey free from gunfire and an opportunity to see this land."

"It should be a very uneventful journey, sir," Wesley said. "Arthur and I will be traveling all the way to Darwin, it seems. Our orders indicate we'll be rejoining our unit soon. I'm looking forward to a more normal type of army service."

Two hours later, the train pulled away from the station with a small jerk, soon increasing speed as it began the long diagonal journey across the hot interior toward its destination. The small towns along the way witnessed several Australian and American army units boarding the train as the journey progressed. They were met with transport trucks at Alice Springs, where the train stopped for two days. Arthur and Wesley looked at each other in a meaningful way at the number of men and vehicles in the knowledge that something was about to take place.

"I asked the officer in charge if I could say a prayer for them before they pulled out," Father Joseph said as they watched the last truck pull away and disappear around a bend in the road.

"I think they're going to need all the prayers they can get," Wesley said. "It looks like something big is going to happen soon. Maybe we'll hear in the next few weeks on the news broadcasts."

After they spent two nights at the lone hotel available in Alice Springs, the train journey resumed a more northerly route before turning northeast, once again toward Noonamah, the northernmost station the train would travel to due to the destruction in Darwin from the February bombing.

Helen and Sally waited at the station with the old sedan Helen had kept at the warehouse. They used their gas rationing stamps for the month to make the trip to meet Wesley and Arthur at the train. Andy's call about a priest and his daughter from Java had their curiosity piqued about the British citizens rescued from Japanese hands.

When the train approached the platform, Wesley looked out the window and waved at Sally, who was clearly eager to see her brother. Helping Arthur carry Katrin and Father Albright's bags and pointing toward the young woman who was hurrying to greet them, Wesley set the bags on the platform and embraced his sister. After a moment, Helen touched his arm and kissed his cheek, saying how wonderful it was to see him. He turned then to introduce the newcomers to her and Sally.

"Helen, Sally, this is Father Joseph Albright and his daughter, Katrin. We met at Java, and they traveled with us to here. I understand they will be staying close by until arrangements are made to get them back to England."

"A pleasure, Mrs. Burns," Father Albright said, shaking Helen's extended hand. "Miss," he said, turning to Sally, "I hear from Wesley that you are a nurse."

"Yes, I am, but please call me Sally. Katrin, I'm glad you're here. Andy said you've had quite an adventure."

"Yes, we did," Katrin replied in distant thought, before looking back at Sally. "One I hope doesn't repeat itself."

"I'm sure it won't," Sally said before taking Katrin's extra bag, remembering her own haunting memory.

"Andy filled us in," Helen said. "And by the way, I'm Helen. I have an empty cottage just down the beach from mine that you are welcome to use, Father Albright. Sally and I opened it up when Andy called, and it's all ready to move into. I'll introduce you to Jane and Peter Romans in the cottage next to you tomorrow after you've had a chance to get a decent night's sleep."

"Thank you, Helen." Father Albright grinned. "But I am Joseph to my friends."

"Then Joseph it is. Wesley, Arthur, I'm so happy to have a chance to see you both again," Helen said, giving each of the young men a motherly hug. "I was afraid you would be in the desert by now and caught up in the offensive that Germany has launched. According to the radio reports, it isn't going as well as first expected. Tell me, Joseph, do you think the Americans will be there soon?"

"I don't know for sure, of course, but my guess is you'll be hearing from them before much longer. Our American friends from Java said the army was gearing up pretty quickly back in the United States."

"Your friends from America?" Sally asked, crinkling her eyes at the unexpected reference to Americans from the other side of the world by British civilians escaping from Java.

"We met a short time ago on Java and became rather close before leaving. Katrin and I had a chance to show them around a bit."

"You can compare notes with Helen and Sally," Wesley said, grinning, as he picked up the bags and headed for Helen's car.

16

"Lieutenant Jones," Andy said, returning to the bridge after a commanders' meeting ashore.

"Sir, we just received a dispatch about Midway Island. The Americans have turned back the Japanese," Brian Jones reported with a wide grin. "And they sank four of their aircraft carriers before the battle ended."

"Now that is good news, Lieutenant. Have you told the crew?"

"No, sir. I thought you might want to make the official announcement."

"Now, hear this: the American Navy has soundly defeated the Japanese Navy at Midway Island—sinking at least four carriers and deflecting a planned invasion. Our ally is flexing his muscle to the despair of the enemy." Andy replaced the microphone and nodded at Jones before returning to his cabin for what might be his last night of uninterrupted sleep for several weeks.

"'Hat'll show tems Japs 'ose superior," Bert said to the ratings standing around him. "Sure wish Ernie twas 'ere ta 'ear. Now, 'e was a sailor's sailor, Ernie twas. Why, 'e took a shot ta da 'eart from tems Japs an' 'e's still a livin', ya knows."

Andy sat down at his desk after Mason left his cabin and thought about the *Mariah*'s upcoming mission. He was glad for the promised fighter cover out of Malta when the group passed through the narrow slot between Sicily and Tunisia. The *Mariah* would sail late that night with a group of merchant vessels that carried the next load of goods to keep a beleaguered England going.

Admiral Edwards told him that he expected the return trip would be loaded with weapons and troops that would work with the Allied armies to bring victory in North Africa. He hoped the tide would turn soon with the Axis armies retreating against a victorious Allied offensive. Maybe then he could look toward the future.

Andy smiled for a moment when he looked down at his desk and saw the letter he received from Sally this morning. She had told him his passengers from a few weeks past had arrived safely and were already under his mother's wing. He also learned that Father Albright was asked to step in at the local church when their priest had taken ill. The bishop had made special arrangements since Father Albright was from England. She finished with words of hope and loving thoughts about a brighter future, which gave him a sense of being grounded while the insanity of war circled around them. Smiling again as he reread the letter, he slipped between the crisp sheets on his cabin bunk and fell into a peaceful sleep.

* * *

Andy stepped to the center of the bridge feeling refreshed and carefully took in the men and ships preparing to sail. They would be joining two corvettes, the *Victoria*—their old friend from Singapore—and another minelayer. The *Victoria* was to drop underwater mines close to the Tunisian coast as they passed the harbor entrance near Tunis. He briefly remembered another time when she was to drop mines in the fifty-by-eighty-mile radius around Singapore in 1940 and the disastrous results of that risky assignment. He hoped the *Victoria*'s current commander was careful and had a bit of luck left to get the job done.

"Let go spring," Andy ordered. "Ahead slow."

Andy watched as his orders to get underway became reality, and the *Mariah* gently moved away from the docking area to take her position near the rear of the convoy. The moon was a sliver in the clear starlit sky, giving a sense of floating unencumbered, until the ship approached the already moving line of merchant ships carrying precious life-giving cargo to a hungry nation.

"Sir, we are in position and sailing at eleven knots as ordered," Mason reported.

"Very well," Andy replied to the routine report. "Post additional lookouts at 0330, Number One. You have the bridge," he continued before retiring to his bridge cabin. Lying on the bunk, he wondered what England would look like after being away for nearly two years. He knew many of the crewmen were eager to see England and home again. His job was to get them there safely, along with their charges' cargo intact.

Eric Edwards sat looking out his office window, contemplating the orders the group faced under the guise of a convoy while waiting to hear if the mission was successful. They would pass between Sicily and Tunisia in about three days, giving the *Victoria* the advantage of darkness to distribute her lethal load. With German bombers once again pounding the small island of Malta off Sicily's southern coast, the underwater mines were essential to deny the German forces in North Africa of sufficient supplies to continue east toward Egypt. If Egypt were lost, it would seal their fate and, with it, the loss of the Suez Canal, denying the Allies safety of passage into the Red Sea and the short passage to the Indian Ocean and Persian Gulf, with its rich oil-supplying ports.

The small island where St. Paul was once shipwrecked during his passage to Rome to face the emperor's judgment was proving to be an essential part of the defenses in the struggle for the territories across North Africa. Perhaps it was because St. Paul had performed miracles and brought the Christian faith to the small outcropping in the sea during Christianity's infancy that God would not let the Axis boot suppress it. The daily flights of bombers and fighters from the beleaguered island holdout in proximity to Germany's supply line and the destruction of distribution facilities along Italy's coastal ports kept vital fuel and equipment from reaching the German front.

The first few days at sea passed without incident. The sun was fairly high in the sky when a flight of Spitfires out of Malta flew overhead to intercept any German who was bent on sinking one of His Majesty's ships. The fighters gave continual coverage before returning at dusk to their precarious island home to continue the battle with Kesselring's heavy bomber attacks from Sicily's Axis airfields against this last holdout.

Andy posted extra lookouts during the early morning watch before the sun broke over the horizon, remembering the broom-stick-like object feathering the sea with his first submarine encounter as a green first officer on his first war mission. He remembered the chill he had felt when he heard the cry that torpedoes were in the water, and he drilled his men until they responded without hesitation while testing his own skills to the dangers that lurked beneath the waves. One wrong move and they could all be beneath the waves when the hungry sea reached out to claim them. Tonight would be precarious with the *Victoria* laying her mines in enemy territory.

The watch ticked slowly through the tense night hours, waiting for the minelayer to return from her mission off Tunis. The idea of the *Victoria*'s rescue craft taking dangerous underwater mines close to the harbor entrance to gain the best chance of sinking any ships and damaging the harbor seemed daft. The odds against the men making the attempt were too numerous to count. The orders were exact: the minelayer was to drop more of the hideous devices farther out to sea in the approach lane. If her rescue craft did not return as scheduled, she was to sail to the predetermined coordinates at precisely 0425 and rejoin the convoy.

"Sir, we're ready," the sublieutenant in charge of the mission reported.

"Very well, I'll see you at the pick-up coordinate at 0345," Captain Merritt replied.

"Do you think they've got a chance, sir?" the first officer asked when the small craft disappeared into the darkness.

"There's always a chance," Merritt replied then turned his thoughts to the mission at hand.

The convoy had veered south shortly before the Spitfires departed when the group leader signaled no bogies in the sky. *Mariah*'s watchkeepers were told to pay close attention to any movement in the water throughout the night that may indicate enemy activity. The watch changed at 0400 with nothing unusual reported. The midnight shift shuffled to their quarters in the hope of a dry blanket and a few hours rest before the new day brought planes diving from the sun or enemy submarines targeting from beneath the ocean waves.

"See anything yet, Bunts?" Mason asked Roger Barnes at about 0420.

"No, sir, not yet," Roger answered. "Wait—just coming on the horizon...it looks like...a ship—heaven have mercy!" he suddenly exclaimed when a huge orange fireball lit the distant sea, followed by the sound of gunfire.

"Sound general quarters," Mason instantly ordered. "Signal the others that attack is imminent."

"Man your battle stations, man your battle stations," echoed across the early morning air while men scrambled to load their weapons and waited for the command to fire.

"What is it, Number One?" Andy asked a moment after the alert sounded.

"Sir, an explosion to the south. It could be the *Victoria*," Mason reported.

"Signal, sir," Barnes shouted. "Mission accomplished—two survivors aboard. Three ships sunk in the harbor and one approaching submarine. Have damage to port twenty-millimeter gun."

"Ask if they need any medical help," Andy ordered.

"Yes, sir," Barnes answered before turning to send the brief message and waited until the *Victoria* responded. "They say it was a bit dicey there for a bit," he finished.

"I would think so," Mason said.

Andy sent men to assist with the repairs to *Victoria's* twenty-millimeter gun the following afternoon while the convoy settled into a zigzag course toward Gibraltar. Once around the large stone edifice at the narrow lane into the Atlantic, it would be a straight course to England's busy ports to unload and wait for the turnaround to escort ammunition and supplies to feed a determined army at the other end of the line. But first, they must reach the Atlantic while avoiding resistance from the Italian Navy and German planes.

"Mr. Jones," Andy called, the day before approaching Gibraltar—a favorite Axis submarine hangout. "Where is a likely spot we might encounter some enemy resistance to our turn into the Atlantic?"

Looking over the chart a few moments, Brian Jones moved a decisive finger to a coordinate where several attacks had taken place over the past six months. Then crinkling his brow a moment, he said, "This is where other convoys have had trouble, but"—he indicated, moving his finger a bit farther along the chart—"I believe it is more likely to be here, because the area marked as dangerous has been avoided recently."

"Explain, Mr. Jones," Andy ordered.

"It seems to me, sir, the enemy would want to surprise us. Once a coordinate is used a few times, it becomes known, and ships will avoid it. However, if I move, the opposition doesn't know where I am, and the element of surprise returns to my favor."

"Yes, that's true. Mr. Barnes, signal the leader. I would like a consultation."

"Sir," Roger Barnes answered before sending the short request.

Andy sent the coded message to the lead ship and waited for her captain to reply. If Brian Jones was right, and he seemed to have a knack for it, the enemy would be waiting near their present course. But if they could throw the waiting wolf pack a curve, the convoy might have a chance to avoid the destructive force. He was sure the Germans would be even more determined because of the attack on Tunis.

Several hours passed before a reply came that a course change would be ordered for 0200 hours, which would take the convoy directly through the center of the wolf's lair. It ended with a personal note to Andy, stating he better be right or this would be a massacre they both would have to answer for—if they lived to tell about it.

"Sir, extra lookouts posted," Mason reported at 0145 as he entered the officer's mess.

"Thank you, Number One. Tell me, do you think Mr. Jones and I are right?"

"Knowing his knowledge about the sea and uncanny ability to pinpoint our position and your own trust in his abilities—yes, sir, I believe you are right. It was a tough decision to make for both you and the captain of the lead ship, but a necessary one."

"Would you have made the same decision in my place?" Andy asked, looking up from his hardly touched plate of scrambled eggs in the officer's mess. He and Mason were having a small late-night snack before going to the bridge to be on hand when the ships passed through the area in question.

Mason set his fork down and took a sip of coffee before looking up at Andy. "It would be easy to say yes or no because it isn't my decision to make. However, I believe if the captain of our lead ship would have taken my word along with Mr. Jones's expertise, or I would have had to make the decision without the other captain—yes, sir, I believe I would have given the same recommendation. It makes sense that the Germans would move their submarines to keep us on edge and attack the convoy from a new position. Is it where Brian Jones believes? No one really knows," Mason ended with a shrug of his shoulders. "But even if not, I don't believe they will be found where we're going."

Looking into Mason's eyes a moment, Andy nodded before setting his plate aside and sipping the cup of steaming coffee before him. "If I'm wrong, it could be a busy night. We've both seen the sudden impact of torpedo attack and what can happen to a convoy. Be careful tonight, Number One. I don't want to break in a new first officer."

"Always, sir. I'll post extra lookouts and have men standing by at their stations until we're well past the area in question."

"Good," Andy replied. "I—"

Andy got no farther as a rating stuck his head into the room and said, "Sirs, Sublieutenant Anderson said there's a signal from the leader."

"Very well," Andy answered as he and Mason rose to return to the bridge.

"Sir," Anderson reported. "We are on course and should be approaching the area in question shortly. The radio room sent this message up from the leader," he continued, handing Andy the small piece of flimsy flash paper.

"He says to keep a sharp eye out and has ordered the merchant ships to keep in formation, no matter what happens," Andy said while scanning the short message. "Helmsman, turn five degrees to port."

"Aye, sir, five degrees to port," was heard in reply as the *Mariah* answered the helm and moved closer to her charges.

Mason scanned the sea, watching for any indication that a submarine might be stalking them with no sightings. An hour into the precarious passage, he went to the bow for a closer look at the waters between the *Mariah* and the convoy. Watching near the wake of one merchant ship, he saw the unmistakable sight of a periscope rise in their path. "Submarine dead ahead," he bellowed toward the bridge.

"Sound general quarters. Signal the convoy. Prepare to depth charge," Andy instantly ordered.

Several minutes passed before the submarine surfaced and signaled the ship. "Thought we had a bunch of Germans. Sorry about that."

"Keep a close eye. It could be a ruse," Andy ordered. "Signal, identify, Mr. Barnes."

"Says they are American submarine number 1620 taking supplies to Malta. They gave the correct code word."

"Helmsman, come alongside," Andy ordered. "If he twitches, fire the 50-mm into the bridge," he said to Mason when he rejoined the bridge watch.

The *Mariah* moved within fifty yards of the surfaced submarine with four extra lookouts training binoculars on the crew and watching for any indication of an attack. Andy waited until he could clearly see the indentifying markings before taking the loud-hailer in his hand. "Welcome to the Mediterranean, Captain. I see you got out of Manila before the fall."

"Hey, Commander Burns, good to see you and your ship again," the sub's commander replied. He remembered the *Mariah*'s visit to Manila and the small dinner party aboard Jerry Davidson's destroyer, shortly before the war broke out, and the stories about her more unusual missions. He liked what he saw and heard during that short visit and was glad to see the ship and her commander were still intact. "Sorry for the scare."

"Glad we identified you in time. I'll have to learn how you got so close."

"Happy to fill you in. The secret is to not have anything that rattles and to coast up slowly on your prey. A wolf pack makes more noise."

"I'll keep that in mind. Safe journey, and watch out around the narrow gap between Italy's boot and Tunis. We made a little trouble there a few nights ago. Malta can use any supplies it can get right now."

"Thanks, we'll keep a close watch," the American captain replied before ordering the watch below in preparation to dive.

Andy ordered that the *Mariah* return to her original course while he watched the small American boat disappear beneath the surface.

Andy was sitting on his bridge chair when the *Mariah* moved into the Atlantic. She would sail several miles west before turning north to avoid enemy guns mounted near Gibraltar, which could target ships in the normal sea-lanes. The convoy faced many possible perils in the weeks to come—Axis planes bombing the ships, attacks by a German wolf pack, the possibility of bad weather and rough seas—prior to turning into the English Channel to face the final challenge before docking at Harwell.

17

Several weeks had passed since Father Albright and Katrin moved into the small cottage on the Timor Sea. Father Albright was spending more time at the local church since taking over the services, and Katrin was starting to feel at loose ends. When Sally mentioned the hospital was short-staffed, Katrin had volunteered as an aide. She enjoyed helping the recovering soldiers and began to consider taking a nurse's training course. She also learned that Jane and Sally helped Helen with the rejuvenated hospital auxiliary and thought it would be something else to help the soldiers who were far away from their families.

The cottage by the sea Helen had offered as a home was peaceful most of the time. The waves crashing against the rocky shoreline had startled Katrin awake in the beginning, making her believe she was still in the caves beneath Surabaya. Fortunately, her unsettling dreams were slowly fading as the peaceful days went by. She was in the middle of clearing away their noonday meal when she heard a knock on the cottage door. *Must be Jane and Sally coming to talk about the hospital volunteers*, she thought.

Arthur Nance tapped again on the cottage door before Father Albright came to see who was calling. "Lieutenant Nance! This is a surprise."

"Yes, I know, sir. Captain Vilmont and I had some business nearby. I thought I'd see if you and Katrin are getting along okay. Is she in by the way?"

"She's in the kitchen, I believe. Come in, and I'll let her know you're here," Joseph said.

"Thank you, I think I will. This is really nice," Arthur said after he was led to the back sitting room overlooking the sandy beach.

"We are very fortunate. As you can see, Katrin has been busy stamping her own style into it. At least as much as shortages allow," Father Albright said. "Katrin, we have company," he called, poking his head through the kitchen doorway.

Arthur rose from his chair and turned around, bringing a slight intake of breath before Katrin walked over to greet him.

"I thought you were still in Darwin," Katrin said. "Has something happened?"

"No, Captain Vilmont and I had a little business to see too. I thought I would stop in and say hello."

"I see. Well, I hope you'll at least join us for dinner tonight," Katrin said. "I actually found a chicken for us to have."

"That sounds very good, but I'm supposed to meet Captain Vilmont tonight for dinner," Arthur said, looking a little disappointed.

"Bring him along," Father Albright said. "If it weren't for the two of you, we might not be here."

"Oh yes," Katrin chimed in with a radiant smile that pierced Arthur's soul by its genuine enthusiasm. "It would be almost like having a house warming."

"Yes, that's what it would be." Father Albright nodded, giving a fatherly smile at his daughter's happiness. *Thank the Lord we lived to see this*, he thought. *I had doubts that still need forgiving. It was His grace that spared Katrin the horrors others are enduring.* "Dinner is at seven o'clock. Katrin, why don't you show Lieutenant Nance the patio we have here?"

"Would you like to see it, Arthur?" Katrin asked.

Katrin led Arthur through the double French doors onto the open patio above the sea. Several bushes and blooming flowers grew along the patio edge before giving way to a sandy path leading to the lapping waves at the shore's edge.

Feeling a little at a loss what to say next, Katrin said, "Would you like some iced tea?"

"That would be very nice," Arthur said. He helped her with the small tray when she returned and pulled the chair out for her to be seated before sitting next to her, sipping his tea. "Are you starting to feel settled in?"

"I've started volunteering two days a week as an aide at the hospital, and Sally and Jane are coming to talk about the next event Helen and the hospital auxiliary are planning," Katrin said.

"You will feel at home before you know it," Arthur said. "Helen is a lovely lady who makes one comfortable, no matter how short a time she has known you."

"Yes, that's true. Oh, look, there's a dolphin out there," Katrin said suddenly, pointing at the sea.

"They sometimes follow a troopship when it's close to land," Arthur said. "I think it has left for now."

"I like to sit here sometimes and just watch the sun reflecting off the water. It reminds me of Surabaya when I was growing up," Katrin said.

"This is really nice," Arthur said, admiring the peaceful view.

The sun was moving the shade farther across the patio's edge when they left the small iron table and chairs, where two empty iced-tea glasses remained.

"Remember, dinner at seven," Katrin said when Arthur prepared to leave.

"We'll be here. Thank you for a wonderful afternoon."

"My pleasure....Arthur," Katrin replied, somewhat awkwardly.

That evening, Joseph Albright answered the door at 6:45 p.m. to Arthur and Wesley and a man in an American uniform whom he did not know.

"Sir, this is Major Palmer," Wesley said. "I hope you don't mind, but he wanted to meet you."

"Of course, we don't mind. Please, come in, Major," Father Albright said, extending his hand.

"Thank you, Father. It's a real pleasure to meet you."

"Dad, did I hear you talking to someone?" Katrin asked through the swing door to the kitchen.

"Come out for a minute, Katrin. Our guests have arrived. Captain Vilmont and Lieutenant Nance have brought a friend, Major Palmer."

"Ma'am, a pleasure, and thank you for your hospitality," Fred Palmer said, taking the delicate hand in his.

Katrin stared a full fifteen seconds before composing herself and welcoming her guests. *It couldn't be,* she thought. *He sounds just like the voice on the radio.*

"That was truly delicious," Wesley commented an hour later, raising his wineglass. "My compliments to the cook."

"Wonderful, Katrin," Arthur said, saluting her as well.

"My dear, like your mother's—exceptional," Father Albright chimed in.

"Very good, and thank you again," Fred Palmer said, looking over the rim of his wineglass as Katrin looked at him curiously once again.

"You're very kind," Katrin managed to answer before lapsing into thought about the stranger at their table.

"Shall we retire to the sitting room to listen to the latest news?" Father Albright suggested.

"I'll be along shortly, Dad. I just want to clear up a bit here," Katrin said.

"Let me help you," Arthur offered.

"I'll take you up on that. Come into the kitchen a minute. I'll find something to keep your uniform safe from spills."

Katrin shut the swinging door and quickly turned to face Arthur. "He's the man that was on the short-wave receiver. I'll never forget that voice. Arthur, what's going on?" she asked, trying to control her breathing and mounting fear.

"It's okay," Arthur reassured her. "He's just here to debrief us. Captain Vilmont and I aren't spies or anything," he said, taking her hand in his and holding it to his chest.

"He isn't English," Katrin said. "That's an American uniform he's wearing. Is he testing us?"

"I don't know. He just said he wanted to meet you and your father when I found him with Captain Vilmont this afternoon.

"You've met him before?"

"Briefly, but I can't really say any more. You do understand," Arthur said, searching her face. *She's so lovely*, he thought as he drew her petite form closer and kissed her before he knew what he was doing.

Katrin looked up at him a moment later with a somewhat mischievous smile before retrieving the hand he still held and began clearing away the evening's dishes. "Shall we join the others?" she asked a short time later.

"Katrin, I…" Arthur started.

"I liked it too, Arthur," she said before pushing the kitchen doorway open.

"Ah, there you are. We were just wondering if the two of you would be joining us," Father Albright said. "The news broadcast should be on in a few minutes."

"It took a little longer than I thought," Katrin said. "Arthur isn't quite as practiced in the kitchen as you, Dad."

Smiling at his daughter's obvious attraction toward the young man she saw as her hero, Father Albright turned to adjust the dials on the ancient, sometimes fickle radio.

"Today marks the beginning of the road back to Japan," the announcer dramatically said in his opening statement. "In a stunning announcement just hours ago, the United States reports victory at sea. After a raging battle between the outnumbered United States carrier fleet and Japan's superior forces, the United

States has halted Japan's march across the Pacific Ocean at Midway Island. American naval aviators struck a resounding blow, sinking four Japanese carriers and forcing the invading forces to retreat. The charred remains of the once feared floating samurai now rest at the bottom of the sea. Meanwhile, in North Africa, British and Australian armies continue to struggle against the German offensive as General Ritchie takes up the reins of engagement. This is the BBC Perth station reporting."

"At least the Americans are fighting back," Joseph Albright said. "Tell me, Major, did you know about the sea battle before tonight?"

"I don't understand what you mean, Father Albright. I'm not privy to that kind of information," Fred Palmer said.

"I just thought you might have had wind of it. You were the voice on the radio just before we met our rescuers after all."

"I see. You're very good. Did you know as well, Miss Albright?"

"I was pretty sure. I'm curious though if there was a chance we might recognize you. Why did you come?"

"I wanted to meet you, both of you," Major Palmer said, nodding at Father Albright and Katrin. "The men said you were very brave. Captain Logan believes they would not have survived without you. I just wish we could have been somewhat quicker to get you out. I also have to tell you that this is top secret. No one can hear your story for a very long time."

"I'm used to keeping secrets, Major Palmer," Father Albright said. "A priest hears far more than most people would believe."

"I suppose that's true." Palmer nodded. "Katrin, what about you? Can you keep a secret?"

"No one would believe me if I told them," Katrin replied. "It's too much like a dream, a very bad one."

"I'm sure you won't have to be concerned, sir," Arthur interjected.

"Then we shall leave it at that," Major Palmer said. "Captain, I need to return to headquarters shortly. Father, Miss Albright, thank you for a most enjoyable evening."

"Yes, thank you," Wesley added. "Arthur, I'll drop the major off and meet you back at the barracks."

"I hope we'll see you again," Father Albright said, walking the two men to the door.

"Katrin, I'm sorry if I was too forward," Arthur said when Father Albright walked Wesley and Major Palmer to the door.

"You weren't too forward," she replied with a smile. "I kind of liked it," she added, feeling the heat rise in her cheeks.

"May I write to you?" Arthur quietly asked with a quizzical look in his eyes.

"I'd like that very much," Katrin answered with a shy smile.

"Katrin, will you see Arthur out when he's ready?" Father Albright asked from the study doorway. "I'm going to read for a while."

"Okay, Dad."

"I should go," Arthur said, taking her hand in his.

"It's okay. Dad's going to read his nightly office."

"I really do have to get back," Arthur said with a slight smile. "We have an early morning."

"I see," Katrin quietly said. "Will you be back?"

"I don't know," Arthur truthfully answered. He looked down a moment before gently putting his arms around her delicate frame and kissing her. "I'll write as often as I can."

"Arthur," Katrin quietly whispered, "I shall miss you. I never thought I would meet someone like you, especially in a cave."

Arthur smiled and put her hands to his lips before stepping out to the roadway.

*　*　*

"All present and accounted for," Sergeant Moore reported, early on a Monday morning in late August.

"Very well, Sergeant," Wesley acknowledged. "We move out in fifteen minutes. Load 'em up!"

"Yes, sir!"

Wesley moved to the front of the truck, where Arthur waited, to report that the last of their equipment was loaded and ready to move out at his orders. The Eighth Army had taken a blow when newly appointed General Stafer Gott's plane was shot down the day after his appointment. He was a legend of the desert and the last of the so-called Desert Rats. Wesley heard, just before their orders came through, that General Bernard "Monty" Montgomery would take command of the Eighth Army. He wondered how long before the Americans would begin an offensive in North Africa as the truck jerked forward on the first leg of their journey toward the desert.

18

"This is the BBC Perth, Australia, station reporting," the news-caster began. "In a daring offensive on September 15, United States forces repelled the Japanese at Guadalcanal. Little more is known at this time as the offensive continues to clear the area of the lawless Japanese invader. And this just in: the British have taken Tamatave, Madagascar, when British troops entered the town and found it undefended after a three-minute bombard-ment by British warships.

"On the European war front, it is reported on Thursday last, Stalingrad is suffering fierce fires from German bomber raids as German troops ram into the city outskirts after twenty-six days of continual fighting. The brave Russian soldiers continue to give ground by inches as they vigorously fight to defend the soil of the czars. This is the BBC Perth, Australia, station reporting."

Martin Jamison reached over to turn off the radio as a bond drive commercial began. "It looks as if the Japanese are starting to see some defeats, but I wonder how much it will take to push them out of all the islands and jungles they've fought their way into. I don't believe Stalin's troops will give ground easily either. I've heard he would rather execute his generals than have them give any of Russia to Hitler's army."

"You're most likely right about Russia, Martin," Quentin Patterson responded. "But as more American forces come our way, the Japs might do more retreating. I heard before the Americans go into a fight, they all yell, "Remember Pearl Harbor," and it fires them up. It looks like the Vichy French don't have any stomach for a fight in Madagascar either."

"We'll have to wait and see what happens there in the next few days. It would sure be helpful to not have Madagascar available to the Jap Navy to blockade the Red Sea and Suez Canal."

"Yes, well, that could be difficult. I wonder how the *Mariah* is getting along in all this."

*　*　*

Andy sat in his cabin, catching up on paperwork, when a knock came at his door. "Come," he called out, looking up from the sheets of reports that kept the *Mariah* at readiness.

"Sir, we just received a signal from headquarters," the runner said, handing Andy the scribbled message.

"Have Mr. Roden report to my quarters," Andy ordered after glancing through the deciphered message a few moments later.

Andy still held the torn piece of flash paper in his hand when Mason reported with question on his face. "We have orders to be an escort to Iceland and back to Harwell," Andy said without preamble. "We leave day after tomorrow at midnight," he went on, laying the message on the small table. "All shore leave is canceled."

"We'll be ready, sir," Mason replied. "I ordered shore leave limited to the canteen after the weekend passed. I figured we would be heading back to Alexandria though."

"As did I." Andy shrugged. "But the navy has its own ideas."

"This could become interesting," Mason commented with a smile.

Andy sat down after he and Mason reviewed *Mariah's* readiness and reflected on their last voyage coming north through the

Atlantic. The wolf-pack attacks were becoming more intense as the German and Italian forces gave ground and saw fewer and fewer supplies coming across the Mediterranean Sea. He had heard the British won Alam Halfa in North Africa—under Montgomery—at the end of August. It was rumored, two days later, Rommel was forced to retreat to save fuel. Now he wondered if the enemy attacks in the North Atlantic were as severe as the previous year.

"Sir, the ship is ready for sea," Mason reported as Andy walked onto the bridge two nights later.

"Thank you, Number One."

"Signal from the tower, sir. We are to join the *Victoria* and leave harbor."

"Very well, release spring," Andy ordered as the *Mariah* began to swing away from the peer. "Slow reverse. All ahead one-third, course two-four-zero," Andy continued as the orders crossed his lips by rote.

"All ahead one-third. My course is two-four-zero," the quartermaster responded.

The *Mariah* quietly maneuvered through the harbor, giving way to a tanker as it crossed her path, before entering the open sea and turning her bow toward the English Channel, where German raids were a distinct possibility.

"Lookouts to their posts," Andy ordered, once clear of the harbor.

The ship quietly cut through the sea toward the coordinates the sailing orders indicated to meet the merchant ships that would once more face the harsh North Atlantic crossing. The crew knew from others who had survived the constant wolf pack attacks that the crossing would be a treacherous journey. The only consoling factor was that the time at sea was not as long as the journey to North Africa. But first, they needed to clear the channel.

The crew knew the pitfalls of not keeping constant vigilance and watched with practiced eyes for the first hint of trouble approaching. The newest crew member stoically stood his watch, trying to emulate those around him as he lifted his glasses to look at the dark rolling water, wondering what there was to see. Something in the distance looked like breakers coming toward the shore, but there was no shore.

"I say," the young rating said, looking toward Tim Parker, who was standing nearby looking about the decks to see that all was in order. "I say...ah...do you suppose those breakers out there could be something?" he asked, pointing over the port rail.

Tim lifted his glasses and looked in the direction the young man indicated. He saw small German attack boats taking shape, coming toward the merchant ships—near the end of their group. "Sound battle stations!" he hollered. "Attack boats approaching!"

Andy threw the covers off from his bunk in his sea cabin and grabbed his hat as his hand turned the door handle that opened onto the bridge. "What is it?" he asked, already in battle mode.

"German attack boats approaching. I ordered a shaded signal sent to the group to warn them of the danger comin' at us," Tim answered.

"Good—that's good, Mr. Parker. You're relieved. Report to your battle station," Andy ordered.

"Yes, sir."

"Men closed up, sir," Mason reported when he came to the bridge.

"They'll be swerving in and out between us and trying to line up to fire torpedoes," Andy stated. "Tell the men to wait until they have a good line of sight to begin firing and to not give them a chance to fire on us."

"Yes, sir," Mason responded as he saluted and went to give the instructions to the gunners.

"You heard the lieutenant," Parker hollered just as the first tracers flew across the ocean toward them.

Mason stood at his station aft, waiting until he was sure the small boats were within reach, before he ordered the first shots fired. The shells were still in the air when a second volley was loaded, and the guns were fired toward the boat approaching between the *Mariah* and a large cargo ship about a half mile back.

The shells fell, straddling the small enemy attack boat, sending splinters flying into the enemy ship and her crew. A third volley fell true and exploded near her engines, causing fires to break out and the boat to slow in the water. A moment later, a large explosion splintered the hull, and the boat soon disappeared beneath the dark rolling sea.

Five more boats continued the attack and damaged one merchant ship—to the point that it had to return to port for repairs. A second ship took minor damage, but her captain signaled he would be able to continue. His signal said he wouldn't be stopped by that puny thing the Germans called a warship. When Roger Barnes reported what the captain had said, Andy grinned and said he was glad the man was on their side.

The next evening saw the convoy turn north into the Irish Sea, where more ships would join the growing bevy of cargo ships out of Scotland. Once the group was complete, the convoy would have air cover for the first day of their journey as they left the Irish Sea. They would then make the run through the cold unforgiving North Atlantic to Reykjavik's sheltered port—where supplies from America waited to feed the English population and an army in need of American lend-lease machinery and supplies—to continue the fight.

"We've been ordered to take the lead," Andy indicated when the turn came. "Double our lookouts. The Germans like to follow a convoy from near Belfast well into the North Atlantic before attacking. We want to find them before they find us."

"Yes, sir," Mason replied before issuing the necessary orders.

The morning continued without any sightings. Andy raised his glasses to search the sea again and observe the merchant ships to ensure they were staying in formation. He swept the sea and stopped when he saw the unmistakable shape slip beneath the waves. Without pause, he pushed the alarm bell that brought the men to their battle stations. In seconds, the crew answered the call without pausing to think what new tactic the enemy might try this time.

"Alert the others. Submarine sighting. Stay in formation. Prepare to depth charge," Andy ordered. "We might trap him with the narrows ahead."

The sun was setting when the convoy passed Belfast and the last of the merchant and escort ships out of Scotland joined them. A few hours later, the turn into the North Atlantic came for the several days' journey to Reykjavik in the open seas. The sighting the previous afternoon and the ensuing depth charging was indecisive as the convoy rolled north—into greater danger.

England's admiralty knew "desperate need" outweighed any consideration to halt the shipping rotation cycle. Men and ships would have to be sacrificed until the navy was able to overcome this merciless weapon in the unending succession of deadly tactics the Germans brought against them.

Two days passed without incident, and the crew was starting to believe the crossing would be a milk run when an explosion rocked the nearest ship in the darkest hours, and flames spiraled into the sky, giving an eerie dim light across her decks. Men, looking like ghosts in the fading firelight, ran to retrieve axes and hoses to douse the fire, to save the ship, before their lives were lost in the cold unforgiving sea.

Instantly, ships' alarms echoed across the sea's empty void to man their battle stations. Another explosion was heard as the small merchant ship lost the battle and began to break up before it slipped beneath the surface, with only a slick of oil from its ruptured fuel tanks as the lone grave marker, which would soon wash away. Only the depths would know how she died and became a tomb to those who had served her needs.

"There he is!" Mason shouted above the din of gunfire. "Twenty degrees to starboard, up ten degrees, fire!" he ordered and watched the shot miss as the surfaced U-boat made a quick turn to avoid the shell coming toward it. "Left, twelve degrees, fire!" he ordered again and watched as the shell hit the U-boat near the side of the bridge before the enemy U-boat disappeared beneath the waves. Other ships were firing on a second U-boat, which slipped away in the darkness without damage.

"Cease-fire" came over the intercom as Andy searched the sea for any sign of the attacking submarines.

"No injuries, sir," Mason reported. "I believe we may have hit one of the U-boats just before it disappeared, but I can't be sure."

"Have the men stand by at battle stations in case they return. We'll have to be ready for daylight and keep a close watch. We're still a few days away from any air cover to help find them. Signal the others to be alert, Mr. Barnes."

"Yes, sir," Roger answered, turning to make the necessary signal to the group.

"They'll have to surface before long and charge their batteries," Andy mused. "Send a coded signal to the *Victoria* to watch for any smudge of smoke that is low to the sea."

* * *

The German U-boat captain quickly pulled the hatch shut and ordered a crash dive as the shells from the destroyer exploded near the bridge. *I hope Wilhelm made it out*, he thought, before turning his attention to the needs of his small command.

"Take her to one hundred feet," he ordered and watched the depth indicator spin as the boat continued its steep dive into the depths. "Silent running. Turn fifty degrees to port, steady as she goes," he continued.

He smiled a half hour later when he could no longer hear any engine noise from the surface. "Well, looks like we outsmarted them. Continue to our rendezvous to charge batteries," he ordered. "Lieutenant, you have the bridge."

Captain Haus retired to his small cabin and entered the latest attack into the U-boat's logbook. He smiled when he wrote that an enemy ship was sunk. *I wonder how much damage Wilhelm's boat took. I hope he's all right*, he thought. *After all, he owes me a glass of ale for that last one.*

* * *

Morning broke with cloud cover and wind, causing the seas to be choppy. Rain soon pelted the lookouts, making watch duty a miserable experience that dulled the senses. The towels that men draped around their necks to dry their faces were soon saturated and cold; even oiled slickers didn't prevent the dampness from penetrating through heavy sweaters and sea jacks. Andy knew the hazards the changing weather could bring, so he sat on his bridge chair to keep a constant watch and encourage his crew to do the same. The rains became heavier as late afternoon approached, making it more difficult to see anything in the angry, choppy seas. But one bridge lookout stiffened, and Andy was instantly at his side.

"What is it?" Andy asked. "Tell me what you saw."

"Sir, it might be nothin', but I think I saw a periscope. But wit' ta seas an' all, I—"

He got no further before Andy said, "Good job, son. Bridge, sound general quarters," he ordered.

Men ran to their stations as the alarm sounded in the pelting rain, telling them to load their weapons and wait for orders to come from the bridge.

"Everything closed up, Mr. Parker?" Mason asked.

"Yes, sir, and we're a watchin' with a close eye," Parker said, just as a rating pointed to the unmistakable shape of a periscope lifting above the rolling sea.

The commence-firing order came a moment later when the sea burst into geysers all around the U-boat. The approaching submarine broached the surface before diving for the depths after her unsuccessful approach into the convoy's midst. Andy signaled the *Victoria* to depth-charge the area in hopes of catching the daring captain of the enemy sub before he could reach the depths and slither away to hunt again. An oil slick reached the surface before the convoy was clear of the area, but it was most likely a ruse. The ships continued the precarious journey with the assumption that the attacks would continue.

Another day passed without incident. The *Mariah* watched the sun set and the stars fill the clear sky. The storms over the past few days had hindered any further enemy attacks, and morning would bring air cover for the approach into Reykjavik. Mason stood the early morning watch, enjoying the calm seas and the kaleidoscope of colors dancing across the wave tops as the sun began to make itself known. He almost missed the quick up and down of the periscope, watching and waiting for a chance to invade the tight-knit convoy before the morning sun made it impossible to approach this near to Iceland.

"Man your battle stations," rang throughout the ship as Mason ordered a signal to the convoy to be on the lookout for approaching submarines. He quickly brought Andy into the picture before leaving the deck for his battle-station aft. The navy knew it had to separate the captain from his first officer to ensure the chain of command remained intact if the bridge was compromised or the captain killed. *Mariah* would still have a commander to step in to continue the fight and bring her back to port.

"Torpedo, port side!" a lookout yelled.

Andy quickly spotted the ugly device and ordered a sharp turn to avoid being hit. The torpedo slid by with only feet to spare as the ship made another turn—to throw the submarine off the scent and to become the hunter instead of the hunted. Mason quickly came to the bridge to report all stations ready.

"Very well, prepare to drop depth charges," Andy ordered. "We're going to end this cat-and-mouse game—right now."

"Yes, sir." Mason saluted before hurrying to the deck to relay the orders.

"Mr. Parker," Mason ordered, "drop depth charges on my signal."

"Yes, sir," Parker responded. "You heard the lieutenant," he hollered at the ratings. "Get 'em ready."

Within moments, the orders came to commence depth-charging as Andy worked with Brian Jones to lay out a crisscross pattern that would pound the invasive enemy boat from two directions using the *Mariah* and *Victoria* as her nemesis. An oil slick appeared shortly after the pounding started, but Andy didn't believe the ruse and continued pounding the sea until he saw the submarine broach the surface and men scramble into life rafts. The submarine soon slipped away for a final plunge into the depths, where the intense pressure against its hull would cause it to implode on itself, leaving nothing but a few fragments of metal to settle on the ocean floor.

"Mr. Barnes, collect an armed guard and tell Mr. Parker to retrieve our guests. We'll turn them over when we reach Iceland," Andy ordered.

Roger Barnes quickly drew a sidearm and collected three other ratings to do the same and follow him to the deck. "Mr. Parker," he said, "Captain Burns has ordered us to collect our guests from the sea and bring the officers to the bridge. He'll come alongside and slow for the operation."

"Bert, Hanson, get the nets ready. Be prepared to keep them on the deck until Captain Burns decides where to put the miscreants."

A half hour passed before all the surviving submariners were brought aboard the *Mariah*. Once on the deck, Roger Barnes and three ratings kept them under guard while Mason conducted the surviving officers to the bridge.

"Well, you don't look as fierce as I anticipated," Andy stated when the two men reached the bridge. "How many men survived?"

"We are a small group," one man replied. "I am the first officer of the boat. The men, they will be treated well."

"As well as we are able to provide," Andy stated. "Mr. Roden, put them in the wardroom and keep an armed guard on them," he ordered then turned his attention back to the officers. "We'll be arriving in Reykjavik by dusk. You will be handed over to the appropriate authorities as prisoners of war."

Nodding at the inevitable, the man said, "Perhaps we would have been friends in another time and enjoyed a shot of schnapps after the war games."

"Perhaps, but it's doubtful. Take them below," Andy said to Sublieutenant Anderson.

"Yes, sir."

Once alongside the dock in Reykjavik, the *Mariah* was met by the military police to take charge of the prisoners. Andy watched from the bridge until the prisoners were out of sight then turned to make the final entry in the logbook about this most recent journey.

19

Jane laid Jimmy in his bassinet and smiled at his sweet face as he lay in a peaceful sleep. The planned rite of baptism was being postponed because the elderly parish priest had recently become seriously ill, and his return was doubtful. There was a recent shortage of newly ordained clergy to fill the void as young men learned the ways of war when it was apparent diplomacy wouldn't bring about a solution to the nations' differences.

Jane and Peter entered the local church the following morning and sat next to Helen, who reached for Jimmy while the young couple bowed their heads in prayer. The small group present for the short Morning Prayer Rite consisted mostly of mothers, wives, and children of army personnel. Jane prayed that the women she saw here would not receive the starkly worded telegram that would tell them their loved ones had been killed in this terrible conflict.

The organist began the processional hymn. Jane and Peter looked at each other in surprise as Joseph Albright processed up the aisle and began the service. A moment later, Katrin quietly took a seat next to Martin Jamison and opened a prayer book as her father said the opening prayers. An hour later, Father Albright greeted the congregation after the service ended with the final "Alleluia."

"Father Albright," Peter said, shaking the extended hand, "it was a surprise to have you preside this morning."

"Yes, well, Father Baxter contacted me and asked if I would be willing to take the service if the bishop approved. I've been given special permission until a decision is made regarding him returning if his health permits."

"Well, your homily will be something to think about this week, with the news that has been coming in lately."

"That is what I hope for, Peter—to have people reflecting on how scripture relates to life today. I see Jane with Helen and your Jimmy," Joseph concluded, waving at the women talking a few feet away.

"Father Albright, we'll see you at the cottage later today?" Helen asked.

"Oh yes. Katrin gave me instruction to be on time. I believe she is finding life here much more normal than it was on Java."

"I hope it returns to normal everywhere soon."

"As do I, Helen…as do I."

The friends from Helen's Landing and their new friends from Java gathered around the rough-board dining table at midafternoon to share a quiet Sunday together. The inviting smells brought a smile to everyone's face at the prospect of enjoying the abundant food, which combined resources gave them, and time to share one another's company.

"I heard several positive comments about your homily today, Father Albright," Dr. Jamison commented.

"Please, call me Joseph."

"Very well. I'm Martin," Dr. Jamison put in.

"And I'm Quentin," Dr. Patterson said. "I only use my title in the hospital, mostly with wide-eyed interns or resident physicians," he finished with a grin toward Peter. "That is, if they haven't experienced a harrowing escape and saved a couple of lives along the way."

"You must have a positive influence on Dr. Patterson, Dr. Jamison. He has improved his outlook over the hardworking resident. Of course, being a second-year resident now gives me a higher status," Peter said with a glowing smile.

"I think all three of you are working overtime right now," Helen put in. "But it is good you can still joke with each other. Tell me though, Peter, have you and Jane set a new date for Jimmy's christening? Sally and I are anxious to become official godmothers."

"Well, we did talk about it, but we haven't set a date yet."

"Peter and I were talking on the way over, and we wondered if it might be possible to have Jimmy baptized now that you will be at the church, Father Albright," Jane inquired, looking up from her plate. "We wanted to wait until he was a little stronger before planning it, and then Father Baxter became ill, and we were at loose ends."

"It would be a great honor to welcome your son into the Church of Christ. But don't you want to wait for Father Baxter to return?"

"I'm not sure about his health improving enough right now," Dr. Jamison put in. "His age and weakening heart are preventing the recovery we should be seeing."

"I see," Joseph said. "I'll speak with him about the christening, and I'll let you know. If he agrees, I would suggest All Saints' Sunday as an appropriate time because we renew our baptismal vows on that day as well."

"That sounds wonderful," Jane said. "We would all be taking the vows that we promise for Jimmy."

"I like that," Helen said.

"Me too," Sally agreed.

After enjoying the various dishes that rationing allowed, the friends gathered around the radio in the small living room to hear the latest news. The tubes were soon warm, and Martin Jamison adjusted the dial until the static was cleared, in time to hear the end of the latest war bond drive.

"We'll have to get into town this week and purchase a bond for Jimmy," Peter commented as the live commercial ended and the newscast began.

"This is the BBC Perth, Australia, station. In a remarkable victory, the British Army has occupied the Madagascar town of Tananarive. Upon arriving at the town's outskirts, it was soon discovered the Vichy government was nowhere to be found, leaving the town undefended by opposing forces. It seems the Vichy French have no stomach to fight under the Nazi's swastika.

"And this just in from the Australian Army: Australian troops have landed on New Guinea and are in a fierce battle to recover ground that the Japanese currently and unlawfully occupy. So far, our forces are holding the beachhead and appear to be moving inland against the Japanese, using some of the same tactics the enemy thought were impossible to bring against them. It seems the Japanese chose the wrong islands to invade as the United States have repelled them at Guadalcanal, and now our own troops are showing them what we can do when a bully comes to visit. Good night from the BBC Perth, Australia, station."

"By Jove, now that sounds more like it. We'll finally see the Japs on the run," Dr. Patterson said, slapping his knee.

"It appears that way, Quentin, but I don't think we can claim victory quite yet," Dr. Jamison said.

"I hope the Allies will clear them from the area soon," Katrin said. "I can't help but think how Dad's parish in Java is suffering because of all this terrible fighting," she finished as a tear slid down her face at the memory of the frightening screams she had heard from what was once a place of worship.

"Gentlemen," Helen interceded, noticing Katrin's obvious distress. "I think we should discuss the upcoming plans for the recuperation center's beginning-of-fall celebration."

"I have to say, it feels more like summer though than fall," Jane commented.

"Katrin, how did the plans with the volunteer aides go?" Helen asked.

"They're very excited about the luncheon plans for the patients, and especially being a companion for the day to them. I'm glad you thought of that, Helen."

"And the local merchants are putting in some small prizes for the soldiers as well," Sally said. "I think they want to thank them for keeping Australia safe."

"Martin, do you and Quentin plan to attend?" Helen asked, looking up from a small notebook, with the event checklist beside her.

"We wouldn't miss it, would we, Quentin?" Dr. Jamison said with a smile toward his friend and colleague.

"Absolutely," Dr. Patterson replied with an answering grin.

"And Peter is going to stay home with Jimmy that afternoon so that I can give my full attention to the event," Jane said with a smile toward her husband.

"Just don't be dazzled by a soldier's tall tale," Peter said lightheartedly.

"I don't believe anyone can top ours," Jane remarked.

"Well then, I believe we are ready for a pleasant afternoon," Helen said. "I was just thinking—oh, I believe my godson wants attention," she said, rising from her chair before Jimmy's parents could respond.

"Now, there's a sweet boy," Helen said, bringing the baby into the room with her. "He reminds me of Andy when he was this age, so warm and snuggly after a nap, before he was fully awake. I do hope Father Baxter will agree to you christening him, Joseph."

"I'm sure it will be okay. I'll speak with him tomorrow."

"I think it's time to take our little one to his bath and bed," Jane said, reaching to take her son into her arms.

Jane and Peter gathered Jimmy's blankets and other paraphernalia and bid their friends good-bye after thanking Helen for a relaxing afternoon and evening. The pathway back to their cottage was a short distance, and soon they had completed their son's evening routine before he fell back into the slumber of innocence.

"I do hope Father Albright will be able to christen Jimmy," Jane said while she and Peter lay next to each other after what seemed like such a normal day.

"I'm sure it will work out," Peter said before kissing her goodnight and quickly slipping into a peaceful sleep.

Jane lay awake, thinking about having their son baptized and what that meant to him and to them. *So many people are struggling to stay alive right now, and our only worry is when Jimmy will be christened,* she thought. *The vows we'll promise for him are serious, and we'll have to work to live into them. I'm just thankful we're together when so many children are without their fathers right now.*

Looking over at her sleeping husband, she smiled a moment and said a silent prayer of thanks that their lives were so normal before praying for the troops who were fighting this war, especially for those serving on the *Mariah*. Her last thought before drifting into sleep was how John was making out as the ship's doctor.

20

"You sent them where!" Admiral Edwards exploded as he grappled with the irony of the *Mariah* sailing into harm's way when he had plans to put her in greater danger with the approaching Allied offensive in North Africa. *Mariah* was to be his flagship for this operation, and he was not happy she was currently anchored in Iceland. He flew to England—at some risk—to meet with the admiralty regarding the upcoming offensive and to finalize his part in it the previous day.

"We have to use whatever ships are available, Admiral Edwards, and the *Mariah* is a destroyer in His Majesty's service if I'm not mistaken," the planning officer in charge pointed out.

"Yes…yes, I know. I need her for another operation when she returns. In fact, I need her commander now—to put the plans in place before we sail."

"Well now, that we can accommodate. We'll have him flown back to meet with you. I'm sure the first officer is capable of bringing the ship to Harwell. After all, he's been aboard her nearly since the beginning of the war."

"All right, we can't change what's been done. Bring Andy back here, and we'll see how Mason Roden handles getting the ship back to England," Edwards said, running a hand through his hair. "How soon can you get Captain Burns here?"

"I'll have the request sent today. I'm sure a transport plane is coming over in the next day or two. Between us and the Americans, we almost have a permanent air highway between Iceland and England."

*　*　*

"Sir," the runner said, holding out a slip of flimsy paper, "this just come, sir."

"Number One, you have the bridge," Andy stated as he made his way to the map room to decode the short message.

"Aye, sir," Mason responded, stepping to the center of the bridge.

The *Mariah* was preparing to sail the following night—to act as an escort for the large convoy that was heading for England. It looked like more than food supplies were being sent by the number of ships lined up at the piers, which were taking on goods and equipment. Everything—from cloth to guns—was being lowered into ships' holds as the cranes busily kept the dock in a constant flurry of movement.

"Admiral Edwards has ordered that I return to Harwell by the most immediate transport," Andy informed Mason upon returning to the deck. "He also ordered that you bring the ship back to Harwell without delay. You sail in three hours, with the *Victoria* at cruising speed."

"Sir, we'll bring the *Mariah* back safely," Mason responded as he grappled with the sudden orders to take command of the ship and not be part of the large convoy returning to England.

Andy went to his cabin and packed his shaving gear and necessary clothing before presenting his orders at the shipping office an hour later. He watched from shore as the *Mariah* put to sea without him. He turned and walked to the adjacent airfield when the ship was no longer in sight for the quick trip back to England. It seemed strange to watch his charge leave the harbor without him. He wondered if other captains had the same empty feeling when their commands put to sea, and they were not aboard.

Andy boarded the transport plane an hour later and strapped in as the plane began its run down the tarmac. It flew over Reykjavik Harbor, following the same direction the *Mariah* would sail. He looked out the small window, following her wake in the water below, until he saw the ship directly beneath him. He could still make out the bridge and deck, but the men were nearly indistinguishable as the plane gained speed and elevation. He was soon above the scattered clouds, and only sunshine reflected off the ocean far below.

*   *   *

The week that followed saw the *Mariah* and her companion making the speed run for Harwell—without incident. Mason ran drills all the way across to keep the men at peak readiness.

"Battle stations, man your battle stations," resounded throughout the ship as men closed up in record time. Mason's lips turned up in a brief smile when he noted the quick response. He was pleased with the seconds they had shaved off their time. However, he wondered if his skills were enough, if he would be able to detach his emotions to make the final decision, right or wrong, to keep the ship and her crew alive. He knew that the cloak of command was heavy, and he knew that the burden had fallen to him to bring the *Mariah* safely to port. He shook off his musings and turned his attention to the task at hand.

He noticed the *Victoria* was also coming to battle stations, and he lifted binoculars to his eyes to try and find the enemy submarine. He was rewarded when he noticed the tip of the periscope reflecting in the sunlight between the wave tops when the enemy took another quick peek. Suddenly a lookout yelled, "Periscope, twenty degrees starboard!"

"Forty degrees starboard. Come to one-four-zero, full speed. Signal the *Victoria* submarine at two-one-seven," Mason said in a smooth succession of orders.

"Forty degrees starboard. My course is one-four-zero," the quartermaster replied.

"*Victoria* confirms submarine position," Roger Barnes reported a moment later.

"Prepare depth charges, set at fifty-five feet," Mason ordered.

"Stand by depth charges, set at fifty-five feet," came the instant reply.

"Commence firing depth charges," Mason ordered a moment later. "Stand by guns."

Tim Parker pulled the line, and the first two cylinders flew skyward before falling into the sea, where tall geysers of water erupted within a few minutes as two more cylinders struck it. *Victoria* crossed *Mariah*'s path and dropped two depth charges before the second column of water settled back into the sea.

The two ships continued to pound the area and were rewarded when oil and other debris began floating to the surface. Remembering Andy's lessons about the ruse that a submariner had used to give the impression of damage or destruction, Mason continued the depth-charging for another half hour before returning to the original course. He hoped the second oil slick and flotsam that came to the surface meant the submarine was no longer able to harm another ship. The convoy was only a few days behind them, and he ordered a coded message to be sent to warn of the danger.

Three more days passed before the *Mariah* and *Victoria* tied up beside each other in Harwell's busy port. Andy was waiting on the pier when the ship docked.

"Sir," Mason greeted Andy on the bridge an hour later. "She had an uneventful voyage, sir."

"Except for the submarine you spotted and most likely sank, Number One," Andy said with a grin. "Come to my cabin. We have orders," Andy continued.

Once the door was closed, Andy pulled a large envelope out of the briefcase he carried and laid it on the desktop, which he had pulled down from the cabin wall. "Admiral Edwards is requesting the *Mariah* as his flagship for this operation. It's a pretty tall order," Andy began. "One other thing—you've been promoted to lieutenant commander."

"Sir, I...thank you, sir," Mason stammered at the sudden increase in rank.

"You'll have your own ship before much longer, Number One. I have to say, I'll miss having you around. But you're ready, probably more so than some of the regulars who command His Majesty's ships right now. But back to business. Here," Andy said. "Read this, and then we'll discuss our plans."

Mason lifted the "Top Secret" sheet and began to read the orders that would send the *Mariah* into a battle, far beyond being a convoy escort. The orders included working with their allies, in a determined stroke, to take back North Africa. The words *Operation Torch* stood out, like the blood of the wounded on a sterile sheet.

"It's pretty ambitious," Mason said after reading the bullet points that clearly outlined the steps of the operation and what each unit was expected to complete.

Mariah would have a twofold roll in the operation. First, she would be an escort to the convoy of men and equipment that was sailing out of England to North Africa. Her role as an escort would then change to that of destroyer, when she would bombard hostile ports—to land troops and equipment for the upcoming land offensive.

"Yes, it is ambitious," Andy agreed. "Admiral Edwards was in on the planning and believes the operation will be successful. He said the Americans have a very large number of ships and men, ready to take the coast of Oran and occupy Casablanca. He wouldn't comment on just how many ships would be part of the operation, but I got the impression it would be a force the enemy would find overwhelming."

"When do we sail, sir?"

"I haven't been told, but it must be soon."

* * *

Wesley had heard about the invasion of New Guinea when his unit reached the port city where they would board the ship that would take them to North Africa. He was surprised they weren't sent on the mission due to their proximity to the area. But command had other ideas apparently. He and Arthur reported in at the port headquarters to find out what ship they were to board.

"Ah, Captain Vilmont and Lieutenant Nance," Fred Palmer greeted them when they walked into the building.

"I'm afraid to ask what you're doing here, Major," Wesley said.

"I had some other business to attend to when I learned you would be passing through. I just stopped to wish you a safe journey. We might have a combined operation in the future, but that will depend on certain things taking place beforehand."

"That was mighty nice of you, Major, but I have to find out what ship we're supposed to report to," Wesley said with a small smile.

"Oh, that won't be necessary," Palmer replied. "Here are your boarding orders. I believe the ship is that nice big one that is tied up to the pier over there," he said, pointing out the window.

Glancing at Arthur, Wesley took the envelope from Palmer's hand and nodded his understanding. He and Arthur bid Fred Palmer good day at the closed radio-room door outside his office when Palmer took out his key to enter the room.

"Well, I guess we better have the men get settled then," Wesley said before shutting the headquarters' door and shaking his head at this new "twist" in the unit's next operation.

The convoy was a slow affair, and the men passed the time playing cards and catching up on their sleep. Sergeant Moore and

Corporal Jenkins advised the unit to get as much rest as possible and to eat three meals a day. "It won't be long before you all will be wrestling with German tanks and dumping sand out of your boots," Moore predicted.

A week into their voyage, Jenkins said, "Sir, I just heard the Australians have fought their way to the Mediterranean in North Africa, and they have the Germans bogged down in the salt marshes near El Alamein. I'm a wonderin' if we'll get there in time to get in on the fight."

"I wouldn't worry too much about that, Corporal. My guess is we'll see plenty of action before much longer," Wesley predicted.

21

Another day and the convoy that Wesley traveled with would reach Alexandria, Egypt. The journey through the Indian Ocean had proven to be uneventful, but once the convoy transitioned through the Suez Canal from the Red Sea, the danger increased. The German Air Corps was only a few hours' flying time away, and the ships faced another enemy hidden beneath the waves, desperate to stop the Axis retreat across the searing desert. He had pushed other dangers that lurked closer at hand to the back of his mind and was startled when sirens blared and saw men scurrying to their battle stations.

Escort ships sliced through the ocean and forcefully signaled the small convoy to stay on station while they dealt with this latest challenge. One small troopship was damaged, leaving men who had never seen a battlefield injured or killed when a prowling submarine landed a torpedo in their midst. The attack was soon over when the escorts dropped depth charges to ward off further interference as the convoy steered toward their final destination.

Twilight was approaching when the convoy entered Alexandria Harbor and tied up at the peer to disembark their passengers. Men with duffle bags thrown over their shoulders paraded down the gangways to line up in units, companies, and battalions within an hour of docking before marching toward the temporary barracks. The British Army was wasting no time reinforcing the troops and equipment on the frontline in the battle for North Africa.

"Sir, we've been ordered to Barracks D," Arthur indicated.

"Very well," Wesley answered. "Sergeant Moore, load them up and move out," he ordered.

"Yes, sir. You heard the captain. Let's move it out," Moore bellowed before leading the unit to the waiting transport.

Orders came for all company commanders to report for a briefing at 06:30 a.m. two days later. Wesley reported to his immediate superior to learn what his unit's assignment would be for the coming attack. He was surprised to see General Montgomery was also there. Saluting, Wesley came to attention. "Sir, reporting as ordered," he briefly stated.

"At ease, Captain," Colonel Gherst replied.

"Thank you, sir," Wesley said, placing his hands behind his back and focusing on a spot just above his superior's head.

"I understand from various sources, you can be flexible when the situation calls for it," Gherst began. "Your little sea adventures indicate you can also use what is available to get the job done. Tell me, Captain, are there any other adventures you might draw on to improvise, should the situation call for it?"

"Nothing I can say for certain, sir. We're an engineering unit and do our best to outsmart the enemy to their disadvantage."

"Yes, well, we would like your unit to be in an advanced position when our next offensive begins," Gherst stated, then added, "What you are about to hear is top secret."

"Captain Vilmont," Montgomery said, "in a few days, Operation Lightfoot begins. We are to take El Alamein before the American Army lands in East Africa with their British counterparts. We cannot lose this battle, Captain. No matter what it takes, we must push Rommel back and destroy as much of his forces as possible."

"Yes, sir. What do you want our unit to do, sir?" Wesley asked.

Smiling, Montgomery nodded to Colonel Gherst to fill Wesley in on the plan and to show him where he and his men would plant devices to slow the retreating German and Italian armies, allowing Allied forces to inflict as much damage as possible. Their unit would work alone and have to depend on stealth and victory by the Eighth Army to not be killed or captured and sent to a German prison camp.

"We'll do our best, sir," Wesley assured them.

"You're darn right you will, Captain." Montgomery briefly nodded before turning to leave the small headquarters.

"I believe the general likes you, Captain Vilmont. Now, as for your transport to the front...," Gherst continued, filling Wesley in on the particulars. Just before dismissing him, he commented on the rescue of his friends from Java. "Joseph always did have a bit of luck in his pocket, but I was more concerned for Katrin after hearing some of the stories coming out of the east."

"Sir, how did you know Arthur and I were there? It's supposed to be top secret."

"I received a note from Joseph with their new address in Australia. And Katrin is my goddaughter. She enclosed a note as well, saying she was fine, thanks to her rescuers and mentioned Lieutenant Nance and yourself."

"Glad we could help, sir."

"Yes, well, you're dismissed."

"Sir," Wesley said, saluting his superior before closing the office door behind him.

"Lieutenant Nance," Wesley said when he entered their temporary home. "Come with me. We have orders."

Wesley soon brought Arthur into the picture and told him the unit would be leaving Alexandria for the front in three days' time. "Have the men check their supplies and then draw as much ammunition as you can get your hands on."

"I think Moore and Jenkins can be of help there, sir." Arthur smiled when he considered Moore and Jenkins' ability to "improvise."

The drive to the front took much less time than the fight to get to the jumping-off point. Burnt-out trucks and two-wheeled track vehicles littered the desert highway as a testament to those who had come and fought before them.

Opening a satchel, Wesley pulled a small set of drawings out and spread them over the hood of the Land Rover. Before leaving Alexandria, he and Arthur were summoned to headquarters and shown the drawings that were given to Colonel Baxter in Australia, shortly before he and Arthur went on their "little adventure," as General Montgomery referred to their trip to Java. Now it was superimposed over a grid map of the area.

"We can use this route to sneak into the town and plant the traps in front of the retreating forces. We'll have to watch for any troops guarding the town," Wesley said.

"What about the locals?" Arthur asked. "We won't know if they're pro-Axis or pro-Allies until we get there."

"First we have to get there," Wesley stated.

Darkness had covered the desert when Wesley's unit moved out across the desert sands. The small town beyond El Alamein was several clicks west. He was told the night artillery fire would keep the enemy forces occupied so they could get into position and plant traps that would hinder Rommel's retreating army.

"Sir, I can make out some buildings just north of us. See—just a dark outline against the sky," Arthur said an hour later.

Stopping the Land Rover, Wesley got out and looked through his binoculars. He saw the faint outline of a walled town in the darkness. "Corporal Jenkins, take two men and scout around the wall. See if any guards are at the gates."

"Yes, sir. You—Thompson, Wheatley—come with me." When the town was about one hundred yards away, he ordered, "Keep low and don't make no noise."

The men crawled the last fifty yards and slid up against the wall. The town appeared to be in darkness, and no noise could be heard from their position. Jenkins pointed to Thompson and indicated he should slide along the wall to peek around the southeast corner and see if there was any sign of activity. A few moments later, Thompson carefully leaned against the wall and moved his head forward—just enough to see around the blind corner. The only thing in sight was a closed gate with no guard stationed outside. From his current position, he couldn't tell if there was a guard in the tower next to the gate. Using hand signals, he indicated Wheatley should find a place to climb the wall and inspect the tower before they moved forward. Several minutes passed before Private Wheatley appeared inside the tower and gave a low whistle that all was clear. Thompson eased around the corner and along the wall another two hundred feet before he could see the next corner in the far distance.

"I nearly had a heart attack when you slipped around that corner," Jenkins said. "What did you find?"

"It's clear on that side. Ain't no guard in the tower neither."

"Okay, I'll do the same on the west side," Jenkins said. He was gone about ten minutes and reported the same on the other side. "Must be a gate to the north. We best get back and tell the captain."

"About time," Sergeant Moore said. "Well, what did you find?"

"Ain't nothin' to the south, east, or west walls. We didn't try the north side, figurin' there's gotta be a gate or somethin' there."

Standing beside Moore, Wesley nodded and said, "Okay, one way in and one way out means the Germans most likely won't enter the town, but the road runs just north of it. We'll circle the town, head north to the crossroad, and set the first traps. There's another village, about two clicks farther up the road, where we can set the rest."

Just then, the sky was lighted as the first artillery began to fire into the German lines. Wesley knew over eight hundred field artillery would fire into the Panzer Army before sappers went ahead of the advancing Allied Army to locate land mines with electric mine detectors and bayonets. As dangerous as it was to be behind enemy lines, Wesley thought he would rather be here than looking for the traps Axis forces had planted. He knew that a sapper's life expectancy was short.

Giving the walled town a wide berth, the small unit headed north and soon came to the empty crossroads. "Get those mines out and set up the fakes we brought to throw them off. Figure about one hundred yards out."

The men began digging in the low brush around the perimeter of the roadway and soon had set several devices that would destroy an enemy vehicle and cause chaos among the retreating army when four-wheeled and track vehicles drove off the road to avoid what appeared to be bombs set to explode along the roadway. If they were lucky, they might even get a tank or two.

The unit was soon moving toward the next town and turned south into the desert to approach without being seen. Once again, Jenkins took the two men to investigate the outskirts of the town before the rest of the unit moved up. This time, there was no wall around the town, but the roadways were narrow. Wesley took out the drawings and checked the coordinates where the army wanted the enemy stopped. "Grab those two bags there," he said, before crouching and leading the group along the narrow road until he reached the first intersecting cobblestone street.

"Lay the explosives here, here, and here," he indicated, pointing at three of his men. "Be sure the wires are fastened tight so we don't have a dud when the time comes."

Moving farther into the town, the rest of the men turned up another alleyway and soon found the next position where the process was repeated.

"Moore and I will take this one up and set it," Arthur said, grabbing the last bag and disappearing into the darkness.

The two men took a quick look around the corner of a building and saw their first enemy soldier, standing in a doorway and smoking a cigarette. Pointing at the man, Arthur indicated they should wait until he turned his back to them and then quietly disable him. It seemed an eternity before the man stubbed out the cigarette with his foot and turned to walk toward them.

"Get back," Moore whispered. "He's comin' our way."

Arthur heard the man whistling as he came closer and soon heard the sound of his boots on the cobblestone street as he neared the corner. Nodding to Moore, he stepped out in front of the unsuspecting soldier and forced him toward Corporal Moore, who knocked him to the ground and soon had him gagged and tied—hand and foot. The two men sprinted up the street and set the last device before dragging the unconscious prisoner back to the rest of the unit.

"And just what are we supposed to do with him?" Wesley asked.

"We couldn't leave him where he was, sir, and gunfire would bring out a lot of Germans that we don't want to see," Arthur said. "I figured we could hand him over when the rest of the army gets here."

"Well, we'll have to find a good place to hide for the next twenty-four hours until they do get here. Maybe he can help us out a little," Wesley said as the man started to come around and then stared in surprise when he saw himself surrounded by British uniforms.

* * *

"This is the BBC reporting," Katrin heard on the nine-o'clock broadcast. "In an unprecedented move, the Eighth Army has opened an all-out offensive to retake El Alamein against fierce resistance by the German Army. News releases indicate the second day of the battle saw the desert lit like day in a two-mile radius as the Luftwaffe bombed Allied tanks and support vehicles, igniting precious fuel and ammunition in the pitched battle. Our forces have joined with the Tenth Armored Division and continue to push against a vicious enemy. In other news, we have learned that eight hundred Vichyites surrendered on Madigascar. This is BBC Perth, Australia, station. Good night."

Katrin turned off the radio and sat for some time, thinking about the desert and wondering if Arthur was okay. His last letter was a short missive—written on the run—saying he had arrived safely and would write again soon. Turning off the small light, she prepared for bed then knelt in prayer that he would be kept safe. She felt helpless—that there was nothing else she could do to help him. Even in the caves of Java, she had felt more capable of being useful than when lying in a bed, listening to the calm sea lap against the shore in the darkness, where the dangers of war felt a world away.

22

"Admiral, welcome aboard," Andy greeted Eric Edwards when the boson's whistle sounded.

"A pleasure, Captain Burns," Edwards replied with a smile and handshake after saluting the colors. "May we retire to your cabin?"

"As you wish, sir," Andy responded as he led the way to his cabin and shut the door behind them.

"I called you, Captain, up on the deck because your promotion has come through. The command board met yesterday and approved it. I think that last sub you got was the most persuasive item on the recommendation. Keep it up, and you'll make admiral."

"Thank you, sir. I'm a little stunned at the short time since my last promotion. It takes three or four years to make captain—that is, if you're going to be promoted at all."

"Well, your performance is a persuasive argument. I'm afraid, before long, we'll need you in a more decisive position. But we'll talk about that later. Right now, we need to get ready for sea."

"The *Mariah* is ready to sail. Would you like to join me on the bridge tonight when we leave the harbor, sir?"

"It would be my pleasure, Captain," Admiral Edwards responded. Once again, he would be the group commander, but another would be commanding the ship he sailed aboard.

Protocol was especially important at this delicate time when England's very existence lay in the balance. The meeting with his superiors this morning was explicit. Montgomery would soon be moving across Egypt with a precise plan and orders to secure the advances before moving forward and beyond his supply line. The navy was to bring men to replace the soldiers lost in battle and supplies—from tanks to tea bags.

Edwards knew the *Mariah* and her captain as an efficient war tool; now they had to become an efficient command tool as well. He expected to soon be drafted to a desk job—with another star on his mortarboard—by the time the mainland of Europe was tackled. He also expected Andy Burns to be the officer who would command a task force to secure a safe corridor before a single soldier set foot on European soil.

A sliver of moon shone in the clear night sky as *Mariah* entered the English Channel. She would join the large convoy sailing to North Africa with equipment and soldiers to rid the land of the Axis swastika for good.

"Lookouts at stations, sir," Mason reported as *Mariah* made her turn.

"Very well. Keep a sharp eye," Andy commanded.

"Tea, sirs?" the young rating asked as he approached the bridge with tin cups and a pouring bucket bearing strong hot tea.

"Thank you, son. Don't mind if I do," Admiral Edwards said, holding out the tin cup as the young rating carefully poured the hot sloshing liquid.

"Ships to starboard!" a lookout's yell pierced the night's calm.

After receiving the correct reply to his challenge, Andy ordered the ships to fall in line until the next group was met with another escort as the convoy came together while passing the various ports leading into the channel. Three more hours passed as each group joined until the convoy grew to nearly two miles long and several ships wide in a box formation, with several escorts to protect them.

"Have the *Victoria* take the rear escort," Admiral Edwards ordered. "We'll take the lead, Captain."

"Yes, sir," Andy quickly replied. "Mr. Barnes, signal the *Victoria* to take rear escort. Tell her to be on watch for any stragglers. We don't want to lose anyone along the way."

"Aye, sir," Roger responded before lifting the signal lamp.

The turn into the Atlantic came under low overcast skies, which gave the convoy a reprieve from German planes. Andy hoped they would get far enough out to sea that enemy planes would not be able to reach them easily. There were enough dangers in the sea as his recent voyage—and that of his first officer—reminded him.

The convoy had continued another day and into the evening hours when the first indication of trouble sounded. "Periscope thirty degrees to starboard."

Andy quickly crossed the bridge and saw the unmistakable broomstick shape lower beneath the waves, just as he raised his glasses. "Sound general quarters. All men to their battle stations," he ordered. "Hard aport. Signal the group that we are under attack," he continued in one breath. "Be on the lookout for more submarines in the vicinity."

"All stations closed up, sir," Mason reported. "No further sightings at this time," he started to say when a lookout yelled, "Torpedo in the water—port side!"

Andy quickly ordered a sharp turn and avoided the devious device before taking a look at the convoy behind him. "Order the convoy to tighten up and to not change course," he ordered. "Signal the escorts to move closer in and to keep an eye out for anything unusual."

He raised his glasses again and saw a small Corvette changing course to move closer to the convoy when a torpedo slammed into her side. She staggered from the force of the explosion but appeared to still have steerage when a second white hot explosion flashed from her side. A second escort moved in and began firing near the damaged Corvette, hitting something low in the water that caused a large explosion, followed by the sound of breaking metal tearing across the ocean.

Andy ordered the men to remain at battle stations another hour before sounding the stand-down. The damaged Corvette was still with them but losing ground as the convoy continued its eleven-knot run to the Mediterranean. Andy signaled the ship's captain to see if he thought they would be able to catch up. The reply that came back was from a mad commanding officer, whose ship was damaged, and he hadn't even been able to get a shot off at the enemy. He'd lost two good men and would be darned if the enemy was going to stop them from reaching their destination. Andy smiled a moment at the reply and told his lookouts to keep an eye on the damaged ship.

The voyage continued another three weeks with intermittent aerial attacks as the Axis alliance flew surveillance over the sea and sent in fighters and small bombers to nibble at the merchant ships moving south. Andy and Eric Edwards both knew the danger was the reports that were sent back to their headquarters about the convoy and its direction. Andy was in his bridge cabin when a more determined attack took place as they approached Gibraltar.

"Where are they, Number One?" Andy asked as he came onto the bridge.

Pointing, Mason answered, "Off our starboard side, about four o'clock," he quickly answered.

The German planes dove toward the convoy in pairs, dropping bombs and strafing the decks as they passed low overhead. Mason quickly went to his station aft and ordered his men to be ready to fire when the planes flew over their deck. He could see the dots take on shapes, which roared toward the *Mariah* at an incalculable speed, as he waited for the order to fire and wipe the sky clean of these screaming pariahs bent on destruction.

"Fire!" Andy ordered when the planes came into range.

With practiced skill, the gunners began firing on the enemy planes to throw them off their attack path. To keep the *Mariah* out of harm's way, Andy watched closely as planes weaved through the defensive fire to see what path they would take to drop their bombs. Soon, the crisscross of planes and canon fire created flashing streaks of continual fire, reminiscent of a demon's howl emanating from the bowels of God's fiery pit—described in countless sermons throughout the ages.

Admiral Edwards stood at the back of the bridge to be out of the way but also to be able to see if any of the convoy ships were damaged or sunk. He knew each ship was vital to the upcoming mission when his group would join with the Americans at Algeria to secure several harbors for the Allied Command to use in the next phase of the operation.

"Fire!" Mason was yelling above the din of 20-mms' cannon fire when a second plane streaked over the decks, spitting angry cannon fire into men and machinery. "Up one hundred, fire!" he ordered again and watched the shell strike a wing, causing the plane to spiral into the sea. A small victory that came too late for the man being carried away to the infirmary and the other rating whom no one could help.

John Hartman worked quickly to stem the flow of blood from the rating whom was brought to him. "Clamp," he tersely ordered, holding out his hand. "Hold this sponge here." He pointed. "Need to stop the flow of blood to see the field and repair the artery," he said, more to himself than to Ethan Harris, his helper in the small operating room. "Ah, there it is. Suture," he flatly stated. "That's better. Now, let's see what else we have here." He continued as he had on Arthur that terrible night, blocking out the dangers surrounding him as he worked to repair the damage the tools of war had ravaged on the body beneath his scalpel.

The fight continued another half hour until the German planes ran low on fuel and had to return to their base—after sinking one merchant ship and damaging two others. Andy put a hand up to shade his eyes as he watched the planes become small dots and then disappear over the horizon. It was nearing sunset, and he believed there would be no more aerial attacks today. The night, however, held another enemy that was harder to see.

"Hold that, there," John instructed as he worked on a wounded sailor near the 20-mm.

Bert continued firing at the adversary that had, again, brought injury to one of his mates. His reward was to see smoke spilling from an engine cowling as it disappeared from sight.

Mason watched John and a rating help the wounded man below before reporting to the bridge. "Sir, two wounded, one dead. No damage to the ship."

"How's that Corvette doing?" Andy asked.

"So far, he's holding on," Mason reported. "According to Mr. Parker, it appears the damage is above the waterline and that helps him, and his crew has steadily worked on repairs since they were hit. But if we get many more attacks like that one, I don't know."

"What about the two merchants that were hit?"

"So far, they appear to be staying in formation, sir. Apparently the damage was minimal, with more smoke than anything."

"Have Parker keep an eye on them. Tell him to let you know if he thinks they won't be able to keep up."

"Yes, sir."

The convoy swept on through another night and day without incident. It would soon be approaching the rally point where they would meet several more ships for the run to Oran's harbor, where the French fleet was destroyed by the English in 1940 to keep it from falling into German hands. Another group was scheduled to take the Port of Algiers. Other ships would split off to secure Casablanca, which would provide a rail line for Allied supplies to move upland and give the ground forces a continual lifeline. With Madagascar nearing the end as a Vichy French stronghold, it was believed that the Vichy French government in Morocco and Algeria wouldn't be in the mood to fight for the Axis alliance.

"Ships approaching to port!" a lookout yelled the next morning.

Andy lifted his glasses and saw a large number of ships on a course toward the convoy. "Send this, Bunts," he told Roger Barnes. Turning to a rating, he said, "Alert Admiral Edwards that the second group is approaching."

"Yes, sir," Roger responded and lifted the signal lamp to send the coded challenge to the approaching ships.

Eric Edwards stepped onto the bridge as the lead American destroyer answered the challenge and then signaled, "Glad you could make the party."

"Captain, we take position behind the American force. We should see carriers before long that will give us the air cover needed to take the ports and establish a beach head."

"Signal the convoy to fall into place and await further orders," Andy ordered. "Number One, you have the bridge."

"Yes, sir, I have the bridge," Mason responded, stepping to the center of the bridge as Andy Burns joined Eric Edwards in the map room and closed the door.

"We sail to these coordinates and wait for the signal to enter the port," Admiral Edwards indicated on the chart. "Can your Mr. Jones time it so we won't be sitting on the open ocean, twiddling our thumbs?"

Andy looked at their current position and ran a finger down to Algiers, where their group was to enter the port and unload the supplies and men sailing in the convoy. He knew timing was important to avoid aerial attack in the narrower sea space and not have the merchant ships panic and try to scatter, making them a simple target for the enemy to destroy.

"I believe he can, sir, if we get some information from the Americans as to when they will secure the port. If not, we'll have to chance going in and possibly have to fight our way in to secure it ourselves."

"Have Mr. Jones plot the course. I'll handle the rest," Edwards ordered.

"Yes, sir." Returning to the bridge, Andy walked to the chart table and quietly explained to Brian Jones the course and arrival time he needed the *Mariah* and her charges to enter the port at Algiers, behind the American warships.

"Not a problem, sir. We often sailed to the port during the fall of the year. You would be amazed at how pleasant the weather is in November: very little cloud cover, with warm days and pleasant evenings to enjoy the sunsets along the seashore. How much leeway would you like to have, in case the French are cantankerous about allowing the Americans and us into the port?"

"Give us nine hours. Any more than that and we become a sitting target."

"Then we should continue at about seven knots on this course, sir," Brian indicated after making a few calculations and rechecking the chart.

Andy ordered the group signaled before returning to his bridge chair to watch and wait for word of the first American signal that Casablanca was under Allied command and that ground forces were moving overland to Oran and Algiers.

23

"The Vichy French government of Madagascar, on Thursday last, officially placed control of the island state in Allied hands. In other breaking news, American and British forces entered the French ports of Casablanca, Morocco, Oran, and Algiers after two days of fighting against the Vichy-controlled naval and land forces at the all-important port cities," the morning news began. "Rumor has it, American general Mark Clark told Admiral Darlan of the French naval force stationed there, he would have thirty minutes to surrender the port, or he would be arrested and his fleet sunk. It appears the admiral thought better of risking the remainder of his fleet and surrendered to the overwhelming presence the Americans had brought to the coastal nations of North Africa.

"Closer to home, the Allied advance continues on New Guinea as American and Australian forces work their way across the malaria-infested jungles against a stubborn Japanese army."

Peter turned off the radio and turned to Jane, who was still holding their sleeping son. He smiled when he thought about Jimmy's baptism the previous Sunday. "I'll take him, Jane," Peter said, reaching to take the sleeping child into his arms. "He's had a busy week."

"I wonder if Wesley and his unit are in Egypt," Jane said when Peter returned from laying their son on his bed.

"It's hard to say. My guess is they are, but we won't really know for some time. Maybe Arthur will write to Katrin or Father Albright, and we'll hear from one of them."

"You're probably right. Sally said Wesley's letters are not real frequent and are pretty brief. I think Arthur is attracted to Katrin. I hope things work out for them."

*   *   *

Father Albright turned off the radio and returned to next Sunday's sermon. His thoughts soon turned to the short note Arthur Nance sent upon reaching what he assumed was someplace in North Africa. Arthur's letter said he was sorry he had to fight in a war that meant killing his fellow human beings. "However," he went on, "I feel it necessary to rid the world of the toxic message the German government, and its current military command, is enforcing." He continued by asking permission to correspond with Katrin in the hope he would one day see her again in better times.

Unable to concentrate on his message, Joseph Albright took up pen and paper and began a response to Arthur's letter.

Dear Arthur,

I have to say, I was pleased to receive your letter. I have to commend you for your concern about your fellow man, but sadly, many wars are fought because a tyrant came to power. It seems the evil of Satan controls their thoughts and deeds, and the innocent suffer—when war erupts— until peace once again prevails.

I believe our Lord weeps at every conflict the world encounters and watches over those who call on him to keep their souls free of darkness. My prayers are with you—and the men in your unit—as you encounter the daily struggles and heartbreak that this war continues to bring to those who must fight the battles and see the ugliness of war. While Jesus said to offer the other cheek as well when struck, He did not say to allow injustice to prevail.

I thank you for asking, and if Katrin wishes to correspond, I have no objection. She is a mature, young woman with a mind of her own, so like her mother.

Take care of yourself and come back to us soon.

Yours in God's love,
Joseph Albright+

He folded the letter and placed it in an envelope with the address Arthur had indicated in his correspondence. Getting up, he placed a stamp on the envelope and put on his jacket. He hoped the short walk to the post office would clear his mind of the recent news about the Allied landings in North Africa and the impending battles that young men like Arthur would have to fight. *How do I preach the Gospel about God's love and celebrate the Eucharist while the news is filled with war?* he wondered when he had returned home and was staring out at the ocean lapping the shoreline.

He thought about the baptism of young James Peter Romans the previous Sunday and smiled a little at the hope of new life and the young parents who would raise him. Helen had taken an active role in getting Father Baxter to be part of the service, with help from Martin Jamison and Quentin Patterson. She and Sally Vilmont made the day a time of celebration, which brought happiness to more than Jane and Peter. The congregation celebrated as well. *Maybe that's where the answer lies*, he thought. *The Gospels speak about hope and love, and that's what last Sunday was about—hope and love.*

"Dad, do you want some lunch?" Katrin asked from the patio doorway. "You look very deep in thought."

"Just a little reflecting is all. I'll be in shortly," Father Albright said, glancing up from his notes. He looked out over the ocean one more time and saw the splendor before him and the power of God's universe that no nation of men could overpower. *I believe a study group during Advent would be a good idea,* he thought. *One that brings out the real message of Christmas in the birth of our Savior. Someday, the war will end, and somehow, those that are left must learn to love those we think we hate. I wonder if the message can be brought to those fighting and struggling to keep the hatred from poisoning their souls.*

* * *

Wesley's unit continued to move behind enemy lines, disrupting communications and destroying as many supplies as possible while Montgomery's forces moved forward. Before leaving the last small settlement, they blew up two fuel trucks en route to Rommel's tanks.

"I think I hear something," Moore said, moving toward the small window to peek over the sill. Carefully sliding to the side of the smudged windowpane, which overlooked the small town square from the abandoned loft where the unit hid, he looked out on the street below. He saw several armored vehicles preparing to leave the square and men spilling out of doorways carrying guns and ammunition. In the distance, he saw a large cloud of dust rising from the east and wondered if it was the British Army coming toward them or the Axis forces regrouping to push the British back again.

"What do you see, Sergeant?" Wesley asked, moving toward the window at the sound of engines starting.

"Looks like they're getting ready to move out and join that cloud of dust just east of us," Moore said, pointing out the window.

"Then it's time for us to make our move. We have a few little items to give our friends to send them on their way."

"Yes, sir." Moore grinned.

Wesley took Jenkins and six of the men with him toward the first set of explosives planted in the adjoining buildings that surrounded the square at the center of the town. Arthur had Moore and the rest of the unit quietly moving toward the outskirts of the cobblestone streets, where centuries of caravans had packed desert sands into a road toward the coast.

Wesley waved his men toward the three placements and ordered them to wait until the German unit assembled in the square. He knew, once the blasts occurred, other units would come running to see what had happened and open fire in all directions, thinking tanks were close by. He and Jenkins crawled along the roof of the opposite building until they could see the soldiers running to their armored cars and tracked vehicles. Some of the men climbed into transport trucks, pulling what belongings they had hurriedly put together, with the sergeant hollering to hurry it up. A few minutes passed before another man appeared, carrying a riding crop in his hand, whom the sergeant saluted. The two men climbed into what appeared to be a command car and indicated the group should move out.

"Okay," Wesley whispered, "here we go." Taking a deep breath, he took careful aim with his rifle and slowly squeezed the trigger, sending the bullet through the back of the German officer's head. Jenkins quickly rose in the confusion and lobbed a hand grenade through the open window of the building opposite them, setting off the pile of explosives, which sent cement and wood splinters flying through the air—striking whatever was in its path.

"Let's move," Wesley hollered, grabbing Jenkins's arm and diving for the relative safety below the terrace roof. "Head for that back doorway. We need to get clear before the next ones go off."

Wesley ran for the open doorway and stopped short when he saw a shadow fall across the opening. Diving behind a table, he pulled his sidearm and waited. A shot from the doorway ricocheted off the opposite wall, and he saw Jenkins grab his left leg and sag behind what appeared to be a bar. Sliding across the floor, he managed to sneak behind the bar and found Jenkins wrapping a piece of torn shirt around his bleeding thigh.

"Went clean through," Jenkins told him. "Didn't hit the bone, thank heaven."

"Okay, we need to get our friend inside to deal with him. I'll make a run for the other side of the room. Think you can hit him when he goes for me?"

"I'll get 'im, all right. Now I'm just plain mad."

Grinning, Wesley nodded then inched to the end of the bar. "Now," he mouthed and ran in a crouch toward the far side of the room—away from the doorway.

Bullets began spattering off the wall when the unknown German began firing toward Wesley. Jenkins rose above the bar and fired at the shadow in the doorway until a gun clattered to the floor and the shadow disappeared in a heap.

"Come on, let's move before anyone else decides to investigate," Wesley ordered, grabbing Jenkins's arm and helping him run out into the roadway and through the empty marketplace to where the rest of the men with Wesley were waiting to scurry to the outskirts of the town. Two more explosions went off, sending smoke and fire into the air when an ammunition depot was torn apart. Out of breath, Wesley's group stopped near an empty German outbuilding to wait for Arthur's team to join them.

* * *

"Sounds like the major started a ruckus," Moore commented.

"We should see something pretty soon," Arthur said. "Have the men take their positions. We don't want to spoil the surprise."

Another five minutes passed before the sound of engines could be heard nearing Arthur's position. Holding up a hand, he signaled the men to wait for the retreating enemy to get closer. He let the first tracked vehicles pass him and head toward the men up the line. He wanted to get the tail end to give them the best chance of escaping before any organized retaliation could begin.

The end of the small armored group drove into view. Arthur pulled the plunger, preparing to set off the explosives that were planted along the desert roadway. When the last armored car was within range, he pushed the plunger down with a swift force, setting off the charges that exploded beneath the last vehicle. Up the road, more explosions were heard as the rest of the charges were set off, leaving only the land mines along the side of the road to take out the ones that survived.

Arthur whistled to his men to head toward the rendezvous point and started to run with his rifle in his hand. He made it to the first piece of cover and waited to see if the rest of his men were coming. Moore slid into the cover, like the American baseball players slide into home plate, which Arthur saw when he visited the United States before the war. Four more men came quickly on Moore's heels, with gunfire coming close at hand, but one man was missing.

"Where's Langley?" Arthur asked.

"He was right behind us," one of the privates said. "I heard the shooting but...," he trailed off.

"We can't wait," Arthur said. "Move it out."

*   *   *

Wesley sat in cover until he heard men coming toward him. He glanced around the side of the building and saw Arthur and four others trailing behind him, with Moore bringing up the rear. Stepping into the open, he waved for Arthur and the others to join him.

"We lost Langley," Arthur reported. "We took out most of the armored cars and heard a couple more explosions after we vacated the area."

"Let's move out," Wesley ordered. "We have to get clear of the area before they find us. I sent Jenkins ahead with the others about an hour ago."

Two hours passed before Wesley and his men were gathered behind the desert sand hills to wait for darkness to fall. Their orders were to return to their own lines and report in to Colonel Gherst. He hoped the Eighth Army was moving their way and they wouldn't run across any German stragglers along the way.

24

Sally turned off the radio and thought about the recent news reports. It looked like the Allies were starting to turn things around in Africa. The news said that Montgomery had Rommel on the run after the British and Scottish First and Tenth Brigades joined with the New Zealand forces. From the little information released to the public, it looked as if the Italians were ready to quit fighting. She had not heard from Andy since his last letter nearly six weeks ago, which said it would be a while before he could write again. She hoped the mail might hold something today as she walked to the post office to send letters to him and Wesley.

Opening the door, she saw Jane holding Jimmy, waiting in line with several envelopes in her hand. "I had to catch up on our correspondence," Jane said when Sally approached.

"I just have one for Wes and Andy," Sally said, holding up the two envelopes she carried.

"Peter wrote a note to John, and I added the latest about Jimmy, then decided I might as well write to Peter's parents and Jim's dad. We finally were able to send a picture of Jimmy to everyone."

"I'm hoping Wes or Andy have sent a letter," Sally said. "I never know when something might come. After listening to the news about the desert fighting and about convoy losses, I wonder if they even get my letters."

"Oh, Sally, I'm sure they do. I think letters to the troops go by air so that the men can hear from home as much as possible. It must keep up their morale to know someone at home is thinking about them."

"I'm sure you're right, Jane. I just get discouraged sometimes when there's a dry spell between letters."

"I bet you'll get one from both of them real soon," Jane encouraged.

"Miss Vilmont," the postmistress called, "I have a letter for you. Looks like it came from England."

Sally took the letter and recognized her mother's handwriting. Smiling, she opened the envelope and began to read about the current news from home. Her mother said they had a note from Wesley that said he and his unit had arrived safely at their destination, and he would be writing to her soon.

> ...and your young man, Andy Burns, came to visit a few weeks ago. He said you were doing well and that his mother enjoyed having you with her. I must write and thank her for looking after you, with the world the way it is now. Not much news here. At least we don't have to wait in long lines for a bag of sugar, the way they do in the big towns. The farm keeps going, and the harvest was good...

The letter continued with news about neighbors and young people she had grown up with. Some of it was sad—about young men being wounded or killed in the neighborhood. Sally smiled when she put the letter back in the envelope.

"Everything okay with your parents?" Jane asked.

"They're fine. Mom said that Andy had stopped there a few weeks back. It must have been nearly three months ago by now though," Sally said, looking at the postmark on the envelope.

"I better get Jimmy home for his nap, it looks like," Jane said when her young son began to fuss.

"Let me see him for a minute," Sally said, reaching to take her godson. "He's getting to be a big boy. I hope his generation doesn't have to see any wars." She handed him back to Jane after snuggling the innocent child close to her heart.

"So do I, Sally, so do I."

Sally walked along the short roadway back to the hospital to check in with the matron before meeting Helen to help carry home what supplies they were able to purchase. *It seemed, before the war, there was never enough money to buy all the things we thought we wanted,* Sally mused. *Now, we find we didn't need them after all and have money to spare.*

*   *   *

Mariah's anchor lay in the captured harbor at Oran. Andy remembered the last time the British visited a French-held harbor in 1940. He still could not understand why the French didn't try to sail to England or a neutral port when it was apparent France was going to fall into German hands. The need to destroy their navy so it wouldn't fall under German control and have so many French sailors die still brought a sense of despair when he thought about the attack and the men who had to carry out the orders. "Come," he said when there was a knock on his cabin door.

"Sir, we've resupplied and are ready for sea," Mason reported.

"Very well. I'll be up in a few minutes. Has Admiral Edwards been informed?"

"Yes, sir. I sent Sublieutenant Anderson to let him know."

"We sail with the Americans as far as Algiers and then join the convoy heading to Alexandria. We'll have air cover from the aircraft carrier still in the area and again when we get near Malta," Andy indicated. "Admiral Edwards told me he didn't know what the admiralty might have in mind after that. Maybe back to the north-south run."

"Wherever it is, the *Mariah* will get us there," Mason said. "The men are fired up after this last mission. I still can't believe that American general. Do you think the Americans would really have sunk the entire French fleet?"

"I got the impression he was serious when we got the signal from our American destroyer friend that he might have to leave us for a while. I think the Americans were in no mood for anyone to stand in their way. I heard that General Eisenhower arrived with his team to take over the whole Allied Army here and means to get his tanks moving into Tunisia before long."

"Well, I'll have to say, once they make up their minds to do something, they sure go all out," Mason observed. "I've never seen so many supply ships in one place in my entire life. And the men pouring out of the troop transporters boggle the mind."

"Let's hope it will distract our German friends while our little convoy continues on to Egypt," Andy said, picking up his hat with the additional captain markings.

Mariah left the sheltered harbor and soon entered the Mediterranean, where she would rendezvous with the convoy. An hour had passed when the first signs of ships could be seen in the distance.

"Send the challenge, Mr. Barnes," Andy ordered. "Number One, bring the men to battle stations until we're sure."

"Sir," Mason answered and went to the loudspeaker. "All men to battle stations. I repeat, all men to their battle stations."

The scurry of feet running to their stations and the sound of guns being loaded and made ready to fire were heard throughout the ship as men swallowed their fear and reported they were closed up. Fingers nervously moved toward triggers and held firing strings in sweaty palms as anticipation built about the enemy waiting, but the order to fire didn't come.

"All stations report closed up, sir," Mason reported.

"We should know in a moment or two," Andy said, more to himself than the bridge at large.

A light began to flash a short reply to the challenge and then went dark. Roger Barnes gave a quick answer and turned to his captain. "Sir, the answer is correct."

Nodding at the information, Andy ordered the men to remain at battle stations until they took their position alongside the rear escort. He swept the sea with his binoculars, aft of their position, to be sure nothing was following the merchant ships and troop transporters now under his charge.

Three days passed without even a hint of the enemy showing any interest in the convoy that was steadily steaming toward Alexandria. Tonight they would pass Tunis and enter the corridor between the boot of Italy, Sicily, and the small rebellious island of Malta. With any luck, the Germans would be preoccupied with the advancing British forces pushing Rommel back along the coastal highway into Libya while the planes of Malta denied enemy ground forces essential supplies.

"Double the lookouts," Andy ordered at dusk.

"Do you think we'll see surface action tonight?" Mason asked as he swept the sea with his binoculars.

"We're close to Sicily and could run across a German convoy trying for Tunis with their own escorts."

"That could prove interesting." Mason grinned. "It would be a dilemma for both sides, whether to attack the warships or go for the merchant ships carrying the supplies. I would guess...," he started saying when something caught his attention.

"What is it?" Andy asked.

Pointing, Mason was starting to reply when a lookout hollered, "Submarine off the port quarter!"

"Battle stations, all men to their battle stations," echoed throughout the ship when Andy instantly ordered the alert to be sounded.

"Here we go," John Hartman told Emil Harris. "Let's get the operating room set up and make sure recovery has enough warm blankets."

Emil nodded and began to prepare the necessary equipment to repair the damage that shots fired in anger did to the human body. "We'll be ready, sir," Harris assured him.

Giving a brief smile, John said, "Yeah, we always seem to be, even when we don't have any notice. Dr. Patterson trained you well."

Emil stayed with the *Mariah* when Quentin Patterson left for shore duty. He missed the older man but decided Lieutenant Hartman was a proficient enough doctor—not as good as Patterson, but then, few were. Hartman did say he was going to recommend that Emil attend the navy's equivalent of nursing school and wrote to Dr. Patterson and even Rear Admiral Jamison to assist in the process. Emil looked back on the day fate had placed him with Dr. Patterson and thanked God for it regularly.

"There, we've got everything out and ready. Hopin' we won't be needin' any of it."

"Yes, let's hope not," John said with a faraway look in his eyes.

Preparations took two and a half minutes as stations reported "closed up," and men squinted into the darkness for a hint of what danger might lie in the sea. Minutes had passed with no order to fire when a small light blinked near the ocean surface. Men wiped their sweaty palms across their trousers and returned them to their guns, waiting for Captain Burns to give the open-fire order.

"Sir," Roger Barnes said, "it's an American submarine. Their captain says they spotted the convoy and started an approach when they realized it was British and American ships. He says they're heading east. Do we want them to run interference?"

"What is the lead escort answering, Bunts?"

"He's telling them to stay on the surface until morning. Sir, lead is saying he wants to get a good look at them at dawn."

"Wants to be sure it isn't a trick. Mr. Anderson, have two lookouts watching all night. Tell them not to lose sight of them," Andy ordered. "Tell the rest of the lookouts to watch for anything unusual. If it is a trick, you can bet there's at least one more, nearby, at periscope depth."

Two more hours passed, and the surfaced submarine continued alongside the convoy, running her diesel engines and charging her batteries. Andy sat on his bridge chair, unwilling to be even a few steps away should trouble start unexpectedly.

"Periscope—two thousand yards, starboard side," a lookout hollered, shattering the night air.

Andy raised his glasses and saw the tip of the scope disappear beneath the surface. "Signal the group. Send a shot across the other one's bow. Turn twenty degrees port. Come alongside that sub before he can dive," he ordered in quick succession.

Mariah glided through the ocean with her bow lined up with the center of the surfaced submarine. Andy remembered his first encounter as an unblooded first officer with a submarine in 1940 and didn't intend to see this one bring destruction to those under his charge.

"Signal the sub to have their captain ready to parley, Bunts. If we don't get an answer, Number One, be ready to put a shot right into the bridge."

Roger Barnes raised the signal lamp and sent the quick message his captain had given him. His knees were shaking inside his trouser legs as the tenseness on the bridge increased while waiting for a reply.

Within a minute, the signal lamp from the surfaced submarine indicated their sonar had picked up the approaching sub. It sounded like an Italian boat by the engine noise. "We can take it," the final signal indicated.

Mariah continued on her course to intercept the submarine in question and was minutes away when Andy heard the unmistakable sound of their signal to clear the deck and dive. He raised his binoculars in time to see the German uniforms as enemy sailors scrambled to get below and close the hatch so that the boat could disappear beneath the waves.

"Fire!" Andy ordered as the U-boat hatch was being closed and the submarine began to dive.

Mason ordered his men to fire the aft guns together, sending lethal explosives that straddled the sides of the surfaced boat and shattered the night's calm. A second salvo was sent, blowing a hole in one of the air tanks and causing the submarine to list along the surface. Hatches were opened, and men scrambled to the deck, pulling rubber rafts out of cargo holds. Soon the enemy submariner was drifting in the sea, at the mercy of another warship coming alongside.

"Signal the lead escort: second submarine in the water, last seen two thousand yards out, and give the coordinates," Andy ordered.

"Sir, lead escort wants us to coordinate depth-charging with the American destroyer," Roger reported.

"Mr. Anderson, get with Mr. Parker and set up depth-charging. We'll do a cross grid," Andy ordered.

The two destroyers pounded the sea while the convoy continued toward its destination. The sun was well above the ocean's surface when the two ships turned back to their original course and increased speed.

As they approached Malta the following day, the welcome sight of fighter planes overhead gave the men a sense of relief that added eyes were watching the sea and sky. Another two days and they would be in Alexandria, where they would have a short respite before being sent out to risk another journey into enemy territory.

25

Martin Jamison adjusted the tuning dial on Helen's radio on Sunday evening in late November and waited for the tubes to warm up before turning up the volume. The fellow refugees of Helen's Landing and Java sat around the small living room and fixed their attention on the illuminated dial, waiting to hear the weekly nine-o'clock news review.

"This is the BBC Perth, Australia, station reporting. Allied headquarters has confirmed that General Rommel, the Axis Desert Fox, is on the run. We have learned that Prime Minister Churchill ordered church bells to peal after the El-Alamein victory from one end of Britain to the other, stating, "Victory marks the turning of the hinge of fate." British commandos and American rangers have successfully crossed into Tunisia to begin squeezing the Axis exploiters out of North Africa and freeing citizens from the Nazi boot of oppression.

"In other news of the week, the United States has landed marines and army troops in the British Gilbert Islands of Tarawa and Makin in the Pacific Theater of Operations, where intense fighting continues against harsh Japanese forces. On mainland Europe, our Russian allies have turned the ferocious struggle at

Stalingrad against Hitler as the Red Army encircles the invaders and cuts off any chance of retreat. This is the BBC, good night."

Dr. Jamison reached over and turned off the radio as a live commercial promoting war bonds began. "I sure hope Montgomery can hold at El Alamein and start the push toward the Americans."

"We haven't heard anything about the Italians—if they're fighting as hard as the Germans. I wonder if there was any significant number of prisoners taken," Peter said.

"I don't know about prisoners, but the note from Arthur indicated that things went okay for their unit. At least, as much as he could tell me," Katrin said. "Dad, did you hear anything when you visited Major Palmer?"

"Not really, my dear. I was simply asking if there might be a way to bring the Gospel to the men fighting these terrible battles. So many men are fighting their own internal battle against the prince of darkness that's troubling their souls. I thought there might be something I could do."

"What did he tell you, Father Albright?" Sally said.

"He just said he would get back with me about it. He seemed distracted when I went to see him. I suppose this latest battle had something to do with his vagueness."

"Yes, I suppose," Katrin surmised. "Well, Dad, I think it's time we retired for the night."

"Same here," Jane said. "We need to get Jimmy into his bed."

The friends gathered the dishes they had brought for their Sunday meal and bid Helen and Sally good-night. After the door closed, Sally thought about Wesley and what part his unit might have played in the second battle of El Alamein. Wesley had hinted he did not believe their role would be that of traditional engineers. Unlike the defensive systems the unit had built in Malaya, this time, it would be destruction. He told her he was melancholy about destroying instead of building: the dream he had always held. "Don't be discouraged," she had said. "Someday, when this is over, you'll have to build a lot of things." Wesley had just smiled and touched her cheek before hugging her good-bye when his unit prepared to leave Australia.

*   *   *

Wesley stopped the Land Rover beneath a sand dune and sent Moore and Private Haines to scout the desert from the top of the dune before moving his unit closer to friendly territory. He watched when Moore and Haines half ran and half slid down the dune within fifteen minutes of reaching a vantage point and scrutinizing the surrounding area.

"Sir," Moore said, short of breath. "There's a small concrete building with soldiers milling around the doorway. It looks like they're piling up storage boxes about one hundred yards from the building."

"It will be dark shortly," Wesley said. "Arthur, take Jenkins and the rest of your group and get to the top of the dune that's about five hundred yards farther down. Sergeant Moore, the rest of us will climb back to the same area you just came from. We'll attack on my signal."

"Jenkins, gather the men and let's move out," Arthur ordered when he returned to the men he had led the previous night. "We attack in fifteen minutes."

Wesley lay prone at the top of the dune and watched the activity below. The small group of men appeared to be hurrying to empty the bunker-like building, loading boxes into a covered truck. He slid a few feet below the peak of the dune and told the men to be ready in five minutes. Taking a small flashlight, he sent a brief signal to Arthur.

"Corporal Jenkins, bring the grenade launcher and set it up here." Arthur pointed. "Anderson, Pool, be ready with the machine gun."

Arthur waited until the first shot was fired five hundred yards away and watched the enemy soldiers scurrying behind their truck. Some others near the doorway to the bunker dove for cover. Arthur counted to ten then ordered the grenade launcher to be fired on the truck. Within a few seconds, the cover of the vehicle burst into flames as a second strike exploded near the back of the truck, blowing the rear axle apart.

The stunned soldiers began to fire wildly at an enemy they could not see. Another grenade exploded, leaving screaming men in its wake, as machine-gun fire raked across the small compound. Wesley watched the mayhem and ordered gunfire to be directed at the entrance to the bunker, signaling Arthur and his men to crest the dune and capture the intact pile of boxes sitting on the ground.

Breathing hard, Arthur slid to his knee and brought his gun up, pointing toward the bunker doorway as the men surrounded the captured pile of boxes. He didn't know what might be in them, but he thought it was something the enemy didn't want the Allies to know about.

Wesley and his group came running to the side of the bunker to approach the doorway and capture the remaining enemy soldiers who were held up inside. Half his men circled to the opposite side and, at his nod, rolled through the open door, bringing their rifles up inside the small windowless room, where a single lightbulb illuminated the interior. The seven men they saw raised their hands in submission and waited for their captors' next move.

"Haines, Anderson, tie their hands and sit them outside," Wesley ordered. "Sergeant Moore, shut down those radios."

"Yes, sir." Moore grinned and ordered two of the men to cut off the switches and disconnect the wires.

"Sir," Arthur said, "these are codes and what looks like operation orders from the German high command. There are also several battle plans in another box. I haven't had a chance to look through the rest of it yet."

"Okay. Have our transportation brought in, and we'll radio Colonel Gherst about our findings. My guess is, he'll send someone to take all of this back to headquarters, along with our prisoners," Wesley answered.

The sun was rising over the desert when several trucks and tracked vehicles arrived to take over the find that Wesley's small unit had captured. He was told several Italian units surrendered during the second battle of El Alamein, with one enemy general barely escaping a burning tank and simply waited until the British arrived to take him prisoner.

"Where is the frontline now?" Wesley asked.

"Just east of El Alamein," the intelligence captain informed him. "Colonel Gherst wants your unit to return to headquarters. He said to tell you good job."

"Thank you," Wesley replied. "We'll get underway in a half hour. I'd like the men to have a chance to grab a meal before we leave."

Four hours later, Wesley reported to Colonel Gherst.

"A fine job, Major," Gherst said when Wesley saluted his superior, standing at attention. "Stand at ease," Gherst continued. "I've set aside a barracks for the unit. I think a few days' rest is in order."

"Thank you, sir. I'm sure the men will appreciate a chance to pour the desert out of their boots."

Laughing at the comment, Colonel Gherst continued, "Your unit helped a great deal with the El Alamein battle. Cutting off resupply from behind the lines caused the Germans to make a rapid retreat. It also gives us time to tighten up our lines and organize for the next offensive. We've heard from the Americans, and they are wasting no time in pushing east. Once Tunisia is secured, we'll be ready to liberate Libya and have a secure coastline to launch aerial bombings on Europe's underbelly."

"Yes, sir," Wesley said.

"I'll have orders for you in a week or two. Until then, you are at liberty to go into the city for a few days, *Major*," Gherst said, emphasizing the word *major*.

"Sir?" Wesley questioned.

"You must still be in the desert, *Major*," Gherst commented, again with emphasis.

"I've been promoted, sir?"

"Yes, indeed—at General Montgomery's command. The bunker your unit captured is a significant find. He also promoted your second to captain, effective immediately. I have both sets of bars here," Gherst said, handing Wesley two small boxes and shaking his hand. "The bars were a gift from the general, for a job well done."

"Thank you, sir," Wesley answered with a tired smile. "Arthur and I will have to send a note of thanks to him."

"I'm sure he'll appreciate it. That's all for now. You're dismissed."

Coming to attention, Wesley saluted his commanding officer before closing the office door behind him.

*   *   *

Sally opened the envelope and savored the three short pages that Andy had written. The long dry spell between letters evaporated as she read his words of hope about the coming year. "I am encouraged," he had written about the Americans landing in Eastern Africa and the defeat of the Germans in the desert. He wrote that he missed her smile and longed to be with her. She folded the letter, after reading it a second time, and put it with the others, which were tied together with a white ribbon. The following day, she was surprised to receive a letter from Wesley:

> ...I'll give your love to Mom and Dad. All is well here. I look forward to a time when we can travel in peace and, once again, see more of each other. I still think about our little jaunt around the bay at Helen's Landing in '41 and

laugh at myself at having been talked into rowing. Take care of yourself, Sis. I'll write again soon.

Love,
Wes

Sally set the short note aside and wondered why her brother was heading to England. She also wondered if Katrin had heard from Arthur and if he was going as well. She shook her head and decided she would learn soon enough about Wesley and his unit. Her mind drifted to the *Mariah* and where it might be today. Andy's letter didn't say if he would be able to write again soon. *So many mysteries*, she thought. Turning on the small radio in the nurse's station, she waited for the afternoon news to begin.

"This is the BBC Perth, Australia, station reporting. According to government releases, General Rommel is still in retreat as the Axis forces limp to the west under constant aerial attack. We are told the pressure will continue until German and Italian forces are cleared from North Africa. In other news, we have learned that American forces have secured the Tarawa and Makin atolls after severe resistance by the Japanese Army.

"In local news, this reporter has learned that a ring of counterfeiters was arrested, bringing an end to the black market sale of ration coupons. In a brief statement, Australian intelligence commented that the use of counterfeit coupons harms everyone with essential goods in short supply. This is the BBC Perth, Australia, station. Good afternoon."

Sally shut off the radio and wondered how anyone could counterfeit ration coupons. No wonder it was so hard to buy things like sugar and tea since people were cheating. Looking at the wall clock in the small nurses' station, she thought she had better get back to the ward to check her patients' temperatures and blood pressures before turning over to the afternoon shift.

26

"Sir, orders from headquarters," the messenger said, handing Andy the coded sheet of flash paper.

"Ask Mr. Roden to join me," Andy ordered, taking the short message sheet and heading for his sea cabin.

"Yes, sir," the rating replied with a salute.

"Reporting, as ordered." Mason saluted upon entering the sea cabin.

"At ease. Sit down," Andy indicated as he shut the door. "We have orders to leave tonight. We'll be sailing with a convoy that's taking the wounded back to England. Even with the hospital ship cross, our Axis friends may try to sink them. We sail with the *Victoria* and one other sloop as escorts. We also have a couple of passengers joining us."

"Passengers?" Mason questioned with a crinkled brow.

"Yes, Major Vilmont and Captain Nance. It seems they were promoted recently."

"Well, at least we know our passengers." Mason grinned. "Perhaps they can fill us in on what is really happening in the desert. Will Admiral Edwards be with us also, sir?"

"Not according to the orders. I am to report to him at 1800 hours. In the meantime, check with Hartman and be sure we're fully supplied. Also, have Jones make sure we have the most current charts and maps of where our allies are located and what the latest intelligence is on the German Navy's whereabouts. We don't want to stumble into the enemy, nor do we want to attack our ally by mistake. We'll make a brief stop along the way to evacuate the latest desert casualties from Egypt at Mersa Matruh."

"I see," Mason answered, deep in thought. "I'll alert Brian and Mr. Parker. It should be a bit like when we evacuated casualties out of France in '40 and Singapore last February. Perhaps, the air cover will be better this time."

"One can always hope. I should know more after seeing Admiral Edwards. Until then, carry on," Andy said.

Andy entered the naval headquarters building and reported to Admiral Edwards's office at 1800 hours as ordered. Lieutenant Gaines stood and saluted before asking how the *Mariah* was faring since he was last aboard her.

"She's doing well," Andy told him.

"That's splendid, sir. I'll let the admiral know you're here."

"Thank you, Lieutenant," Andy said, taking a seat in the waiting area.

Admiral Edwards stood in his office doorway and waved Andy in a short time later. "Gaines here will have additional orders for you before you leave headquarters," he indicated as the lieutenant left the office and closed the door behind him.

"In a nutshell, the *Mariah* will be carrying a few more passengers to England. They will board at 2200 hours. Have them ushered below and placed wherever convenient until you are at sea. I'm sorry I can't say more right now. They will explain once the *Mariah* leaves her last port."

"I understand, sir. I believe the crew will miss having you with us on this voyage."

Smiling a little, Eric Edwards replied, "I'll miss being aboard, Captain. I also wanted to tell you I've been in communication with Martin Jamison. We've had some concerns over a troublesome malaria outbreak and complications among the wounded, with all the heavy fighting in the marshes. You know, I never thought about swamps being around the North African coast. Most people just think of arid desert around here."

"How is Dr. Jamison?"

"He's very busy, but we might have to move him here before much longer."

"If the *Mariah* is sent back, it will be good to see him again. In the meantime, she and her crew are ready for sea."

"Good luck, Captain Burns," Admiral Edwards said, answering Andy's salute and then shaking his hand in dismissal.

Andy returned to his stateroom and gathered a few items before entering the bridge in preparation to sail. The sealed orders that Gaines had handed him were in the safe in his sea cabin, along with the orders to sail to England. He greeted Wesley and Arthur when they boarded the ship at 2000 hours and congratulated them both on their promotions.

"I fear it will bring more difficult assignments," Wesley responded with a smile while shaking Andy's hand. "Arthur and I seem to have met some unusual characters in our travels the past few months."

"Yes, I would agree," Arthur said. "But we've also made a couple of friends along the way."

"It always helps to have a friend or two in life," Andy noted. "Mr. Barnes, please show our guests to their quarters."

"Sir," Barnes saluted before asking Wesley and Arthur to follow him. "We have a double cabin that should work out just fine for you," he indicated as they entered a passageway near the mess room.

The *Mariah* left Alexandria without fuss and soon took the lead position in a convoy of four hospital ships. Their other passengers were made comfortable in the wardroom, where an army colonel handed Mason their orders and asked that they not be disturbed. "Unless, of course, the ship might be taking on water," he remarked with a grin.

"Permission to enter the bridge," an unknown voice said a few hours after the *Mariah* entered the Mediterranean.

"Permission granted," Mason answered, turning to see the same colonel walking toward him.

"I thought I'd get a breath of fresh air before daylight. This must be a bit unusual for your crew."

"A bit," Mason agreed. "But we've had unusual orders a few times prior to this. If you need anything, just ask any of the crew."

"Thank you, we'll try not to get in the way. I understand your other two passengers made it aboard as well."

Sliding a sideways glance at his visitor, Mason simply nodded without comment. He thought if Wesley and Arthur wanted these men to know they were on the *Mariah*, they would let his inquisitor know.

"It's all right, Commander. We have orders for them once we leave the area. I'm sure we'll see them in the morning."

"Perhaps," Mason agreed. "As I said, if you need anything, please feel free to ask."

Nodding, Colonel Gherst bid Mason good-night and left the bridge. He was pleased the first officer didn't volunteer any information about Major Vilmont or Captain Nance. He also hoped the voyage would be without incident. Things were going well in North Africa, it seemed; and before long, it would be time to tackle Europe. He thought 1943 would prove to be an interesting year for both sides.

*   *   *

Martin Jamison turned off the small radio in his office and turned again to the letter from his friend Eric Edwards. The malaria outbreak and problems with tropical disease in North Africa was becoming a hindrance to the British, especially since the rainy season had begun and equipment was bogged down, slowing the British advance. "We need expert help," Edwards's letter indicated.

The latest news reports stated that the British had opened a campaign at El Agheila against Rommel's forces, and a forty-mile line of defense was broken, forcing Rommel to retreat. The Desert Fox was cut off from a rear guard by a British column that sped across the desert from Agheila. By December 19, Rommel was still in retreat; and in the East, British forces had successfully advanced forty miles into Burma, ousting the Japanese Army along the way.

Dr. Jamison set his friend's letter aside and rocked back in his chair. He would have to go to Egypt to see for himself what medical problems they were facing. He would need Peter and Quentin for certain and wondered about taking Sally and asking if Jane would also be able to come. The problem was, what to do about Jimmy? He knew Jane wouldn't leave him, and the only possible way for him to move to Egypt would be for Helen to accompany them. He wanted Jane and Sally because of their specialized training in tropical disorders. He was planning to see Helen tonight to discuss the Christmas party plans for the recovering soldiers and sailors at the army-navy recuperation home. He decided to ask what she thought of Eric's request and his idea to move on to Egypt. A move from Australia would also mean getting replacements for everyone at the hospital.

* * *

"A wonderful meal, even with the shortages," Dr. Jamison said to his friend.

"And you always savor a home-cooked meal, Martin," Helen replied. "Shall we listen to the latest news?"

"I'll get the wireless warmed up," Dr. Jamison said.

"This is the BBC Perth, Australia, station reporting," the newscast began. "According to latest reports, the Desert Fox is still in retreat as our forces strengthen their presence in recaptured ground. On other fronts, England has experienced a lull in the Blitz as the RAF continues their nighttime raids on German-held territory in Europe.

"In local news, the ration-stamp–counterfeiting ringleader, who was recently captured, has faced Australia's justice with a twenty-year sentence at hard labor. The defendants' attorney has agreed to a plea that would allow the remaining defendants to be inducted into the army and sent to the frontlines for the duration of the war. Should their wartime service not be acceptable, they will face an additional ten years behind bars. Good evening from the BBC Perth, Australia, station."

"It appears the British are making headway," Dr. Jamison stated with a faraway look in his eyes.

"Yes, so it seems. Martin, do you have something on your mind?"

"You know me too well, Helen. I received a letter from my friend Eric Edwards today about some of the problems they're facing in North Africa. It's the rainy season, and a great number of our troops are bogged down in the marshes off the coast. Eric said a malaria outbreak has occurred, along with other problems the wounded face because of the tropical conditions. He wants me to go there with a team to help."

"I see. That would mean taking Quentin and Peter along—for an indefinite period of time."

"I would like to have my old team from Helen's Landing too, including Sally and Jane. The problem is, what to do about Jimmy? I know Jane won't leave him here, and I agree—he needs his mother. As his godmother, would you consider making the move as well? Everything would have to be cleared with Eric or his superiors, but it would have to be soon to be of any help to them."

"Let me sleep on it, Martin. A lot will depend on whether Jane and Sally are willing to make the trip. We wouldn't be very far from the fighting, even if we're in Alexandria. Remember, the battlefronts changed pretty quickly the past two years."

"Yes, I know, but I think this time is different, with the Americans closing from the West. As for next week, is everything in place for the Christmas celebration?"

"Martin, of course, our auxiliary ladies are very excited about Father Albright coming to give a Christmas Eve service right at the recuperation center and visiting the hospital staff. Joseph said he and Katrin are looking forward to being part of the celebration and the gift exchange with all the patients. As to your other question, I'll let you know in the morning."

A short while later, Helen closed the door behind her friend and went to the small kitchen to clear up. She was deep in thought when Sally came through the doorway after her hospital shift to find her slowly wiping a plate dry.

"You look far away," Sally commented.

"Oh, just something Martin said tonight. Well, I'm off to bed. Good night, my dear."

"Good night," Sally replied as she watched her mentor and friend head for her bedroom. *Wonder what got into her all of a sudden*, she thought.

Helen sat in the small rocking chair near the corner window in her bedroom late into the night in thought. She knew Martin wouldn't ask her to leave Australia unless he thought Eric Edwards's request was more important than he had let on. She opened her Bible and read the soothing verses from Christ and came across Psalm 37:10 when she turned to the Old Testament. "In a little while the wicked will be no more. You may look for them, but they will be gone." "Guide me, Lord," she prayed. "I put all of us into your hands." Smiling, she pulled the sheet over her shoulder and soon fell into a peaceful sleep. The decision was made; there was no need to ponder it any further.

27

The *Mariah* quietly docked at Mersa Matruh with the crew at their battle stations while ambulances delivered wounded men to the waiting hospital ships for the long journey back to England. The five-week voyage would see some depart this life before reaching their homeland while others would show the small signs of recovery anxiously awaited by their caretakers. Andy knew the dangers the convoy would encounter and would use the tools he was given to allow these men—who had fallen in the fight for freedom—a chance to return to their families.

"It's a little like the last time we sailed from Singapore," Brian Jones said as he watched the parade of ambulances shuffling back and forth from the field hospital.

"Yes, I guess it is somewhat," Andy agreed. "We sail at dusk. Mr. Jones, you have the bridge."

"Sir, I have the bridge," Brian replied.

The *Mariah* slipped her moorings and pointed her bow west for the tenuous journey to thread the mercy convoy between Malta and Tunis and sail beyond Palermo, where the Mediterranean narrowed and U-boats waited near Cagliari in the Tyrrhenian Sea. Once through the tight squeeze at Gibraltar, where the Mediterranean spilled into the Atlantic, there would be room to maneuver more freely. Even with the number of Allied ships and planes in the area, the Axis war machine was still a force to be reckoned with, and Andy felt a need to be on the spot should the enemy come hunting his prey.

Several days passed without incident as the *Mariah* led her charges through waters bordered by German-held territory. Rain fell, which prevented aerial attacks, but also prevented friendly air cover out of Malta. The choppy seas made watchkeeping more difficult—a periscope could go unnoticed between the unsettled seas. Andy felt the tensions mounting as the days passed, waiting for the enemy to make his move. Soon they would approach the narrows at Gibraltar and be committed to the precarious passage into the Atlantic. He wondered if the ships in the small convoy would still be intact for the approaching Christmas the crew anticipated.

"Double the watch," Andy ordered at dusk as the *Mariah* made the first course change near Gibraltar.

"Aye, sir," the sublieutenant on bridge duty replied.

"Send a signal to the group to be extra alert while we make the course change."

"Captain Burns is antsy," the captain of the closest hospital ship commented when the signal was deciphered. "I don't believe any German ships will be attacking us. We are a hospital ship after all."

"Sir, look," a bridge lookout said, pointing, when a flare went up near the convoy and the sound of approaching engines filled the air.

Andy pressed the alarm before boat engines were heard in the distance, bringing *Mariah*'s crew to battle stations. Men prepared their guns by rote, following the steps drilled into them through countless practices and the lessons of battle. Some crossed themselves as they made the guns ready, praying they would survive to see another sunrise. Some wept in their soul, knowing that men would die this night in the violence.

"Dirty buggers, comin' after 'ospital ships," Bert said to the new gunner at his side. "Ernie would be thinkin' the same. Glad 'e's out of it though," he concluded, shaking his head.

"Watch your front. Wait for the signal to fire," Parker hollered to the gunners under his command.

"All men at their stations. Ship ready for battle," Mason reported within minutes of the alarm sounding.

"Very well. Send a messenger to our passengers to stay out of the line of fire. We'll wait until they're closer to open fire. Mr. Anderson, do you see anything?"

"Sir, low in the water. Looks like a small craft approaching. I count three—no, wait—four heading toward the second hospital ship."

"Smart, putting another ship between us and their target. Helmsman, bring her around to two-one-zero, increase to twenty-three knots. We'll swing out and fire once we clear the first ship."

Minutes passed in slow motion as the *Mariah* made the sharp turn and brought her guns to bear on the approaching menace to her charges. Lookouts called out overlapping targets as *Mariah* cleared the first ship and bore down on the enemy craft attacking the unarmed hospital ship under her care.

"Commence firing," blared across the decks, sending tracer rounds flashing through the air until they zeroed in on the first attacking boat. A four-inch shell exploded on the deck of one craft, obliterating it in minutes. A third craft took hits from the *Victoria* and turned away when smoke began to belch from the engine compartment. The fourth boat sped around the starboard side of the ship being attacked, only to take a shell from the protective sloop before speeding after its companions.

Watching the short action through his binoculars, Andy saw the last craft limping away with what appeared to be damage near its bridge. He ordered a signal sent to the ship under attack to see if there were casualties or damage.

"Sir," Roger Barnes said a few minutes later. "Their captain reports his navigator was killed. No other casualties and no damage reported."

Sighing, Andy nodded. "Tell the captain I'm sorry. Then signal the group that we enter the Atlantic in forty-five minutes."

"Yes, sir."

The convoy sailed well out into the Atlantic before turning north on to the second leg of the journey. It was December 23, and soon the *Mariah* would celebrate the birth of Christ while men made war across the globe.

* * *

Helen watched the last decorations being put into place, remembering when Andy was young, and Ralph would put the Christmas train around the potted palm tree they used each year since arriving in Malaya. The tree was planted each New Year's Day until the Traveler's Palms lined the property that overlooked the sea, where she and Ralph had carved out a life. This year, no palm tree would be planted in Malaya, and no celebration of Christ's birth would be experienced by those who were caught up in the swift tide of battles throughout the region. This year, the fortunate few who made it out of Malaya and Java would celebrate by service to others.

"Helen, the decorations are wonderful," Jane said when she entered the recuperation center. The seaside resort, being used as a temporary army-navy recuperation center, was festive with donated decorations strung along the lobby entryway and a variety of glistening Christmas balls and tinsel, brightening the various common rooms. Some of the recovering soldiers and navy ratings had even taped colorful handmade paper wreaths to bedroom doorways.

"The auxiliary ladies went all out. We even have traditional English crackers for the men. But where is my godson?"

"Peter will be along with him in a little while. I wanted to get here early to help with any last-minute details. We're very excited about Jimmy's first Christmas. We found a box in the attic with decorations and set them out. He seems quite fascinated with the Nativity set when the sun reflects off the star above the stable."

"Here's Sally." Helen smiled. "Well, I believe everything is in place. Joseph and Katrin should be along shortly."

Martin Jamison and Quentin Patterson joined the women, along with Peter and little Jimmy, in the large room set up for the early Christmas Eve service. Katrin slipped into a seat beside Jane just as her father stepped up to the podium to begin the mass. Katrin's thoughts drifted to Christmases before her mother died and the beautifully prepared church at Surabaya. She watched her father read the Eucharistic prayers to bless the bread and wine in preparation for those present to receive the body and blood of Jesus and wondered if the civilians who didn't escape Java were hearing the Christmas message tonight. She still shuddered when she remembered the screams heard from the church above their hiding place and the fear that penetrated her soul.

Father Albright patiently administered communion to men needing help to sip the chalice and aided others still trying to adjust to a limb missing or an arm in plaster. Katrin knelt at the makeshift communion rail and crossed herself before holding her hands up to receive the body of Christ. After taking the sip of the blessed wine that followed, she returned to her seat and prayed that Arthur was safe this Christmas Eve and able to receive the good news of Christmas—wherever he may be.

The service ended with everyone singing "Silent Night" before men who were ambulatory began shuffling back to their rooms and the small treats that awaited them. Nurses and volunteers wheeled the less fortunate to the beds reserved for those who had lost limbs to land mines or to infections that were out of control by the time help arrived. Some of the men would find ways to prematurely end their life rather than continue as less than whole while others would reach deep inside themselves to find new avenues to pursue and live life to the fullest.

"A wonderful service, Father Albright," Jane said when the men and hospital personnel had departed. "Just two short years ago, we celebrated Christmas with no war around us and enjoyed plentiful traditional dishes, with little thought about the rest of the world. Now, we celebrate this holy season with a world gone mad. I remember last year, wondering if a bomb would fall on the church while we prayed for peace. Your message reminded us that Christ is the Prince of Peace, and we have hope in Him that soon this will end."

"Yes, Jane, that is true. His grace is all around us. We only need to accept it. It looks, though, like young Jimmy is ready for slumber," Father Albright said when he noticed the inquisitive eyes of an hour ago becoming heavy.

"He'll soon be in his bed and sleeping soundly." Jane smiled. "I'm looking forward to being at Helen's tomorrow with everyone. It will be a little like the Christmas of 1940—before war upset our world. I hope Jimmy never sees the seamier side of man's character."

"When men accept the lessons given in the Bible and set a pattern to live accordingly, the world—as we know it—will change and become a more peaceful place."

"Jane, we best be getting home," Peter called from the doorway. "I've settled my patients in for the night. The men were pleased with their treats. I believe several will have notes from home tomorrow, and there are several parcels to be dispersed. Father, we'll see you at Helen's tomorrow."

Touching Jimmy's head, Father Albright said good-night. "Sleep in peace, little one," he softly said then watched as Jane carried her sleeping child out the door.

28

The sun edged its way above the cold rolling waters in a wondrous display of beauty on Christmas morning. The sea curled aside the transparent liquid-diamond surface as the ships continued north toward the English Channel and on to Harwell, where they would rest before making the trek back to Alexandria with the next supply of men to feed the unceasing war-machine appetite. *Mariah*'s crew watched the sky, hoping clouds would cover them to prevent the Luftwaffe from attacking and from giving their position to the greater threat of a wolf pack that was looking for a chance to sink a British warship.

"Captain on the bridge," the rating said when Andy walked onto the bridge from his sea cabin.

"Good morning, sir. Happy Christmas," Mason greeted with a salute. "There were no sightings during the night. We are currently on course at eleven knots, and all ships are in their correct position."

"Thank you, Number One. Happy Christmas to you as well," Andy replied. Taking his glasses, he swept the sea for any irregularity. "It appears quiet for now. Ask our guests to join us on the bridge for the Christmas service at o-eight-hundred—provided Gerry doesn't interfere."

"Yes, sir," Mason responded. "I believe the men are looking forward to the special meal that cook is planning today. It is certainly different from our last Christmas in Malaya. From the latest news reports, it looks like the Allied armies have the Axis on the run in Libya and may be in Tunisia soon. If things continue in their current mode, the Axis will run out of real estate."

"Yes, and the Americans are—," Andy began when a runner approached with a message.

"Sir, message from headquarters."

"Thank you, that will be all," Andy said, taking the message and quickly decoding it. "The Vichy French Admiral Darlan was assassinated yesterday—by a French patriot. It appears that a General Giraud has taken over. The controversy over the Darlan-Deal in Britain and America, making him commander of all French forces, his self-nomination as high commissioner of France for North and West Africa should come to an end now."

"Well, nothing was done by the French in Tunisia to stop the Germans from sending additional forces into Tunis. Our men will have to fight rested troops to take the port cities and secure the capital. Maybe this Giraud fellow will be a bit more cooperative with the Allies."

"Yes, well, I'm sure our superiors have made the Allied position clear by now," Andy replied.

Andy closed the navy service book an hour later and wished the men a Happy Christmas before inviting the passengers to join him in the officer's mess.

"Gentlemen, we should be arriving at Harwell by New Year's—that is, if our Axis friends don't cause difficulties between now and then."

*   *   *

The convoy arrived at Harwell, after a quiet Atlantic voyage, the second Monday of January to the news that a German panzer division withdrew in Southern Russia to avoid being encircled by attacking Soviet forces. Andy told the admiral in Harwell the increasing cloud cover prevented German planes from sighting the convoy during the last week of the voyage. Admiral Benson—looking toward the window that overlooked the harbor, at the increasing snow and wind whipping across the water and heavy clouds moving in from the west—nodded in understanding.

"You've done well, Captain Burns, since taking over the *Mariah* from Edmon. By the way, he asked after you the last time he was here."

"He's doing well then?" Andy asked. "Maybe I'll get a chance to see him before we sail again."

"Perhaps," Benson replied. "The crew has a week's leave, and I'll have a relief crew covering the ship—say, starting at o-seven-hundred tomorrow."

"Thank you, sir. I believe the men will enjoy the break."

"That will be all for now, Burns. Report in next Monday," Benson said in dismissal.

Andy had Mason follow him into his cabin upon his return. "Have a seat, Number One."

"Thank you, sir."

"Starting tomorrow, the crew is on a week's leave. Admiral Benson will have a relief crew covering the ship. My guess is: we'll be back at sea within a week of returning."

"I'll have the repair list ready and will make sure our supplies are ordered before leaving," Mason said.

"Good. Let Tim Parker know about the leave, but I don't want the crew alerted until morning to keep them alert. They'll have time enough to think about girls and getting drunk."

Grinning, Mason said he would be sure no rumors were started, which would distract the officers or crew in tonight's wardroom rehashing of the war news.

"So Stalin held, and the Germans rolled the dice—once too often—and lost," Brian Jones commented that evening in the wardroom after switching off the wireless set.

"It appears so," John replied.

"Let's hope they can exploit the German defeat and start moving them out of Russia," Mason commented. "Well, gentlemen, I believe I am going to call it a night."

"Sir, is there any news about leave?" Sublieutenant Anderson asked.

"Not at this time," Mason replied. "Perhaps tomorrow we'll know something. After all, we just got in."

"I hope we get a few days. I'd like to visit my village while we're here."

"I'm sure we'll know something by tomorrow. Well, good night all," Mason said, moving toward the wardroom doorway.

*　*　*

"And this just in," the newscaster excitedly stated. "A release from the War Department reports that German panzers have withdrawn in Southern Russia to avoid encirclement. This is a significant blow to the German Army and a personal blow to Hitler. In other news of the week, it appears Australian and United States' forces are fighting back the Japanese at Buna in New Guinea. This is the BBC Perth, Australia, station reporting. Good night."

Helen turned off the radio and turned to her guests. "It appears to be getting better. Maybe Hitler will give up," she hopefully said.

"I wouldn't count on it, Helen," Martin Jamison said. "But at least things seem to be turning around. Now, about my proposal to go to Cairo—has everyone thought it over?"

"Jane and I talked it over, and as long as Jimmy will be safe, Jane will volunteer to go," Peter said. "Would she remain in Cairo?"

"I don't know, but my feeling is probably not. I think, once the Allies invade southern Europe—and I don't see any other way for them to keep the Axis out of North Africa if they don't—we could possibly be moved to England."

"Do you think it would be safe to travel there, Dr. Jamison?" Sally asked.

"In time, I think it will be. But we'll have to wait to see what the future brings."

"That's true, Martin," Quentin commented. "I would say, for now, we should concentrate on the medical issue in North Africa and see what February may bring to our current enemies. Since the Americans came into the war, Japan has seen some defeats. And now Germany has suffered a loss in Russia."

"That's true," Jane said. "When do you want to leave for Egypt, Dr. Jamison?"

"I'll check with headquarters, but I think in the next few days. How soon can everyone be ready?"

"I would say by next Wednesday, Martin," Helen said. "Sally, will that work for the hospital?"

"I think so. Matron knows Dr. Jamison wants me to go with him and Dr. Patterson, so she only scheduled me for tomorrow. Katrin, will you be able to leave the nursing program here?"

"Yes, I was told my credits could be transferred under Dr. Jamison."

"I also talked with the bishop," Father Albright stated. "He agreed the soldiers in Egypt need us there. There's a newly-ordained priest from the area that he will place at the church here."

"Very well then. I'll let headquarters know," Martin said.

"Now, let's enjoy our evening," Helen remarked. "Let's toast the new year in the hope of peace in 1943."

"To peace in 1943," everyone echoed and raised their glasses.

The friends parted well before midnight after enjoying a short time of celebrating the coming of 1943 and singing a few songs around the old upright piano, with hope that the new year would see the end of the war. Sally went to her room after everyone was gone and reread the letter Andy wrote during the *Mariah*'s last voyage. He told her of his hope for the future now that the Axis was on the run in North Africa and the Japanese seemed to be losing to the Americans.

> ...and I want to say, I love you, Sally. I know this should be done in person, but I don't know when we will see each other again. So here goes: Will you be my wife? There, I said it. I don't know how else to ask you. I just know I want you to be a part of my life. There isn't much to offer, but once the war has ended, I think we could settle in England. Please think about saying yes.

Smiling, Sally held the letter for some time as she prayed for the men aboard the *Mariah*. "I love him, Lord. Please bring him back to me," she whispered before pulling the covers over herself.

*   *   *

It seemed the day of departure was upon them before Jane could catch her breath. Dr. Jamison was able to arrange for all of them to be on the same army transport, stating, "The men will need more than medicine to recover," referring to Father Albright and Katrin accompanying the rest of his small entourage.

"Well, we're on our way," Peter commented as the plane rolled down the runway. "I've been reviewing malaria symptoms and made a short list for the field medics. Hopefully, they can tell the difference between a common cold with fever and chills and a malaria attack."

"Usually, a couple of other things come with the chills. The stomach upset is mistaken for a bout of flu until the patient doesn't get any better and lapses into unconsciousness," Quentin Patterson replied.

"That's why I asked to have the field doctors rotate to Cairo for a couple of days to go over the problems of malaria symptoms and some of the other problems with infection in a tropical climate," Martin Jamison said. "The three of us might need to go into the field to help identify the patients that need to be moved to Cairo and those that will recover more quickly and will be able to return to their units in a week or two."

"Looks like Jimmy is enjoying the plane ride," Peter said with a smile. "Hey, little one, come here and see your dad."

Jane and Katrin talked while Helen and Sally dozed until they landed to refuel before the final passage to Cairo. So far, the flight was uneventful, and Father Albright said he believed they were being watched over because they were on a mercy flight. "The suffering of the soldiers and the people of North Africa will surely soon be over, and the medicine you bring to them is an integral part of that healing."

The flight, while holding an element of danger for those aboard, continued toward Cairo on a steady flight path. The moonless sky gave the plane a sense of floating in a darkened void until the stars shone clearly when they approached the Cairo airport.

Two days passed before Admiral Jamison indicated things were in motion. An army escort would be taking them to a neighborhood in Cairo at nine o'clock the next morning.

"Here we are then," the young lieutenant said when everyone was in the hotel lobby, where they had been staying until a more permanent arrangement was made. "I'll be taking you to a small area where we have some temporary housing arranged."

"Is it near the hospital?" Dr. Jamison asked.

"Yes, sir, just a few blocks away. The houses are furnished, and we've stocked the larders so you can settle right in."

"That's very kind of you," Father Albright said. "I guess we should have our luggage loaded and be on our way."

29

Andy placed his hat squarely on his head and took one last look around his cabin. He wouldn't be returning until the ship docked again at Alexandria. He spent his short leave visiting Sally's parents for a day before heading to London to meet Wesley. He told Sally's father he wanted to formally ask for his permission to marry Sally. "I wouldn't feel right if I didn't talk with you, sir."

Mr. Vilmont saw the lines around Andy's face and the look of strength in his eyes. He knew Andy was regular navy and had seen some gruesome fighting in the last three years. He also knew, by his daughter's letters, she was certainly smitten with the man who was sitting across the kitchen table from him. He didn't know it was the *Mariah* and Andy Burns's skill that had saved her and her brother on that fateful day off Banka Island. "I have no objection if Sally is willing."

"Thank you, sir."

Sally's mother smiled to herself as she came into the kitchen after hearing part of the conversation. *He'll make her happy*, she thought.

"Well, Mother, it appears our little girl has herself a navy man," Mr. Vilmont said when she came into the kitchen.

"Really now, what makes you think that, Eric?"

"Young Andrew here wants to marry our Sally."

"Well now, that is nice," Mrs. Vilmont responded. "Welcome to our family, Andy. I'm sure the two of you will be very happy."

"Thank you, ma'am, but she has to accept first." Andy smiled.

"Well, we'll see what the future brings," Mrs. Vilmont responded.

*   *   *

"Crew is at their stations, sir. Anchor is up and down," Mason reported when Andy crossed onto the bridge.

"Very well, anchors away, all ahead slow."

"Yes, sir, anchors away," Mason responded. He watched the orders become a reality while the men on anchor duty scrubbed the chain, washing away harmful debris and saltwater as the electric motors, deep within the ship, reeled the large anchor up from the harbor floor.

"All ahead slow," the quartermaster answered to Andy's order as *Mariah* began to move into the harbor waters in preparation to leave the port.

Soon the ship was navigating toward the channel, where a new convoy was forming to transport men and equipment to the desert. According to the latest newscasts, the African campaign was moving forward, and the American and British forces were starting to squeeze the Axis troops into a smaller pocket where the final blow could be delivered.

Andy was pleased to learn, when he returned to Harwell, that Captain Edmon was able to return to shore duty after surviving the horrific wounds he received when the *Mariah* escorted the *Royal Yacht* into the Atlantic during the worst of the 1940 blitz. Edmon said the ship looked pretty good, considering the abuse she received in Singapore.

"Keep an eye out for those dratted German wolf packs," Captain Edmon warned before leaving the ship when Andy invited him to have dinner in the mess with the officers.

"Ships to starboard!" a lookout yelled.

Raising his glasses to see the ships approaching out of the snow that was beginning to fall, Andy returned his thoughts to the job at hand. He knew thirty-five ships were scheduled to join the convoy during the night and head toward the Atlantic before sunrise. If they were lucky, the snow would continue and give them cloud cover to keep the Luftwaffe from finding them. He also knew the weather was a double-edged sword that could hide a periscope in the choppy seas.

Ships continued to move into view, looking like ghosts pushing through the veil of separation, for another three hours before the convoy turned their bows due west and began the voyage toward the Atlantic Ocean with purpose. The *Mariah* slowed until the last ship passed her bow to take the rearguard position to the vulnerable merchant ships—so vital to keep the army moving now that the Free French were moving toward Montgomery's Eighth Army. The last the crew heard, it looked like the Germans were on the run in Libya, and the two armies would soon link together.

* * *

Katrin turned the radio on low until the evening news broadcast began. She and her father leaned into the set as the announcer began the latest report from North Africa: "This is the BBC Cairo station with the weekly news review. On Sunday last, Soviet troops opened offenses at Stalingrad, Leningrad, and the Caucasus. Very little information is forthcoming, but it is believed, by the Allied partnership, that the fighting is intense."

After a short break for a soap commercial, which ended with a catchy jingle sung by a local men's trio, the broadcast continued: "We have just learned that Free French forces have merged with the British under General Montgomery in Libya. Allowing little time to regroup, British forces have started an offensive attack to take the capital city of Tripoli, thereby compelling the last of the Axis Army to retreat out of Libya. Allied headquarters is releasing little information about this latest offensive, stating, and I quote, 'Loose lips sink ships, but they also defeat armies.'"

Katrin said she wondered if Arthur was on his way to Tripoli. "I haven't heard any news from him since his last letter that said he wouldn't be able to write for a while."

"I'm sure he's thinking about you, Katrin. We'll keep praying for an end to this madness and the safety of his unit," Father Albright said. "I think there's more," he continued, turning the radio up again after the latest bond-drive commercial ended.

"I have just been handed this news release," the announcer said with excitement. "In an announcement earlier today, the government of Iraq has declared war on the Axis powers this sixteenth day of the new year. It appears that soon most of the world will be against Hitler and his henchmen. This is the BBC Cairo station reporting. Good night."

Father Albright switched off the radio and sat back on his chair with a small smile. "I believe things are definitely turning around, Katrin. A couple of weeks ago, the United States and Australian armies beat back a Japanese attack on New Guinea, and now it looks like the German Army is on the run in Libya."

"I hope you're right, Dad. I hope it's over soon."

"I'm sure it will be, my dear. Well, I'm going to my room to meditate a bit before turning in," Father Albright said, leaning over to kiss his daughter on the cheek.

Katrin sat for some time, looking out over the small garden area and watching the stars emerge in the sky. With the blackout, it was easier to see the night sky, even in the city. She had turned out the lights and left the blackout curtains open while she thought about the many changes in her life since the war had come to Java.

I wonder how many other people have seen so many changes, she thought. *Lord,* she prayed, *please keep the soldiers safe. Please bring*

Arthur through this. I know there are many soldiers on both sides that would rather be home with their families. I hope it is your will to end the hatred and the killing soon. I ask you to strengthen those that were left behind to the mercies of the invaders in the East. I still hear the screams of the young woman that terrible night in Java and pray that she finds solace in your mercy and grace. I thank you for saving us and ask for your forgiveness for my fear and doubts in those darkest days on Java. Your grace brought us through to a new life and to new friends whom I am grateful to know. I ask you to bless my father and give him the words of encouragement that are needed to help the broken, wounded soldiers brought here from the battlefields of this terrible war. Heal their minds and bodies and let your Spirit walk with them through their dark valleys. In the name of your Son, Jesus, amen.

While Katrin watched the night sky and prayed, Sally wrote her reply to Andy's letter. She had thought about it for some time and prayed often about the man she had grown to love.

My Dearest Andy,

I have given your proposal a great deal of thought. I believe our children will find it very amusing to know that their father put his proposal in a letter, saying he most likely was too nervous to do otherwise. My dearest one, you know that I love you and will be your wife at the earliest possible moment.

I wrote to my parents to inform them I plan to say yes to your proposal and that I hope they will understand if we are unable to marry in England. I did say we would come to them as soon as this war will allow, and I hoped that Helen would be with us as well.

Mother wrote that she is looking forward to that time and finally meeting the woman that took Wesley and me under her wing. She said in her letter, she did not believe that Wes and I would be here today without her. I didn't tell her the rest. I thought it best to wait until she can see us both—safely, in her kitchen.

I pray for your safety, and that of the crew and the ship, each day. Please let John know about our plans and that someday I hope he finds peace within himself.

I love you,
Sally

Sally reread the short note before folding it and placing it in an envelope to mail the following day. Smiling, she picked up Andy's letter and decided it was time to let Helen and Jane know she and Andy were planning to marry. She decided to read the letter to them and Katrin when they met tomorrow, after posting her reply. They were to meet with Dr. Jamison and Dr. Patterson later in the day and decided to have lunch together and start making plans for things that could be done for the troops—after being wounded or suffering a malaria attack—in the hospital.

*   *   *

"He's sleeping in such peace," Jane said of their son to Peter. "He's going with me tomorrow to meet with Dr. Jamison and Dr. Patterson. Helen, Sally, Katrin, and I decided to meet beforehand and make some preliminary plans for the hospital in Alexandria for the patients and overworked staff once the Germans are definitely out of Tripoli and being forced out of Tunisia. We believe it should be safe to be there by then. The Americans are already bringing nurses into Algeria."

"We'll see what the next few weeks bring and go from there," Peter replied. "Well, I'm for bed. It's been a busy couple of weeks getting here and getting settled in. I believe, before the week is out, I'll be heading for some of the small outposts to help with the outbreak."

"Just make sure you're careful and remember to take care of yourself," Jane quietly said.

"I'll be careful and back before you know it. Remember, we're going to grow old together and wonder where the years went," Peter said, taking Jane into his arms and kissing her.

"Peter," Jane whispered, "I love you so much. Please come back to us." She looked up into his eyes and brought a hand up to gently touch his face.

30

The black clouds and heavy snows gave way to rain before the skies began to clear and the seas became calmer. It was ideal weather for the Luftwaffe to search out ships and alert their naval friends. Andy knew the enemy would be more determined to stop any supplies, or fresh troops, from reaching North Africa since the Eighth Army had marched into Tripoli the previous day. The week had also seen the besieged troops in Leningrad, Russia, link up with relieving Russian troops and the United States and Australian forces joining together in New Guinea.

"I'll be in my cabin," Andy said, lowering his glasses after scanning the sea. "Call me if there's any irregularity," he ordered before leaving the bridge.

"Yes, sir," Sublieutenant Anderson replied. He had spoken with Mason Roden the evening before and learned the northern route in the Atlantic, between Iceland and England, was plagued with German submarine attacks. He also knew that the wolf packs were moving south to stem the flow of supplies and men who were pouring into North Africa from the United States and England.

"Keep a sharp lookout," Anderson said to the bridge watch. "I don't want to run into trouble without warning. Captain Burns is counting on us."

Two days later, during the early evening watch, Roger Barnes commented, "I wonder if the Germans are too busy trying to stop the Eighth Army to pay any attention to a convoy heading toward Gibraltar."

"Let's hope they continue to ignore us," Mason replied.

The sun slipped beneath the horizon, leaving the ocean a dark rolling abyss with a sliver of moon rising on the horizon as stars began to dot the clear sky. Brian Jones began to update the navigation charts with star readings to verify *Mariah*'s exact location on the ocean. Roger Barnes stood by his side, taking down the longitude and latitude, as Brian carefully read the sextant, the same instrument sailors of centuries past used to navigate the vast liquid desert that separated the land that men fought over to gain power over the masses.

"You hold it like this," Brian was explaining when a shout from the starboard watch broke the calm routine of the bridge.

Andy rose from his bridge chair and scanned the ocean for any sign of irregularity. He waited for another watchman to give the alarm, but none came. A half hour passed, and no other sighting was reported. He scanned the ocean once more but did not see anything out of the ordinary.

"Keep a sharp eye out," he ordered the bridge watch. "I'm going to lie down for a bit. Call me if there's another sighting."

"Yes, sir," Anderson replied when he reported for his late-night watch rotation. Unease filled his thoughts as he drank the warm tea meant to keep him alert an hour later. *It was a night like this when my sloop was sunk in '41*, he thought. He checked the chart to see how close they were to the turn at Gibraltar before scanning the ocean once again. *So far it's quiet. Let's hope it stays that way*, he prayed.

Three more hours passed before Mason Roden entered the bridge to begin his predawn watch. He reviewed the log, noting the earlier navigational readings and a note from Captain Burns about a possible sighting.

"Everything quiet, Anderson?" Mason asked.

"Yes, sir. Nothing since that last possible, which could have been a piece of garbage one of the transports threw overboard that didn't sink right away."

"Yes, that could be an explanation. You're relieved, Lieutenant."

"Yes, sir, I am relieved," Anderson replied, making a final note in the log and returning to his bunk for a few hours' rest before the next cycle of watchkeeping came his way.

Mason made a careful sweep of the ship's lookouts to be sure each one was on station and keeping a close vigil before raising his glasses and scanning the wave tops and convoy to assure himself the vulnerable merchant and transport ships were keeping stations. He knew the formation was meant to deflect as much opportunity for the enemy as possible and aid the few more heavily armed escorts in defending them against armed aggressors. He saw one ship that was well out of formation and sent a scathing signal to pay attention to their navigation and hold station. He watched until the delinquent watchkeeper brought the ship back on course. Three hours later, he witnessed the sun rise out of the sea, offering clear skies and little disturbance beyond the water curling aside, as the ships passed across the ocean surface.

"Morning, Number One," Andy said in greeting when he strolled onto the bridge before lifting his glasses to scan the sea and take inventory of the watchkeepers on duty. "It looks like a nice day to be at sea. I wonder if *Gerry* will come to the same conclusion."

"I was wondering the same, sir," Mason responded. "So far, this has been a pretty tame journey, and it's making me very nervous."

"I don't think we'll see anything until—"

"Planes—eleven o'clock!" a watchkeeper shouted.

Quickly turning to sight the intruders, Andy ordered all stations sounded before raising his glasses to get a better look at the approaching planes. "Looks to be six in formation," he said before sending Mason to his station at the aft antiaircraft guns. "Keep an eye out for a second wave," he commented as Mason descended the bridge ladder and ran to his duty station.

Mason watched the planes turn and begin their descent, putting the sun behind them to impair the ship's defenders from sighting in on them. At four hundred feet, the planes began to splay bullets across the convoy ships' decks, knowing the small caliber deck guns were no match for a small target moving over 150 miles per hour. Mason watched as the second plane turned and began ascending out of his dive and coming within range of his guns.

"Up one hundred, fire!" he hollered as the gunners adjusted the guns and fired another volley that exploded near the tail of the departing plane. At first it appeared to be a miss, but then the plane seemed to stop in midflight before turning at an impossible angle and diving into the sea. The small victory was soon forgotten when another plane strafed the bridge before turning away toward land.

"They must have been coming off another run when they spotted us," Mason commented. "Good shooting, men. We got one of them. Clear away and be ready for another wave. I'll report our good fortune to the bridge."

"Sir...," Mason started to say, stopping midsentence.

"It's all right, Number One, nothing fatal," Andy commented.

"Yes, sir," Mason continued. "We sent one into the drink. No damage reported."

"Sir, signal from the leader," Roger stated. "'Good work, no ships damaged.' That's all, sir."

"Very well." Andy winced when he moved his arm, and a wave of pain shot through him. "Take over, Number One. I'll be in sick bay for a bit. Keep an eye on the merchant to port. He's all over the ocean."

"Yes, sir. Told him last night to keep any eye to his navigation. If we have a serious attack, they could very well be our weak point," Mason answered.

Andy started to leave the bridge and stumbled a little, leaving a trail of blood dripping off his hand. "Porter," Mason ordered, "give Captain Burns a hand."

"I'll be all right," Andy said.

"No argument, sir. Porter, give the captain a hand."

Porter steadied Andy and helped him through the map room and down the ladder to the lower deck to sick bay. John Hartman saw them coming down the narrow corridor and ran to help his captain onto a bed.

John quickly cut away Andy's shirt and saw where a bullet had entered his upper chest near his shoulder. Feeling along his back, he felt the bullet just inside the skin.

"It looks like a clean shot," John said. "I'll have to turn you onto your side to get the bullet out. Harris, help me get this wedge behind his back," John ordered. "There, that's better. We'll have to knock you out to do this, sir."

"Yeah, I figured you would," Andy said. "Make it quick. I have a feeling we'll have visitors by tonight—if not before. Those planes will radio our position to their headquarters, and I'm sure the German telegraphs are burning up the wires to get the information to any submarine in the vicinity."

"We'll worry about that later, sir," John said as Harris began to put ether on the mask that he placed over Andy's face.

Two hours passed before John was satisfied the wound was clean and no damage had been done to any vital organ. He placed sterile bandages over the entrance and exit wounds and immobilized the arm to keep it from irritating the injured area. He knew it would take at least three or four months for the wound to heal properly.

Andy woke up in his cabin with Emil Harris sitting at his bedside. "What time is it?"

"It's 1830 hours, sir. Dr. Hartman asked me to let him know when you woke up," Harris commented as he opened the cabin door.

Andy felt around his shoulder and discovered it was bandaged rather heavily and his right arm was taped across his chest. He tried to roll over but decided it was too much effort at the moment. He wondered how he had gotten down to his cabin and into his pajama bottoms.

"Good, you're awake," John said. "The bullet went straight through and fortunately didn't hit anything vital. The bad news is, it will take quite a while for it to heal properly. I'm sorry, sir, but once we dock, I don't think you can go out again right away."

"We'll see what transpires between now and when we dock in Alexandria. How soon can you get me to my sea cabin?"

"Sir, I really don't think—,"

"Lieutenant, unless I'm too severely wounded to function, get me to my sea cabin. If the Germans come tonight, I'll need to be on the bridge."

"Sir, Mr. Roden is in command right now," John said. "He told me to remind you of Captain Edmon, sir."

"Yes, Troy Edmon, I remember. However, he was in much worse shape. I'll make a deal with you, Lieutenant. Should the Germans come tonight, you get me to the bridge. If not, then I'll be content to stay here until tomorrow when I'm sure I'll be feeling much better and able to resume my duties."

"Yes, sir. We'll talk about it tomorrow then," John said as he closed the cabin door behind him.

He probably thinks I'll be an invalid by tomorrow, Andy thought. *I sure hope the Germans don't come calling tonight.*

Andy drifted into a light sleep and vividly saw the plane coming toward the *Mariah* begin to fire his cannon and strafe the bridge. The bullet coming toward him took on the image of a swastika with a laughing face before slamming into his body and causing a searing pain, which made him gasp, before he awoke in a cold sweat. His chest and shoulder throbbed like it was on fire, and sweat beaded across his face. Throwing off the cover, he managed to sit up on his bunk and eventually got to his feet. He went into his small private bath and splashed water on his face with one hand. When he looked into the mirror, he saw the face of Troy Edmon—looking at him from his hospital bed. *Trust your first officer*, the image reminded him. *If you don't, ask yourself: is it you or him, and then take action.*

"Yeah," Andy whispered. "But it's my ship."

31

The *Mariah* docked in Alexandria's large harbor after traversing the Mediterranean Sea corridor without incident the prior week. Since the fighting in North Africa was pushing the Axis Army into a pocket, the American Navy was on hand to secure the area for needed supplies to reach their army, making the seas around North Africa less dangerous at the present. Once the *Mariah* was moored to the dock and her engines were at rest, Mason reported to Andy Burns.

"Sir, ship is secure at the dock, and the wounded are being transferred. I have arranged for a nurse to accompany you to the recovery hospital ashore. She should be here shortly."

"Thank you. My grip is ready if you could send one of the ratings to bring it on deck. I don't think I'll be gone for too long. Take care of the ship, Number One."

Giving his captain a grin, Mason assured him that all would be in order for his return.

Andy slowly climbed the steep metal stairs to the main deck, using his good arm to hold on to the rail while trying not to bump the other heavily bandaged arm held securely in a sling. He looked around the ship out of habit before starting toward the gangplank. The officer of the deck was on hand, along with the boatswain, to see him over the side, where he saw Sally waiting on the pier. Breaking into a wide grin, he waved and began walking toward the pier.

"I have no idea how you got here, but I can't think of anyone I'd rather see right now," Andy said, wrapping his good arm around her and kissing her. "I think you must be real and not a hallucination from the medications John Hartman's been giving me."

"Andy," Sally whispered, holding back the tears that wanted to come. "I've missed you so much. Thank goodness you're still in one piece. I have a car waiting at the roadway to take you to the recovery center. Dr. Jamison said you had to go directly there, and he would take a look at you."

"Admiral Jamison is here? How did that happen?" Andy asked as they made their way to the transport car and got in.

"Dr. Patterson and Peter Romans and Jane are here with little Jimmy, along with your mother. Admiral Edwards sent a request that Dr. Jamison come because of the malaria outbreak and other difficulties with the wounded here. He put a group of us together, and Admiral Edwards set it up. We flew into Cairo a few weeks ago. We were moved here last week," Sally informed him on the ride to the recovery center.

"It sounds like a lot has happened since you accepted my written proposal. I have since spoken with your father, and he has consented to our marriage, if you are willing to be my bride. So, Sally Vilmont, will you accept in person?" Andy asked with a slight show of returning spirit in his eyes as they pulled up to the requisitioned hospital recovery center.

"Well, since you have spoken with my father, and since you have now asked in person, how could I say no? Oh, Andy, I do love you so very much and want to spend a lifetime with you."

"In that case...," Andy softly said before drawing her to him and kissing her. "I found this in a small shop in England and have been keeping it in my pocket," he said, fumbling to put his right hand into his pocket and draw out the small box. "Open it."

"All right," Sally said with question on her face. Inside the box was a small jewelry box that held a lovely emerald ring surrounded by tiny diamonds in a gold setting. "Andy, it's beautiful." Sally breathed before throwing her arms around him and kissing him.

Taking the ring out of the box, Andy carefully slid it onto the third finger of her left hand and brought it to his lips. "When do you want to be married?" he asked.

"As soon as it can be arranged. I don't want to wait for you to return again."

"We'll tell everyone once I'm out of the recovery center, if that's okay with you."

"I think that's a grand idea. Maybe we could have everyone together—like old times."

"I like that idea, yes. I like that idea very much."

Dr. Jamison met them at the door to the large building that was set back from the road, with pleasant gardens and walkways, to give the recovering patients a peaceful place to heal.

"Andy, it's good to see you, but I'd prefer you not to be a patient. John sent over the chart, and it looks like you're healing, but it will take some time to get back the full range of motion in your arm again. It looks like he did a good job patching you up, from the notes in your chart. We'll let you get settled in, and we'll take a look at it and get some x-rays tomorrow. Your mother will be along later today to see you."

"Thank you, Admiral," Andy said with a salute to his superior officer. "I don't think I'll be here for too long. There are plenty more who need the bed more than me."

"Well, we'll see how things go along," Dr. Jamison said noncommittally.

Sally helped Andy get settled into his room and said she would be back that evening to spend some time together. "I think

Dr. Patterson will be along as well." Throwing a kiss from the doorway, she left to return to her duties.

*   *   *

John Hartman left sick bay after the last patient was taken ashore. He was concerned about Captain Burns and wanted to talk to the first officer about how the captain returning to the ship too soon could hinder his recovery.

"Commander Roden, do you have a moment?"

"Yes, come in, Lieutenant. What can I do for you?" Mason asked.

"I'm concerned about the captain. He indicated returning before much time has passed, and I'm afraid, to do so, he'll try not to show his discomfort during rehabilitation. You know him better than I do. I thought you might be able to speak with him about it. His injury is serious, and he could have some debilitation without hindering the recovery."

"Well, I wouldn't worry too much about it. I've just learned that Dr. Jamison is at the recovery center in Alexandria, along with Dr. Patterson and your friends—the Romans and Sally Vilmont. I'm pretty sure Dr. Jamison won't release him until he's sure of his recovery. And I know Dr. Patterson won't."

"I'm relieved, sir. Do you know how long Jane and Peter will be here?"

"I don't know the details, but I believe it's a long-term assignment, or at least until the army finishes pushing the Axis out of North Africa."

"I'll have to contact them tomorrow and make arrangements to see them and my godson. I don't believe Jane would be here without Jimmy."

"That shouldn't be a problem. The crew will have leave for the next fifteen days, so you can go ashore and relax."

"I hope you'll get a chance to do the same."

After John had left, Mason closed the door to his cabin and ran a hand through his hair. He knew from experience the *Mariah* would have a fairly quick turnaround, and he wondered if Andy Burns would be back to take her out again. *If not,* he thought, *who would be the new captain of the* Mariah, *and would he be able to work as well with that person as he did with Andy Burns?*

He turned on the radio in his quarters and decided to see what indication he might get from the latest news broadcast as to when the *Mariah* could be at sea again. He fiddled with the dial until he picked up a signal then sat down to listen as the announcer began the evening broadcast.

"This is the BBC Cairo station reporting," the announcer began. "The Axis Army was sent packing when the British Eighth Army marched into Tripoli on Saturday last, followed by French forces on 26 January. The campaign continues to pressure the Nazi invader as Allied forces push across Libya to sweep that country free of the last remaining enemy holdouts.

"In other news, we have learned that Guadalcanal is now free of all Japanese presence on the disputed island. Apparently, they slinked away under the cover of night, fearing the Allied Army coming for them with a vengeance. This is a victory to be celebrated, along with the United States and Australian troops joining forces in New Guinea to bring that same fighting force to clear the enemy's presence there. It appears, as the first month of 1943 draws to a close, the enemies of the Allied forces are sharing in defeat in large numbers. This is the BBC Cairo station, good night."

Mason turned off the radio and thought about the newest developments on the war fronts, wondering how it would affect the *Mariah*.

* * *

"It looks like you're starting to have some improvement," Dr. Patterson told Andy a week after he arrived at the recovery center.

"How soon before I get sprung from this place, Doc?"

"Perhaps in a day or two, but that doesn't mean you're released back to the ship," Dr. Patterson cautioned. "I'll talk with Martin and see what he thinks about you staying at your mother's for the rest of the recovery period."

"That would be an improvement."

Andy looked around the small confining space after Dr. Patterson had left and thought about his cabin aboard the *Mariah. What happens if I'm not ready by the time the ship receives orders?* he wondered.

It was the following Monday before Andy was released, with strict instructions from Dr. Jamison that he was not yet ready to return to the *Mariah.* "She'll get along just fine with Mason Roden in charge," he said. "I'm letting you go to make room for the number of malaria patients we're starting to take in. Helen said she would be sure to keep you out of trouble."

Laughing a little, Andy replied, "Well, she's had plenty of experience there. I remember growing up, she got me down from a tree at least twice a week and kept me from exploring too far into the jungle. Until I could go into the fields with Dad and help, she had her hands full. I imagine Sally will have something to say about it too."

"Yes, what is it between the two of you?"

"When I found out you would release me today, I asked Ma to set up a friends-of-the-family get-together for next Sunday after church. I'll fill you in then. Here's Sally to wheel me to the door."

The week passed quickly until Sunday arrived. After the church service, Andy greeted Dr. Jamison and Dr. Patterson at the cottage door when they arrived. "I believe everyone else is in the front room," he said, leading them into the large room that faced the sea.

"Helen," Dr. Jamison said, "it smells wonderful in here. You always come up with something to whet my appetite."

"Well, I did have a little help from my friends, Martin. Now that we're all here, Andy, what did you want to tell us?"

Sally came and stood beside Andy, and he took her hand in his. "We wanted you all together to let you know we are going to be married as soon as possible," Andy announced before kissing Sally's ring finger and then her lips.

"That's wonderful," Jane said before embracing her friend. "Have you set a date?"

"Andy, Sally, I couldn't be more pleased." Helen smiled, giving both a kiss on the cheek. "Martin, I have a bottle of champagne I've been saving, and I think it's time to open it."

Andy heard a knock on the door and went to see who would be calling on them since all their friends were in the front room. When he opened the door, John Hartman stood on the stoop and gave a look of surprise when he encountered his commanding officer.

"Sir, I'm sorry. I didn't know you had company. I'll come another time," John said with a salute.

"Don't be silly, Lieutenant. Come in and join us."

Removing his hat as he came into the front room, he was a little surprised to see everyone together as if nothing had changed, and they were at Helen's Landing—with the exception of two additional adults and Jane holding his godson. "Hello, everyone. It looks like we're all together like we were back in Helen's Landing. So this is my godson? Let me have a look at him. He's quite the boy. Hey, little fella, I'm your Uncle John," he said, touching Jimmy's cheek.

"John, it's wonderful to see you," Helen said, embracing him. "How has my son been treating you?"

"Ah, just fine, Helen, just fine."

"Father Albright, Miss Albright, it's good to see you in much better circumstances," John said when he turned to the others in the room.

"Dr. Hartman, we still talk about your skills in saving the soldier who came with the rescuers. I honestly didn't think he would survive after all that time without proper medical care," Father Albright said, shaking John's hand.

"Please call me John."

"John," Sally said, coming up behind him. "It's wonderful to see you, especially today."

"I found the corkscrew, Helen," Dr. Patterson said, coming from the kitchen with Dr. Jamison in tow, holding the bottle of champagne.

"Well, John Hartman, it's good to see you, son," Dr. Jamison said, extending his hand.

"Thank you, sir. What are you celebrating?"

"Ah, they haven't told you yet? Andy and Sally have just announced their engagement."

Turning to Sally, John smiled before bringing her hand to his lips. "That's wonderful. I'm very happy for you, my friend," he said, looking into her eyes. Turning, he said, "I'm happy for both of you. Congratulations, sir. I hope you have many years of happiness."

"You're staying, of course," Helen said, handing him a small glass.

"Thank you. I remember how delicious the food was at these gatherings. But I have to ask, where is Peter?"

"He'll be here shortly. He had duty at the hospital this morning," Jane answered. "I know he'll be thrilled to see you again."

An hour later, Dr. Jamison said, "That was a wonderful meal as always, Helen. Even with the ration shortages, you ladies always seem to give us a delicious meal."

"I agree," Peter said. "My belt just keeps getting tighter."

"Remember, rice with no sauce," Jane said with a laugh. "Oh, I think I hear Jimmy wanting attention," she said, excusing herself to tend to her son.

"Father Albright, how did you and Katrin come to be here?" John asked.

"Martin arranged it. I wanted to bring the message to the severely wounded and those who are maimed for life, that they are no less of a man than when they joined the army or navy. In a time of crisis, we sometimes forget God is always there for us. So many become despondent, and I've heard tales of men withdrawing from society when they return home, or even finding a way to end their life."

"Yes, I see that when there's no choice but to amputate or when I have to tell a man he won't ever see again."

"That was the hardest part for me on the *Mariah* too, John," Dr. Patterson said. "I sure hope this is the last war we'll ever see. Man has to learn sometime that war isn't the answer."

"You're right, Dr Patterson," Peter said. "Hospitals are overflowing with the seriously wounded and the severely burned that will be permanently scarred. It seems the leaders of every nation would do better if they stopped war. The Hitlers and Mussolinis of this world need to wake up and realize that their heavy-handed rule only leads to disaster and death—not to mention, the Japanese."

"You're right, Peter," Dr. Jamison said. "Andy, you're awfully quiet."

"I'm just thinking of the men on the *Mariah*. She's only one destroyer amongst so many, but her battles have been fierce at times, and we've lost men in the process. It staggers the mind to think of the many that won't make it from all the ships in this war right now."

"How about we listen to the evening news to see if there is any good news?" Dr. Jamison suggested. Turning the radio on, he waited for the tubes to warm up before turning up the volume and adjusting the dial.

"This is the BBC Cairo station reporting," the announcer began. "On this first Sunday of February, we will look at the week past. Our Russian allies have ended the battle at Stalingrad with the capture of one hundred seven thousand German troops. It is reported among them is General Field Marshall Friedrich Paulus. British Broadcasting in London reports for the first time, the German public was informed by the Nazi government out of Berlin about the defeat on the Russian front.

"Meanwhile, in North Africa, Rommel is once again on the run and has moved into Tunisia. The Allied troops have cleared the last remnants of the Axis Army out of Libya and are continuing to bring the war to Rommel's army by moving into Tunisia in the wake of the Germans' retreating dust. This is the BBC Cairo station reporting. Good evening."

"It appears the Germans will soon have no place to run," John said.

"It looks like the army has finally closed the door to Egypt, and with the Americans coming from the other direction, the Germans will be running out of real estate before long," Peter said.

"It does look that way," Dr. Patterson agreed. "I think I'm going to stop by the hospital on my way home, so I'll bid you all a good evening. Helen, thank you for a wonderful afternoon."

"You're most welcome, Quentin."

"Good night, Doc," Andy said. "I'll be by tomorrow for our session, and perhaps we can arrange to have lunch together afterwards."

"That sounds good, Andy. I'll see you then."

Soon the rest of the friends began to thank Helen for a wonderful afternoon and for the shared meal. Little Jimmy yawned at all the fuss around him, bringing a laugh to everyone before he was taken home to his bed.

Closing the door, Andy came back into the front room and brushed a kiss on Sally's cheek before relaxing into a chair. "Ma, Sally, this was a great day. Sally, we need to start thinking about making plans for a wedding."

"Yes, we do. Helen, what do you think about having it here and just a few friends to join us? I know it would be lovely to have a large affair, but with my parents in England and Andy maybe having to go back to the ship before long, I just don't see it practical to make big plans."

"The important thing is for the two of you to be happy," Helen began. "I think we can put something very nice together."

"I think it will be wonderful," Sally said, with a happy smile.

32

Arthur Nance slithered through the shallow ditch and along the damp grasslands until he reached the cover of the thickly grown trees. Taking his time, he arranged the explosives on the tall straight tree trunks and set the timers. In theory, the trees would fall across the road, just past the blind curve, and stop any pursuing enemy troops. Once he was done, he crawled down the sloping hillside until he was out of sight of the road and then did a quick run back to where Wesley and the other observers waited.

"Well done, Arthur," Wesley said. "I didn't see you until you stood up at the bottom of the hill. Now we'll see if our little trap will work."

"We should see the—"

Arthur got no farther when the first tree started to fall toward the road. A minute later, the second and then the third was heard to crack, completely blocking the narrow roadway. The location was selected because of the drop-off at the north side of the road and the steep slope just beyond the roadblock that even army vehicles couldn't navigate. Unless a tracked vehicle or tank were present, the road would be impossible to traverse without first removing the heavy trees.

"It looks to be sufficient for our needs, Major. Will you be able to expand on the size of the roadblock?" Colonel Gherst asked.

"It shouldn't be a problem, sir. We'll need the rest of the unit though to do anything requiring something larger."

"Yes, well, we'll see what can be arranged. Shall we return to base?"

"Yes, sir."

Wesley and Arthur left Colonel Gherst's office after reviewing further suggestions and explaining the technicalities of making a series of engineered problems for the enemy in combat. They were told to put everything together on a topographical map of an area encompassing about seven square miles but did not know the location of the topography or the weather conditions that might be encountered.

"Sir," Arthur began, "I'm not sure just how accurate we can be. Without specific information, we don't know what atmospheric conditions might be encountered."

"Yes, I know. However, I have a feeling the sea won't be far from where we'll be."

"I'll start with that assumption then," Arthur said.

"Do it with and without those conditions. That way, we'll have the best-case scenario for whatever our colonel and his superiors have in mind."

"The preliminary drawings will be ready the day after tomorrow," Arthur concluded.

"I sure wish the rest of the unit was here. Sergeant Moore is proving to be pretty good at making practical suggestions when we start putting something like this together. And Corporal Jenkins is pretty good at improving our transportation setup and getting extra gear in place," Wesley stated. "I still don't know why we came all the way to England with Andy Burns just to do a few drawings. Something has to be brewing," he brooded, rubbing a hand over his chin a moment then shaking his head. "Once the drawings are ready, I think we'll take a few days to visit my parents' farm. It will give us both a break and time to clear our heads."

"That would be very nice, sir. Are you sure your parents won't mind my tagging along?"

"You don't know my mum. She'll try to fatten us both up with her special treats and most likely will fuss over us until we're ten miles down the road on the way back."

Arthur laughed at Wesley's description and said he'd be sure to get done as quickly as possible—to enjoy being fussed over.

*   *   *

Wesley and Arthur returned from the barn after helping Wesley's father water and feed the livestock. The train ride to the local station consisted of a series of transfers until they boarded the local weekly six days ago. When they finally sat down at Wesley's parents' kitchen table, Wesley's mother managed to have a cup of real coffee and an apple dessert, which melted in their mouths. Reaching over to the small side table, Wesley's father turned on the radio and fiddled with the tuning dial until the evening news broadcast began.

"This is the BBC London station reporting. It has been a busy week in the East since our last weekly review," the reporter said with an attention-getting voice. "After fierce fighting, the Americans have captured Guadalcanal from the Japanese. This is the first major achievement of the American offensive in the Pacific War. The newly secured airbase, known as Henderson Field, will offer the availability of air coverage in the Solomon Islands and will reduce the threat of a Japanese invasion of New Zealand and Australia." A second war bond commercial followed, along with an advertisement for kitchen utensils, before the news continued.

"In other news, it is reported that after careful consideration of several candidates by Allied Command, United States General Dwight D. Eisenhower has been selected to command the Allied armies in Europe. Meanwhile, in North Africa, Rommel's Afrika Korps has evacuated Libya and moved into Tunisia.

"This just in: We have learned that, as American forces cross into the narrow waist of Tunisia, German forces, under the leadership of General Rommel, have counterattacked, taking Sidi Bouzid and Gafsa. It is reported there was fierce fighting as the Americans regrouped with assistance from our British reserved forces and have denied the Axis forces an exit through the narrow mountain passes, pushing them into retreat through Kasserine Pass. This is the BBC London station. Good evening."

Wesley's father reached over and turned off the small radio when a live soap commercial began before the evening programming.

"It appears the Axis Army is having a tough time of it. I wouldn't be surprised to see them pushed into the sea before much more time passes. After that, I'm guessing we'll be clearing the islands in the Mediterranean in preparation to invade someplace in southern Europe," Wesley said.

"I hope it isn't Greece again," Arthur commented. "It didn't go so well there the last time, as I recall."

"Well, wherever it is, I'm sure we'll be better supplied," Wesley said. "Mum, that was a terrific dessert. Any chance a fellow could get seconds?"

"I think I can arrange that. Oh, by the way, we received a letter from Sally just before you came. She and Andrew Burns have set a date to be married. She said he was wounded and would be in Alexandria, Egypt, for a few months. I'm sure she sent a letter to you as well, Wes."

"It probably will catch up with me in about a month, the way we've been moving around lately. What did she say about Andy Burns's injury?"

"She said he would be fine as long as he does what the doctors tell him. She's sure to keep an eye on him too. I just wish we could all be there, but with this terrible war going on, it just isn't possible. She did say that as soon as they could get to England, they would come to the farm and stay with us a while."

"He came here, you know, a few months ago," Wesley's father said. "He said he wanted to have our permission to marry Sally before making anything official. I thought that was pretty decent of him. The way things happen nowadays, a lot of girls just run off and marry anyone they please, and the parents don't even know who the man is."

"Andy wouldn't do that, Dad. He's a pretty good guy, and Sally will be happy with him. I hope you get to meet his mother as well. Helen is a special lady. Someday, Sally and I will fill you in about our adventures before landing in Australia."

"It will make for interesting listening," Arthur said. "Well, I think I'm going to retire. We will have an early start in the morning. Mr. and Mrs. Vilmont, thank you for opening your home to me. I've had a very nice time with you."

"You're welcome anytime, Arthur," Wesley's mother said.

"Good night, Arthur. I'll be up in a bit," Wesley said.

After Arthur had left, Wesley's dad said, "A nice young man, Wes. What happened to him in Malaya?"

"Arthur was wounded rather badly. I didn't know if he'd survive, but he's pretty tough. I really can't say much more."

"I hate this war," Mrs. Vilmont said, clenching her fists before abruptly leaving the room.

"I didn't mean to upset her. I'm sorry, Dad."

"It's all right, son. She just sometimes gets to missin' the old days—when you and your sister were here. Can't say I blame her. Well, I'm off to bed. See you in the morning."

"Good night, Dad." Wesley sat in the darkened kitchen for some time, remembering the men lost in Malaya and the desert fighting. He wondered what Colonel Gherst might have in store for them next.

*   *   *

The countryside opened up as the train filled with men wearing military uniforms from nearly every Allied nation of the globe. Wesley and Arthur found a convenient spot on the floor and settled in for the short run to the next station, where they would change trains for the morning run to the small town above their current base.

"It shouldn't take but fifteen minutes to get to our next train," Arthur commented.

"I hope nothing holds us up at the station. I hate wandering around a station, waiting for the train to get in."

"It was very kind of your mother to pack us a lunch. The selections at a station's canteen are pretty much like eating cardboard."

"Mum thinks we're both too skinny. I wouldn't be surprised to find the rest of the apple dessert in with our sandwiches and the rest of what's in this box. I can't complain though. It'll probably be the last home-cooked food we're likely to see for some time."

Wesley and Arthur were lucky to find the train to their base as it was just pulling into the station. Once they handed over their tickets, they climbed aboard and found an empty seat. The whistle blew a loud cry, and the train jerked forward to begin the last part of their journey. Both men nodded into a deep slumber before the train had covered the first five miles.

"Sirs, wake up," the conductor said, shaking their shoulders. "We're about to pull into your station. Wouldn't want to miss your stop now, would we?"

Wesley and Arthur blinked a moment before opening their eyes. "Oh, thank you," Arthur replied.

He and Wesley stretched before standing up to retrieve their overnight bags and headed for the exit to the station's platform. They noticed another train across the tracks and watched while a group of men, with their backs to them, stepped down. Looking about a bit, the men turned around and followed one another toward the station-house platform.

"That's Corporal Jenkins, sir," Arthur said in surprise. "I think that's Moore—a couple more back. Wonder what they're doing here?"

"Yes, what are they doing here, indeed?" Wesley asked. "Sergeant Moore, over here!" Wesley called out.

Picking up his pace, Moore climbed the steps to the platform and saluted. "Sir, reporting for duty."

"At ease, Sergeant. Do you have your orders handy?"

"Yes, sir," Moore answered, reaching into his duffel bag for the unit's orders. "We got them about ten days after you left, sir."

"Interesting. Well, get the men together, and we can make the march to the base. It's not far."

"Yes, sir," Moore replied to the orders given. "Corporal, get the men in order for the march to the base. Major Vilmont and Captain Nance will be coming with us."

Saluting, Jenkins turned to the men and hollered for them to fall in and to be quick about it.

"I see Vilmont and his unit just entering the base, sir," Colonel Gherst's aide said, looking out the office window ten minutes later.

"We'll let them get settled in and then start the maneuvers the day after tomorrow. The major said his unit was one of the best at this kind of thing. I sure hope he's right."

* * *

Wesley signaled his sergeant to move the men across the road unseen. Fifteen minutes passed before the last man hustled into the trees and disappeared in the underbrush of the training grounds. This was the third time the maneuver was repeated, and each time, the results were the same: the men came to the edge of the woods, where a stream gently rippled across a stony bottom, with a high bank on the opposite side. The men waded across the shallow waters and sought exposed tree roots, pushing out of the thick foliage, to use as handholds to pull themselves up to the ground, which ran parallel to the flowing stream.

Jenkins peeked above the bank and looked for any sign of human presence before hoisting himself up onto the bank and signaling Sergeant Moore the all clear. "I thought North Africa didn't have any woods," Jenkins commented when Moore joined him.

"It doesn't—at least not where the army is right now. I've a feelin' the army has something else in store for us," Moore answered before turning to wave the rest of the unit to climb up the bank.

"It looks good so far, sir," Arthur said as he watched the exercise through binoculars. "Moore and Jenkins have gotten the exercise time cut down by about seven minutes since the first time."

"Tomorrow we move to temporary quarters in northern Scotland. I don't know what this is about, but I don't believe it has anything to do with the current offensive in North Africa," Wesley commented. "Once the men make their way to the roadway, send the truck to pick them up and take them back to base," he ordered before starting the Land Rover to head back to headquarters.

"Major Vilmont, Colonel Gherst will see you now," the aide said.

"Thank you, Corporal."

Wesley entered his superior's office and saluted, waiting for Colonel Gherst to respond.

"At ease, Major. Have a chair," Gherst said, looking at the man whose unit was more than decimated in Malaya after fighting the invading Japanese at close range and paving the way for the army and navy to evacuate as many as possible before the door closed on that bloodied battlefield. He also knew that Vilmont was part of the group that went to Java and rescued his friends, the Albrights. He didn't know about the equipment Wesley and Arthur had secured in the fairy-tale cave of light well beneath the occupiers' feet.

Colonel Gherst closed the folder on his desk and looked at the man who would lead an important phase of the battle plan: when the Allied armies began an offensive against the Axis armies on the European mainland in 1943. He knew Vilmont's unit was well-trained and had proven themselves in the battles of North Africa. The major had done well to train a new unit and move forward after the disasters of Malaya.

"Major, your unit will be flown to Wick, in northern Scotland. The base there is mostly Royal Canadian Air Force, but the major share of the unit is currently on assignment elsewhere. You won't be there for long."

"Yes, sir. The men will be ready to move."

"Yes, well, that's fine. Tell me, do your men get seasick?"

"No, sir. The men do fine at sea. Is there a reason the colonel asks?"

"Just wondering. You will be in charge at the base for now. I and a few others will join you in a month or two. By the way, have you heard from the Albrights lately? My mail hasn't caught up with me, for a while now."

"I received a letter the other day from Katrin. She said her father will be presiding when my sister marries Captain Burns, commander of the *HMS Mariah*. Unfortunately, my parents and I won't be able to attend since it's in another part of the world."

"Oh yes, I remember that name. Joseph said something about him in a letter that I received about six months ago. Seems he made an impression on him."

"I like Andy. He's a good man. My second corresponds quite often with Katrin. They met in Australia. Captain Burns's mother helped Katrin and her father get settled while they were there. They're in Cairo, the last I heard from my sister."

"I wonder how they managed to get to Cairo," Colonel Gherst said. "I've known Katrin since she was a youth. I remember it was hard on both of them when her mother died so quickly from leukemia. Well, your orders will be ready shortly. That will be all for now."

"Yes, sir," Wesley said, rising to leave.

Wesley met Arthur at the officers' club and filled him in on where they were going over a scotch and soda. "The next time you write Katrin, you might ask her how they met Colonel Gherst."

"I remember her telling me on our voyage back to Australia that Gherst had left the radio that they used to contact the Allies. She said he also taught her how to hide from anyone pursuing her and to not leave a trail. He must have been afraid of her being caught in the closing trap long before they were stranded in Java."

"I wonder how he got away from Java," Wesley said. "I guess we'll find out when he lets us know. I'm for some supper and an early bed. How about you?"

"That sounds like a good idea. We might not have many regular meals ahead of us. I'll tell Sergeant Moore to have the men turn in early."

Wesley turned off the light in his shared quarters and lay staring at the ceiling for some time, wondering what the army had in store for them. He finally drifted into sleep and dreamt about crawling through an endless maze of brush and never quite making it to the clearing, where his men were waiting to be rescued from a danger only he could see. He awoke in a cold sweat and padded into the bathroom to splash water on his face. He looked up into the small mirror over the sink and wondered how much longer the war would hold him and his men in its grip.

33

Andrew Burns looked at the *Mariah* peacefully residing at the dock, waiting for orders to embark on her next voyage. The deck was deserted at this hour, except for the watchkeepers and OOD, when he walked up the gangplank. His arm was no longer in a sling, but any sudden movement soon reminded him to be careful. Mason Roden met him at the wardroom doorway.

"Sir, I didn't know you were coming. Please join us."

"Thank you, Number One. I believe I will."

Andy sat on his favorite chair, where he and Dr. Patterson had sat across from each other when he was the first officer, enjoying a gin and tonic and discussing recent news events. Accepting a drink, he said, "I've come to talk with you, Number One. Sally and I plan to marry in a few days, and I would like to have you as my best man."

"Sir, I'm…I don't know what to say. Thank you."

"You might consider saying yes."

"I mean…sir, of course, I will."

"I think you can call me Andy, under the circumstances."

"Thank you, and please call me Mason."

"Very well, Mason. Father Albright will perform the ceremony at my mother's house a week from Saturday. The rest I've left in her and Sally's capable hands. I don't know how long we'll be here, but I plan to be ashore as long as possible."

"You don't need to worry about the ship. She'll be ready when we're called on again."

"Yes, I know she will be. I'm going to recommend that you receive your own command, when one becomes available. You've certainly earned it."

"I...," Mason began, at a loss for words. "It seems you've brought two very large surprises today. I just hope to live up to your expectations."

"Troy Edmon told me, when I took over command of the *Mariah*, to trust my first officer. He said, if I didn't, to ask myself if it was him or me and then to take action. Well, First Officer, you've proven yourself. Now it's time to move on. You'll find your own style, just like I did. I couldn't be Troy Edmon, but I did take a little of him—and many others—with me when I put on the cloak of command."

"I'll do my best," Mason said. "I think I understand what you mean about commanding a ship. I've been given a good teacher, but also some large shoes to fill. The *Mariah*'s been a lucky ship, with her crew and those who led them."

"Yes, she's a lucky ship, and she needs strong leaders to keep her lucky. Command is lonely in the end because your sole decision determines what the final outcome will be. We can never go back and change it—once the decision has been made. A commander needs to be confident, even at the darkest times."

"Like when we turned into our own smoke screen off Banka in '42 and went after that Jap destroyer?"

"That's one instance. There were others before my time. But now they're history, and it's time to move forward. Well, I best get back. I said I wouldn't be long."

"I'll see you to the pier."

Saluting the flag, Andy stepped onto the gangplank. "See you a week from Saturday," he said before disappearing into the busy pier.

*   *   *

The night before Andy and Sally's wedding, the wedding party gathered at Helen's for a short rehearsal and dinner before tuning in the radio to hear the latest news.

"This is the BBC Cairo station reporting. With help from the British, the Americans are on the move again in Tunisia, and the Axis Army pulled back through the Kasserine Pass on Monday last. After fierce fighting against a stubborn line of Axis troops and tanks at what is being called the Mareth Line in southern Tunisia, the Allies are beginning to see chinks in the armor. According to government sources, Allied forces are inching their way through and will soon bring the Axis Army to its knees."

The announcer continued, following a war bond appeal, "In other parts of the world, the United States and Australian naval forces have sunk several Japanese troop transports in a course of three days, denying the enemy reinforcements in the East. Meanwhile, in the United States, their congress debates the continuance of the lend-lease plan. His Majesty's government awaits word regarding this most necessary support at a time when British land forces have effectively fought and won pitched battles in North Africa. This is the BBC Cairo station reporting. Good evening."

Martin Jamison reached over, turned off the radio, and sat back on his chair. "Well, let's hope the United States continues the lend-lease with England. It's the only way we'll have the equipment to push the Axis right out of Africa and Europe."

"I don't believe they'll stop now, Dr. Jamison," Andy said. "After all, we are allies."

"Yes, but politicians can be fickle," Dr. Patterson noted with some excitement in his voice. "Why, I remember when…well, that was another time," he sheepishly trailed off when Dr. Jamison cleared his throat.

"Why don't we set the war aside for an evening and concentrate on the wedding tomorrow?" Helen said, looking at Andy and Sally sitting together, holding hands.

"An excellent idea, Helen," Father Albright said. "I think, besides a baptism, this is one of my favorite things about being a priest."

"Dad always hummed at home when a wedding was taking place," Katrin said with a faraway look in her eyes. "Mother had said, he was singing to the angels about a happy event."

"That is a really lovely way to put it," Jane said before her attention was diverted by Jimmy, who started rubbing his eyes with a tiny hand. "I think Peter and I need to get Jimmy home and into his bed," she continued with a tender smile. "I'll be here at one o'clock tomorrow afternoon, Sally."

"I think I'll be going too, Helen," Dr. Jamison said. "I'll see you tomorrow. Quentin, do you want a lift home?"

Helen closed the door behind Mason and turned to see Andy smiling at her from the living room doorway. "I wanted to say good-night. Ma," he said, bending to kiss her cheek, "take care of Sally when I'm at sea. She puts on a good face, but I know she feels things deeply."

"Yes, I know she does. I'm sorry her parents and Wesley can't be here tomorrow. I plan to take a lot of pictures to send them. Sally will be all right. We'll take care of each other."

* * *

Father Albright gave Martin Jamison a nod, letting him know the guests were seated and the groom was in place, before he walked down the hallway and knocked on the bedroom door.

In the bedroom, Sally said, "It seems like only yesterday, I was getting you ready for your own wedding, Jane. Now I know why you looked a little dazed that day. My stomach is in knots right now. I'm so nervous."

Jane smiled at her friend. "I know what you mean. But I have to say that married life is quite nice. I know you and Andy won't have the settled life that Peter and I have been blessed with at this time, but I believe the two of you will weather the uncertainties and have a wonderful life together."

"I'm counting on it," Sally said just before opening the door to Dr. Jamison, who was going to walk her into the front room to take her wedding vows.

Andy caught his breath when he glimpsed Sally—framed a moment in the hall archway—and thought again how lucky he was to have found someone like her. Not only was she beautiful, but she had spirit and kindness in her heart. He knew no other person would have penetrated his soul as she had done.

"Let us pray," Father Albright began. The ceremony came from the Anglican Book of Common Prayer, and soon the words of commitment, repeated before God, began.

The vows were said with the couple facing each other and holding each other's right hand. Their wedding bands were blessed as they repeated the words "With this ring, I thee wed." Father Albright then wrapped his stole around their joined right hands as a symbol of tying the knot. Using the words from the marriage rite, he then declared, "In as much as Andrew and Sally have taken solemn vows in the presence of Christ, by the joining of hands and the exchanging of rings, I pronounce them husband and wife. In the name of the Father, and of the Son, and of the Holy Spirit, Amen," he intoned, while making the sign of the cross over their joined hands. "Those whom God has joined together, let no man put asunder." Father Albright then invited the newlyweds and their guests to share the bread and wine of communion, making it their first act as a married couple.

"Congratulations," Mason said to Andy as the guests mingled around Sally. "I hope you will have a very happy life together."

"Thank you. I believe we will. I wanted to let you know that I spoke with Admiral Edwards, and he agreed that you are ready for your own command. He's put you on the list for the next command board meeting in June."

"That's pretty quick."

"A part of our times, but I believe you're ready. Edmon was right when we talked last, that a man can only learn so much from where he's at. It's your time, Number One."

"Perhaps we'll be on the same convoy duty."

"We'll have to see what fate will send. I believe, at the moment, I see my wife looking our way," Andy said before walking over to Sally.

"Andy, you looked to be deep in conversation over there," Sally said with a smile.

"Congratulations to both of you," Dr. Jamison said after coming up to the newlyweds.

"Thank you, sir," Andy acknowledged. "Sally and I are very happy you were able to be with us today."

"I believe your mother is signaling the two of you."

"Andy, Sally, Martin just informed me you can feel free to go away for at least ten days. He said he wouldn't release you to the ship until Quentin examines your arm. I took the liberty of getting train tickets to Cairo, which leaves the station this evening at seven o'clock."

"Helen, that's wonderful. I don't know how we'll ever thank you for this wonderful day, and now, a chance to escape together," Sally said with glowing eyes. "Oh Andy, we'll have such a wonderful time in Cairo."

"Did I hear someone say Cairo?" Father Albright asked. "Katrin and I are going there for a few days next Monday."

"Well, perhaps we'll see you there," Andy said. "We'll be there for a week or more before returning to Alexandria."

"Dad, Helen asked to have you bless the meal before everyone sits down," Katrin said, coming up to them. "Sally, you look absolutely gorgeous. You're a lucky man, Captain Burns."

"Don't I know it. And please, call me Andy. All of my friends do, and since you're Sally's friend, then you are mine as well."

"It's been some time since we met on that unexpected cruise, and your mother took us under her wing. I'm happy to say you are a friend," Katrin said with a smile. "If not for that, Dad and I might never have known any of you, and we would have missed out on meeting some really wonderful people."

"Glad we could help," Andy said before escorting Sally and Katrin to the small dining room.

"Before we toast the newlyweds and dine, I've asked Joseph to say grace for us," Helen said to the small assemblage of friends.

"Let us bow our heads," Father Albright began. "Gracious Father, we thank you for this special occasion and ask your blessings on those that have witnessed the marriage we celebrate today, as Jesus celebrated a wedding where he performed his first miracle. We ask that you watch over Andy and Sally and grant them a long and happy life together. We ask you to bless those who are unable to be here today and to bring an end to the fighting that prevents their presence. Protect our men in uniform on land, sea, and air, we pray. And now, Father, we ask for Your blessing on this wonderful food that is given to us by Your grace. Amen."

"This meal is wonderful," Peter said. "I can't remember when we've had such a feast, and fresh chicken as well. Helen, I don't know how you managed with all the shortages."

"I had a little help from my friends," Helen said. "Peter, I'm afraid tomorrow it will be rice with no sauce," she continued before laughing at the shared joke from Peter and Jane's first dinner party in Malaya. It seemed a lifetime ago, and yet it wasn't even three years since that time of false peace. *So much has happened since that innocent time*, she thought.

"I have to agree with Peter," Father Albright said. "My waistband will have to be enlarged if this continues."

"Ma, wonderful as always," Andy concluded.

"Let's toast the newlyweds before we send them on their way," Dr. Jamison said. "Here's to a long life, happiness, and the blessing of children."

"Well, I believe the best man is supposed to say something," Mason began. "I don't really know where to begin. First, I wish you both much happiness. I have to say, I don't believe I could have had a better teacher than you, Captain. Here's to a long and lasting friendship with you and your lovely bride."

The rest of the friends around the table offered their wishes for happiness and a long life together. When the meal was cleared, a small wedding cake was served before Andy, Sally, and their guests gathered around the radio to hear the latest broadcast.

"This is the BBC Cairo station reporting," the announcer began. "The Australian Navy has announced the sinking of eight Japanese ships that are believed to be troop transports in conjunction with United States naval forces. This is seen as a great victory in the fight to prevent the Japanese from threatening Australia's sacred shores. In the meantime, fighting continues in Tunisia to force the Axis Army out of North Africa," the announcer stoically stated. "In local news…"

The broadcast faded, and Dr. Jamison reached to turn the radio off. "It sounds as if the Japs are starting to see the seamier side of war—with the previous loss of ground, and now, the number of ships sunk."

"Maybe they'll rethink their position and stop this awful fighting," Jane said. "I remember saying, when they bombed Pearl Harbor, that they didn't know what they had started. America won't let up until they surrender."

"You think so, Jane?" John asked. "I know in '39 and '40, they had wanted to stay out of a war. I think President Roosevelt wanted to help, but his hands were tied with your congress."

"I don't know, John," Peter said. "Their lend-lease program helped until the United States was forced to enter the war. And now, their link to Australia is certainly helping to keep the Japs away from there."

"Well, whatever the reason, I'm glad they're on our side," Dr. Patterson stated. "I still say, man has a long ways to go before he learns that war isn't the answer."

"Here, here," Mason agreed. "Sir, I'm sorry to break this up, but I have to get back to the ship."

"I think Sally and I should get ready to leave for the station as well, if we're going to make the seven-o'clock train. They don't always run on an exact schedule," Andy said.

Jane helped Sally into her travel clothes and hugged her friend, wiping a tear from her eye. "I'm just so happy for you."

"I know you are. I remember feeling the same when you and Peter were married. Jane, no matter where we wind up, I don't want to ever lose our friendship."

"Don't be silly. We'll always be friends. We could be on the other side of the world, and you would be my best friend."

"And you mine. Someday this awful war will come to an end, and our lives will be more settled. I know Andy will still spend time at sea, but at least we'll be in a settled place."

"You'll travel the world in peacetime once this war is over and have a great many stories to tell us. Peter and I have talked about where we want to go when the war comes to an end and are debating between England and returning to Helen's Landing."

"Andy said he wants to retire from the navy and settle someplace near the sea. We might just manage to be together yet."

"Well, right now, it's time for you to be on your way. I'll see you when you get back," Jane said.

Father Albright placed the two small suitcases in the car that the parish provided him in preparation to drive the newlyweds to the station after their good-byes to Helen and their friends.

Sally threw her bouquet for the fun of it, and it landed in Katrin's hands. "Oh my gosh!" Katrin said, beginning to blush.

"Guess I'll have to start watching the mail more closely," Father Albright said, smiling, before driving Andy and Sally to the station.

34

"If I have to crawl through that bog one more time, I'm going to send the cleaning bill for my uniform to Churchill," Wesley told Arthur as they climbed into the truck, which would drive the unit back to their barracks.

"That's not such a bad idea," Arthur said. "I wonder if there'll be any mail when we get back."

"I certainly hope so. It's been nearly three weeks since we last had any mail. The men are starting to grumble."

The bumpy drive over narrow English back roads finally ended. The men quickly dismounted to head for their barracks to wash and change into dry clothes. Some laughed about the mud and grime on their faces and clothes. "We best see some mail," Wesley heard as the last of the men left the trucks.

Wesley and Arthur entered the officers' quarters and found several letters stacked on their beds. "Hey, it's a letter from my sister. She was supposed to be marrying Andy Burns a couple weeks ago," Wesley said, tearing the envelope open. "She says she is very happy, and the wedding was very nice. Apparently, they were able to spend a week in Cairo before Andy had to get back to his duties. Ha! It also says here that your girlfriend caught the bouquet."

Blushing a little at the last remark, Arthur opened the letter from Katrin. He spent several minutes absorbing the words of encouragement and love that she sent. He did notice she didn't mention catching the bouquet when telling him about Sally and Andy's wedding day.

"You look very serious," Wesley said after a few minutes.

"What? Oh, just concentrating is all," Arthur absently said. "Did your sister say anything about Cairo in her letter?"

"Not much, just that she wished I could have been with her, along with our folks, of course. Speaking of my parents, they have invited us to return to the farm before we ship out again. I talked with Colonel Gherst yesterday, and he said we could go next week—after that, not to make any plans. I think our training is coming to an end."

"I've wondered after seeing the new companies of British and American special forces coming onto the base. I just wonder what they have in store for us."

"I never thought, when I went to engineering school, that it would lead to what we've been doing," Wesley thoughtfully said. "Well, anyway, I told Ma to expect us next week."

"I'd like that," Arthur said. "I enjoyed the quiet and working in the barn last time. It's relaxing, and you don't contemplate the future when the cow is eyeing you while you're milking her. My only thought is to keep her from giving me a kick for taking milk from her baby."

"She does have a way of giving a look," Wesley said with a laugh. "Well, I'm for a shower."

* * *

All too quickly, Wesley and Arthur found themselves on the return trip after the week with Wesley's parents whisked by. Two days after returning to base, Wesley was summoned to Colonel Ghersts's headquarters, finding several other officers present. After a half-hour wait, the men were summoned into a large room, where chairs and a podium were set up, and a covered map was in the front. Colonel Gherst entered the room with a two-star general and mounted the podium with a folder in his hands, bringing everyone to their feet.

"Gentlemen, please be seated. I would like to introduce General Chase," Gherst said with little ceremony. "He will address you regarding the missions you have been training for."

"Thank you, Colonel Gherst. Gentlemen, tomorrow you and your units will begin the journey to your next assignments. My aide will have an envelope for each commanding officer at the end of this meeting."

The special forces and engineering units are to move ahead of the armies to sabotage enemy installments and clear difficult emplacements that could hold the army's forward movement for several weeks. "Even tanks can't clear everything," General Chase stated. "In regards to the final decision of where the next offensive will occur, you can be certain it will be someplace in the Mediterranean once we conclude the current action in Tunisia. In conclusion, all personnel are confined to the base until our departure time."

Wesley returned to his quarters and found Arthur sealing an envelope in preparation of heading to the officer's club to mail it. "You might see her sooner than you think," he said. "We move out tomorrow. If you don't mind, I'll walk with you to the club."

"You're more than welcome to come along, sir. What makes you think I'll see Katrin soon?"

"I just have a feeling we'll be in Africa before we move to our next job."

Wesley and Arthur entered the officers' club to find several officers having a last drink at the bar while waiting for the evening news to begin. Taking a small table, they each ordered a whiskey and soda.

"Arthur, I'm going to recommend you have your own unit after this operation. I believe you're ready to move out on your own. I'm also going to recommend you be promoted to major. You've certainly earned it."

"Thank you, sir. I don't know what to say."

"Say you'll do the job and come out in one piece. Other than that, there isn't much more to say."

"I'll get the job done, sir," Arthur said with determination. "We need to end this madness as soon as possible and return people to a normal life with the expectancy of being safe in their homes. When this is over, I want to marry Katrin, if she'll have me, and I want to ensure she and any future children we might enjoy are not threatened by war."

"It's as good a reason as any to finish the job," Wesley said as their drinks arrived.

The room suddenly became quiet when the evening broadcast began. "This is the BBC London station reporting. The government has just released the latest news from North Africa. After German counterattacks at Medenine failed, it appears General Rommel, the Desert Fox, has left North Africa, leaving his troops to fend for themselves as American and British troops close in. In other news, the United States House of Representatives voted to continue the lend-lease plan on Wednesday last.

"On the European front, German troops have entered Kharkov after fierce fighting with the Red Armies. The German Army lost the town a month ago to Soviet forces but, at present, have retaken it. At this time, Stalin has not commented on the loss. This is the BBC London station reporting. Good evening."

The bartender reached over and turned the radio off when a new soap commercial began and rang the bell at the bar. "Last call," he yelled. Squadron commanders and their lieutenants began to shuffle out the door a short time later, with the knowledge that they had enjoyed their last evening in the officers' club for the foreseeable future. Tomorrow, their men would be informed they would be leaving England. Until they were aboard the troopships, none of them knew where their next port of call would be located.

35

Katrin opened the letter from Arthur and slowly read the two pages, telling her that he missed her bright smile and the scent of her hair. He also said it would be a few weeks before he would be able to write again. She looked up at the picture of him she kept on her dressing table and whispered a prayer for his safety. After reading the pages again, she placed this latest missive with the other letters Arthur had sent since meeting her in the top of her bureau. She gently ran her fingers over the stack of envelopes that she would open and reread when longing to hear from him and knew she wouldn't until the mission was completed.

"I had a note from Helen," Father Albright said when Katrin joined him on the small patio. "She says that Andy and Sally arrived nearly on time in Alexandria. Apparently, they are currently staying with her. She says here, let me see, oh yes, 'Andy is still waiting to be released back to the ship.' She does say things are getting fixed around the cottage though, and she and Sally are taking full advantage of him being there."

"I'm looking forward to returning and having more to do. I get restless just sitting here in Cairo with nothing to occupy my time," Katrin said.

"Major Palmer stopped by yesterday when you went to the marketplace. He just wanted to know how we are doing."

"I think he's making sure we don't give away any secrets," Katrin said with a thoughtful look. "I believe he has something to do with what Arthur will be doing as well. Even though he's from America, I think he works with our British intelligence as well. I just hope he doesn't send Arthur into a more dangerous situation than he's already been through."

"I'm sure he won't. Well, now, are you packed for tomorrow morning? You know we leave at dawn. I just hope the train will be on time."

"I'll be ready, Dad, don't worry."

Joseph Albright smiled and said he was sure everything would go as planned. He talked about the new work he would be doing with wounded troops being evacuated to the rear from the intense fighting taking place at Medenine. "Maybe with Rommel out of North Africa now, the Allies will be able to occupy Tunis and end the struggle there. Without their general, the Germans may be less inclined to continue fighting a losing battle."

Sunrise the following morning found Father Albright and Katrin boarding the weekly train to Alexandria. With shortages and few conveniences present since the war entered North Africa, they carried a small basket with sandwiches and water to see them through the day.

* * *

"I believe you can return to service, Andy, but you'll have to continue the exercises I gave you to keep improving the arm motion," Quentin Patterson said at Andy's latest checkup.

"Thanks, Doc. I'm not sure if I'm pleased or not. I'm starting to get used to married life."

Grinning, Dr. Patterson replied, "It appears to suit you. Between your wife and your mother fussing over you, it has to be rather pleasant after being at sea during a war. I remember our escapades before being assigned to Singapore and after the Japanese invaded Malaya. It cannot have improved much since then."

Grimacing, Andy said, "No, it hasn't improved any. Well, I better let Sally and Ma know their repairman won't be available for much longer."

Sally greeted Andy at the door to the cottage and saw the changed look in his eyes. "Dr. Patterson cleared you to return to the ship," she said, without preamble.

"Yes. He said I'd have to continue the exercises to avoid stiffness, but the arm is doing well. He also said I won't need to use the sling anymore."

"How much time do we have?"

"Today," Andy replied. "Let's spend it enjoying each other's company."

Swallowing the lump in her throat, Sally gave a small smile and said they would have a picnic near the water.

*　*　*

The boson piped Andy aboard when he boarded the ship early Tuesday morning. "We're glad to see you back, sir," the boson said before the OOD saluted and said he was happy to see him recovered from his injury.

"Gentlemen, it's good to see the ship is in good shape. Please have Commander Roden report to my cabin," Andy ordered.

"Sir," the OOD said and turned to a rating to issue the order.

"Reporting as ordered, sir," Mason said when he knocked at Andy's open cabin door.

"Come in and sit down, Number One. I asked a rating to bring us coffee and some snacks while you bring me up to date."

"Thank you," Mason said, taking the chair across from Andy's desk. "We've been resupplied, and I had the fuel tanks filled yesterday. We've been here for some time, and I'm sure we'll have orders soon."

"You're most likely right. Have you had any communiqués about enemy activity in the area?"

"No, sir, not much, even between Tunis and Italy recently. We did get information regarding U-boat activity in the Atlantic though."

"It's usually been on the northern route for the most part," Andy said. "I don't recall there being as much on the north-south run."

"No, not as much," Mason said. "However, the mid-Atlantic isn't covered sufficiently with planes or ships, and there's rumor that is soon going to change."

"We'll have to see what develops. In the meantime, Admiral Edwards asked that both of us meet with him on Thursday. I believe we'll soon be in combat, with the door closing on the Germans in North Africa. My guess is, we'll start softening up Sicily, and possibly even the boot of Italy, in preparation to invade there."

"I agree," Mason said.

Thursday morning found Andy and Mason outside Eric Edward's office, where his aide placed them in a small windowless waiting area until the admiral was available. A half hour passed before the aide returned to direct them to Admiral Edward's inner sanctum.

"Captain Burns, Lieutenant Commander Roden, good to see you," Edwards said, returning the salute that both men gave upon entering the room. "It reminds me of Singapore—with one exception."

"What's that, sir?" Andy asked.

"This time, we're planning an invasion, not an evacuation. Monty says the Germans will be out of Tunis by the middle of April. I think it will be a bit longer. I do believe we will see a successful effort from the west now that the Americans have regrouped and stiffened up their forces. They also made some command changes since we had to rescue their offensive. I hear General Patton is like a tiger on the prowl with his tank division."

"You mentioned invasion," Mason commented with interest.

"Yes, Commander, that I did—and the *Mariah* will be a part of it. Andy, I know you have given a lot of yourself since taking over the *Mariah* from Troy Edmon, as well as you, Mr. Roden. I want both of you to participate in the final planning stages of the bombardment that will take place prior to landing troops to the north. That's all I can say for now."

"We're at your service, sir," Andy said. "How long will we be in port?"

"I've pulled the ship from convoy duty until further notice. Until I give the orders, you are free to stay on shore as long as you can be on board within an hour's notice. Leave the information with my aide if you leave the port area."

"Thank you, sir. I believe my wife will be happy to hear that," Andy said with a small smile.

"I thought that might please you, Captain. Seriously, I believe it will be at least another month, perhaps six weeks, before we're on stand-by. I'm sure the final planning will take place in the next two or three weeks. That's all for today. Oh, and Mr. Roden, the command board will meet in June, and I've placed your name on the list for command. I agree with Captain Burns that you are more than ready."

"Thank you, sir," Mason said before saluting and leaving the admiral's office.

36

"General Patton of the American Army leads his tanks into Gafsa, Tunisia," the evening news report began. "This is the weekly update from the BBC Cairo, Egypt, station. Since General Patton's tanks entered Gafsa, General Montgomery's forces have begun to break through the Mareth Line in Tunisia in an effort to break the stubborn defenses in place. It is believed that this is the last effort by the Germans to prevent being pushed into the sea or captured at the hands of the Allied forces, bringing strong offensive measures against the waning German lines.

"In other news, we have learned a covert Axis spy ring was captured outside Alexandria when a nearby neighbor heard some intermittent Morse code interfering with his radio reception. It turns out the house—two doors down the quiet neighborhood street—harbored three enemy spies that were watching the Allied airfield and reporting flight patterns to Berlin. The men are now in Allied custody and will be spending the rest of the war behind barbed wire, where they can do no harm. This is the BBC Cairo, Egypt, station. Good evening."

Andy reached over and turned off the radio when the latest cereal commercial began. A week had passed since his meeting with Admiral Edwards, and he shared his time between being with Sally and Helen and the ship.

"We likely won't see the new cereal on the shelves near here anytime soon anyway," he commented.

"You're probably right," Father Albright said.

Helen had invited Father Albright and Katrin to join her, Andy, and Sally that evening after their arrival in Alexandria. Joseph would be leaving Alexandria with the next army medical group to move closer to the British lines. He insisted that, this time, Katrin remain in Alexandria and continue her interrupted nurse's training work with the local hospital.

"I don't believe I'll be in any danger, but I know your mother would be very displeased if you were allowed to accompany me on this trip. Besides, Peter will be with me for a short time because of the malaria threat, and Jane and little Jimmy will need some company while he's gone," he told her.

"Dad is getting excited about being able to go with Peter when the medical people move forward," Katrin said. "He's been packing and repacking the last two days, trying to decide what he should take with him. I said to pack light and take the bare minimum. I don't believe they'll have room for any civilian luggage."

"Katrin is right, Father Albright," Andy confirmed. "You'll be lucky to have a change of clothing and your prayer book if you're going to be close to the front."

"Well, it won't be for a week or two at least," Father Albright said. "Helen," he began, changing the subject, "that was a wonderful meal. Katrin and I are very fortunate to be included in your circle of friends."

"Joseph, I enjoy your company as much as my friends that were left in Malaya. I pray for them to come through this safely. A few of them made it out before the invasion, but so many just couldn't believe the war would invade their lives, and it was too late. I know the Johnsons, our closest neighbor, went to Singapore several weeks before we left Helen's Landing, but I've not heard any word if they escaped or not. I do know they missed the *Bengal Princess*, which the Japanese sank, because it only took women and children, and Deloris didn't want to leave without Frank. I may never know what happened to them."

"Ma, some of the people are hiding in the jungles and working with our navy and army, providing information about the enemy. Maybe the Johnsons are with them," Andy said. "I know Frank was pretty savvy about the surrounding hills."

"I hope you're right, Andy. Well, now, what do you say we talk about something more pleasant? Katrin, would you like to help us with the Easter egg hunt this year? I know the local children are looking forward to it, and the patients are already talking about having something to look forward to. Matron said, even the staff are hopeful we'll do something to spice up their routine for a day."

"I'm looking forward to it. With Dad most likely being away for Easter this year, I'm a little at loose ends. It won't be quite the same with him gone."

"Helen," Sally said, "I know the nursing staff is ready to help and, of course, Jane has already started looking for some of the trinkets we'll need. As far as the children's part, I talked with one of the bakeries in town, and they said they would help make candies and other treats—as much as the rationing will allow. I suggested contacting some of the other bakeries in the area and working together to defer some of the sacrifice the ingredients will require."

"I also talked with Jane, and she said the Sunday school teachers are ready to help organize the children's Easter egg hunt on Saturday afternoon and will find volunteers to hide the goodies," Helen said. "Joseph, it will be a bit unusual to not have you with us for Easter, but I know the men on the line will be grateful to have you there. I'm going to suggest that Katrin stay with us while you're gone. That way, she won't just be on her own—that is, if you would like to come here, Katrin."

"Helen, that would be wonderful. I'm not really afraid to be alone, but with all the extra people here, I would feel more secure. But I don't want to be an inconvenience. You already have Andy and Sally here."

Helen pooh-poohed the idea that Katrin would inconvenience her. She said, that way, their planning for the hospital auxiliary and community events would be much easier, and Sally could help with her nursing studies. "Besides, when Andy has to return to the ship, Sally and I will need the company."

"Helen," Father Albright said, "I'm grateful. It will be a great relief to me, knowing that Katrin is with friends while I'm away. But, for now, I think we should get back to our cottage. I thank you for a very pleasant evening. I'm looking forward to when our times together don't involve radio reports about a war."

"Here, here," Andy said, raising his water glass. "I'm looking forward to an ocean deployment that only involves maneuvers and heading for a tropical port. Sally, you'll have to fly out to meet the ship, and we can be tourists."

"I'd like that," Sally said with a lingering smile.

"Good night, Helen, and thank you for having us," Katrin said. "I'll let you know when Dad is leaving, and we can talk about my coming here then. Andy, Sally, it was good to see you again. I'm glad you're getting some more time together after Cairo."

*   *   *

Three more weeks passed before Andy received a message by courier from Admiral Edwards, telling him to report to his headquarters the following Monday.

"Captain Burns, this way," the aide said, leading Andy to a small conference room, where two other captains and Mason Roden were seated. Eric Edwards followed a moment later, with a two-star admiral and a three-star admiral. A captain, carrying a packet marked "top secret," followed them into the room.

"Gentlemen, please be seated," Admiral Edwards said as he took the chair at the head of the table. "We're here to finalize the navy's involvement with the upcoming invasion of—," he said then stopped a moment and looked toward the three-star admiral who had not yet been introduced.

"I believe we have to let these men know the location to better assess the needs that will arise," the three-star said.

"With the American tanks defeating the Germans at El Guettar, Tunisia, and our British breakthrough at the Mareth Line in southern Tunisia in late March, we anticipate invading Sicily or Sardinia by late May or early June. Admiral Barlow is here to lay out the navy's timeline for the bombardment that will be coordinated with the American Navy's participation, Admiral."

"Thank you, Eric. Captain Hardee will pass out a detailed map of the area with navigational markings where the initial bombardment will take place. There are five numbered copies. Your names will be placed alongside the map number issued. Along with the map, you will receive top-secret orders that coincide with your map. Each map indicates the coordinates for the group that you will be leading."

"Sir," Mason interjected, "I don't have a command. I'm not sure I should be here."

"Eric?"

"Lieutenant Commander Roden is here because he is first officer of the *Mariah* and will be coming before the command board tomorrow at his captain's—and my—recommendation to be given a command. It is my belief that he will be commanding his own ship prior to the invasion and will be working with Captain Burns with the destroyer group," Admiral Edwards responded.

"I see," Admiral Barlow said, rubbing his chin a moment. "Mr. Roden, what you hear today, no other first officer will hear prior to the day before sailing. Since Eric is recommending you have a command, I will move forward trusting in his judgment."

"Thank you, sir," Mason responded.

"You may not have heard this yet. Today, Sfax seaport was bombed in preparation to take the port and the city. Once North Africa is secured, we'll move some of our ships forward in preparation to soften up the landing areas for the army and the marines. It's the navy's job to prepare the ground for the least number of casualties ashore. I want you to study the maps you've been issued and return next week with recommendations to improve our participation for the most effective outcome. Also check what the currents might be in your particular areas throughout May and June. Captain Hardee, do you have everyone's signature for their packets?"

"Yes, sir."

"Very well. Are there any questions? No? Carry on then," Admiral Barlow said and sat down to confer with Captain Hardee.

"Jeff, you have anything?" Admiral Edwards asked the two-star sitting at the end of the table.

"Not at this time, Eric."

The meeting broke up five minutes later, and the men gathered their papers and left for their various ships to review the information presented and then lock it securely in the ship's safe. Andy and Mason boarded the *Mariah* then adjourned to Andy's cabin.

"Sir," Mason began, "I'm a little overwhelmed to be included in this. I don't even have a safe to put this packet in at the moment."

"May I suggest the packet be placed unopened in *Mariah's* safe until after tomorrow? I have a feeling you'll be opening it after that."

"Thank you. I wonder what ship they might give me. I mean, all the destroyers in Alexandria already have a commander."

"Yes, they do. However, that can change, as you well know from past experience. Tell me, Number One, do you feel ready to face the challenge that command will bring?"

"You mean, making the final decision for the ship and her crew? Yes, I'm ready to lead a crew. I'll miss the *Mariah* and the men I learned from since those first days: Brian Jones and his navigational skills and Tim Parker are each unique. And who wouldn't want to have another Ernie and Bert—two of the best gunners—until Ernie was wounded. I still miss Quentin Patterson, who had a certain panache about him, even though John Hartman is a perfectly adequate replacement."

"I thought the same of my first ship. I wondered how I would adjust to the new crew and ship when I was promoted to sub-lieutenant and moved twice before being promoted to lieutenant and navigational officer. It suddenly hit me that, one day, I would be captain and started watching my ship's commander. I noticed he treated the ship like his child—to be guided and trained to respond. It was then that I knew my first command would be the hardest to give up, if and when the time might come."

"I believe you will be with the *Mariah* for quite some time yet," Mason said.

"Perhaps. But someday she'll have a new commander and move on without me. I thought of that a few months ago when you were left in command, and I watched the *Mariah* leave the port without me. I have to say, it was a hard pill to swallow. I'm sure Troy Edmon felt the same when he watched me sail away with her, leaving him behind."

"I guess all of us face it one day. Which reminds me, we had a signal that Mr. Barnes is due to return to England for his next level of training. We'll receive a new ensign to take his place when the time comes."

"Very well. I'll write a letter about his service aboard the *Mariah* for his packet. He's done well and proven himself to be a good sailor."

"Yes, he has. I'll let him know. I'm sure it will please him to have that on record," Mason said. "If there's nothing else, I'll set up the watch schedule before dinner."

"Carry on, Number One," Andy ordered.

After Mason left, Andy opened his packet and began to study the map. Five locations were indicated and four other unnamed destroyers as part of the group. He read through the two-page sheet of orders with dispersal assignments for the *Mariah* and the four other ships. The last paragraph indicated one destroyer would move into a small bay to land a group of engineers in a remote location.

He thought for some time about the operation and made a few notes in the margin of the orders that might keep the ships a little less vulnerable to enemy attack.

37

Joseph Albright left the last tent of wounded soldiers, twenty-five miles from the front, and looked up toward the evening sky. He marveled at the beauty of the desert and the sun sinking behind the distant hills. *How can man destroy each other when God provides such magnificence?* he wondered. He entered the tent that he shared with a young lieutenant, who was fresh out of his medical internship from England, and smiled when he noticed a letter on his bunk from Arthur Nance.

> Dear Father Albright,
>
> I wanted to write to you before seeing Katrin again to ask your permission to seek her hand in marriage. I know that a war still needs to be won, but I find myself unable to think beyond the fact that I am in love with your daughter.
>
> I do not know when I will see Katrin again in person. Her letters fill me with encouragement to give my best effort in my work to bring a swift end to this madness. I look to the future when times are settled and we no longer have men killing each other because their leaders cannot use diplomacy to settle differences.
>
> I cannot tell you my whereabouts at this time or what my work involves. I pray that the war will end soon, and

we can all return to a normal life. I can be reached at the
return address on the envelope.

Respectfully yours,
Arthur

Father Albright laid the letter aside and picked up the second
one, which was from Katrin. She wrote about the upcoming Easter
activities and what Lenten Bible studies were being offered. "It
isn't the same without you though, Dad." She mentioned hearing
from Arthur and that she missed him, "and you, of course, Dad."
She also said she didn't know when Arthur would be able to
write again. He laid the second letter aside and sat on his bunk in
thought for some time until his bunkmate entered the tent.

"I tell you, Father Albright, I wonder about some of the
doctors here at times. I'm sure that at least four of our patients
are showing signs of malaria, but I'm told I don't know what I'm
talking about—that it's just some flu symptoms going around. I
remember when we went to Cairo before being sent to the front
and what the doctor and his assistant, who gave the seminars
about the disease, said."

"You mean Dr. Jamison and Dr. Romans?"

"Yes, that's right. How do you know them?"

"We met about a year ago in Australia and became friends. Dr.
Jamison is noted for his expertise in tropical illnesses. I'm sure the
other doctors are just being cautious about starting a scare that
could hinder the army from bringing a swift end to this fighting
and killing."

"We'll see, but I think they're wrong, and that one of those
two doctors will have to come and see for themselves who does
or does not have malaria and bring the medicine for it."

The lieutenant went to the mess tent to find some dinner
before he would turn in for a few hours' rest until his shift began.
Joseph said he would be along in a bit then took up the two letters
again. He liked Arthur Nance and was sure that Katrin cared a
great deal about him, but did she love him? was the question. *I'm*

just being sentimental because it's been just her and me for such a long time. Lord, guide me, please, he prayed before tucking the letters into his kit and going to join the lieutenant.

* * *

Peter set the last patient chart on his makeshift desk and thought about the seminars he and Dr. Jamison had given the previous month. The malaria outbreak seemed to be coming to an end, and he wondered where he might be sent—now that the fighting in Africa was drawing to a close. He was glad to see an end to the struggle here but knew there was all of Europe to free before this war ended.

"Peter," Jane said when she entered his small office space. "I'm going to Helen's to pick up Jimmy."

"What...oh, okay."

"What has you so deep in thought?"

"Oh, nothing really. I was just thinking about what it will be like when the fighting ends in Africa. Each day seems to bring it a little closer."

"Maybe the news tonight will have something about it. It's been a couple of weeks since we've heard anything of substance. I suppose it's like when the war began, and the government wouldn't let any news about the current fighting be released."

"Perhaps. Well, I'll see you and Jimmy at home," Peter said as he kissed Jane before she left for Helen's.

Peter reflected a while longer about what the future might bring. *I'd like to serve at least a short while aboard a ship,* he thought. He looked at the wall clock and started at the approaching hour then quickly cleared his desk before closing up his small office and heading toward the house that he and Jane had found on the edge of the city.

* * *

Helen turned on the radio and sat down on the rocker near the window when the news began. Andy and Sally had decided to spend the evening in town, knowing that soon Andy would be at sea again. He didn't say anything about what his orders may be, but the women knew—by the faraway look in his eyes—that the quiet days of normal life were about to end.

"This is the BBC Cairo station reporting," the announcer began. "The American Army released the news on March 23 that their tank divisions defeated the Germans at El Guettar, Tunisia, squeezing the Axis Army farther north. In a like effort, we have learned, through Allied sources, the British have broken through the Mareth Line in southern Tunisia, sending the entire German Army on the run toward the port cities along the northern coast of this small country. In response to the German lines moving north, the Allied air forces have begun to bomb the last ports in Tunisia that Hitler's navy could use to evacuate their overwhelmed ground forces.

"In other news today, it was announced that ration stamps will marginally increase to families with small children as basic supplies begin to flow into the area. This is the BBC Cairo station reporting. Good evening."

Helen turned the volume down when a recording of the London Symphony began to play. *I wonder if this last fighting in Tunisia is what has Andy distracted. Maybe the ship will have to blockade the approaches to the port in Tunis or Sfax*, she thought. She sat for some time, thinking about the *Mariah* and her crew, while the soothing music softly filled the room. Looking up through the window at the star-scattered sky, she whispered a prayer for safe passage, knowing the *Mariah* would soon face a new challenge.

Two more weeks passed with little word about the mission the *Mariah* would lead coming out of headquarters. Andy reviewed the orders several times, with little change to his initial margin notes. He decided there was nothing more he could do until

Admiral Edwards contacted him and the others involved to report for a review of the mission.

The news indicated the fighting in Tunisia was becoming even tougher for the Germans when the Americans coming from the west and the British from the east linked up near Gafsa. On April 10, it was reported that Sfax seaport was taken, but heavy fighting continued as other German holdouts moved north after the official surrender by the Germans on April 11. Andy reached over and turned on the radio in his cabin then adjusted the dial until the newscast began, wondering if it might be announced that the final surrender had come in Tunisia.

"This is the BBC Cairo station reporting with the week in review. After the surrender of Sfax on Sunday last, the final holdouts of Hitler's Afrika Korps surrendered in the northern corner of Tunisia on Monday, leaving few German forces to carry on the fight for the Axis powers. In other parts of the world, the RAF carried out a nighttime raid on Stuttgard, bringing the war into Hitler's backyard.

"This reporter has learned that Berlin radio is purporting the discovery by their Wehrmacht the mass graves of Poles they say were killed by the Soviets in the Katyn massacre on Tuesday last. Our Allied leaders are investigating the report but believe it is another attempt by Hitler's Germany to cause dissent among the Allied forces. This is the BBC Cairo station reporting. Good evening."

Andy turned off the radio and indicated that the rating standing at the doorway should enter.

"Sir, a message from headquarters," the young man said, holding out the hastily scribbled message.

"Thank you. Wait just a moment in case there's a reply."

"Yes, sir," the young rating said, standing at attention in front of Andy's small cabin desk.

"At ease, son. Tell me, what do you think of the ship?"

"She's a beauty, sir. 'T'aint seen one like 'er in trainin', I's can tells you. Why, the *Mariah* is the best ship a sailor can get. I 'ad to be ta top a me class ta gets assigned ta 'er."

"Why is she so popular back in England?" Andy asked out of curiosity.

"She's got ta best a luck in 'er. Story goes, she whipped more-'n-one enemy ship tryin' ta sink 'er. And she's said to 'ave done somptin' important early on in ta war. But I guess you'd knows 'bout tat, sir."

"Yes," Andy replied with a faraway look in his eye. "Well, I hope she keeps her luck a bit longer," he said before decoding the short message. "Send a message to headquarters stating that Mr. Roden and I will report as indicated tomorrow," he ordered, returning to his role as the ship's captain.

"Aye, sir."

"Carry on," Andy said before dismissing the rating and reflecting on the stories about the *Mariah* going around England's training grounds. *If the new recruits are talking about her, we can bet the enemy knows something about her. I hope she isn't a marked ship, especially with a new mission coming up in enemy territory.*

* * *

Andy finished his weekly report and sent the package to headquarters before closing his cabin door and climbing up to the bridge. He saluted the officer on duty and reviewed the log for the day with its routine entries. He noticed, for the past several days, Mason was conducting drills with several scenarios in preparation for their mission. The men grumbled, but Mason and Andy knew that without the daily exercises, the ship would not be prepared for what they were about to face.

Entering the map room, Brian Jones noticed Andy on the bridge and opened the map-room door. "Sir, I didn't know you were aboard. Commander Roden said he would be ashore for the day and left me in charge, so to speak."

"Not to worry, Mr. Jones. I just wanted to catch up on some paperwork before returning ashore. I'm beginning to learn why other captains had spent so much time away from the ship when they were in their homeport."

"Married life is agreeing with you, then," Jones commented.

"I believe it is, yes. Tell me, do you have charts for the island formations in the area and near Italy?"

"I was just going through them in the map room. Would you like to see?"

"Yes, perhaps I should take a quick look at what we have. Has anything new been sent recently?"

"No, sir, only what we've had all along. Here they are, sir."

Brian stood back as Andy studied the charts of the surrounding islands. He paused over Sicily a moment and tapped his teeth with the pencil he held before stepping back and looking out at the bridge area. After a few minutes passed, he thanked Brian and descended to the deck in preparation to leave the ship.

Brian was picking up the charts to place them in the map drawer when something caught his eye. He studied the slight dot on the map for several moments before thoughtfully replacing it in the map drawer.

38

"Martin, Quentin, what has you looking so startled?" Helen asked when the two men arrived at her door.

"One of the American doctors doing his two-week malaria training came out of the radio room at the hospital all excited," Martin began.

"It seems that Admiral Yamamoto's plane was shot down by P-38s over Bougainville, and there are reports that he didn't survive the attack. Yamamoto is the chief architect of Japanese naval strategy," Quentin said.

"If the report is confirmed, it's a major blow to the Japanese," Martin stated.

"Could that mean they would give up the fight?" Katrin asked, coming from the kitchen when she heard Helen talking to someone.

"I wouldn't go that far," Quentin said. "But it's a major blow to them."

"Maybe Andy will have heard something. He had to go to the ship before coming back here after church today," Helen said. "He and Sally should be back before long."

It was well past dinner before Andy returned to Helen's cottage. He came into the living area where all the friends were gathered just as Martin Jamison was tuning in the evening broadcast.

"When you said for me to come ahead, I thought you would be back sooner," Sally said with question in her eyes. "We saved you a bit of the roast mutton we managed with our pooled ration stamps."

"Things took a little longer than I anticipated. Is it time for the news broadcast?"

"Just coming on," Peter said. "I wonder if there will be anything about Yamamoto's plane being shot down."

"I hope it means the Japanese will give up," Jane said when the broadcast began.

"This is the BBC Cairo station reporting," the announcer began in a solemn voice. "Today, after careful scrutiny, it is believed that Japanese admiral Yamamoto is dead. According to a news release by the American military, Yamamoto's plane was attacked by American fighter planes near Bougainville. The short statement did not indicate what air group was involved in the attack, stating they did not want them designated for annihilation by the Japanese.

"In other news, Christians marked the beginning of Holy Week in Jerusalem with the waving of palms where it is believed Christ entered the city prior to his crucifixion. This is the BBC Cairo station reporting. Good evening."

"I wonder what the Japanese will do now," Katrin said. "I...I wish Dad was here...," she trailed off, looking out the large window toward the enclosed garden. She still heard the screams from Java and hoped the Japanese would be done with the killing and torture they engaged in at the beginning of the war. She gave a small smile when little Jimmy crawled across the floor to her and lifted his arms up to sit on her lap. *At least he's oblivious to all this terrible killing*, she thought as she reached down to pick him up.

"He likes to snuggle," Jane said, beaming at her son cuddling with their friend. Looking at Katrin's troubled look, she said, "Isn't your father returning for Easter?"

"Yes, he said he would be home by Tuesday. I'm looking forward to having him back home again. His last letter was very sketchy, stating he's been busy with the troops and didn't have much time for writing. Usually, his letters are chatty, with some antidotes about his service. I suppose he's just tired with not being used to the army's routine."

Andy turned off the radio and sat for some time, listening to the conversation around him. He was pretty sure he would be returning to the *Mariah* before the month was out.

"A penny for them," Sally said that night when she and Andy retired to their bedroom.

"What? Oh, nothing really. I was just thinking about the ship and the fact we've been in port longer than usual."

"Do you think something significant is about to happen?"

"Probably no more so than usual—that is, if you can call our current situation usual," Andy said with a small smile. "Right now, I think I'd rather think about my wife." He reached for her to hold her in his arms as he lay down beside her.

"Andy," Sally whispered, "I want to give you a child, a son that will know his father helped to bring peace back to the world. I love you so much."

Reaching to kiss her, Andy murmured that he thought of her as the most precious thing in his life and gathered her into his arms with growing passion. Their words of love brought tenderness to their lovemaking until they were one with each other in the grip of passion.

When they were spent, Sally quietly said with a slight tremble in her voice, "I hope the Lord has smiled on us, and we have conceived a child tonight."

"As do I," Andy softly said before once again putting his arm around her and drawing her close to him to sleep.

* * *

Andy and Mason entered Admiral Edwards's office and saluted then stood at attention with their eyes fixed just above the admiral's head.

"Sit down, gentlemen. We have a lot to cover."

"Thank you, sir," they both responded as they drew their chairs closer to Eric Edwards's desk.

"As you know, the battle for Tunis is winding down, and we are preparing to strike at the islands just south of the boot of Italy. However, because of the increased German U-boat attacks in the Atlantic, the Americans are reluctant to make that move until something is done about the threat to their supply ships and men coming across before the landings begin."

"That seems reasonable, sir," Mason ventured. "I mean, it would be good to have the supply line less threatened."

"What do they want us do to, sir?" Andy asked with narrowing eyes.

"Well, they need to have some destroyers, with antisubmarine depth charges aboard, to help their long-range bombers sink as many U-boats as possible before the invasion begins. I have orders here for the *Mariah* to lead four other destroyers into the Atlantic near Gibraltar and sink as many U-boats as you can find. I know it's like looking for a needle in a haystack, but we have to try," Edwards said.

"A little like when we went looking for that destroyer in '42 out of Singapore," Mason said.

"Yes, somewhat," Edwards agreed. "As I recall, you sank that ship and opened the way for the refugees to pass through the Bangka Strait. Hopefully, you'll have the same results this time."

"We'll certainly try for them, sir," Andy said. "When do we sail?"

"Day after tomorrow," Edwards stated. "My aide has the orders. Captain Burns, you will serve as Captain of Destroyers.

I have every confidence you will complete the mission and return unscathed."

"Thank you, sir. We'll do our best to help open the waterways at Gibraltar and bring the group back intact."

"I'm sure you will. That is all. Good luck," Edwards said, dismissing Andy and Mason and shaking their hands before they closed the admiral's door and walked down the corridor to pick up the *Mariah*'s orders.

Once out in the sunshine, Andy turned to Mason. "I think you were right back there. It will be a little like '42, looking for that destroyer. I don't have to tell you that the mission is important. You'll have to run the ship while I try to determine where we should be looking. I feel more strongly than ever that you'll be commanding your own ship very soon."

"Sir, I'll give you all the support you'll need on the mission. I know the men will as well."

Turning toward his number one with a lopsided grin, Andy said he knew the *Mariah* would come through. "Now to go home and tell my wife I have to leave for a bit," he concluded. "I think that will be harder to do than to fight the Germans."

*   *   *

Sally knew when he opened the kitchen door that Andy had something on his mind. She set down the dish towel she was using and put her arms around him then told him to sit down and tell her what had him looking troubled.

"We have orders for the day after tomorrow," Andy said. "I don't know how long we'll be gone, but I suspect not more than a few weeks. You can't say anything, not even to my mother, until after we're gone. She can only know that my leave is up, and I have to report back to the ship. Sally, I'm to lead the group on this mission. I only hope I don't make the wrong choice and lose a ship and men because of it."

"Andy, you've led men and ships in the past and always watched out for the ship and the crew. That's why you're such a good choice to lead this mission. I know you'll do everything in your power to bring everyone back safely."

"You always make me feel right about things," Andy said. "I wish you were on the ship with me when I have my doubts."

"I wish I were with you too," Sally said, moving closer to lean against his chest and feel his arms encircle her. She sighed in contentment when Andy held her to him and rested his chin on her soft auburn hair.

39

Tim Parker closely watched as the depth charges were loaded into the racks. He noticed Bert telling a young rating to watch what he was doing: "Don't want ta be leavin' this life just yet." The sky was clear, and Mason had ordered extra lookouts just in case the Germans decided it was a good day to try a raid on the port. Tim thought it was unlikely, but one couldn't be too careful these days. A lucky hit in the right place, and there wouldn't be enough left of the *Mariah* to send to the scrapyard, not to mention the destructive force the explosion would have on the ships around them.

"All right," Tim bellowed to those on deck when the operation was completed. "I don't want to see no smokin' on this here deck. Is that clear?"

"Yes, sir," the ratings halfheartedly replied.

"I can't hear you!" Tim hollered.

"Yes, sir, Sublieutenant Parker!" the ratings loudly answered.

"All right, you're dismissed," Parker stated in his no-nonsense voice of authority.

The *Mariah* left port and was soon sailing with her companion destroyers into the Mediterranean Sea on a course heading due west. Andy consulted the chart and ordered the group to continue on its present course and speed and to keep a sharp eye out for submarines and aerial attack. Several days passed with no contacts. The Germans were occupied with trying to salvage what was left of their attempt to send troop transporters into Tunis to evacuate isolated pockets of troops and left the skies over much of the Mediterranean free of attacking planes for the present.

Andy ordered additional lookouts for all destroyers when they passed between Tunis and Italy's most southern shore in case they ran across a German transport group and support ships. Three days passed with no sighting, and he gave a slight smile when he picked up that some of the crew thought he was like a fussy old man fearing the dark. *Better to be thought of as a fussy old man than to be caught off guard*, he mused.

On April 26, the radio room picked up an Allied broadcast, and Andy ordered it to be put over the loudspeaker for the crew to hear. "This is NBC news reporting from somewhere in North Africa. Today, in a tenacious move, the British have taken Longstop Hill in Tunisia, a key position on the breakout road to Tunisia. Allied command states it is only a matter of days before the countries of North Africa are freed from the Axis swastika and returned to their rightful governments. In the meantime, British and American air forces continue to keep up the pressure on German strongholds in Europe with continual day and nighttime bombings, destroying factories and disrupting supply lines.

"In other parts of the world, pressure is continuing to force the Japanese Army to retreat, leaving behind vital supplies in their rush to evacuate whole island groups. This is NBC news reporting." The broadcast ended with the sound of the NBC trademark gongs.

"I guess we showed t'em Germans," Bert said to his fellow gunners. "I bet Ernie t'was all ears at ta news 'bout ta Japs. 'E t'was ta best gunner dis 'ere ship ever seen, Ernie t'was," he assured everyone.

"Keep a sharp look out there," Parker ordered.

"Aye, sir. We 'as just 'memberin' Ernie an' 'is keen eye wit ta guns. Wish't 'e t'was 'ere right now," Bert said with a faraway look on his face.

"He was that," Tim agreed. "Right now, we need to keep focused on spotin' a submarine tryin' to come after us. Holler if you see anything unusual in the water."

Another day passed before one of the destroyers signaled a possible sighting. Andy ordered the group to deploy in the predetermined pattern and watch for any sign of the enemy. An hour passed with no other sighting, and the group moved another two clicks on the chart toward Gibraltar. Nighttime was fast approaching, and Andy wondered if the sighting was a scout from a wolf pack, who might bring more than one submarine into their midst.

"Mr. Jones, what kind of depths do we have in a fifty-kilometer radius of our present position?" Andy asked.

"Over seven hundred feet, sir," Brian answered. "Over here," he continued, pointing his pencil at a small area, "we have even deeper water."

"Could a submarine hide beneath a water layer and follow us until his friends arrive?"

"It's possible, sir. However, they would have to charge their batteries before daylight in order to remain there."

"Yes, that's so. I'm concerned we might be moving into a trap with subs on both sides of us, preventing an escape route if we run into two wolf packs. Is there sea room to make a move north or south for about fifty kilometers before returning to our westerly course?"

"Sir, you don't paint a very nice picture of our immediate future. If we were to turn at this point," Brian said, putting his pencil on the chart, "we would be able to have about fifty to sixty kilometers to maneuver in and throw them off. That is, if we're being chased by one group into another."

"Very well, set up the coordinates, and I'll order the course change. We can't let them have it all their way."

"Yes, sir. The course is two-one-three."

"Mr. Barnes, signal the group to set their course at two-one-three."

"Sir," Barnes responded.

Mason blew into the voice pipe to order the course change five minutes later and watched as the *Mariah* made the turn with the other ships following. He scanned the deck watches to be sure they were watching the water as the *Mariah* made her turn before taking up his glasses to scan the water again. A yell from the starboard watch brought instant attention to the area in question.

The unmistakable wake of a periscope being retracted near the destroyer aft and starboard of the *Mariah* brought the crew to their battle stations. Andy ordered the group to take action and ordered the depth charges to be prepared. Within minutes of these orders, the destroyers began a pattern to give continuous depth charging to the area around the last known coordinates of the submarine stalking them. Andy hoped there was only one and that it hadn't notified its fellows that destroyers were in their path.

Water erupted from the sea as the charges exploded in the depths, sending showers of saltwater across the decks of the ships as they crisscrossed one another's paths in continuous depth charging. At one point, a small oil slick appeared, and Andy ordered the depth charging to continue until a large disturbance rose from the sea and a substantial amount of debris came to the surface.

"It looks as if we sent this one to the bottom," Mason stated.

"If not, it can't continue to attack," Andy said. "I think we'll run one more pattern a little farther south and then return to our course. That way, we may throw them off if they're still able to function."

A half hour later, the group was back on its southerly heading with no other sightings reported when it turned back to the west again. Andy could only hope the maneuver had thrown their pursuer off and would avoid being caught by another submarine pack moving west toward the Atlantic. He knew the worst attacks were taking place in the mid-Atlantic where it was hard for ships to have air cover. A few more days of sailing would tell him if he was right. Admiral Edwards had told him the Americans would be sending long-range bombers to cover the area where his group would be hunting the enemy. He anticipated today was only a skirmish, and a bigger battle lay ahead.

*   *   *

The transport ships docked in the early evening of April 30 and began to disgorge their passengers in companies onto the shore. Wesley left Arthur with the men while he reported into headquarters and secured quarters for his unit. He gave orders for the men to report to their barracks, and he and Mason headed for the officer's quarters.

Arthur waited out a long Saturday and Sunday morning before being informed their unit would have a ten-day leave. He quickly donned his dress uniform and checked his right-hand pocket before heading out the barrack's door.

"Hey, where you going so quick, Arthur?" Wesley asked.

"I'm off to see Katrin."

"Wait up and I'll walk with you as far as the hospital. I'm going to see my sister and find out how she likes married life."

The two men left a short time later and walked into the hospital together at Alexandria. Wesley smiled at the young women behind the desk and said he was looking for Sally Vilmont and Katrin Albright.

"Oh, you mean Mrs. Burns? She was married a few months ago to that handsome captain of a destroyer, you know. Katrin isn't here today, though," one of the girls replied.

"Yes, that's who I mean—Mrs. Burns," Wesley answered with a slight smile.

Sally was sputtering under her breath when she came out of the nurses' station at the disruption to her routine until she saw her brother. "Wesley! I didn't know you were coming," she said, throwing her arms around him and kissing his cheek. "And, Arthur, you're here as well. Katrin will be happy to see you, I'm sure."

"Yes, well, might she be at home?" Arthur shyly asked.

"She's at Helen's while her dad is off in the desert. I'm going there in just a few minutes. Why don't you both come along?"

* * *

"I have company," Sally said when she walked through the cottage doorway.

"Is Dad back from…," Katrin began before she saw Arthur standing just inside the doorway. "Arthur," she whispered before running into his open arms.

"I can't believe it's really you," Arthur murmured, pulling her closer to him.

"Who's here?" Helen started to ask when she came in from the sitting room and saw Arthur and Katrin along with Wesley standing with Sally. "What a surprise!" she said. "Do you get to stay longer than a few hours?"

"We have leave for a few days," Wesley said. "It's wonderful to see you, Mrs. Burns," he continued, embracing the woman who had become more than a friend to all of them.

"Mrs. Burns, it's wonderful to see you again," Arthur said, leaning over and giving Helen a peck on the cheek.

"Let's not just stand here. Come in and rest a bit," Helen said. "I want to hear everything that's happened to you both since the last time we saw you."

"We can say we've shaken the sand out of our boots," Wesley said.

"And we've had some training in our itinerary," Arthur commented.

"I see. Well, I suppose everything is classified still. I'll be glad when the world returns to normal, and there aren't so many secrets," Helen said.

"We did get to meet General Montgomery," Wesley said, thinking it might be of some interest and divert the conversation.

"You met Bernard?" Helen said. "What did you think?"

"You know him?" Arthur asked, somewhat surprised.

"Only casually. He was at a couple of gatherings I attended in England shortly before the war broke out and I returned to Malaya. He seemed pleasant enough, but I didn't really pay a lot of attention. Maybe I should have."

"He appeared very confident that we would soon be moving toward Italy and on to occupied northern Europe."

"And your thoughts, Wesley?" Sally asked.

"He's likely right, but I think his time frame is a bit off. What do you think, Arthur?"

"Oh, I don't know. He could be right. Our next move will tell the tale, I think," Arthur responded, letting his eyes drift toward Katrin.

Noticing Arthur's eyes on Katrin, Helen said, "Sally, why don't we see what we can come up with to give Wesley and Arthur some dinner? Wesley, you want to join us in the kitchen?"

"Can I help you, Helen?" Katrin asked.

"No, why don't you take Arthur out on the patio and keep him company."

"I think she knew I wanted to see you alone," Arthur said after they were on the patio.

"Why?" Katrin asked, looking up at him.

"Katrin," Arthur began and then fumbled a little with his jacket pocket. "Katrin, I wrote to your father and asked if I could…that is…," he trailed off, starting to feel his cheeks burning.

"Yes, Arthur?" Katrin said with a look of innocence in her eyes.

"Well, would you consider—oh heck, will you marry me?" Arthur finally blurted out, looking down and shaking his head at how he botched his proposal. *She probably thinks I'm a fool,* he thought.

Gently lifting his chin with her hand, Katrin looked deep into his eyes and saw the look of despair, combined with the unmistakable love he felt for her. "How could I say no to such a definite proposition? Yes, Arthur, I'll marry you."

"Really!"

"Yes, really."

Arthur opened the small box, showing her a tiny diamond ring, which he slid onto the third finger of her left hand. He held her hand in his, looking at the ring on her finger, then looked into her eyes and felt drawn to her lips. He held her in his arms for a long time, content just to be near her.

"Maybe we should rejoin the others," Katrin suggested.

The week seemed to fly by, with news that the British Seventh Armored Division, the Desert Rats, were among the first to enter Tunis once the last German line was blown open. In the meantime, the Americans reached Bizarre, Tunisia.

* * *

"And this just in," the announcer excitedly stated in the middle of the May 9, Sunday evening, broadcast. "German and Italian forces have surrendered to the British in Tunisia. Hitler can yell from Germany to his commanders in Africa to not surrender, but when the fight is untenable, even Hitler's commands go unheeded. The end of fighting in North Africa can't be far away. This is the BBC Cairo station reporting."

Dr. Jamison switched off the radio and returned to the patient files on his desk. *Churchill must be elated at the news,* he thought. *At least the malaria epidemic is ending here. Still have to keep a close watch in the islands though. Tom Linn is coming here from Australia. Maybe he can fill me in on his observations from his time with the underground in the Pacific. His letter said he wanted to discuss some medical issues that he ran across.*

Sighing, he put the last file down and prepared for bed. *I wonder how Andy is doing tonight?* he thought just before drifting to sleep.

40

Andy lay on top of his bridge cabin bunk and thought about the past few days of searching out German submarines. He heard by coded message that the Americans were having some success with long-range bombers in the Atlantic, but he knew the only real way to confirm a kill was to be nearby. So far, they had only engaged one submarine, and he was beginning to wonder if this would be a wild-goose chase. His doubts were soon dispelled with a cry from at least three lookouts reporting submarine sightings.

"Two periscopes spotted there and there," Mason tersely said, pointing toward the north and northeast of the *Mariah* with general quarters still ringing in the air.

"Notify the group. Send the prearranged signal 'fish in the sea.'"

"Torpedo in the water!" a new lookout exclaimed.

"Where?" was the only word Andy uttered before an explosion to their port signified one of the corvettes with the group was under attack.

"Hard a-starboard," Andy ordered.

"Turning to starboard," the quartermaster calmly replied.

"I see him, sir, and another there," Mason said, pointing to the two surfaced submarines.

"Prepare torpedoes," Andy ordered. "I'm going to try to take the lead one out. Have the gunners fire fifty degrees beyond to see if we can discourage his companion. Signal the group to prepare depth charges and begin the prearranged pattern. Let them know our intentions."

Andy went to the torpedo-sighting device and lined up on the submarine turned toward the corvette, giving a rare side shot at the small boat. He watched when the torpedo entered the water and sliced into the German U-boat, with a fiery explosion that caused the enemy boat to heave above the sea before disappearing beneath the waves. Cannon fire followed toward the companion boat, which quickly dove for cover and then faced the depth charging that began a few moments later.

A half hour passed before a large amount of debris and the unmistakable oil slick of a destroyed submarine rose to the surface. Andy kept the crew on station another hour before releasing them from general quarters.

"Sir, message from headquarters," the runner said, handing Andy the sheet of flash paper.

"Mr. Jones, you have the bridge. Number One, you're with me," he said. "We're to return to Alexandria," he said, a few moments after entering the map room. "Admiral Edwards sent the orders himself."

"It has all the appearance of something being in the air," Mason commented. "I'll have Brian plot a new course and signal the group."

"Ask the radio room to try and pick up the latest news about the war in the desert."

"I'll take care of it, sir."

Andy sat down in the map room after Mason left to carry out the routine orders and get the group headed back toward Alexandria. He knew the fight was pretty much over in Tunisia and wondered if the British would return to England to invade Europe in the coming months or try for Italy first.

"Sir," Mason said, breaking into Andy's thoughts, "we just heard the German Afrika Korps and Italian troops have surrendered to the Allied forces in North Africa. The Allies captured 275,000 Axis troops since last week."

Grinning a little, Andy went to the bridge and picked up the microphone. "Now, hear this," he began. "This is the captain speaking. Our army brethren have persevered in North Africa, and the Germans and Italians have surrendered. This is a debilitating defeat of Axis troops and a major victory for the Allies."

Cheering could be heard across the water as other captains gave the news to their crews. Andy was sure this had something to do with the orders they had just received and returned to his bridge chair to savor, for a moment, the victory just won before the next challenge came to the ship and her crew.

*   *   *

Sally waited, with Admiral Edwards beside her, as the *Mariah* moved into her position along the pier at Alexandria. The group had traversed the Mediterranean from Gibraltar to her present port without incident. It appeared for the moment that the Axis armed forces were not in the mood for a fight in the Mediterranean.

"All stop," Andy ordered.

"All stop," the quartermaster replied.

Mariah's engines became quiet, and soon the gangplank was in place. Andy wrote an entry into the log regarding their arrival at Alexandria and went to his quarters to pack his kit before going ashore. He noticed Admiral Edwards waiting for him and a smiling Sally at his side. Coming up to them, he saluted his admiral before taking Sally into his arms and kissing her.

"Welcome back," Admiral Edwards said. "I know you want to get home, but I need you to come to my headquarters for a moment first."

"I'll meet you at the canteen," Andy said to Sally before following Eric Edwards back to his office.

"I'll be brief. Your mission was a success, and it drew out some other U-boats the Americans were able to destroy. We intercepted a German dispatch stating that about forty or more U-boats were lost, with only thirty-four Allied ships sunk. For now, the U-boats are being withdrawn from the Atlantic, which is good, because it will open the corridor to the Americans when we make our next move."

"It's good to know our tactics are working," Andy said. "We did lose a corvette though."

"She slinked into the first Allied port on the Mediterranean and is under repair. We couldn't have done that a year ago. Now, for the next thing on the agenda. Andy, upper command has reviewed your suggestions for the Allies' next offensive. They want you at headquarters when that takes place."

"But, sir, what about the *Mariah*?" Andy asked in astonishment.

"I believe you have a first officer you had recommended for command. It is my considered opinion that he should have that command, and the *Mariah* is the ship he should command. Now, I know you think of her as your ship, but remember when Troy Edmon had to let you take command."

"Now I know how he felt. It's a hard pill to swallow," Andy said. "How soon before he takes over?"

"Oh, I think the first Monday in June would be a good time. Gives you time to turn over everything to him and let the crew know. Any thoughts on who might make a good first officer for him?"

"Brian Jones," Andy instantly replied. "He's steady and knows the sea. He also served aboard a cruise ship as first officer before joining the navy when the war broke out. He's got an uncanny way of knowing within a half mile where the ship is at any given moment. I think he's related to Davy Jones, the way he can navigate."

"*The Spirit of the Sea*. Well, I'll take it under advisement and run it past Roden once he learns he's taking command. Now, go see your wife."

Saluting, Andy left Admiral Edwards in a melancholy mood. It would take some getting used to not being aboard the ship when she left to go into harm's way the next time. He waved when he saw Sally and quickly walked over to meet her.

"You look like you've got something on your mind," she said when he came closer.

"I'll tell you once we're away from the docks."

Crinkling her brow a little at Andy's answer, she led him to the car on loan from Dr. Jamison and drove back to Helen's cottage.

Entering the door, Andy took Sally's hand and led her into the small kitchen. He shut the door and gathered her into his arms and kissed her before saying he wouldn't be leaving her for a while. "I'll be on shore when the next move is made against the Axis," he told her. "Admiral Edwards said the brass want me around for the planning of the navy's part for the invasions that are coming."

"You're not going to be on the *Mariah*?"

"It's time for her next commander to write in the logbook. Mason Roden will be taking command the first Monday in June. He doesn't know it yet. I'll tell him when I go back tomorrow to start her turnaround process."

"Andy," Sally softly said. "I know the ship is important to you, but I have to say, I'm glad you'll be here with me for now. You see…well, um…remember what we talked about the last time you slept on shore?"

"Yes, about when the war is over, where we might go."

"Well, yes, we did talk about that, but we also talked about other things. Things closer to home."

"Wait a minute," Andy suddenly said with a light coming into his eyes. "Do you mean what I think you mean?"

"We're going to be parents. What do you think?" Sally said with a mischievous grin.

"Wow! This is the best news ever. I don't think the war being over could top it," Andy said, gathering her into his arms again.

"Andy," Sally whispered with a tear trickling down her cheek, "I can't wait to give you a son."

"I'll take whatever we get. One as beautiful as her mother wouldn't be all that bad."

"There you are. I thought I heard the car on the driveway. Sally said it wouldn't take long to get you when the *Mariah* docked, Andy," Helen said, walking into the kitchen. "What has the two of you looking so excited?"

"Ma, Sally and I are going to be parents. You'll get to be a grandmother before much more time passes."

"Andy, don't joke about something so important," Helen admonished.

"He's not joking," Sally said. "We'll have a little one around Christmas. What a way to celebrate." She smiled.

"Oh, Sally, Andy, I couldn't be happier," Helen exclaimed before hugging both of them. "Wait until Martin hears about this."

"I can't wait to tell Jane. I've been bursting to tell both of you since I found out for sure."

"She'll be as excited as you were for her," Helen predicted.

*   *   *

A week passed, and Andy was preparing to leave the *Mariah* for the last time. He looked around the cabin and made sure he hadn't left anything behind. He smiled a little when he thought about the first time he had laid on the bunk and was unable to sleep, feeling like a child with a new toy. He knew the *Mariah* was much more, but the feeling from that first night stayed with him beneath the surface when it was time to take her to sea and face the enemy—with the final decision for the ship and the crew in his hands.

"Well, Number One, she's all yours," Andy said when he entered the wardroom to say good-bye to the officers.

"Sir, I'll take good care of her. We'll miss you, sir," Mason said. "I just spoke with Admiral Edwards, and he has recommended Brian Jones as first officer. I think he'll be a good one."

"I'm sure he will," Andy said. "I better get on the deck and officially turn her over to you."

"Yes, sir."

Andy walked onto the upper deck and saw the crew formed into position to receive the orders of turning the *Mariah* over to Mason Roden as her new commander. He looked at the men whom he had led for over three years and felt a sense of pride in what they had accomplished. Then clearing his throat, he read the short dispatch from the admiralty, placing the ship under a new commander. "And I know you will continue to give your all," he concluded.

"Dismissed," Mason said as his first order to the waiting crew.

Everyone gathered around Andy for a few minutes and said good-bye, stating he was a first-rate captain.

"Sir, I've been privileged to serve with you," John Hartman said, shaking the offered hand. "And tell Sally I'm happy for you both, with the news of the new baby coming."

"I'll do that, Lieutenant."

The boatswain piped Andy over the side, and the *Mariah* became a statistic in his file of service well done.

"Captain Burns," an unknown commander hailed.

"Yes?" Andy answered.

"Admiral Edmon asked me to give you this," the man said, holding out an envelope.

"Admiral Edmon?" Andy asked. "You don't mean Troy Edmon, do you?"

"Yes, sir, the very same," the man said before taking his leave.

Andy opened the small envelope and read the short note.

It looks like we'll be working together again, Number One. Stop by headquarters tomorrow morning and we'll catch up.

It was signed simply *Edmon*.

Andy thought the next months could become very interesting with Edmon back in the picture. He put the short missive in his pocket and walked to the car he had at his disposal to return home with the remainder of his belongings from the ship. He decided, hefting the large bag into the small car, that it would be a good idea to be more discerning about his personal items the next time he was at sea.

"I'm home," Andy called as he entered the cottage, only to discover he was alone. He decided to listen to the afternoon broadcast to see if he could learn anything about how the rest of the war was going. He turned up the volume when the broadcast began at the top of the hour.

"Good afternoon, this is the BBC Cairo station reporting. The Americans have confirmed that all Japanese forces have abandoned Attu Island in the Aleutians and are believed to have been taken away in the darkest hours of the night. Also, on the same day as their Memorial Day celebration, American B-17s bombed Naples, Italy, for the first time. In other news, we have learned on Friday last, General Henri Giraud has officially become the commander of the Free French forces in North Africa.

"Closer to home, just outside Cairo, a small bus with military on board overturned on a curve, leaving several soldiers with injuries, but no deaths have yet been reported. This is the BBC Cairo station reporting. Good afternoon."

Andy reached out and turned off the radio and leaned back on his chair to contemplate what Edmon might want to discuss. He had made some suggestions to the plans given him regarding the navy's involvement with the invasion of one of the islands off Italy. He didn't know which island would be invaded, but he had suggested, with its proximity to Malta and the air cover available now, that Sicily would be a logical choice. It also presented a logical jumping-off point for the invasion of Italy for many of the same reasons. He sat for some time, thinking about the plans, and brought his head up with a start when the kitchen door opened, and Sally walked in to find him dozing on a chair.

"It's rather pleasant to come home and find my husband asleep on his chair."

"I must have dozed off," Andy said with a yawn. "I'll have to start working around the house to keep from making it a habit."

"How did it go today?" Sally asked.

"With the ship? It was a little melancholy, but it's all right. It's time for Mason to take command, and he'll do a fine job. I had a note from Troy Edmon, the *Mariah*'s previous commander. He's here in Alexandria and a one-star admiral. He asked me to see him tomorrow. It could prove to be an interesting meeting."

* * *

Andy waited for some time before an aide escorted him to Troy Edmon's office. He was surprised to find Eric Edwards there as well. He saluted both men and waited until Admiral Edwards told him to have a seat.

"I suppose you wonder what this is all about," Admiral Edwards began.

"Well, I have learned over the years that the navy has a reason for its actions. It's good to see you looking fit again, Admiral Edmon."

"Yes, well, thank you, Number One. Admiral Edwards and I discussed your comments about the upcoming invasion and found them to be very astute. We want you to join our team to finalize our strategy for the British Navy's part in that invasion."

"It would be an honor to be a part of that. Are you sure you want me here and not on a ship?"

"I thought you might think that way," Admiral Edwards said. "As you know, we all take a rotation on shore duty. But this is different, Captain Burns. We need your fresh ideas to use our resources to their best advantage, as well as keeping those resources—and that includes the *Mariah*—as safe as possible. For the first time, we have an advantage, and we want to exploit it as much as we can."

"An advantage, sir?"

"You'll be brought more into the picture once we put our proposal together and take it to our superiors. We have a week to complete the plan," Edmon said. "I want you to review what you recommended, expand on it, and meet with me the day after tomorrow."

"And, Andy," Admiral Edwards said, "be as direct as you are when commanding a ship."

"I understand, sir."

"My aide will give you the most recent update. The plans are not to leave the building and must be placed in the safe in the office you'll be using whenever you leave the room—even to visit the head," Edmon said with a pointed look. "Well, that's all for now. My aide will show you where your office is and get you anything you might need."

"Thank you, sir," Andy said before saluting and leaving the room. He was met in the corridor by the same aide who had conducted him to Edmon's office. He was already thinking about how to expand on the comments he had written on the outline he had received shortly before the *Mariah* sailed on her last mission. Once in the small office with the door closed, he turned on the radio that sat on the windowsill to catch the afternoon newscast.

"This is the BBC Cairo station reporting," the announcer said. "Just ten days ago, the Japanese abandoned Attu Island in the Aleutians, and it was announced this morning that they have also abandoned Kiska Island in the Aleutians. This was the last foothold held by the Japanese in the western hemisphere. This latest victory frees the United States from the possibility of attack on their western coast.

"England continues to fight an air war over Germany, with the American Army Air Corps assisting with daylight bombing raids well into German-held territory, denying the enemy vital goods. It is reported, civilian morale is high as news of the Axis defeat in North Africa was announced over London BBC. This is the BBC Cairo station. Good afternoon."

Andy switched off the set and began writing his plan for a strategic naval bombardment of Sicily, where he felt the next offensive should take place. If Sicily became the target, he noted, the air resources on Malta would be in easy range—to not only provide fighter protection for the fleet but to also send bombers to further soften up the landing areas. He continued with the number and type of ships necessary to support the landing forces and search for submarines that could disrupt supply lines and hinder the swift conclusion of the battle.

As he continued to lay out the reasoning behind the suggested strategy, he began to wonder what part Wesley and his unit might have in the greater picture of the coming battle. He smiled to himself for a moment when he thought about letting Wesley know he was about to become an uncle. *I wonder what he'll think of that.*

41

Wesley walked across the small compound and entered Colonel Gherst's outer office area. The aide finished addressing the envelope he was typing before looking up and acknowledging Wesley's presence. "Good morning, sir. Colonel Gherst is with someone at the moment. Please have a seat and I'll let him know you are here as soon as he's free. I know he wants to discuss something with you."

"Thank you, Corporal," Wesley replied then retired to a small waiting area within the rows of file cabinets lined up like walls in order to create offices and private spaces for army personnel to work and visitors to wait. Wesley looked at his watch a half hour later and was about to say something when the aide called him.

"Morning, Vilmont," Colonel Gherst began. "Your unit will be going in early to help displace any traps the enemy may have placed before the next offensive begins. I believe you'll be sailing to your objective shortly."

"Yes, sir," Wesley acknowledged.

"It's not just another job this time," Gherst said. "This time, the British have specific time lines to meet along with the Americans. We're to get the job done quickly so we can move forward and get the Krauts out of Europe altogether. Montgomery and Eisenhower are already discussing with their governments which of them will be the overall strategist for Europe."

"I'd heard the rumor that Montgomery wants the job, but a decision has not yet been made. I would imagine the results of this next campaign will have some bearing on it. I also heard the Americans have some mighty tough generals on the ground and want to get their men moving before they become lax and forget what they learned in the desert."

"Yes, I've heard the same. Now, to business. You'll be sailing in advance of the troopships with one of the navy destroyers. They'll move as close to shore as possible. You'll have rubber rafts to move your supplies and unit to shore. The specifics, with map coordinates, will be with your orders aboard the ship when the time comes. Head inland quickly and wait for the army to catch up to you to evacuate back to the rear."

"We'll be ready, sir," Wesley assured with confidence.

"Very well. You are dismissed. And Vilmont—good luck," Gherst said before acknowledging Wesley's salute as he left the room.

*　*　*

Andy entered the small conference room with his notes and maps and took a seat next to Troy Edmon. A few moments later, Admiral Edwards entered with two army generals, and the meeting began.

"Admiral Edmon, Captain Burns," Edwards began, "I believe you have a presentation for us to consider."

"Yes, sir," Edmon said. "Captain Burns and I believe it would be best to invade Sicily at these coordinates at the southern tip of the island and work our way to Messina, just across the strait from the tip of Italy. With the additional air support out of Malta only sixty miles from the battle zone, we could have nearly continuous coverage of the area. Captain Burns has put together a plan for naval support that lists the ships and time lines for preinvasion bombing of military installations, as well as the best beaches for landing troops, tanks, and equipment to support the ensuing battles."

"Tell me, Captain, do you have any experience in strategic planning?" a two-star general asked.

"In a sense, sir. I commanded the *Mariah*, a destroyer, since late summer 1940 and participated in several sea battles, as well as smaller missions, when the ship was called on. I am familiar with how the tide effects the ease of a landing on beaches, as well as what conditions are needed for a naval force to be in place, at a given time, to bombard a shoreline before ground forces land," Andy stated. "I have copies of the plan, along with map coordinates, for you here," he continued, passing out copies of the plan to the men at the table. "I have been informed, for security reasons, each of you will need to sign your copy and add your name to each sheet of paper. I've kept it to three sheets to lessen the chance of anything being misplaced."

The meeting continued for another hour, with the army generals asking questions and referring to the map coordinates, as Andy walked the small group through the landing and first days of anticipated battles against opposing forces. He also indicated that their counterparts in the American forces would have their own ideas about when and where the landings should occur.

"Well, gentlemen," Admiral Edwards said as Andy concluded his presentation, "I believe we can meet later today to discuss these ideas before presenting them to our superiors. Remember, these plans are top secret, and no one is to view them. This meeting is concluded."

"Captain Burns, stay a moment," Admiral Edwards said as the men were leaving the room.

The door closed, and Eric Edwards smiled for the first time since the meeting began. "A credible presentation, I believe. A lot will depend on how Eisenhower receives the plans being presented, but I think things are leaning toward Sicily. The decision will be made in the next day or two, and we'll see things move quickly. His General Patton is already straining at the leash to get moving again, along with our British troop commanders. Too much time out of the battle zone, and the troops get bored just sitting around."

"I remember, from when the *Mariah* was kept in port longer than normal. Also, anticipation of what's to come next when idle for too long can be problematic."

"It won't be long now," Edwards said with a distant look in his eyes. "Well, I must get back to my office. Good work."

"Thank you, sir," Andy said, rising to leave and saluting his admiral before closing the conference room door to return to his small office. He placed the papers he carried in the office safe then went around the corner and tapped on Edmon's door. "Come," he heard before opening the door and taking the chair across Edmon's desk.

"We'll be at sea by July," Edmon predicted. "I anticipate being with one of the destroyers during the bombardment. My guess is we'll be transferred to the next liberated area before winter comes."

"If we liberate Sicily this summer, we very well could see Italy invaded by early fall. That would undermine their current government and possibly topple one of the Axis partners. There were some powerful people that didn't want to partner with Germany, and they might use force to bring an end to the fighting."

"You could be right. We'll have to see what the next few months will bring," Edmon concluded.

Andy left the building an hour after conferring with Troy Edmon and headed home as if it was a normal day for dinner and an evening listening to the radio. A week passed with no news regarding the plans Andy presented to the small group of army-navy personnel. He turned the radio on Thursday evening and sat down to hear the nine-o'clock news.

"In a brief news release, the RAF reports Allied bombing of Sicily and the Italian mainland for the first time. No other information was related. This is the first bombings in the area since Friday last, when British forces secured Pantelleria and Lampedusa between Tunisia and Sicily, after several days of heavy bombing attacks. In other news, it appears—"

Andy switched off the radio and looked out over the water for some time. He wondered when the decision was made and anticipated the *Mariah* would soon be sailing—without him in command. Sally found him sitting in the rocking chair deep in thought an hour later and asked what had him looking so serious.

"Oh, nothing. Just thinking about the future a bit is all. Didn't mean to wake you."

"I wasn't really sleeping. What has you looking so distant?"

"I'm thinking about the next move...and wondering when it will be."

"Why don't we sleep on it?" Sally said, reaching out her hand.

Andy turned off the small lamp on the stand next to the chair and slipped his hand into Sally's. He believed the upcoming invasion would be soon by the number of soldiers he saw reporting in each day at army bases and sailors preparing ships for battle. He also knew waiting for word of the outcome, instead of being engaged in the battle, would be far more difficult than anything he had faced thus far in this war. He wondered when the *Mariah* would sail and what she would face in the battles to come. He turned his head once more to look at Sally peacefully sleeping beside him and smiled before allowing himself to drift into sleep.

42

Mason walked onto the bridge and quickly looked around the ship—his ship. He knew, from talking with Andy Burns, the decisions he will make will affect every person aboard her. His new first officer stood a few feet to his side, waiting for the first command to bring the ship to sea. Mason watched the navigator, come first officer, bring the ship to battle readiness, with a sense of determined ease about his duties. He remembered the first time he went to sea as first officer, wondering if he would live up to the position with Andy Burns in command.

"Sir," Brian Jones said. "The ship is ready for sea. Passengers are aboard and housed in the wardroom. Equipment is below decks."

"Very well," Mason responded. "Let's take her out. Let go moorings. Let go spring," he ordered and watched as the ship began to swing out into the harbor. "Left rudder. All ahead one-third."

"All ahead one-third," the quartermaster responded.

The crew quickly curled the mooring ropes to prevent them from tangling in the screw and took their places for leaving harbor. Once the *Mariah* was freed from the land, the Union Jack was raised at the piped command, and the ceremony of leaving harbor began. The only difference from peacetime was the number of lookouts on duty who were ready to sound the alarm should the enemy choose that moment to make an appearance.

Mason scanned the sky when the *Mariah* entered the Mediterranean Sea a half hour later. "Post lookouts, general routine," he ordered before moving to the captain's chair. It felt strange to be sitting down while others carried out the routine chores of a ship at sea. He knew *Mariah*'s previous commander had felt the same way when he sat in the chair for the first time. Troy Edmon was the captain then, and Andy Burns, as first officer, had to take over when the captain was severely wounded on that special journey the *Mariah* made out of London in 1940. It didn't seem possible that three years had gone by, and the world was still at war.

* * *

Andy Burns watched the *Mariah* leave the harbor, feeling like a father watching his child leave home to venture out on its own. He then wondered how he would feel when his real child began the journey to adulthood. He knew this was the beginning of the next step to free Europe from the Axis swastika that covered the land like a shroud. More ships were preparing to sail within a day or two, and other harbors farther west were loading men and equipment to land on the enemy's next stronghold. He had heard the Americans were also preparing to land at the enemy's doorstep in the fight for freedom.

"Burns," Edmon said, walking into Andy's cubicle. "I see the *Mariah* has sailed. I had felt the loss when you sailed her away the first time, watching out the hospital window."

"Does it get any easier?"

"You learn to live with it. Admiral Edwards wants us to report to him right away."

"Thank you, sir. I'll be right there," Andy responded before reaching for his hat from the top of the file cabinet.

Andy and Troy Edmon were ushered into Eric Edward's office without ceremony when they arrived across the compound. "I won't beat around the bush," Edwards said. "We are going for Sicily on July 10. Command wants an observer aboard one of the ships bombarding the shoreline prior to the landings. I'm sending you, Troy."

"Yes, sir."

"It will be a short mission. You fly to Tripoli on the sixth and board the *Victoria*. I think you're familiar with her."

"Yes, sir. Her captain is a good man."

"Yes, well, your orders will be ready by the fourth. I don't need to tell you this is top secret."

"Yes, sir."

"Once the initial landing takes place, I have orders for you to sail with the *Mariah* to England while she does escort duty. I believe they have a job for you in planning for the big one to come across the English Channel."

Giving a brief smile, Troy Edmon nodded before saying he was sure Hitler would be quite surprised at what the next year may bring. Turning to Andy, he said, "Number One, keep your head down. I might just have a job for you in a few months' time."

"I'll do my best, sir."

*　*　*

Wesley entered Mason's cabin and took the seat across from his desk. "It seems a little strange the first time in this cabin that Andy isn't here. I can't say that Sally is sorry he isn't here though. Let me congratulate you on your promotion as commander."

"Thank you, Wesley. I know it will take a little getting used to. I'm just glad the crew was left intact. It will make it a little easier at the first sign of trouble, knowing what to expect from them."

"That is a plus these days. I'm glad I still have Arthur, but he should be leading a unit of his own. I'll miss him when the time comes. Well, to business. I understand my unit's orders are in your safe. Might I take a look at them, now that we're at sea?"

"Of course. I have them right here," Mason said, placing a sealed envelope on his desk.

Wesley unfolded the short, terse bullet-pointed orders and quickly read them before extracting the map and reading the orders more slowly while referring to the map periodically. He then slowly folded the pages and put them back in the envelope with a thoughtful look on his face before handing the packet back to Mason.

"Is something wrong?" Mason asked.

"What? Oh, no...I was just trying to visualize the area where we'll go ashore. I'll have to bring Arthur up to speed, and I'm sure he'll have some ideas as well."

"We'll be at the coordinates tomorrow at about midnight. My orders are to send you ashore, using the rubber rafts, and to sail to new coordinates to give you the best opportunity to get ashore without being discovered. If you run into trouble at the beach, the *Mariah* will send the tender as close to the shore as possible to pick you and your unit up. It would mean a bit of a swim."

"Since I'm not one for dipping into the sea, I guess we better not run into any trouble."

Wesley left Mason after sharing a cup of coffee and relating that just before leaving for the mission, Sally had announced that she and Andy were going to have a baby, which brought a broad smile to Mason's face. He walked down the familiar passage, remembering the other times he was aboard the ship, and hoped the outcome of this mission would be as successful. Maybe the *Mariah* was a lucky ship, as the scuttlebutt below the decks had said.

Entering the wardroom, Wesley signaled Arthur to join him. "We have orders to land on a beach on Sicily and move inland to disrupt communications and work with the paratroopers to secure bridges at certain strategic points. The landings will take place the day after we go ashore. Now I know why we spent so much time crawling through the mud in England. I'll bring the orders down tomorrow afternoon so that you can study the map coordinates, and we can decide how we want to deploy the men."

"That sounds good, sir. When will we be going ashore?"

"A little after midnight tomorrow night. There's supposed to be an abandoned building, not far from where we go ashore, that we can hold up in once the shelling starts."

"The chaos should work in our favor," Mason said. "We can also set out some traps before daylight to help add to the disruption the Axis armies are about to behold."

The *Mariah* slowed until she glided to a halt at the designated coordinates the following night. The lower deck was suddenly awash with men and equipment, which was to be put over the side as quickly as possible.

"Get those rafts in the water," Tim Parker ordered. "Quickly. You're slower than an old man after a few pints at the local pub."

"How's it going, Mr. Parker?" Brian Jones asked.

"Fine, sir, just fine. But I'll be a lot more at ease once we're underway again," Parker replied. "You there, get that box over the side. Be quick about it," Tim hollered to one of the men standing on the deck.

"Carry on, Mr. Parker," Brian said before returning to the bridge to report on the progress.

"How much longer, Mr. Jones?" Mason asked.

"Shouldn't be long, sir. Tim Parker has everything under control."

"Always good to know he's on the deck at times like these," Mason responded then turned to Wesley. "Best of luck. I'm sure I'll see you around," he said, extending his hand.

Shaking Mason's hand, Wesley nodded then clambered down to the deck where Arthur had the men and equipment on the rafts. Wesley quickly scrambled down the net, signaled to let go of the ropes, and began paddling toward the shore. He watched, when they were about two hundred yards away, as the *Mariah* slowly moved away from the area. It seemed an eternity before they landed on the beach.

"Okay," Wesley softly said. "Let's get this equipment unloaded then hide the rafts in those bushes over there."

The men soon had the boxes of explosives and their machine guns out of the rafts and then headed inland. Wesley halted them when the building where they were to hide came into sight. "Sergeant Moore, take a couple of men and make sure the building is clear," he ordered.

"Percy, Oran, come with me," Moore ordered before starting toward the building.

Using hand signals, Moore directed the two men to circle around to the back while he looked in the small front-door window. No light came through the curtain over the window, and there was no sound coming from inside. He waited for the other men to return before deciding whether to walk in or to use another strategy.

"'T ain't nothin' behind the place," Oran reported. "I tried the backdoor handle and 't isn't locked."

"Okay, we go in through the back," Moore decided. "Be ready, in case we run into somebody."

A half hour later, the last of the equipment was stored inside the empty building. When Moore and his two helpers entered the building, the only thing they found was an old wooden boat with a hole in its hull.

"Well, at least headquarters got something right," Arthur said once they were settled inside. "Do you want me to take a couple men and set a few traps for our German friends farther inland? I think there's a town about two or three miles up that road at the top of the hill."

"I want to take a look at that map again first," Wesley said. "We could split up and meet back here at o-four-thirty," he continued, tracing his finger over a line on the map. "How about here and here?" he indicated, looking over at Arthur, who was also closely studying the map.

"I'll take Jenkins and a couple of men with me, and we might get some transportation as well," Arthur said.

"Okay, get those explosives and timers there," Wesley indicated to Sergeant Moore and pointed to several men to help them.

Five minutes later, the two groups cautiously walked up the hill to the side of the road and worked their way toward their first objectives.

43

Helen answered the front door of her small Alexandria residence when Martin Jamison arrived for the dinner party with the friends from Helen's Landing and Java. She had discussed, a few days previous, the possibility of them moving back to England now that North Africa was free of the Axis-occupying armies.

"Helen, I've brought a friend to join us this evening who might be able to help with getting us back to England," Martin said when Helen opened the cottage door. "I want you to meet—Admiral Eric Edwards."

"A pleasure to meet you," Helen said. "There's always room for another at our table."

"That's very gracious of you, Mrs. Burns," Admiral Edwards replied.

"Ma, is that—Admiral Edwards, I didn't know you were coming," Andy said, somewhat surprised. "Please come and join me in the sitting room. My wife will be out in a moment."

"Martin, what's this all about?" Helen asked after Andy escorted Admiral Edwards to the sitting room.

"I believe, a way to get back to England. When will the others be here?"

"They should be arriving anytime now."

A half hour passed before Jane and Peter arrived with Jimmy. Katrin and Father Albright were a few minutes behind them.

"Now that we're all here, let's go to the dining room and talk while we have our dinner. I think Jimmy's waited about long enough for his supper," Helen said.

Once settled, Helen asked Andy to offer the blessing. He ended by asking for guidance to those planning where the armed forces would be moving to next.

"Eric, why don't you explain to everyone how a move back to England might be accomplished?" Martin Jamison said once their plates were filled.

"Well, it's pretty simple, really. You see, Martin, Captain Burns, and Lieutenant Romans are under my command, and I am able to order them to any location where they might be needed. Since Captain Burns and Lieutenant Romans are also married, the navy will, if not a danger to civilians, relocate spouses and children to where their men are reassigned. Now, as for Captain Burns's mother, she is living with Captain Burns and, consequently, considered dependent on him for shelter and necessary essentials."

Peter looked up from his plate with a look of astonishment— that his fate rested so precariously in the hands of one man. "You mean, sir, that should you determine one of us was needed any place in the world, you could send us there?"

"That's it, precisely, Lieutenant. On the other hand, the navy doesn't move personnel without carefully considering the individual's job description, and tries to match that person to the most appropriate assignment."

"I think Admiral Edwards is saying, there has to be a specific job vacancy before anyone would be relocated," Andy explained.

"That's good for most of us, but what about Father Albright and Katrin?" Helen asked. "We can't just leave them here should Andy, Peter, and Martin be relocated."

"Yes, Eric, what about them? Also, if I were sent to England or any other place, I'd want to take Quentin Patterson with me. He's essential to my team and also one of the best surgeons England has produced in the last few decades."

"Katrin and I would be subject to the Church of England," Father Albright said. "The bishop would decide where I am assigned, and Katrin, of course, would come with me. However, she is engaged to Arthur now and, when married, will go wherever he may be assigned, unless it's in a combat zone. I believe he plans to return to civilian life as an engineer once the war ends."

"I just want to be sure any move is safe for Jimmy to travel," Jane said. "Our little adventure when we had to leave Helen's Landing was dangerous enough. We should be cautious about any definite plans until we know how we would get there."

"I agree, Jane," Sally said. "Andy, a lot would depend on whether you're at a base or at sea as to where Helen and I should be. Admiral Edwards, you've given us a lot to think about."

"Nothing would be done until we are closer to clearing the Axis armies and navy out of the Mediterranean," Eric Edwards said. "Right now, that is our focus of concentration. The navy will focus on the next steps to ridding the world of the tyrants that are currently cursing the world with their grab for power."

"Would anyone like more of Katrin's dessert?" Helen asked, to bring the dinner party back to a normal sense of conversation.

"Thank you, no," Peter said, laying down his fork. "Even Jimmy isn't able to eat any more," he said when he observed his son pushing the spoonful of food being offered away from him.

"He takes after his father," Jane said with a small grin on her face.

"Why don't we retire to the sitting room and catch the evening news?" Andy suggested.

Andy turned on the radio and let the tubes warm up before turning up the volume and tuning in the local BBC. The group of friends heard an excited announcer begin the broadcast:

"This is the BBC Cairo station reporting. In an all-out offensive, the British Eighth Army landed on the southwestern tip of

Sicily on July 9 with General Montgomery leading our troops. The Americans, with Lieutenant General George Patton commanding, landed as well, along a hundred-mile strip. Heavy naval and aerial bombardments of enemy positions allowed approximately 150,000 Allied troops to reach the Sicilian shores and bring heavy armored equipment and numerous tanks to support the offensive. According to official reports, the landing went without a hitch, and German and Italian defenses were light.

"In other news, this past Monday, the Red Army has taken Belgorod while the battle in Kula Gulf, near the Solomon Islands, has ended. This is the BBC Cairo station reporting. Good evening."

Andy reached up and turned off the radio when a new hair tonic commercial began. "Well, it looks like the waiting is over for our next move against the Axis," he began to say when the phone rang. He rose to answer it in the hallway alcove. A few minutes later, he returned and said, "Admiral Edwards, we have to report to headquarters. I believe it might have something to do with what we just heard on the radio. Sally, Ma, don't wait up. It could be a long night."

"I thought we might have to return," Admiral Edwards responded. "Mrs. Burns, thank you for a delightful evening and a good meal before the long nights begin at headquarters."

"You're most welcome. Please join us anytime," Helen replied, offering her hand.

"I better get back to the hospital as well," Dr. Jamison said. "Peter, once you get Jane and Jimmy home, report back to the hospital. We better set up some plans for the wounded that will be evacuated back to us."

"I shouldn't be very long," Peter answered.

"Helen, a delight as always," Father Albright said as he and Katrin left. "Don't worry about us. I'm sure the Lord will send Katrin and me where we will be needed when the time comes."

* * *

Wesley carefully peeked over the rocky mound at the remaining Italian defenders on the outskirts of the town. Their orders were to create chaos a few hours before the shelling was to begin. He was wondering if the invasion would continue on schedule when he saw storm clouds approaching the area. He signaled for Sergeant Moore to join him and pointed to a building about one hundred yards to the left. Pointing to three men, he indicated they should maneuver around the perimeter to the other side of the building beneath a small knoll. Moore nodded, and the men carefully moved out of sight for several minutes before Wesley saw the signal that they were ready.

Wesley and another man in the unit pulled the pin on two hand grenades and counted to five before throwing them beneath the armored truck sitting at the main roadway into the village. A moment later, the truck was destroyed, along with the two men standing beside it. Wesley and his men quickly ran into the building on the corner and took the explosives they carried to the upper floor before more soldiers arrived. They were in a prime position by the time another truck arrived, led by an armored car containing two officers and their driver.

Wesley waited until all of the men were out of the truck and one of the officers was giving orders before signaling Moore with a mirror to begin the attack. Two explosives fell onto the top of the truck, which exploded a moment later, lifting it off the roadway and depositing it twenty feet away on its side. Several men were wounded in the blast, and a few began firing their machine guns wildly toward the rocks, spitting up bits of stone and gravel. The firing stopped when the officer in the armored car quickly stood up and shouted orders to cease firing. He looked up at the building to see if someone was on the roof and missed the next move made when Moore and his squad charged over the knoll of the hill while Wesley and his men pointed machine guns down through the building's upper windows, indicating the remaining Italian soldiers should drop their weapons.

"A very clever move. My compliments," the Italian officer said after the enemy soldiers and their weapons were gathered up. "Tell me, might you have an American cigarette?"

Wesley reached into his pocket, offered the man a Pall Mall, and lit it before speaking. "Are there any more of you in this lovely little village?"

"I'm afraid I cannot tell you that," the officer replied, sending a cloud of smoke toward the heavens. "It is something you will have to discover for yourself."

"Very well. I'm sorry, I don't know your name."

"Captain Marino, Italian Army. What will you do about my wounded men?"

"We'll do what we can, Captain. If you have a doctor in the village, it would be beneficial to summon him here until our medics arrive."

"I cannot do that either."

"Very well," Wesley said. "For now, you will join your men in the building behind us."

Wesley followed the captured Italian captain into the building and told Moore to do what he could to make the wounded men comfortable. He ordered two other men to move the bodies of the dead out of sight and to put the armored car behind the building. He wondered how Arthur was coming along with his area, a few kilometers farther inland above the village.

* * *

The *Mariah* moved into position among the British naval vessels, preparing to bombard the eastern Sicilian shoreline. The heavy summer storm, which nearly cancelled the operation, was abating as Allied forces descended on the small island in force. Bomber planes out of Malta would soon be overhead, ready to drop their payloads on strategic inland positions, giving the army a chance to come ashore and establish a beachhead before moving inland to secure the island.

Mason ordered the ship to slow when the lead ship signaled the group was in position. Their orders were simple: attack with full strength along the assigned shoreline to soften up the enemy's defenses. Mason wondered how Wesley and his unit were faring and where they would be while *Mariah* pounded the beaches with artillery fire. He remembered another time the *Mariah* had been sent to soften up the beaches before the doomed British soldiers landed on the southern Malaya Peninsula in a desperate effort to stop the flow of the Japanese driving through the jungle toward Singapore.

"Sir, signal from the leader. Two minutes," Roger Barnes reported.

"Very well," Mason replied. He keyed the bridge microphone, causing the speakers to crackle for a moment, before he spoke. "In less than two minutes, we fire our guns to help the army successfully land on Sicily. I know you will all do your best to hit our assigned targets and bring victory against the occupying enemy that we face. Stay alert for enemy ships and let our gun barrels become hot from a quick reload to fire at the Axis resistance. Fire!" he ordered a moment later and listened as the first shells expelled themselves from *Mariah*'s guns, followed by a second and third explosion of fire, before the first shells hit the shore.

"Up two hundred, fire!" Tim Parker ordered as he followed the shells to shore through his glasses. Judging by the impact point, he discerned the gun-angle adjustments until he saw the shells causing damage to emplacements along the beaches.

Mason watched as Brian Jones descended the ladder as first officer and realized, once again, that command meant being alone yet surrounded by subordinates while waiting for information so that the right decision could be made for the ship and her crew. He had to trust not only his first officer to bring the good and the bad to his attention, but also his new navigator to keep the *Mariah* on the correct course. He hoped, as Andy Burns had hoped, that the newly promoted officers, himself included, would have time to learn the jobs of war in order to keep the *Mariah* safe.

The bombardment continued into the morning hours while bombers flew overhead in greater numbers. The crew witnessed landing craft nearing the shore, with several thousand troops scrambling onto the beach against little resistance as Operation Husky unfolded before them. The guns continued to fire farther inland while more bomber planes flew farther inland to shatter strongholds and break the resistance to the liberating forces coming ashore.

"Sir," Roger said in the early afternoon. "We are ordered to cease-fire after the next run and return to Alexandria for further orders."

"Very well," Mason responded. "Mr. Anderson, set a course for Alexandria."

"Yes, sir," Anderson replied. "If we turn southeast to course one-two-seven at a speed of fifteen knots, we will arrive at Alexandria by the afternoon of the twelfth, sir."

"Very well. Helmsman, set a southeast course of one-two-seven, speed fifteen knots," Mason ordered.

"My course is southeast at one-two-seven, speed fifteen knots," the helmsman crisply replied a few moments later.

"Mr. Jones, you have the bridge," Mason said. "I'll be in my sea cabin if you need me."

"I have the bridge," Brian Jones answered and stepped to the center of the bridge. He hoped for a quiet voyage and time to drill the men until he was confident they would all respond when the time came to defend the ship against attack and until he was surer of his own abilities in a time of trial.

* * *

Arthur carefully looked around the corner of the ancient building along the quiet street. He saw one Italian officer's car, two per-

sonnel trucks, and one guard walking out of the building. He signaled one of his men to look along the next street to be sure this
was the only place where anyone was present. His small group
had heard the armored car leave earlier from the other end of
town. A sudden burst of gunfire in the distance brought several
men running out of the building, boarding the trucks, and an
officer and a driver got into the car. Arthur counted to ten then
signaled for the charges that they had planted during the night at
the edges of the town, to explode.

"Get to the next block," Arthur whispered to his men and
ran at a crouch to the cover of a small garage, where he watched
the rest of the people from the barracks building empty into the
street. The personnel truck shifted into second gear before the
next explosion sent it careening into a storefront.

"Hats got 'em," Private Hardy said.

"There's still several more to deal with," Arthur said. "Get
the other men and go to the flower shop that we reconnoitered
earlier. Keep out of sight."

"We'll be careful, sir. What will you be doin'?"

"I'll be along in a minute. I want to see what that officer
will do next. If it was me, I'd be mighty cautious before making
another move."

Arthur watched the Italian officer look about, confused, until
he ordered the remainder of his guard force to begin scouting
the area in pairs for the cause of the explosions. Arthur saw some
men starting toward the old garage that he was behind across the
street and decided it was time to retreat to the flower shop for
better cover.

"I didn't think you'd ever get here," Private Hardy said. "We
was gettin' worried."

"The enemy guard force split up into pairs to look about the
area that we just left. Give them about another five minutes then
set off the next explosion. I want to draw them closer to Major

Vilmont's position so that we can take them from both sides before the bombardment starts."

Arthur and his men continued the cat-and-mouse game by setting off two more explosions, which drew the remaining officer and his men toward the building where Wesley was waiting for the signal to attack from the south while Arthur's men drew closer in from the north, until the remaining enemy was in a pocket, surrounded by Wesley's unit. A loud whistle brought Sergeant Moore from the west, Jenkins from the east, and Wesley and his two men from the south.

"Tell your men to drop their weapons," Arthur instructed the officer in perfect Italian when he suddenly appeared with a machine gun in his hands at the side of the car, where the officer and his driver sat at a standstill. "I wouldn't consider doing anything such as trying to draw your pistol," he said a moment later to the driver. "I really don't want to use this. Now, slide out real easy and walk over there with the rest of those men. You can leave your guns behind."

The rest of his men came out from their hiding places and quickly gathered up the guns while Moore came running in from the west and Jenkins from the east. Wesley approached a few moments later and saw the situation was under control.

"I heard gunfire earlier. Is everyone okay?" Arthur asked when he saw Wesley approaching.

"We had some resistance, but none of our men were injured. We have prisoners. Some of them are wounded. I see you managed to take some as well. We're set up in what looks like an old shipbuilder's shop. We should be out of the line of fire there."

Wesley's unit, along with their prisoners, entered the old shop and settled in to wait for the army to come. At o-four-thirty, the first shells whistled overhead and landed about five hundred yards from their position.

"Hope they don't take out shipbuilding shops," Moore said.

"As long as we stay put, we'll be okay," Arthur said. "I expect we'll see some of our own before too much longer, coming over the hill out there."

"Just as long as they don't mistake us for the enemy," Private Hardy said.

"That could be interesting," Wesley said. Turning to Moore, he said, "Make sure the prisoners are secured and set up a guard schedule, Sergeant."

"Yes, sir. Jenkins, come with me. You heard the major."

The shelling continued into the morning as Wesley's unit kept watch for the first British soldiers from the beachhead to come up the sandy hill.

44

Dr. Jamison sat down in his office and tuned the wireless set to catch the noon broadcast. Quentin Patterson sat across the desk from him and leaned forward when the announcer came on the air.

"This is the BBC Cairo station reporting. Today, Allied command released this brief statement, and I quote, 'On Friday, July 9, British Eighth Army, under General Montgomery, landed on the southern tip of Sicily. This is part of a full-fledged invasion of Nazi-held territory by Allied forces along a hundred-mile strip. The offensive, named Operation Husky, has seen light resistance from the enemy, allowing our forces, armed with tanks and armored vehicles, to push north from the east and west to rout the enemy from the island.

"In other news, we have learned on Monday, July 12, Russian tanks engaged German Panzers near Prokhorovka, Kursk, in the Ukraine. After an unprecedented exchange of fire between the opposing tank divisions, the Soviets defeated German defenses and called it a 'pivotal turning point in the battle for Kursk.' This is the BBC Cairo station reporting. Good afternoon."

"Well, Martin, it looks like the Allies are on the move again," Dr. Patterson said after Dr. Jamison switched off the radio.

"Yes, it does seem that way."

The two men talked for another fifteen minutes about critical patients and what remedies to use before leaving to make afternoon rounds. Once orders were written, the nurses were able to carry many of them out with minimal explanation because of the treatment plans Peter had sketched out for the most common battle injuries.

* * *

A week had passed since the invasion of Sicily began, and Wesley's unit was once again working under Colonel Gherst as an engineering unit. They were moving with a company from Montgomery's Eighth Army to build a temporary bridge so that tracked and armored vehicles would be able to cross the small river beneath the next town on the map to be liberated. Wesley knew it could be dangerous work. He only had to remember the other bridge in France that he and his men were sent to destroy to stop the Germans from crossing the river when he was wounded and evacuated by the *Mariah*. He shook his head when he thought about the odds of ever seeing the ship again, let alone how she had saved the refugees from Helen's Landing when the Japanese nearly caught up with them.

"Major, we'll be at our destination in a few minutes," Moore said, cutting short Wesley's musing.

"Thank you, Sergeant. Tell the men to be ready to get this job done quickly. The first company of tanks is just a few hours behind us. Post a couple of men to watch for any Germans that might be about as well. I don't fancy spending the rest of the war in a cold prisoner-of-war camp."

"Will do, sir. I t'aint got no desire ta spend time with t'em no accounts."

Arthur soon had the first span of the bridge ready to be laid and ordered the truck that brought it to be moved out of the way. He was bending over to check a connection when a bullet whistled overhead from the other side of the river. Quickly rolling under the truck, which now had a flat tire, he squinted into the sun that reflected off the water and saw movement in the bushes on the riverbank.

"That was gunfire," Wesley hollered. "Get that army captain on the radio and tell him to get a move on. We're under fire," he ordered.

Jenkins scrambled to the Land Rover at the rear of the small column of vehicles, grabbed the portable radio, and began calling for the army unit behind them. "I don't care what he's doin', Private. Major Vilmont said to get him here pronto."

"This is Captain Hendricks. What do you need, Major? Over."

"We're under fire. We need some guns up here right now if you want to cross that river anytime soon," Wesley said.

"There's not supposed to be anyone within five miles of this place," Hendricks said. "You sure it's on the other side of the river and not one of your men accidentally shooting off their gun?"

"Look, Captain," Wesley said as another bullet ricocheted off one of the bridge spans, "I don't care what your map says. Get some men here now. That's an order. Out."

Wesley signaled for Private Hardy and another man to move farther east while he sent two more men west to see if they could determine just how many hostiles were on the other side of the river that weren't supposed to "be within five miles of them." He wouldn't risk trying to flush them out, until he had a better idea of what they might be up against. His concern was whether or not they had a radio to call in reinforcements that would halt the operation altogether.

Fifteen minutes passed before Captain Hendricks pulled up and hopped out of his Land Rover. He started walking over to where Wesley was crouching behind a transport truck when a bullet struck the dirt a few feet from where he stood.

"Now you believe me, Captain? I've got a couple of my men scouting the situation to see how many might be over there."

"So much for intelligence. I'll get the unit moving. Maybe we can fire a couple of mortars and rout them out."

Private Hardy and the other man scurried to the back of the truck where Wesley and Captain Hendricks were and reported not being able to see anything from farther down the river. A few minutes later, the two men from the west said the same. "And Captain Nance is still under the truck at the front there," Hardy said. "Every time he tries to move back, they shoot at him."

"Okay, see if you can give him some cover fire. Maybe he can roll to the other side of the truck and work his way out of range," Wesley said. "Captain, how long will it take before your artillery gets here?"

"Should be here now," Hendricks replied. "I told them to move it along."

Arthur heard the machine-gun fire from behind him and knew this was his chance to make a break for the rear. Carefully inching his way to the opposite side of the truck, he rolled out and quickly pulled himself up into a crouch and ran. Bullets whistled over his head and spit at his heels as he made the effort to get out of the enemy's line of fire. Hardy and Jenkins continued to send machine-gun fire across the river until Arthur came up alongside them. He moved behind the truck that they were using for cover and collapsed to the ground, feeling like his lungs were on fire from the exertion.

"Thanks, fellas," he said between breaths. "That was a close one."

"Yes, sir," Jenkins replied. "You best catch your breath before we make a run for the back of the line here."

Hardy turned around, looked at Arthur, and exclaimed, "Sir, you got blood comin' outta your side here. Corporal Jenkins, we need to get 'im to a medic an' quick, it looks like."

"Just a scratch is all," Arthur said. "Nothing to fuss about. Let's get back to Major Vilmont."

The three men made their way to the back of the small convoy, where Wesley was talking to the artillery officer about getting the mortars across the river and not to hit his bridging equipment. It took another twenty minutes to get the artillery gun in place and set up the trajectory before the guns opened fire and sent the shells soaring into the place where the attack on the engineers began. Captain Hendricks placed a few men farther along the river to intercept any enemy soldiers who might escape the artillery bombardment. Ten minutes later, all was silent, and a few men from the army unit took one of Wesley's rubber rafts to cross over and see if any more Germans were about the area.

"Sir," Arthur quietly said, "the first span is ready to be placed."

"Arthur, you don't look so good," Wesley commented. Then he saw where Arthur's side was bleeding. "Corporal, take Captain Nance to the rear for medical attention. Arthur, why didn't you call for help?"

"I thought it was just a scratch. Must have hit a vein or something," Arthur said, holding his side. "The rest of the components are lined up and shouldn't take more than a couple hours to span the river now that the bullets have stopped flying," he said before carefully getting into the Land Rover beside Jenkins.

* * *

Katrin came in from the small patio when she heard her father close the front door. "Hello, Kitten, I'm home," Father Albright said as he closed the door. "I've got mail."

"Glad you're home," Katrin said, leaning over to kiss his cheek.

"I think Arthur has written from the looks of it. He might be swimming in the Mediterranean, the way the army is moving through Sicily. You'd think Hitler and Mussolini would just give up as listlessly as their army is resisting the Allies there."

Katrin opened the letter, and her face changed as she read the short missive Arthur had sent.

"What is it?" Father Albright asked when he saw her sudden look of alarm.

"Arthur says he's writing from an army hospital that's set up in the rear of their lines. He says, 'I just got a scrape on the side, but it nicked a vein, and they had to sew me up. Doctors say I have to stay here another week before I can get back to my unit. I feel fine and think they're wasting a bed that someone else could use.'"

"It sounds like he'll recover fully. I wouldn't worry, Kitten. We'll add him to the prayer vine on Sunday, just to be sure."

Giving a small smile, Katrin said it was a good idea. By the time they were to leave for Helen's to meet with Dr. Jamison and the others, she felt better about Arthur's recovery when she remembered he was in God's hands through their prayers. She hoped Dr. Jamison would bring news about returning to England. She remembered very little about her native country since she was only a small child when her father took the post in Surabaya. When she was old enough, she went to a British school that was established for the children of diplomats at the consulate and wasn't sent to boarding school in England—like so many of the landowners' children. She thought it odd that she was British and unfamiliar with nearly anything about England.

* * *

All the friends gathered around the rough wooden table and quietly ate the mixture of dishes from one another's pantries. Andy was thoughtful as he looked at the men and women gathered together and thought about his role in their lives. The *Mariah* had inadvertently affected each of them when he was her commander. The chance encounter with the *Angelica*, his family's yacht, and the orders to rendezvous with a barely seaworthy boat that brought Father Albright and Katrin to the *Mariah*, seemed so unlikely.

The past week, Andy was busy following the progress on Sicily and what aid the navy would need to bring to support the Eighth Army as it continued the drive toward the north end of the island. This Wednesday evening gathering was a short respite before returning to headquarters to continue the planning stages for the next big move—Italy. He wondered how long it would take before Hitler ordered reinforcements to support the German Army on Sicily. He was informed, the day before, about the ruse the Allies used to convince the German high command that the invasion would take place at Sardinia or Corsica, west of Italy. The latest intelligence reported that German ships were still concentrated around these same islands, leaving the supply corridor to Sicily as an open waterway to the well-established docking areas.

"Well, now, that was mighty tasty," Dr. Jamison said, breaking the silence.

"Yes, very good," Peter agreed. "I think Jimmy liked the mashed potatoes from the look of his face," he continued, smiling at his son.

"We'll just clear up in here and then we can retire to the sitting room and catch the evening news," Helen said, rising from her chair.

Andy turned on the radio and let the tubes get warm before tuning into Cairo BBC radio. Jane came in and sat down with Jimmy on her lap just as the broadcast began:

"Ten days after Allied troops landed on Sicily, the first bombs have fallen on Rome. Pilots and crew members of the Catholic faith were given the option of not flying the mission in the off chance that a bomb could land in Vatican City, but no one stayed behind. Our brave Eighth Army continues to push the enemy out of Sicily while RAF bombers and fighter planes cover the sky, sending the enemy scurrying for cover in their relentless attacks against Axis strongholds.

"On a local note, the American USO has invited British troops to attend the scheduled USO entertainment show that will take place next month in Tunis. British command states it is just another example of Allies working together to keep troop morale at its highest level. This is the BBC Cairo station reporting. Good evening."

"It looks like we'll be in Italy before much longer," Peter commented after Andy had switched off the radio.

"We need to finish clearing Sicily first," Andy remarked. "But I have to say, by all indications, it won't be much longer before we take the island."

"Do you think it will mean reassignment?" Sally asked.

"I don't know," Andy said. "A lot depends on where any of us may be needed as Admiral Edwards said."

"That's true, Andy," Martin Jamison agreed. "However, I believe the main invasion of Europe will be across the English Channel. Remember, Switzerland lies between France and Italy, and they are a neutral country, as well as Spain. Also, getting men and equipment to the mainland would be much easier from across the channel."

"I'm sure you're right, sir. But for now, we need to keep our advantage in the south. Italy will be the next step. I don't think France, or any other country in northern Europe, will be considered until Italy is stable," Andy stated.

"Do you think we'll be able to move to England, Andy?" Sally asked.

"I'm sure at some point—once the present campaign is won."

"Why then?" Father Albright questioned.

"The retreating forces will be less organized for a time and also making plans to defend Italy—as the next logical move."

"But won't they still be flying over the Mediterranean?" Peter asked.

"Yes," Andy agreed, "but not as far east. More likely near their ports and airfields. We'll just have to wait and see how the offensive goes on Sicily. Once that's over, I expect command will start rearranging its assets. Don't get me wrong. North Africa will still be an important advantage for the Allies with larger airfields to launch bombing runs, not only into Italy but southern Germany as well."

"I think we'll have to see what the navy decides for us, it looks like," Jane said.

"Yes, that's so," Dr. Jamison agreed. "However, I have a feeling the navy will want Andy and our team in England before any offensive starts across the English Channel."

"They might want to have your experience as a ship's captain," Peter put in. "They also might want to have some medical resources up and running before the invasion of Europe would occur."

"Helen, didn't you say your English estate was around Ipswich?" Sally asked.

"Yes, but at this point, no decision has been made about the property. It only came to me in the last month."

"My mum said several of the larger estate homes were being used as recovery places for wounded servicemen. If the house is large enough, it might be something the navy would be interested in using for sailors," Sally said.

"It's possible, and Ipswich isn't far from Harwell, where a major port is located," Andy said, considering the idea more closely. "We'll just have to wait and see what develops in the next few weeks and go from there."

"All this war talk," Helen said. "As much as I'd like to move to England, it's depressing. It's just like before the Japanese invaded Malaya. Right now, I'd like to think of something more pleasant. Jane, have you and Katrin started plans for the summer celebration at the hospital?"

"As a matter of fact, we have. And we have Sally to help us, now that the matron believes she should stop working. I thought we might gather at our cottage tomorrow and finalize everything over lunch."

"That sounds lovely," Helen said. "Father Albright, we can depend on you for the special service?"

"I already have the readings chosen."

"Then it should be a success," Helen said. "I know the war is at the center of everything we do right now, but somehow, it feels as if we're fighting it too when we do something good for the men that have to leave their families and fight against that evil."

45

"All stop," Mason ordered when the *Mariah* settled into her place alongside the dock.

"Sir," Roger Barnes said, "signal from headquarters."

"Thank you," Mason responded and took the coded message to the map room. He returned to the bridge a few minutes later still holding the decoded message in his hand. "Mr. Anderson, plot a course to these coordinates. Mr. Jones, come with me," he ordered.

Mason and Brian Jones entered Mason's sea cabin and shut the door. "We're ordered to escort duty the day after tomorrow. How are our supplies?"

"I just made a list. It's a short one and shouldn't be difficult to fill."

"Very well then. Talk with Mr. Parker about ammunition needs. Just before Captain Burns left, I spoke with him, and he had a few of the men take stock, just to be sure we were fully loaded."

"I'll make sure of it, sir. I also wanted to run some drills while in port, just to sharpen my own response to how the men react."

"Good idea. Add in a fire drill as well. Hopefully, the Germans will be more concerned with what's going on in Sicily than to bother with a convoy. I expect we'll get further orders by morning.

Until then, carry on," Mason said, remembering how many times he had heard those same words and now knew that ship commanders, the same as first officers, used them when there was nothing else to be said.

*　*　*

Ten days had passed since the *Mariah* received her sailing orders and left Alexandria to journey west through the Mediterranean Sea and into the north-south Atlantic passage to England. Against all odds, Britain held out against German efforts to bring her to her knees in the early stages of the war. Now, she was the solid ground for B-24s and American fighter planes that carried out daytime bombing missions against the Nazi war machine while the British continued the nighttime raids. However, even with goods and war materials from America, it was oil from the Middle East that kept the American Army Air Force and the British Royal Air Force in the skies over Germany.

"Tomorrow, we pass Gibraltar and move into the Atlantic on the next leg of our voyage," Brian Jones commented midway through his afternoon watch.

"Yes, that's true," Mason agreed. "Do you believe we'll run into any more attack boats like the last time?"

"It would surprise me, sir."

"Why?" Mason asked with interest. He felt Brian was a good first officer and knew he had experience as a first officer before the war on a cruise ship. He also knew Brian was more familiar than anyone else aboard the *Mariah* with the coastal waters, where they would soon be passing.

"Two reasons, really," Brian responded. "Since the invasion of Sicily, the German and Italian Navies have been more concerned with our forces taking the island and, possibly, invading Italy. Also, intelligence tells us that most of the German Naval Forces in the area were concentrated around Corsica and Sardinia. We passed between Sardinia and Tunis two days ago."

"That's true. Tonight, however, we commit to narrower seas leading to Gibraltar, where we might have to deal with U-boats lingering in the area, hoping to catch some of the Allied warships moving back into the Atlantic."

"I'll double the lookouts until we're well away from Gibraltar," Brian replied.

"I agree, Number One," Mason said, having just passed on one of the lessons he learned under Andy Burns. "Once we're north of Spain, we'll have to hope for rain clouds to keep the Luftwaffe on the ground instead of hounding the convoy the rest of the way to England."

"Sir, signal from the leader," Roger reported. "He says to add more lookouts when we approach Gibraltar."

"Send signal understood," Mason ordered and returned to the captain's chair on the bridge after scanning his glasses one more time over the sea's surface. *Andy Burns had once said he felt a twitch of approaching danger when things were too calm. Now I know what he meant,* Mason thought.

*   *   *

"Palermo has fallen, and our troops are on the move again," Admiral Edwards said at the morning officers' conference. "As to our ships, the convoy that left here on the fifteenth will be passing Gibraltar tomorrow night. We have a battle group here," he indicated, pointing at the map. "And the Americans are here," he said, once more indicating an area on the map. "We've had good air cover with the planes out of Malta and the carriers in the area."

The conference lasted another fifteen minutes before breaking up. Andy picked up the dispatches he needed to review and headed toward his small office. He spent another half hour reviewing the dispatches and making notes for others to enforce before turning his chair toward the empty harbor. He had watched the *Mariah* leave for convoy duty the previous week and wondered when he might see her—and the men he shared watches with before becoming her commander, her protector—again. He shook off his wandering thoughts then concentrated on the job at hand.

> ...aboard the *Victoria*. While the aerial photos gave good information regarding larger installations, reconnaissance of smaller gun emplacements and concentrations of enemy personnel near landing areas would improve offshore artillery fire on specific targets to better aid the initial landing craft against heavy enemy fire. I also recommend...

Andy continued reading Troy Edmon's eyewitness account about the bombardment of Sicily prior to the army landing on the beaches. The year 1943 was becoming a pivotal year for the Allies, and he wondered what his part might be in coming events. Smiling for a moment, he thought about the other event that would change his and Sally's life forever. *Yes, indeed*, he thought, *1943 certainly is a pivotal year.*

* * *

Helen and Sally met Jane and Katrin the last Monday of July on the hospital lawn and sat down at a small table to review their latest efforts to cheer up the recovering wounded and the overworked staff.

"I believe we have everything in place," Helen said, putting another tick mark on her list.

"It will be a fun summer outing for many of the men and nursing staff," Sally said. "I remember, not so long ago, feeling overwhelmed sometimes with the continual increase in patients coming to us. I just hope we can convince our head of nursing to come along this time."

"I'll speak to Martin about getting her to agree," Helen said.

"Do you think he would say that she had to come along?" Katrin asked.

"No, but he can be persuasive. Now, as to a few prizes, what do we have?"

"Several, actually," Jane answered. "It seems a lot of the merchants in the area have benefited from all the army and navy personnel coming and going and want to be known as generous when one of them has fallen for the cause."

"Food is in place, and we have plenty of volunteers to help with the patients. I think that covers it," Helen said. "I did want to ask you, Katrin, how is Arthur coming along?"

"I had a letter yesterday, and he said he's back with his unit already. Apparently, it wasn't anything serious, but Wesley was being cautious—after his last experience."

"That is good news," Sally said. "I hope he's able to get back here soon."

"It would be wonderful to have all of us together again," Jane said. "It's hard to believe so much time has passed since our escapades on the *Angelica*. So much has changed since we were forced to leave Malaya."

"At least some of it's been good," Sally said. "Little Jimmy's birth, and now Andy and I are going to have a child. Katrin and Father Albright are safe, and she met Arthur."

"Those are good things," Helen said. "I also think, as bad as war is, things are starting to turn around, and we'll have peace again." Looking at her watch, she started and said she had to run and meet Martin before going home. "I'll see you at home," she said to Sally before quickly walking across the lawn to go meet Dr. Jamison.

"Come," Dr. Jamison said when he heard a knock on his office door. "Helen, I was beginning to wonder if you were going to stand me up."

"Sorry I'm late, Martin. Our planning session went a little longer than expected."

"How are things going for next week's outing?"

"Running smoothly. We just want to be sure the head of nursing joins us on this one. Sally thinks it's important for her to get away for a few hours."

"I'll mention it. Anything else?"

"I had a letter from our attorney in England yesterday," Helen said. "It seems the navy would like to use Ralph's family estate holdings for a small nursing home, similar to what we saw in Australia. I'm concerned about the main house being used when no one from the family is there to look after things. Since his brother had no heirs and his sister never married, the holdings came to me. In time, Andy and Sally will inherit it."

"How far is it from London?"

"It's north of London, a couple miles outside Ipswich, overlooking a little bay. It seems Ralph's family liked being near the sea, no matter where they settled."

"Did the attorney say if there was a deadline?"

"He didn't really say in so many words. I got the impression it's for something yet to come. I'm hoping to get back to England before an answer is needed, or the navy decides to use their authority and simply tell me they will be using it."

"You would be compensated if that happened," Dr. Jamison pointed out.

"Yes, I know, but it is a lovely, well-preserved manor house, small by British standards, but it does have three large rooms that could be used to house recovering soldiers. I stayed there when I was in England before the war broke out. Ralph's sister went to London shortly after I left and was killed in one of the first air raids, and now his brother is gone, so the house is empty. I did manage to have one of the locals watch over the buildings and keep the heat on through the winter so the pipes won't burst. I also said to continue using the fields to grow much-needed vegetables for the area. I know we talked about it the last time we were all together, but then it was just a hypothetical circumstance, and now it has become a reality—sooner than anticipated."

"I'm sure it will be fine. Until you can get there, I think you've done everything you can."

"I'm sure you're right, Martin. I'm sure the navy will be careful, if the need to use the estate arises."

After Helen left his office, Dr. Jamison switched on his radio to catch the news report. Today, the announcer sounded a bit excited as he began the broadcast:

"This is the BBC Cairo station reporting," the announcer hurriedly began. "In a surprise announcement today, the British government reported that Prime Minister Benito Mussolini's fascist government is overthrown. Little more is known about the upset in the Italian government or what affect it will have on the future of Italy in the war. In the meantime, the British Eighth Army, under General Montgomery, and the American forces, under General Patton, continue their battle against determined German troops in the mountainous northeastern Sicilian terrain.

"In other news, a brief news release out of London today reports the RAF bombed Kiel, Germany, in a heavy raid on Friday last, inflicting substantial damage. This is the BBC Cairo station reporting. Good afternoon."

* * *

Father Albright switched off the radio and thought about the news that Mussolini's regime was overthrown. He hoped it would mean the Allies wouldn't have to fight to rid Italy of the Axis influence. He turned back to his letter to the Arch Bishop of Canterbury. He didn't know if the letter would help him and Katrin return to England, but at least he was expressing his concerns about being of service to the young men who were putting their lives on the line to bring peace back to the world.

> My daughter's fiancé is an example of a young man that was wounded when the Japanese invaded Malaya, and again in the recent battles in Sicily. I feel a ministry—to the hospitals where these wounded and often maimed men return to England from the fields of battle—is crying out to be fulfilled.

The letter continued another page before Father Albright closed with blessings to the bishop and his staff.

"Dad, you out on the patio?" Katrin called when she returned from the meeting at the hospital.

"Come and join me," Father Albright said.

"Who's the letter to?" Katrin asked when she sat down at the small table.

"I've written to the archbishop in the hope of returning to England to serve there. I don't know how much good it will do, but I felt it necessary to express my feelings at least. Now then, how are the plans for the outing next week?"

"I have to say, Helen is really good at getting things organized, and Jane and Sally seem to have a way with getting merchants to donate things. Everything is in place, and all we have to do is hope the weather is pleasant."

"I'll put in a good word for you above," Father Albright said, patting Katrin's hand and watching her smile at his words.

"Dad, I hope your letter will help. I know you want us both to be in England, and I agree with you. I don't remember much about it and would like to see the country of my birth. You might even get a parish there."

"We'll see what the Lord brings," Father Albright said.

46

Admiral Edwards returned to his office, following a morning conference, and called his aide. "Call Rear Admiral Edmon and Captain Burns and ask them to come to my office right away," he said, having earlier decided to wait on sending Edmund to England.

"Yes, sir," the aide responded with a salute before returning to his desk and lifting the phone to carry out the orders he was given.

"...so we will have to..." Andy was saying when Edmon knocked and opened the door to tell Andy that Admiral Edwards wanted them.

"Come in, gentlemen," Eric Edwards said when his aide ushered the two men into his office. "I've just come from a consultation with my superiors, and things are going well in Sicily. It appears the Italians began leaving the island right after Mussolini was removed from power. The Germans are continuing to fight and slowing things in the mountainous terrain. My army counterpart says the Americans are as tenacious as ever, and their General Patton is determined to keep moving toward Montgomery's Eighth Army. And that brings us to the next big one ..."

"Italy, sir?" Andy asked.

"Italy is certainly on the table. However, I was referring to the invasion of German-occupied Western Europe. The navy will have a large role to play in preparing for the crossing of everything—from tanks to paper clips. But first, we need to eliminate as much of the threat to the numerous ships that will be involved in the operation as possible."

"Are we looking at ambushing German convoys in enemy-held waters?" Edmon asked.

"It will involve more than that, Troy. We have to destroy harbor emplacements that the air boys can't bomb and not lose ships in the process. Therefore, by the end of the month, you both will receive orders returning you to duty in England. You will each be assigned to specific installations and will take charge of the group. Captain, I understand your family has a place near Ipswich."

"Yes, sir. My mother was the last survivor, and the property came to her. Sally and I hope to live there after the war."

"I think it will be much sooner, Captain Burns. Troy, I know you have a home near York."

"Yes—yes, I do. But what does that have to do with orders to return to England?" Edmon asked.

"Nothing, really. I just thought we might get you both assigned near your families during the planning stages. Once operational, you'll be commanding a group or directing the operations from shore. I wanted to give you a heads-up so that you can start wrapping things up here. That's all for now, Captain Burns," Admiral Edwards concluded.

"Yes, sir," Andy replied, saluting his admiral before closing the door on the two admirals.

"Okay, Eric, now that Burns is gone, what's really going on?" Edmon asked when the door closed.

"We're sending Burns to Harwell to lead a flotilla of five destroyers that will be responsible for putting pressure on enemy shipping in the channel. There will be other assets involved, but we need to cripple the Hun as much as possible to invade Western Europe."

"And my role?"

"You will be part of a larger task force in the North Sea, waiting to sink any German battle armada sailing out of Norway or northern Germany. And this time, we'll have air cover to help with the operation."

"A pretty tall order. It will take a well-organized plan to catch their navy."

"Yes, it will. That's why you're going to be part of the planning before the ships go to sea. You have a good head for strategy, Troy. That's why I asked for you."

"I'll do what I can, Eric. I just hope we have the firepower to decimate their naval capabilities."

"As do I, Troy," Admiral Edwards said, looking off into the distance, remembering how the Japanese decimated British forces in Malaya for a moment. "Well, that's all for today," he concluded a few moments later.

*　*　*

Quentin Patterson and Martin Jamison sat down at the small table in the cafeteria and scowled a little at the lunch offerings on their tray. The radio was on in the background, playing some popular tunes, before the noontime news broadcast came on.

"Well, it looks eatable," Dr. Patterson said, poking the casserole with his fork.

"At least it isn't another day of fish cakes," Dr. Jamison responded with a small chuckle.

The two men ate in silence for a few minutes before the news broadcast began. "This is the BBC Cairo station with the week in review," the announcer began. "This past Sunday, the first day of August, the Ploesti oil fields in Romania were heavily bombed. Our brave Allied Air Forces risked the long missions, with many losses, to deny the Axis forces the fuel that keeps their tanks and airplanes moving.

"The famed American General Patton, while touring an army hospital on Tuesday, slapped a soldier when he learned that the man was not wounded and was under observation for war stress. He stated that he would not allow a coward in the same room with wounded soldiers. This incident has received a great deal of attention in the American press.

"Our Eighth Army continues to battle against a ferocious German enemy in the mountains of Sicily while Patton's army presses northeast, pushing the enemy closer to the sea. In the east, the Allies have won the battle of New Georgia in the Solomon Islands, defeating another Japanese stronghold on the march toward Japan. This is the BBC Cairo station reporting. Good afternoon."

"I've never heard of a general slapping a soldier in front of witnesses," Dr. Patterson said. "I wonder what came over the man to lose control like that?"

"I don't know, but it can't be good for his career. He could lose control of himself in a battle situation and cause a lot of casualties," Dr. Jamison said.

The two men continued talking for a few more minutes about the latest progress in the east before returning to the floor to make afternoon rounds. Dr. Jamison returned to his office an hour and a half later and found Admiral Edwards waiting for him.

"Eric, this is a surprise. What brings you to visit our humble establishment?" Dr. Jamison asked.

"I want to talk to you about moving to England, Martin. We need to prepare for when we will invade occupied Western Europe. Your team has a proven track record. This area will become a backwater to the war once the campaign on Sicily is completed."

"Is that why you were so willing to come to Helen's a few weeks ago? Did you know then that we might be sent to England?"

"I didn't know but suspected something was in the air. How long would it take you to prepare to leave?"

"I'd like to talk to Quentin and Peter about it. As far as putting things in place here, I would say a month. What about Andy? Will he be transferred as well?"

"I couldn't say," Admiral Edwards said. "You know it's against regulations to discuss such things."

"Yes." Martin Jamison sighed. "I can guess, though. Very well, Eric. I'll talk to Quentin and Peter, and we'll start putting things in place here. I know how the navy works, and I know one way or the other, you will get us there. I haven't forgotten about how I was duped into active service in Singapore when Wesley was building those emplacements at Helen's Landing in the early days of '41."

"It was one of my better moments," Admiral Edwards said and chuckled at the memory. "You did a fine job, as I recall. As to your team, I'll let you know more specifics once things are in place. I might even waggle a promotion for Patterson and Romans."

"That would be nice, especially for Peter. He's a skilled doctor, and a little higher rank is in order."

"Glad you approve. I have to get back. I'll be in touch soon," Admiral Edwards said before leaving Dr. Jamison to contemplate what the future might bring.

47

The wave tops glistened like sparkling jewels as the rays of sunlight danced across the ocean surface. Men stopped for a moment from the early morning routine to take in the sight that sailors wait to see, when angels sprinkle a hint of color from heaven's radiant, precious gems into the sea. The prisms of light were mesmerizing, until a lookout shouted, "Torpedo in the water—twenty degrees to port!"

Brian Jones sounded the alarm, bringing men to their battle stations with adrenalin flowing at the sudden break in the peaceful early morning routine. "Turn thirty degrees to starboard," he quickly ordered while scanning the sea for another torpedo that might be coming toward them.

Mason jumped up from the bed in his sea cabin and quickly donned his jacket and hat before hurriedly coming to the front of the bridge to assess the situation. "What do we have, Number One?"

"Torpedo spotted in the water twenty degrees to port. I ordered a thirty-degree turn to starboard just before you came on deck, sir."

"Tell sonar to start pounding the water for him. Signal the convoy that we have a U-boat in the area and to be on the alert.

Prepare depth charges and have Mr. Parker report to the bridge," Mason ordered.

Tim Parker climbed the bridge ladder a few minutes after the order was given. "Reporting as ordered, sir," he said, saluting his captain.

"I want you to take Bert and another rating to the depth charger and wait until sonar has a contact. Once I give the order, have the two depth-charge throwers ready to drop two drums at fifty feet from one, and another two drums at seventy-five feet from the other, simultaneously. We might catch him trying to dive after making an attempt on the convoy."

Tim cracked a half smile at the order. "It might just do some damage that way," he said. "We'll be ready."

"Sir, do you think there could be more than one?" Brian asked.

"I don't think so yet. I'm hoping we can catch this one before he can contact his buddies to catch us tonight," Mason answered. "Mr. Barnes, do we have a reply from the leader?"

"Just coming in, sir. He says to stay alert, and he's ordered the convoy to tighten up. He also said good work."

"About all we can do is wait to see if anything develops. Check with sonar. See if they have a contact."

No contact was made, and no other ship had reported seeing evidence of a submarine in the area. Mason sat on his chair and contemplated the situation. He knew several U-boats were sunk shortly before the Allies began the offensive on Sicily. The *Mariah* was part of the operation that sank some of those U-boats and cleared much of the Atlantic, in anticipation of merchant and warships making the crossing from America into the Mediterranean Sea to support Operation Husky. The *Mariah* was off the western coast of France though now, closer to German-held territory.

Morning gave way to noon with the men continuing in the normal four-hours-on–four-hours-off routine when, once again, the alarm began to sound. "All men to battle stations," they heard as their half-eaten sandwiches were hastily tossed aside when seamen scrambled to report to their battle stations. Guns were cocked and ready—with men's index fingers lightly resting against the trigger—waiting for the order to fire.

"Leader reports planes just east of us," Roger reported.

"Planes to port!" a lookout suddenly yelled.

Brian Jones quickly left the bridge to report to the aft gunnery station. He had been under fire many times aboard the *Mariah* as her navigator, but now he had to depend on another to keep the ship on the correct course and avoid collision with an excited merchant ship swerving through the dangerous waters.

"This is the captain," Mason said over the loudspeaker. "Fire at will," he ordered when the planes began to dive out of the sun toward the large convoy.

The 4.7-inchers began continual fire at the diving Stukas, descending at an incredible speed with the intent of dropping bombs on the merchant ships in the convoy. The first plane dropped its bomb and began to pull out of the dive. The merchant ship it aimed for swerved just as the bomb left the plane and was missed by mere feet, sending machine-gun fire after the departing enemy plane. More bombs exploded, which caused towering geysers of seawater to wash across decks, making them slippery and more hazardous for runners to move where needed.

Brian watched a diving Stuka, with its horrible squawk, heading for the *Mariah* and waited until it was within range before ordering his guns to fire. He remembered his father once stating while he was growing up that to be successful when hunting, one must lead the game a bit so the bullet arrives when the animal reaches the correct spot to make the kill. This wasn't game hunting by any means, but these mechanical birds were out to kill him and the ship, so the principle stood, and he adjusted his guns accordingly.

Mason followed the order of the battle while steering the *Mariah* to avoid collision and falling bombs. So far, no damage was reported, and the men were holding off the buzzing planes that were plaguing the convoy with cannon fire. He knew more planes might arrive, with more bombs and cannon fire, until the sun set. He was sure their early morning encounter with a U-boat was responsible for the raid on the convoy. He started a moment when a Stuka exploded not far from the aft deck of the ship.

"Up one hundred," Brian ordered. "Fire!" he yelled above the din of gunfire a moment later. "Reload, fire," he said again. Sweat was dripping from his forehead, and his hands were clammy as the battle continued against the weaving planes that were headed toward the ship. "Fire," he ordered again and saw the first signs of damage to the oncoming plane. "Fire, down fifty, fire!" he yelled on top of the previous order.

The plane wavered when a shell passed through its right wing, but the pilot adjusted and continued his dive. The second heavy hit to the fuselage wasn't as easy for the pilot to pull the plane out of its tendency to fall from the sky. The third hit went through the engine and ignited the fuel lines before the fire spread to the fuel tank and engulfed the fuselage as the plane nose-dived into the sea, exploding on contact.

The battle continued another twenty minutes before the planes left the convoy to assess the damages. One merchant ship reported two sailors killed in the battle, and another reported some light damage. After checking with the other stations, Brian reported to the bridge.

"Sir, no damage to the ship and no casualties, two sailors killed on a merchant ship. I've ordered the decks cleared of shell casings and to be ready for a second attack."

"Good," Mason said. "If there's a bombing raid over France today, it might keep them off our backs until sunset."

The convoy continued north with the precious cargo to feed the hungry British population. The oil they carried was destined to supply more ships to bring men to the battlegrounds, soon to be opened once Sicily was cleared of the German influence.

Mason wondered what Italy's role would be in the war, now that Mussolini was toppled from power. He also wondered how Hitler would react to the news that one of his allies was gone.

Night fell after a tense afternoon of anticipating another aerial attack. The convoy continued pushing toward England under a clear sky, silhouetted by the moon shining brightly and bathing the sea in a pale light. It was the ideal cruise-ship night for romance under the stars, but tonight, lookouts scanned the sea for any anomaly that suggested trouble was among them.

The watch changed, and Lieutenant Anderson came on duty. He reviewed the log before scanning the sea and convoy with his glasses to be sure all was in order. A half hour after beginning the watch, a messman brought him a hot mug of tea. "Quiet night," the rating said when he handed Anderson the steaming mug.

"So far, it is," Lieutenant Anderson agreed. "Another few days and we're in the home stretch."

"I'm lookin' forward ta seein' the…" the man began. "What the…heaven have mercy," he whispered when he turned to see what had suddenly lit the sky as bright as the sun.

Anderson was already sounding the alarm, calling men to their stations, with his eyes on the spiral of white hot light emanating from what seemed to be the very surface of the sea itself. The sound of sirens blowing from other ships in the convoy, combined with the delayed din of the blast, which nearly deafened him as he struggled to maintain his composure and give the orders to bring men to their battle stations.

Mason was the first to rush onto the bridge from his nearby sea cabin, still buttoning his shirt. "Report," he ordered.

"Sir, the explosion of a merchant ship. Men are at battle stations. No other information to report at this time."

"Very well. Report to your station."

Brian Jones reported to the bridge a few moments later. "Is it a U-boat attack?"

"I'm not sure, but it could be. So far, no one has reported any sighting on the surface. I can't believe they would attack from below the surface in the dark. It would be too hard to see the target. Go around the ship and make sure the men are alert. Check in with Tim Parker on the 50-calibers to see if he's sighted anything also."

"Yes, sir," Brian replied before leaving to check the gunnery stations and talk with the officers in command at the port and starboard stations to be certain each man was watching for any sign of a U-boat. He checked with Tim Parker just before returning to the bridge.

"No sign of a U-boat," Tim said. "Might have struck though and dove real quick-like to get a new position and hit and run again."

"I don't like that scenario," Brian said. "I wonder—," he began when another explosion, closer to the *Mariah*, interrupted him. "There," he said, pointing over the rail. "See it, just beyond that merchant there."

"I see 'im," Parker said. "He's gunned 'is engine to get between them two, behind us, there."

A sudden din of 50-caliber–machine-gun fire was heard from the two merchants struggling to ward off the pariah that stalked them. *Mariah*'s guns joined the growing firepower being pelted at the lone U-boat when the merchant ships cleared the area where it briefly sat on the ocean's surface.

"She's diving!" Mason hollered. "Set up a grid to depth-charge. It can't be too far down, so set the charges for fifty feet," he ordered.

"Parker's at the depth charger," Brian reported when he returned to the bridge.

"Very well," Mason said. "The leader is sending another ship to help with the depth charging, to hammer him as hard as we can. Go back down to the depth-charging station and report anything unusual."

"On my way," Brian said as he hurried down the bridge ladder and ran across the deck to where Tim Parker stood.

"Commander Roden wants to know about anything that might indicate we've hit the U-boat or its whereabouts," Jones said when he arrived.

"Right now, I think she's pinned down between us and that other destroyer there. If we can keep her pinned, we'll get her," Parker surmised.

"Very well. Send a runner if you see anything else," Jones said before turning to report back to the bridge.

The two ships pummeled the sea with explosives, changing the depths to prevent the U-boat from escaping to haunt another convoy. Geysers of water still hung in the air when the second ship began another run, sending depth charges deep into the sea, to find the illusive U-boat that sank two of their charges.

"Be quick there," Parker barked at the rating, setting the depths for the barrel-like devices.

Again, *Mariah* crisscrossed the grid and set her charges at a shallower depth when a slick of oil appeared. A lookout spotted the slick and reported it to the bridge. "Make another pass," Mason ordered.

Mariah crossed the same section again, signaling her counterpart to close in and drop charges a few hundred yards beyond to clinch the U-boat's fate. A larger slick of oil surfaced when the sonar room reported sounds of metal breaking up. Mason signaled his counterpart what their sonar indicated and learned the other ship was picking up the same indications. Ten minutes later, the two ships turned north to catch up with the convoy.

Three days passed with no more enemy attacks until the convoy made the turn into the English Channel—the final leg of its journey. The brief BBC newscast, picked up out of London, said the Allies had the Japs on the run with the battle off Kolombangara in the Vella Gulf and the battle of New Georgia won in the Solomon Islands. Very little was said about the continued fighting in Sicily or bombing raids over Europe.

"We should be in Harwell soon," Brian commented.

"This is the most dangerous part of the voyage," Mason said. "We can't relax our guard until we're in the harbor gates, and then only slightly. The enemy likes to attack when we're close to our destination, knowing many sailors are thinking about home instead of keeping his mind on the job at hand."

As if on cue, three enemy planes swooped toward the convoy, strafing the decks in several passes. *Mariah*'s crew fired her guns at the low-flying planes, chipping wings and nicking fuel and oil lines, until a flight of RAF fighters chased them away. The friendly planes returned a short time later and waggled their wings over the ships that were steadily plowing through the water.

Mariah completed her journey on Monday, August 9, having travelled several thousand miles in hostile waters. "All stop," Mason ordered when the ship was positioned in her allotted space along the quayside at Harwell. He remembered another time the *Mariah* was docked at Harwell, a time when London was under siege, and he could see the glow of the burning fires. The ship had since seen a number of battles, with many of her companions resting on the sea's bottom. He watched a moment as the crew threw the mooring ropes to the men on shore, who were waiting to secure them to the dock, and gave a sigh of relief that they had survived another dangerous journey. He prayed he would be given the time to continue honing his skills to keep the ship and her crew safe.

48

Sally was surprised to hear Andy coming home in the middle of the day. "Is everything all right?" she asked.

"Yes, nothing wrong. I just received orders to report in at Harwell on 15 September. The orders include you and Ma traveling there as well."

"Andy, that's wonderful! We'll finally be able to see my parents, and they'll be able to meet Helen."

"What about me meeting someone?" Helen asked when she came into the sitting room.

"I have orders for England, Ma. Not far from Ipswich actually. I'm to wrap things up here in the next few days and be prepared to move by the middle of August. The navy can move quickly when it wants to. You and Sally are to be ready as well. Admiral Edwards said, since we have a place to live, the situation is a little different than it normally would be. He also said something about Dr. Jamison needing his team but didn't elaborate."

"I'm sure Martin will let us know when he can. Sally and I will start making arrangements to close up the cottage and be ready when you tell us, Andy."

"It's going to leave Father Albright and Katrin here if the church doesn't agree to move them, if Dr. Jamison is going and wants his team with him," Sally said. "Peter and Jane will be coming too as part of the team."

"We'll just have to see what will happen. Joseph did say he wrote to the archbishop, stating he thought he needed to serve in England with the wounded men that will be evacuated there once the Allies invade occupied Europe," Helen said.

"Let's pray the bishop listens," Sally concluded.

The second week of August came with little news about the fighting on Sicily, other than the Allies were pressing forward against a stubborn enemy that didn't realize their struggle was hopeless. Katrin switched off the radio and reopened the letter from Arthur to read it again. She prayed for his safety—and a time when they would be able to be man and wife in a peaceful world.

The news that her friends would be leaving soon left her feeling at loose ends about what to do to fill her time outside of helping at the hospital recovery center in Alexandria. She was sure once the struggle for freedom moved farther into Italy, few soldiers would remain, and additional civilian help would not be needed.

"Katrin, are you here?" Father Albright called from the kitchen doorway. "I have good news."

"What is it, Dad?"

"I don't know how it happened, but the church is sending us to England—Harwell, in fact— where all our friends are going. It's the answer to a prayer." Father Albright beamed at the welcomed news.

"But, how...when...I mean, you only wrote a few weeks ago. Are you sure?"

Handing her the short telegram, he said, "It's right there. I'm sure something will be following shortly, unless the mail is delayed."

"It just says you'll be receiving instructions shortly. Dad, this is wonderful news. I can hardly believe it! I have to let Sally and Jane know that we'll be coming after all."

"It's good to see you smiling," Father Albright said, giving her a light kiss on the cheek. "I'm going to go over to the center for a while this afternoon and let Martin know the good news we've just received."

*   *   *

Martin Jamison was reviewing patient files and making some final notations when Joseph Albright knocked on his open door. "Well, come in, come in. What can I do for you?" Dr. Jamison asked.

"I just wanted to tell you that I received a telegram today from the church. Katrin and I will be going to England after all."

"I was hoping you would hear something soon," Dr. Jamison said. "I told Eric what a difference you made for many of my patients that were despondent after losing a limb or marred for life. I don't think some of them would have made the adjustment if it wasn't for you."

"I simply reminded them that the Lord loves them. At first, many that were badly scarred said no one else would, until they began talking with the female nurses and volunteers. Once the first interaction took place, most were ready to talk about their anger and fear of facing their family at home. Parents and wives may have an initial reaction, but the love they hold for the individual overcomes a scarred body. The Lord walks the journey back to wholeness with them. They only need to accept His grace to bring the peace that they seek."

"That's just it, Joseph. You have a way of convincing them that it's true."

"Any servant of the Lord can do that."

"No, that isn't really the case. You see, the men believe because they can see that you believe. Not all of the Lord's clergy bring that special gift to the table, and I told Eric that."

"I see. That's a tall order to live up to, Martin. I hope you aren't disappointed. Even a priest has his doubts at times. When I hear the news and the number of men suffering on both sides, not to mention the women and the children caught in the struggle, I get discouraged."

"We all do at times," Dr. Jamison said, looking off into the distance a moment. He was still waiting for Tom Linn, his Malayan-born protégée, to check in with him. He was beginning to wonder if Tom had survived his service as a doctor in the underground in the east. "Anyway, we'll all be at Helen's on Sunday afternoon, and we can discuss everything then," he continued.

The week passed, and it appeared the last German troops were being pushed into a corner near Messina. Even with the controversy in the press regarding General Patton's behavior toward another battle-stressed soldier, it didn't detract from the Americans advancing to meet General Montgomery's Eighth Army closing in from the west.

Andy left his small makeshift office at naval headquarters for the last time on Sunday morning, August 15, after decoding the last dispatches out of Sicily and reviewing the initial plans for the invasion of southern Italy. It looked as if a two- or three-pronged attack was planned to secure essential ports for supplies and men to continue the battle north to free Rome from the fascist hold and bring security to the Vatican against a possible German looting of treasure and artifacts.

It would take longer, he knew, for occupied Europe to see the Allies crossing their shores. First, the German Luftwaffe needed to be neutralized to allow men a fighting chance to get off the beaches. The factories, where tanks and planes were manufactured, had to be pulverized and naval ports destroyed to deny the enemy their use. The more enemy assets destroyed on the ground increased the chances that an invasion would succeed. Even then, it would be a hard-won victory to finally bring Germany to her knees and end the killing on all fronts.

Taking a final look at his surroundings, Andy picked up his hat and strolled out of the office into the fresh breeze coming off the sea. He knew Troy Edmon was being sent to England as well and wondered what part he might take when the battle for Europe came. He hoped he would be able to one day tell the tale to the child he and Sally awaited and introduce him or her to the man who taught him on a special ship about true honor and leading men.

* * *

Peter laid his fork across his plate with a contented sigh at the Sunday repast that not even rationing could denigrate. "That was delicious," he said with a lopsided grin. "I couldn't eat another bite."

Laughing a little, Jane said he would have to have rice with no sauce tomorrow, a joke between them that started when they first married. "I think Jimmy agrees with his father," she commented when the child pushed away the spoon she was offering.

"Martin, will you warm up the radio while we clear away in here?" Helen asked. "Andy, I wonder if I could get you to lift that large pot for us in the kitchen before joining the men."

"I'll take the little man with me," Peter said, lifting Jimmy from the wooden high chair, which Jane had found in a secondhand store when their son began sitting up and wanting to sit by them at the kitchen table.

The doorbell rang, and Quentin Patterson went to answer it since everyone else seemed to have a job to do. He was a little taken aback to see Admiral Edwards on the doorstep. "Please, come in, sir," he said after a moment of staring at the unexpected visitor.

"Oh, Admiral Edwards, come in, sir," Andy said when he came out of the kitchen. "I'm glad you could take the time to come."

"No bother, really. Things are rather quiet at the moment. Ah, Martin, there you are. Is everyone here then?"

"I believe so, Eric. Why don't we go into the sitting room? I believe you've met Father Albright."

"A pleasure to see you again, Father," Eric Edwards said, shaking Joseph Albright's hand. "I suppose you all are wondering what this is all about. I'll explain as soon as the ladies join us. It's quite simple really."

"Admiral Edwards, I wondered how Katrin and I fit into something that is really a military matter from what I can discern," Father Albright said.

"I believe Martin will have to explain a little, but I have to say, I agree you need to be with the group we are sending to England. Your part in it is as important as the physical needs that the doctors and nurses attend to."

"Joseph, we can only do so much to heal a person. Medical science is improving every day, but the physical healing is only the outer shell to the inner healing. That's where your special gift is needed most," Martin Jamison said. "As I said earlier this week, you truly believe, and the men feel that when you talk to them. I wish you had been with us in Malaya when so many of the men we saw needed that reassurance from someone they felt knew something about their inner pain and would take the time to listen to their doubts."

"But I don't understand how the archbishop could have made such a decision so quickly about moving a priest to another continent. That is something that is deliberated for some time before the final decision is made."

"I'm afraid I have to confess, the navy spoke with the archbishop and related the time constraints being imposed at this time," Eric Edwards said. "My counterpart in London made a call to Canterbury, and the church was most sympathetic to our request."

"I see," Father Albright said. "I wonder if my letter to him was read before the request was made. It doesn't matter now. The bishop has sent his instructions, and I will follow them. Martin, I must confess you have placed me in a difficult position. I don't have any special in with our Lord. I simply know he loves everyone, even those we are fighting right now, and will enter the heart of anyone willing to let him. That love is the power that brings inner healing."

"And reminding our wounded men about that love is why we need you, Joseph," Dr. Jamison said as the women joined them in the sitting room.

"Eric, a pleasure to see you again," Helen said. "I wish you had joined us for dinner though."

"Thank you, Helen, but I had another appointment before coming here today. But let me get to why I'm here," Admiral Edwards began. "It is no secret that Sicily is all but concluded. I expect, before the week is out, the island will be in Allied hands. That said, it is also no secret that the likely next move will be to invade Italy and try to help the new government rid their soil of any fascist personnel. It won't be an easy task with their government in turmoil, the country infested with Germans ready to take over, and their army in chaos. But it is still the lesser problem facing our own military."

"It sounds pretty dreadful to me," Helen said.

"Yes, but the bigger picture is the rest of occupied Europe. That's where all of you come into this. Helen, I understand that you have a large house near Ipswich, which is fairly close to Harwell. The navy has approached you about using it as a possible halfway house for recovering personnel that would eventually return to duty."

"I've received a letter about the possibility but haven't made any final decision. I feel, first, the property needs to be examined, and I would need to be there if it is used for such a purpose."

"Martin, you want your team, as you call it, together when the navy sends you to England. That means Lieutenant Romans and also Mrs. Jane Romans, Mrs. Helen Burns, and Mrs. Sally Burns as well," Admiral Edwards said.

"Don't forget Quentin," Martin Jamison replied.

"I haven't forgotten Captain Patterson. He will be accompanying your team, Martin." Reaching into the small case he carried, Admiral Edwards drew out an envelope and handed it to Dr. Patterson. "These are your travel orders," he said, handing Quentin Patterson the envelope.

"It appears my future is decided for now," Dr. Patterson said, taking the envelope. "Wait, did you say captain?"

"Yes, your official promotion is included with the travel orders. I have two for you as well, Lieutenant Romans. One is your travel orders, along with the necessary paperwork for your wife and child to accompany you. The second is something I've been debating for a bit, but I believe your work merits a small promotion to lieutenant commander, effective on Monday next."

"Thank you, sir," Peter managed to say to the unexpected promotion. The navy was slow to promote their temporary—wavy navy—personnel, and he was sure Dr. Jamison, as Rear Admiral Jamison, had something to do with the unforeseen rise in rank.

"Peter, that's wonderful," Jane said with a radiant smile as their friends reached out to pat his back and congratulate him on the promotion.

"Captain Burns has his travel orders and the paperwork needed for his wife and mother to travel with him already. After some paperwork was shuffled from one office to another and all the red tape taken care of, I have also brought the necessary passes for Father Albright and Katrin to travel with you. I explained to my superior, it would be much easier to have all of you together as a group. He did argue that Captain Burns was not part of the medical team, but I pointed out that his wife was, and it was just simpler to arrange transportation one time as opposed to separate arrangements."

"How will we get there?" Katrin asked.

"It will be a rather circuitous journey, I'm afraid. We need to keep you out of enemy territory as much as possible for your safety. That's all I can say for now. Be ready to leave this Thursday for Cairo. Once there, you will be given further travel instructions. And Mrs. Romans, I would make sure you have plenty of supplies for your son's needs on the first leg of the journey."

"Jimmy won't be in any danger, will he?" Jane asked with concern on her face.

"I don't believe so. I wouldn't allow you to go if I thought there was real danger involved. I just meant it will not be convenient to purchase some of the things a toddler needs for part of the journey. Some of the places where you land, at first, will be rather desolate, I'm afraid."

"We'll be prepared," Peter resolutely said.

"I believe all of us will be prepared, Eric," Helen stated.

"Very well then. I'll see you tomorrow, Martin, to go over the final plans."

"That was interesting," Sally commented after Admiral Edwards left them. "I wonder why he's so mysterious about everything."

"Loose lips sink ships, as the Americans say," Andy answered. "Truthfully, I think he plans to send us by air, and he doesn't want us to make a comment that might get to the wrong person. As tight as security is, we still have the possibility of impostors in our midst. Remember Alan from the hospital at Helen's Landing?"

"How could I forget?" Sally said with a shiver.

"I know, darling, and I'm sorry I brought him up, but that is why we have to be careful for now."

"Why don't we listen to the nine-o'clock news?" Helen said, changing the subject. "Martin, I believe you have the tubes warmed up. Andy, will you tune it in for us?"

Andy adjusted the dial until the end of the latest bond drive came in clearly before the news started. "This is the BBC evening news, Cairo station, reporting," the announcer began.

"In an all-out effort to bring the fighting on Sicily to an end, General Patton's tanks have broken through a difficult line of defenses and are, once again, on the move to meet General Montgomery's Eighth Army. The enemy continues to put up resistance but is being forced into a small pocket near the port city of Messina. It is reported that many prisoners have been taken by the Allied forces, meaning they won't be able to fight again against our brave men on the ground.

"It is reported by the BBC out of London that another black-market ring has been broken. These thieves, who take much-needed items to sell to the selfish among us, will see a hard road ahead. The police reported items, from children's shoes to canned meat and petrol, were found in the small country warehouse outside of London's suburbs.

"And this item, just in over the wireless: the United States has taken Kiska Island in the Aleutians. No other details are available at this time. Good night from the BBC Cairo station."

The friends prepared to leave when Andy switched off the set. Everyone said good-bye and thanked Helen again for the wonderful Sunday gathering.

"It will be our last normal Sunday for some time," Helen commented as the door closed, and she returned to the sitting room.

"I think things will be more like Helen's Landing when we get to Ipswich," Andy said. "I wonder if Wesley will be assigned to Italy or returned to England after Sicily."

"I just pray he's safe," Sally said. "He's seen so much of the fighting. All he wanted was to be an engineer and build things—not destroy them."

"He'll get his chance once this is over. With so many bridges and buildings destroyed, engineers will be needed, along with architects and builders, to restore normalcy again," Andy said.

"I suppose you're right," Sally agreed with a yawn. "I'm going to turn in," she said after yawning again.

"Me too," Andy said, following her toward their bedroom. "Ma, you turning in?"

"I think I'll stay up and read a bit. You two go ahead," Helen said. She sat for some time looking out the window, in thought about the request the navy was making to use the house in England as a recovery center for ambulatory patients. The instructions weren't clear about nursing staff and which doctors would be on site. She was sure Martin and Quentin would be closer to the naval hospital and most likely Peter as well. She thought Joseph and Katrin would be nearby from the way Eric Edwards talked this evening. First, they had to get to England.

49

The friends heard the news on Tuesday that Operation Husky—the Allied invasion of occupied Sicily—had come to a close when United States troops, under General Patton, marched into Messina to find the enemy gone. It appeared the Germans had evacuated men and equipment while forcing their rear guard to fight and die to allow the evacuation in secret nighttime crossings between the island port and the tip of Italy. The planes out of Malta continued to bomb and strafe any army trucks and trains on Italy's mainland in an effort to destroy as much as possible before the inevitable next move by the Allies took place—to invade Italy.

Katrin rejoiced that Arthur's unit would be resting, but she would not be able to see him before leaving for England. She wondered when she would see him again. She heard a knock on the kitchen door and opened it to find Wesley Vilmont standing before her.

"This is a surprise," she said. "Does Sally know you're here? Where's Arthur?" she asked when she didn't see him standing nearby.

"Is your father here, Katrin?" Wesley asked with a troubled look.

"No...no, he isn't. Is something wrong? Where's Arthur?" she asked again, beginning to tremble inside.

"I'm sorry, Katrin. I was hoping your father would be home. Arthur, well, he...he didn't make it on our last mission. His last thoughts were about you," Wesley said before gathering her into his arms when the tentative tears turned into a flood of despair at the realization that she would never see Arthur again.

"What...what happened?" she asked, trying to pull herself together. "When did it happen?"

"We were setting some traps near the Germans when a machine-gun nest fired on us. Arthur managed to throw a grenade that saved the rest of the men with him. By the time I got there, it was too late to do anything. He handed me this and said to be sure you got it," Wesley said, pulling a letter out of his coat pocket.

"I pray he didn't suffer," Katrin said, taking the letter with shaking hands.

"He was only conscious a short time before the end. By the time the medics caught up with us, he was gone. They said he wouldn't have felt much pain. We were all with him. I'm afraid there isn't much more I can tell you," Wesley said.

With tears streaming down her face, Katrin sadly nodded and said. "At least he wasn't alone." She heard the door open a moment later and ran to her father, throwing herself against his chest in desperate tears.

"What's all this?" he asked in confusion and then saw Wesley standing in the sitting room doorway. "Wesley," he quietly said. "It's Arthur, isn't it?"

"I'm afraid so, sir. He died in Sicily, just days before the end came. He asked me to see Katrin and bring her the letter that he wrote the night before. I have to be back to my unit the day after tomorrow, but I promised Arthur I'd make sure I saw Katrin."

"That was very kind of you, Wesley," Father Albright said. "I'll stay with Katrin. You go and see your sister now."

"I will, sir, thank you." Wesley left and walked the short distance to Helen's cottage and knocked on the door. He felt as if he'd been through a storm after seeing Katrin. He'd lost a good friend as well and didn't relish the thought of having to give the news to his sister and the rest of their friends here.

"Wesley!" Sally exclaimed when she answered the knock at the kitchen door. "How on earth did you manage to get here?" she asked, throwing her arms around him.

"It isn't very far, and I hitched a plane ride. Sally, I have some bad news."

"What is it?" she asked, showing concern when she saw the pained look on her brother's face.

"It's Arthur. He—," Wesley started then, taking a breath at the pain he felt at his own loss, said, "He was killed a few days ago in Sicily. I just came from telling Katrin. Her father's with her, but she needs her friends."

"Oh no! Oh, Wes, this is awful," Sally said with tears in her eyes.

"What's awful?" Andy asked, coming in from the patio. "Wes, this is a surprise. What's awful, Sally?"

"Andy," Sally said in a broken voice, "it's Arthur. He was killed in Sicily. Andy, it's awful. Katrin must be beside herself. Jane and I have to go to her. Let Helen know when she gets home. I … Wesley, how long will you be here?"

"I have to go back tomorrow. Is there a hotel room around here?"

"You'll stay with us," Andy said. "Sally, help me get Wes settled in before you tell Jane."

"Yes, I suppose that's best. Oh, Wes, I'm so sorry. I know you were friends. I just can't believe it."

The news about Arthur's death added to the cloud of despair moving through the parish. Not only were they losing a fatherly confidante, but now they were faced with a casualty of war close to home. The women left behind and the men too old to fight gathered to pray, offer their condolences to Katrin, and talk with

Father Albright before returning to their own homes, wondering if the same heartbreaking news would come to their door one day. Helen, Sally, and Jane took turns sitting with Katrin, trying to console her as best as they could, knowing there was little they could say to ease her pain.

"I feel so helpless," Father Albright said. "What can I say to my daughter right now? Arthur is with God, but that is little consolation when the wound of death is fresh, and a young life is cut short—as so many have been in this war."

"Dad," Katrin softly said from her bedroom doorway. "I know Arthur is with God. It's just that I miss him so much…," she faltered and lowered her head a moment. "I wish we had married before he left, but he wanted to wait until the war ended. I was ready to wait for him, but it will never be now. I want to thank all of you for coming. There really isn't much else anyone can do. Dad, could we have a small memorial gathering before we have to leave?"

"Of course, Kitten."

Katrin held her prayer book in the church the next afternoon but didn't really see the words as her father read the burial rite. Her friends surrounded her, but she only felt the loneliness so deep within her soul, which no one could fill with Arthur gone. She looked down at the ring on her finger through her tears, facets of sunlight reflecting off the small stones across the pew in front of her. *The light is gone now*, she thought before turning the ring so the beauty of their reflection was hidden.

"Give rest, O Christ, to thy servant with thy saints."

"Where sorrow and pain are no more, neither sighing, but life everlasting," the mourners responded.

The words of the rite continued another ten minutes, intended to bring comfort to the living and dedicate the departed soul to God.

"In sure and certain hope of the resurrection to eternal life through our Lord Jesus Christ, we commend to Almighty God our brother Arthur."

The words continued to the end, with those attending praying the Lord's Prayer. When it was over, Katrin thanked her friends for coming before returning to the cottage where Arthur's last letter lay on her bedside stand. She held it for some time before putting it in her overnight case. *I'm not ready to read the words of hope for the future that he sent,* she thought. "Arthur, how will I go on without you?" she whispered into the empty room. Mechanically, she began to pack her bags for the journey that lay ahead. Maybe the distraction of a new place would help with her grief, but she doubted it as her hand, once again, settled on the letter. She fingered it and slowly lifted it into her hand before reaching for the letter opener on her dressing table. Taking the pages out, she looked at their reflection in the dressing table mirror before lifting them up to read.

She placed the pages back into the envelope and carefully placed it in her small case. She knew, no matter where she was, there would always be a hole in her heart—where he once lived in joyful anticipation of a future together.

The sun shone on the horizon when Katrin rose from a restless night, two days following the memorial service. The dark shadows under her eyes attested to her silent tears and lack of sleep since learning Arthur was gone forever. *Why?* her mind screamed. *Why was he taken when I prayed for his safety? Lord, what is it you want from me?* She heard her father stirring and put her thoughts aside as she dressed for the long trip that lay ahead.

Helen saw Katrin coming through the train depot door and embraced her, whispering words of encouragement. "I know you have to walk through this valley, but know you're not alone," she told her. "Now, then, is everyone here?" she asked when Jane and Peter appeared with Jimmy a few minutes later.

"I believe so," Andy said. "The train for Cairo should be here in about ten minutes."

"Then the journey begins," Helen said.

* * *

The roar of the plane's engines covered the sound of the soft crying at the back of the plane when the young woman put the letter down in her lap. The attendant wondered what it might contain that would bring such a reaction and quietly walked down the narrow aisle to see what might be done.

"It's all right," the young woman said. "I...it's all right."

Katrin raised the letter again and read the last paragraph once more:

> I struggle each time another trap is set off, knowing a life is lost because of my work. This war will change all of us before it ends. My only consolation is to know that you are waiting until I come home, and we will be together for the rest of our lives. I love you, my dearest one. I miss your gentle smile and the softness of your lips when we kiss. Say a prayer for my soul to be at ease and for this war to end soon.
>
> Love,
Arthur

I'll keep you in my heart, Arthur, she thought, placing the letter back in its envelope. Drying her eyes, she looked out the small plane window at the stars lighting the sky. As Helen said, "The journey begins."

EPILOGUE

The late August sun settled into the sea, casting the last vestiges of golden light across the busy harbor. The *Mariah* sat at anchor, soaking in the warm summer breezes gently blowing across her decks while her crew prepared her for sea. Soon, she would feel the pulse of fresh oil surging through her pipes and fittings when her engine, her heart, beat once again, causing the screw to turn her propellers and move her across the water.

Lieutenant Commander Mason Roden boarded the ship with a sense of purpose, holding new orders that would send them on the next mission the *Mariah* faced. He didn't see the golden fingers of light reaching out to gently touch the curve of the bow or reflect off-deck fittings and gun emplacements. Tomorrow he would inform his first officer about their upcoming sailing orders. Until then, *Mariah* would patiently wait to feel the salty spray of the sea across her bow as she carried her charges into dangerous waters.